THE NIGHT SHERIFF

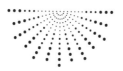

THE NIGHT SHERIFF

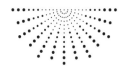

PHIL FOGLIO

Trade Paperback ISBN: 978-1-952825-44-6
Ebook ISBN: 978-1-952825-45-3
Cover Art copyright © 2021 Elizabeth Leggett, Portico Arts
Interior layout and design by Kind Composition
Prince of Cats Trade Paperback Edition 2021
Prince of Cats EBook Edition 2021

Published by Phil Foglio In Association with
Prince of Cats Literary Productions
New Jersey, USA 2021

CHAPTER ONE

I soar over my kingdom.

It's early evening and the vast shield of the night sky lies above me. I miss the stars of my youth, the vast tapestries of patterned lights that wheeled down the seasons, the endless display of celestial majesty. There are stars visible, but they are a paltry remnant that makes mock of my memories. The moon is still there, of course. I think I would have gone mad if that ancient sentinel and nighttime companion had also been obscured by the enveloping vapors of this land's machines.

As it is, I must concede that there are more of them these nights than there were even twenty years ago, a welcome trend, if it continues. The air is cleaner, though now I hear tell that it is the very glow of the city lights that work to obscure the heavens. If it isn't one thing, it's another.

Even after all this time, I will admit that the counterpane of lights below still causes an inrush of breath in wonder and delight at the beauty that humanity creates all too inadvertently, but these glowing confections, even with their dancing neon and sheets of LEDs, compare poorly to my no doubt jaundiced memories of the skies of yore. Call me a traditionalist.

Directly below me, the castle is lit with a particularly

revolting chartreuse and pink lighting scheme. The surrounding streets and buildings are wreathed with several million lights, and hidden projectors shift colors to cheerful effect. The hidden speakers play a compositional hash of tunes, mixed and reengineered to bring a smile of memory to lips and a continuous current of energy to tired limbs.

The crowds below are clamorous and giddy with an excitement that even the most jaded of them are surprised to find still lurking within their breast. It is the time of night when even feet that have walked a league or more in fits and starts find themselves quickening as they head for a final rendezvous, jollied along by the strolling vendors selling balloons and glow sticks, assorted snacks and light-up toys.

More and more of our guests are beginning to line the central streets, staking out a tiny, impermanent claim, a temporary place of refuge against the crush of strangers, girt with insubstantial boundaries that hover scant inches away. Yet I have seen people defend these phantom territories more vigorously than they would their homes, even though, in an hour or so, these impermanent estates will dissipate into history without a second thought.

They gather to witness the nightly parade. You'd think these early defenders to be premature, considering that many of them begin settling as much as an hour before the first funambulist strides forth, but grim reality justifies their actions, as by the time the opening marching band strides down the boulevard, the seething crowd of watchers will easily be a dozen people deep, and many a tardy tot will have to be hoisted up on the shoulders of their sire to see the passing carnival in all its glory.

The shops lining the streets are beginning to see their final sales rush, though this early frenzy will be dwarfed by the mob that will descend upon them after the parade itself, as the people, energized by the procession of monsters and wonders that have pranced past them, belatedly realize that the time left to buy that last souvenir before they must depart is dwindling quickly.

The lights of the pavilions and the rides keep them from seeing me as I glide on by overhead. I swoop closer and taste their emotions. Youthful joy and excitement, with occasional dots of parental exasperation. Nothing untoward.

I sail past the bronze statue of Bartholomew Zenon, the man responsible for it all, his hand companionably slung about the shoulder of Preston Platypus, the company's world-famous mascot. Even now, visitors are draping themselves over the statues, getting photographed one final time before they leave for the evening. I sniff deeply, tasting the winds, and leave the center of the park behind me. Like the moon pulling the tides, the incipient parade's gravity has reached out to the park's extremes, beguiling guests towards the heart of my kingdom, leaving the outer reaches quieter, reserved for those who care not for parades or crowds, as well as the assorted vendors who remain to tend to their needs and desires.

I enjoy this, sailing alone above it all, but I'm feeling a bit peckish. I settle down atop the mountain the *Awesome Avalanche* ride bursts forth from, and even as I allow my own weight to manifest, I feel the all-too-familiar figure of Bone Cat coalescing upon my shoulder.

"Took you long enough," the familiar voice mutters in my ear. I reach up and stroke the cartoonishly absurd earbones atop his head. He drapes himself across my shoulders with a purr reminiscent of an idling chainsaw. He's happy tonight.

Below us, the periodic bursts of terror as the riders see the drop before them are an adequate snack, but I'm in the mood for heartier fare. I settle down, and fold into myself so that anyone actually looking would just think me another faux rocky outcrop. I allow my senses to spread, seeping throughout this corner of my kingdom like a questing, invisible fog. It's a weekday, so the crowds are slightly smaller. Early summer, so the night is warm, not that it ever really gets cold in Southern California, not cold like it used to get back home.

Occasionally I miss the cold. Real cold, the kind that used to come with the winds that screamed down off the mountains in the dead of winter, sending the peasants huddling up against their fires, their livestock, and each other for comfort and warmth. I liked the way the cold felt. The physical sensation. It made my skin tighten, and I felt more sleek and—I guess the modern word would be *aerodynamic*. Silly, really. But as someone who appreciates the subtly different *types* of fear that people are capable of generating, I will confess that the fear of the cold was a seasonal favorite. It was so *primal*. Ah well, different days, different ways.

Who else is back here, walking the dark paths? There are still those visitors, young and old, who are simply questing towards the next ride. This is a special time for them. The park is emptier, the lines are shorter, and their own exuberance adds to the experience of others like them, multiplying the effect and filling the very air with a sense of adventure.

Strolling amongst them are people moving at a more sedate pace. They are not here for the rides, or the souvenirs. I recognize many of them. Older couples. More interested in each other than in yet another spectacle. The myriad of lights and the exotic foliage is merely a backdrop to the quiet magic and excitement they have brought with them. People who have come to the park because it *is* a park. A few acres of grass and trees, ponds and romantic lamp-lighted darkness far from the cares and concerns of the surrounding city that might as well be across the salty sea. A familiar, safe, and comfortable place inhabited by sleepy birds, recorded crickets, and animatronic animals. Keeping it that way is why I'm here.

A child is crying. A quick sharpening of focus and I can ignore it. Simply another tyke stuffed full of sugar and over-stimulated by wonders, being dragged towards the entrance by determined parents. I sigh; another section perhaps—

Suddenly I feel claws prick my shoulder. "Death is abroad tonight," Bone Cat whispers.

I hate it when he does that. *He* claims that Death is, in fact, an anthropomorphic entity that he can actually see, even though I cannot. Now, while I can attest that the supernatural world overlays the mundane, and that there are additional layers of reality that are unperceived by the majority of people, I still find it disquieting that there may be *further* levels that even *I* cannot see. Personally, I believe that he is yanking my chain, as the kids say, but I must acknowledge that he is always accurate. "To the North," he whispers.

I allow myself to tumble backwards, unfurling myself into the air, and take an immature pleasure in my companion's yowl of annoyance as he fades away. To the North. Let's see ... there's Monte Cristo Island, the Lost Temple, Kukuanaland, the Happiness Machine—

And there it is. In the back. Away from the great ever-changing clock and the crowds waiting for the boats. The service door used by park personnel is hanging open. That is very much against company policy. I swoop down and see that the lock has been broken. A moment later I'm in the anteroom, Bone Cat again upon my shoulder. Even back here the ever-playing music hammers at my ears. I consider taking one of the microphone-equipped headsets hanging from the rack, but I need to stay flexible. Unnoticed by most people is a small tube hanging from the ceiling. I blow into it and then speak clearly, "There is an intruder inside." I glance at Bone Cat, who nods. "I have reason to believe that he or she is dangerous."

Less than thirty seconds later, a small green person with an immense nose and an intricately knotted beard pops out of a small door. Automatically my hand grips the nape of Bone Cat's neck. There is no time for his usual foolishness. This is Punch-Press, a senior gremlin. We bow to one another. "Old Tool," he greets me with his usual grin. Gremlins are a cheerful bunch, as a rule. Bone Cat sniggers even though that's been my name amongst the gremlins for fifty years. Partially because that is the sort of name that the gremlins themselves have, but mostly, I believe, because they cannot manage to pronounce my real one, and gremlins hate to do something incorrectly.

He opens a larger door, and we head into the backstage area of the ride. "Found your guy. He's in Asia." Ah. Towards the center of the ride. Punch-Press continues, "There is something seriously wrong with him."

Terrific. "Shut down the ride at *once*. Put up the 'Repairs' sign."

"Oh, we closed it down as soon as he started goin' nuts." I didn't like the sound of that. Gremlins have a great deal of pride, and even the intimation that that they have allowed the machinery to go out of kilter would be regarded as a slap in the face. To do so voluntarily underlines that they regard the situation as serious. The gremlins are still smarting from the bad reputation they were saddled with during the Second World War.

Gremlins started out as an admittedly mischievous, but mechanically proficient clan of kobolds or some such living deep within the Harz Mountains of northern Germany. They had been known to the locals for several centuries, and there was a working détente between the two races, one that had actually showed signs of thawing as the creatures became more and more intrigued by the complicated mechanical marvels that humanity was beginning to cobble into existence.

They had actually aided the Germans during the First World War, but it had been a strictly mercenary arrangement. They never cared about nebulous things like sociopolitical conflicts. But carburetors, now *that* was a thing a gremlin could understand (and improve).

But it meant that they were in the German records when the Nazis took over, and all too soon they were forcibly conscripted. Their caverns were captured, and they were moved *en masse* to laboratories and workshops.

Even then, the Nazis could have pulled it off. Put a gremlin in a well-stocked workshop and keep him fueled with beer and sour milk and they'll do anything you want. But Nazis do not seem capable of letting someone do something just because they actually enjoy it. They bullied and threatened them, tortured their young and their elders, and cut them off from their beer.

Stepping back here, I will concede that Germans, even Nazis, take beer pretty seriously, and the stuff that the Gremlins brew up can only be called "beer" because the science of brewing reluctantly concedes that certain processes produce substances that, technically, must be called beer. At least, that was the case back then. I think today you could legitimately classify it as biohazardous industrial waste. It is entirely possible that when they destroyed the Gremlins' ancient brewing equipment, the Nazis believed they were doing them a favor.

What they actually did was open a third front in the war against Germany. The Gremlins managed to escape and began sabotaging the Nazi war machine. All well and good, but as I mentioned earlier, they really had no grasp of the finer details of human tribalism, and so, all too soon, they had spread from Europe to England and from there to the Americas, where they continued their depredations against mankind's machinery in a very egalitarian fashion.

It wasn't until after the end of the war that people like Mr. Mortimer and myself could spare the time to deal with them. By that time, of course, they had settled into their new homes, and discovered that there were benefits to living in places full of machinery, as opposed to mountain caves. Luckily, it was rather easy to turn them from sabotage to more creative pursuits. Allowing them to rebuild their terrible brewing machines was a major step, and many of these are now spread throughout the technological infrastructure of the world.

However, machinery changes. Perhaps you've noticed public clocks in your city that no longer function. Why don't people repair them? The answer is because ever since the early 1950s, *people* had never *had* to. Each clock, every public fountain, every children's science museum once housed a family of gremlins who kept things working, all for a few bottles of milk, the cost of which was tucked away in a nebulous part of some institutional or civic budget.

But today's younger gremlins are more interested in the new machinery. Satellites, the internet, and self-driving auto-mobiles are the snares that catch a young gremlin's fancy. The older ones, the ones that grew up on simpler, more primitive machinery, such as clock towers, railroads, and air traffic control systems, are dying off, or at least retiring to more hospitable climes—such as theme parks in southern California. Say what you will about the rides here, very few of them employ what you would call cutting-edge technology. All the more reason why the gremlins here will bristle at the intimation that they have allowed the ride to break down. But it is the quickest option. The music, of course, has not stopped, but I can already hear a rising susurrus of noise from outside, as hundreds of guests are informed that they have stood in line for the last hour to no avail.

We arrive at the observation point for the Asia Room. Someone has been here, and no mistake. Brightly costumed dolls continue to dance and sing, but someone has cut a swath of destruction through the heart of them. Dolls have been smashed and mangled, tossed aside and battered even as they continue to move, juddering and sparking as they try to perform their eternal routines. The effect is quite alarming.

I hear a small sob, which allows me to find the real people amongst the false. The girl is young, maybe eight, dressed in a space princess costume possibly purchased this very day. "He snagged the girl out of a boat," Punch-Press muttered. "She was sitting by herself in the back, and I don't think the people in the front even noticed." Her parents will certainly have noticed when the boat exited without her.

The man is maybe twelve years older. Dressed in a somber outfit covered by a bulky coat that I would have thought too warm for the mild California night. He is kneeling in what looks to be prayer. Even from where I am, I can feel the emotions pouring off them. The girl is terrified. She is also in actual physical pain, and I now see that she is handcuffed to the man, who has closed the cuff too tight upon her slender wrist.

"That's him," Bone Cat whispers. For once he is deadly serious. "Death is poised behind them both."

I can believe this. The man is clearly on edge. His emotions are complicated, and, it is obvious to me, chemically enhanced. I taste fear, of course, but there is also a great *anticipation*, which I do not like at all. I have been a hunter of men, among other things, for a very long time, and this fellow here is acting *different*. Now after a thousand years, you'd think different would be good, and if it was just the two of us, I might be in a better mood to savor the peculiarity of the situation. But the little girl changes everything. The prayer thing is throwing me off. It tells me that there is an element of religion here, and that can be tricky, because logic may no longer apply.

Normally I would just swoop in from behind them and put the girl to sleep, but I want her away from this fellow. I must've muttered something to that effect out loud, because Punch-Press nods. "We can do that, Old Tool. You get that chain on her wrist cut, and we'll have her a hundred feet away in three seconds." Gremlins are not known for boasting or exaggeration (unless they're talking about gear ratios, and then they just can't help themselves), so I must assume he knows what he's talking about, but cutting the chain will be easier said than done. It is steel, one of the metals most resistant to mystical influence. Punch-Press seems to read my mind (though I don't think he can actually do that), and hands me a small bolt cutter. I consider it, and the germ of a plan comes to me.

A minute later, I rise from behind a two-dimensional mountain. I will try to talk to this fellow in a calm and sensible manner at first. I can always kill him. The last thing I want at this point is panic, so the two humans see a tall, thin man of indeterminate age, wearing a long multilayered brown coat, a wide, flat brim hat, and an employee badge.

After seeing a rather unflattering picture of myself in the 1970s in some ridiculous Fortean magazine article, I have made it a practice to consciously change my appearance every couple of years. It is a nuisance to keep myself abreast of acceptable fashions, but I refuse to try to scare ne'er-do-wells while wearing bellbottoms. Being caught on camera is something I had to come to terms with decades ago, and I am probably the most photographed "imaginary creature" in history. If that's to be the case, then at least I will look good. "Hello, young fellow, young lady," I call out. "I think you might be lost."

They stare at me. I raise my hands to show that they are empty, and I give them a friendly, closemouthed smile. Oh, look how harmless I am!

Disappointment. Impatience. Rage. These are the emotions that seethe through the young man, and they are not the reactions I expected. He grabs the little girl and holds her before him. I freeze.

"I don't want *you*. I've come to face the Demon," he growls.

It's never good when you can *hear* the capital letters. "I'm afraid I don't understand—"

He cuts me off cold by shaking the little girl. "The monster that stalks this godless place. Zenonland. The one your corporate masters allow to feed off the unsuspecting."

How does he know I exist? Although I must take exception with that whole "feed off the unsuspecting" nonsense. I mean, it's *technically* true, but the way he puts it makes it sound like a *bad* thing.

He continues. "I have been charged by an agent of the Almighty! I must face this monster! Bring him to me or—" His hand gently encircles the little girl's throat.

I shrug off the first layer of glamour and look significantly less human. "I am here," I growl.

The fear pouring off the girl actually raises a notch, poor

thing, but there is no fear at all from the young man, which is unnatural. Believe me, I know. No, he now feels a sense of triumph. Of imminent fulfillment tempered with a growing sense of ... wait ... is that *disappointment?* What? Am I not *monstrous* enough for him? I like this less and less. "I am here," I repeat. "Now release the girl."

"Nooo," he muses as he looks me over, "I don't think you're what I'm looking for at all. That which I seek is *grander* than you. I seek the true evil at the heart of this place. I'll keep this pawn right here."

"You cannot keep her from *me*," I growl as I step forward, and he scoots the girl behind him, while continuing to look at me. Perfect. This allows Bone Cat to pop up and snap the bolt cutter closed on the chain between the man and the girl. It parts with a faint *click*. Faint, but loud enough that this fellow hears it and spins around ready to grab the girl—only to see her drop out of sight through the floor. The gremlins have done their job.

He spins back and finds me standing before him. He stares up into my face and begins to stammer out some prayer. I ignore it and fully dismiss the glamour. I savor the look on his face when he realizes that what he is seeing is neither mask nor makeup. Sometimes I tailor their perceptions a bit, make myself look more like whatever nemesis is ensconced within their own head. But this fellow doesn't need that extra effort. I am sufficient.

He screams so hard and for so long that I worry that he'll pass out, which is always time-consuming. But, thankfully, his survival instincts take over and tell him that he has to shut up and run. I lazily unfold an arm and grab hold of his outfit. Again he screams, but my grip is like iron, and I begin, leisurely, to draw him up towards me. Then—*then* the fear pours off of him. Great waves of it breaking against me. I almost close my eyes to savor it, as it has been so long since I've felt such a rich, raw fear. But no, as I have discovered by watching several television shows devoted to cooking and cuisine, visual presentation and the appreciation thereof really does enhance the dining experience.

I read him, skittering across his mind. Oh, I can't read his thoughts, per se—and thank goodness for that—but the impressions and emotions I get are messy enough. He is different from the usual sweepings of rapists, kidnappers, and pedophiles I'm allowed to harvest. No, this fellow sees himself as some sort of ... of holy warrior. One who volunteered to perform some great noble sacrifice in order to destroy a greater evil, which is presumably myself. Well, it takes all types, I suppose.

The crazy doesn't stop me from relishing the experience. The way his eyes roll up into his head. The way his lips pull away from his teeth. The frantic gyrations, which add a most comical touch. It is delightfully perfect, and indeed even better than I had expected, as, when I grin, revealing my beautiful teeth, the fellow's heart breaks apart. He dies of fear, within my grasp, inches from my face. This is a rare feast indeed, and I feel the empty places in my body filling up with that exquisite energy that sustains me and helps me keep body and soul together. Well, mine, anyway. His soul drains outward from the still-twitching meat. I languidly ensnare it and examine it with the same air I recognize in human connoisseurs examining a wine bottle they have recently emptied. It ripples and strains within my grasp, mewling in terror at its immobility. This does not bother me, as a little suffering is good for it. A tired epigram to be sure, but one that I can assure you is quite accurate, at least the way I do it. Let me see ...

A young soul. Hardly surprising, old souls are usually too experienced to get caught up in religious nonsense like this. Absolutism requires inexperience in order to survive. Time to begin rectifying *that*.

I send a claw deep within the seed of self that desperately wants to move on, and I send it the scariest message I can, under the circumstances. *"If I catch you doing this again, it'll be even worse."* This produces a final jolt of ethereal terror, light and crisp, without all those meaty glands to back it up, like the memory of a perfect dollop of sherbet at the end of a splendid repast. Delightful. I mentally unflex—and it's gone, squealing away into the æther. And while I am standing there like a self-satisfied ninny, his coat falls open, and I see the explosives. My start of recognition is great enough that his hand, which had been clutching what I belatedly recognize as a dead man's switch, relaxes its grip ...

And the world goes white.

It was not a terribly *large* explosion, as these things go, and I can desolidify myself pretty quickly, but still, when I come to, it is to discover myself plastered in a relatively thin layer against a shattered wall. How tiresome. I metaphorically grit my teeth and begin pulling myself together. I pause to rest and see Punch-Press sitting on a smoking puppet, talking to Bone Cat. Neither looks very happy. When they see that I am coming around, Bone Cat, at least, looks relieved. Punch-Press scowls. I can understand his feelings and try not to take it personally. The gremlins are responsible for the maintenance of the Happiness Machine, and I must assume, because they are cantankerous creatures, that since I am the lone survivor, they will blame me for this.

I make a final effort and assume a reasonable semblance of humanity. My ears finish reforming, and I can hear noises from the outside. The shouts of the park staff, the cheers and hollers of a crowd that has gotten an impromptu fireworks show, and—

The music. The music has stopped.

Punch-Press sees my realization. "At least a quarter of the mechanism is blown to shit. That moron managed to fuck up everything. He couldn't have picked a better spot if he'd tried." He ran a hand down his long nose. "Beginner's luck," he said with a grudging admiration. Gremlins still appreciate a nice bit of sabotage.

"The girl?"

Punch-Press waves a hand. "She's fine. We dropped her forty feet and caught her in the Number Three Drenching Tank." He shook his head. "She seems to think this is all a dream or something." I can easily believe it. I have seen the Gremlin's underground lairs, illuminated by their furnaces and forges, swarming with hundreds of small green bodies that you think are industriously laboring away within clouds of steam and sparks until you realize that they're actually singing and dancing and frolicking. Not that they *aren't* laboring, but they see no reason why they cannot do both at once. The simplest way to explain it is to just say that they really like their work.

Punch-Press continues, "A bunch of the third shift got injured, but nobody too seriously, and nobody died." He kicks a tattered bundle of rags. "Except for Captain Suicide here."

"Does anyone outside the ride know that he was in here? That he had grabbed the girl?"

He shook his head. "Nah. If she has parents here, they're still outside."

This is not unreasonable. Many of our older guests elect to sit out rides they have experienced a dozen times already. But they will be frantic. I rise to my feet and sway a bit. I'll sleep well tonight. "Bring me the girl and bag up our bomber. I'll pick him up later this evening." I look around again at the destruction. "Surely your people saw this coming. Why didn't you—?"

"We didn't see *shit*," Punch-Press snarled. "This didn't show up at *all*."

This is surprising. After the war, the Gremlins tried to figure out where everything had gone wrong. They decided that they would never have gotten into that particular predicament if they could have seen into the future, and so they built a device that lets them do that.

Gremlins deal with problems *differently*.

Oh, it's not a perfect system, of course. I'm told there are too many random variables taking place from minute to minute to be able to determine things like horse races, lottery numbers, or what you'll say at ten o'clock next Tuesday, but more general things can be foretold with uncanny accuracy. Over the years it has proved remarkably useful, which is why this lapse is so disturbing.

Punch-Press points an accusatory finger at me. "But how did this clown get a bomb *into* the park in the first place?"

That is a very good question. The security people at the gates don't bother with the modern fad for high-tech security theatrics. They just smile and apologize and paw through everything that comes through the gates the old-fashioned way. It seems inefficient, but a properly motivated and well-paid human being is infinitely more sophisticated than any machine. This is one of areas where the Zenon Corporation does not stint, and on a busy day, there can easily be several hundred security screeners. This diligence has paid off, as there has never been an incident involving weapons in the park. Until now.

I shoot an inquiring look at Bone Cat, who knows what I want. "Death is no longer here." That's something at least.

Several minutes later, outside the ride, a shout of recognition causes two frantic parents to whip around in time so that the little girl cannons into their open arms. After a round of hugs and recriminations, they realize they are not alone. As usual, even though they are looking at me, they are more fixated upon Bone Cat, who is leaning against my leg, with a smug grin upon his face. "I'm guessing you're Delores's parents," I say.

"What happened?" the father shouts at me. He is upset. He is not alone in this, and this is understandable. Many people are listening. The Happiness Machine has smoke pouring from its roof, and even as we stand there, a section collapses in on itself, causing the crowd to scream and surge backwards. And a surprisingly substantial crowd it is, even though the parade can still be heard thumping and booming from beyond the Zeppelin pens.

I address not just him, but the surrounding crowd. "There was a gas leak, I'm afraid. We don't know how it happened ... yet. Luckily, one of our staff members realized what was happening, and he got your little girl to safety." I raised my hands to forestall any questions. "He's fine, and no one else got hurt, but the

Zenon Corporation and I, personally, wish to apologize most sincerely to you and your family. I hope you will accept this small token of our desire to make up for the scare—" I produce the ultimate goodwill incentive: Free Lifetime Passes.

The crowd around us *ooohs* in appreciation, while the man himself is shocked into silence. He gingerly takes the three slips of cardboard and examines them with justifiable suspicion, but they are quite legit, as he will discover when he presents them to the main office in order to be registered.

I continue. "I must say, sir, ma'am, that your Delores is a mighty brave little gal. She followed our man's directions and saved everyone a lot of trouble."

This is indeed what Delores would remember. The whole family thanks Bone Cat and I effusively and hurries off, marveling at how real my companion looked. They are ecstatic over their new treasure, and I am instantly forgotten, as I should be.

I then spend the rest of the evening helping the staff herd the gawkers away from the smoldering building as the safety barriers are set up. Luckily it's not too long until the park closes for the night, and the Sweepers, as we call them, usher the last guests towards the gates. As they clear out, I give a heartfelt sigh. A job well done and a most satisfying meal. I can feel Bone Cat waiting expectantly, hand held high. I reach up and with the tips of my fingers give him his high five. As I do so, I feel a twinge in my shoulder. Evidently I still have some healing to do.

I tell the security people, who have taken over the site, that I am leaving. As usual, their reaction is mixed. They are unsure how to treat me, even after all this time, but no doubt the instructions they had received at their first orientation still hold. *"He has seniority. He will always have seniority and is to be obeyed."* People tend to get nervous around something as open-ended as that.

Back in the late nineties, there was a security officer who had worked with me for close to thirty years. I can't blame his curiosity, I suppose. Towards the end, he spent entirely too much time and effort trying to find out who I really was. The answers he dug up so unnerved him that it was easy to convince him that I had planted a false trail just to throw him off. Unlike other former employees, he's never visited. Perhaps that's for the best. His efforts weren't wasted, though, as it pointed me towards all the remaining records that had to be scrubbed clean. There's no place for real mystery in the Kingdom of Magic and Mystery. These days, because of me, security personnel are rotated across the various parks. Keeps them flexible is the official excuse. I try not to envy them.

I find a secluded spot and launch myself upwards. I drift high overhead, watching our guests pour out across the pavements, climbing aboard the fleets of buses that carry them off, or just scurrying across the street that I can never bridge to the cheap motels that line the avenue amidst the twenty-four-hour family style restaurants and souvenir shops. Lazily, I loop the perimeter, a ritual I have performed every night for close to sixty years now, and one that still gives me the same satisfaction.

I then swing back towards the heart of the park. No doubt the crowds that recently left, pushing their way out into the comfortably lit night, would be surprised to see the way the park lights have been cranked up and multiplied. The harsh glare washes away the charm that is present even under broad daylight, but it makes things easier for the thousands of people on the Night Shift that now roam the grounds tidying, cleaning, repairing, replacing, and preparing for a new inundation of expectant visitors on the morrow. The area around the Happiness Machine is a hive of activity, of course. I see actual non-company police there now. There is no way it will be open tomorrow, or even, in my opinion, by this time next week. I wonder how long it will be closed.

I am pensive, as I circle the park. A bomb. I have seen many things in my time here, but this is an unwelcome first. Pessimistic elements within the company had been expecting something like it for some time, of course, but not quite like this. If anything, we had feared a full-blown terrorist attack—replete with hostages and a simultaneous micromanaged social media blitz. That would certainly generate a great deal of publicity and outrage. But there is none of that here. Frankly, I believe we might even be able to sweep the whole thing under the rug, and upon due consideration, I realize that I'm the only employee that knows what really happened. I'll tender a factual report to Mr. Shulman, of course, but first I will look about the park on the ground level, to make sure there is nothing else out of the ordinary.

I land. "Do you sense anything else amiss?" I ask Bone Cat after he reforms.

He taps out a little melody on his ribcage with his thumbs while he concentrates ... then shakes his head. "Still nothin'." He hesitates. "But ... it's weird. I've really got used to the Happy music stuff, you know? It's strange not to feel it anymore."

I shrugged, then reconsider what he's saying. "Wait ... are you telling me that you could hear the music of the Happiness Machine all the way over here?"

He stared at me. "You *couldn't*? It filled the entire park."

Well, *intellectually* I knew that. "Filled the park" doesn't even come close. It's supposed to affect the entire planet, but I hadn't known that Bone Cat could *hear* it all the time. No wonder he was mad.

We tabled this discussion as I turned down the nearest lane and began to encounter other employees. You might not think that I would be a people person, but you would be quite wrong. Ordinarily, this is one of my favorite times of day, once Bone Cat is safely hidden away inside an inner pocket. Our guests might be credulous enough to believe him a bit of special effects wizardry, but most of our employees are knowledgeable enough about the current limits of technology that they recognize him as something truly inexplicable in a heartbeat, which makes him a bit of a conversation stopper.

We wander about the park, and I listen, taking secondhand delight in the overheard accounts of their travels and family dramas, politics and romances. In many ways, Zenonland is a community, bound together by the company we serve, with its own mores, politics, and customs, and thus, although I exist on its fringes, I take comfort from its familiarity.

Several of the secret gates swing open and the large street clearers rumble forth, their huge mechanical brush wheels scrubbing away at the streets. They are one of those modern inventions that I always find delightful.

Today, of course, the employee talk is mostly about the Happiness Machine. There has never been a catastrophic failure of a ride such as this, even at the company's nadir in the seventies. There is even talk that the entire park might be shut down while inspectors go over everything. This is certainly a possibility, but I think the political influence wielded by the company might prevent that. There will be more outside inspectors, of course, a fact that the gremlins are all too aware of, and by the time they are done, there will be textbook evidence of a perfectly normal gas leak caused by simple human—not gremlin —error. I make mention that I was there when the "leak" happened. This is interesting enough that it temporarily overcomes the disquiet people normally feel when dealing with me, and thus I am able to add my take on things directly to the information exchange market.

But the Happiness Machine is not the only news of interest abroad tonight. As we walk along, I see clusters of people gathered about monitors showing a number of different late-night news programs that are discussing the top business news. Apparently there has been some sort of coup in the upper boardrooms of the Zenon Corporation itself, and the current CEO, Mr. Robert, has been forced out. There are numerous clips of him actually being dragged off of the company property by Zenon security, while he rants and shouts. This makes for excellent television, and everyone is wondering what is going on. Personally,

I'm surprised. Mr. Robert seemed to be firmly in control of the board, and the company was doing quite well under his watch. Even more intriguing, no one is forthcoming with the identity of the new CEO, and there is rampant speculation as to his or her identity, which is to be revealed at an emergency stockholder's meeting which has been called for later this week. This is all of great interest to us, as for our company, the arrival of new management is always a tricky thing, even without all of this drama.

The Zenon Corporation used to be family run, but those days are long over, and today, even the most bureaucratic and sheltered student of accountancy understands that we are something *different*. Whenever a new boss takes over an established firm, you hear about things like "corporate memory" and "traditions." A new boss always likes to place their own stamp upon a recently acquired company. But trying that with the Zenon Corporation causes problems that are rife with the possibility of potential social media disaster.

Our company has produced a plethora of films and stories that have resonated with the young, sometimes to an astonishing degree, and the company works very hard at strengthening these bonds with the buying public, as it helps sell merchandise.

But what the businessmen were slow to understand was that in reality, the Zenon name was not marketing shirts, or plush toys, or anything material. They were marketing stories and dreams. They were crafting role models and exemplars. They were giving young people good memories and examples of how to behave in difficult situations. They were providing comfort in a confusing world and showing people that while things could get very bad, they could get better. These are things that all people, especially children, want and need to believe, and thus the Zenon Corporation, to a greater or lesser extent, influenced the world.

All well and good. But that sort of influence can be a two-way street. If you take it upon yourself to tell people how to live their lives, even tangentially, then they will take an interest in how you live yours. This is where things got complicated. An individual person is easy to judge, but since the death of Mr. Bartholomew, there has been no single person to act as a public lightning rod for our customers' interest, and, indeed, the company makes an effort to present itself as a faceless aggregate, elevating no single standout creator, but presenting itself as a jolly team that regularly spits out enthralling entertainment. The unintended consequence of this is that people are interested in the company as a whole, which is bewildering for corporate types who assume that the public will care as little about the inner workings and politics of our company as they would about a manufacturer of plastic chairs.

As a result, the Zenon Corporation is quite possibly unique, in that there have been best-selling books written about our supposedly secret business workings, decision processes, and traditions. In self-defense, the inner circle of the corporation tends to keep sensitive secrets close to their vests. I, myself, am one of those secrets. A little bit of information that new bosses have to be informed about in awkward face-to-face meetings. Some things shouldn't be written down where shareholders and institutional biographers could discover them.

I expect that I'll have another interview with another new boss, who will no doubt have ideas about how "things are going to change around here." Bone Cat and I enjoy those meetings. We really do. I shall talk to Mr. Shulman about this new regime when I see him this evening. He pays a lot more attention to the power struggles within the company, and actually has dossiers on any group or individual that could potentially become his boss. These have served him well, and I have occasionally found them very useful. No doubt it will be a refreshing change of topic after he's done shouting about the whole "bomber" thing. Besides, it will be a brand-new opportunity to submit my own little project to a fresh set of ears. I mention this, and Bone Cat groans. "Nobody is going to listen to your stupid idea." To myself, I must admit that history supports him, but in my heart, I know I'm right. We shall see.

Ah, and now the true high point of my day. The reason why, if I'm to be honest, I am not already bothering Mr. Shulman. Bone Cat emerges from a pocket and swarms up my arm. "Hey, slow down, Valentino," he says with a smirk, and I find that I am indeed walking a bit faster as I turn onto the boulevard next to the great pylons. I straighten myself and ease my stride. "Silence, churl," I snarl.

The kiosk is one of the smaller ones. It sells little metal pins and buttons depicting the various cartoon animals that romp across the park. She's there, as she is five nights a week. Her face looks tired. It's been a busy day, as I can see from the number of hooks hanging half empty. She looks up and sees us, and the way her face lights up does more to make the world a beautiful place than all the fireworks that have illuminated the park since it opened.

"Sheriff," she says demurely. She's the one who gave me that particular sobriquet. For decades no one had ever really known what to call me. The name on my badge is difficult to pronounce for anyone not born within sight of those far eastern mountains, and, as I have mentioned, my job title is unspecified. But the very first night she saw me, as I loomed up out of the darkness, she smiled that beautiful smile and said, "Why, you must be the Night Sheriff." And the name has stuck.

She is one of the youngest souls I've ever met. I believe that this may very well be her first trip through, to be honest. She is fascinated by Bone Cat and is one of the few to whom he has fully revealed himself. She doesn't believe he's a special effect, of course, but what makes her different is that she does not want me to explain him but is determined to figure "how I do it" herself. As a result, she tends to greet us with some new theory or other. These are always wrong, but never fail to be entertaining, and on slow days can easily provide the nucleus of an evening's conversation. These conversations are far-ranging, as everything is so exciting and interesting to her, even while hauling out boxes of ridiculous pins and restocking thousands of little hooks night after night. I always offer to assist, and the quiet pleasure I get working beside her would be positively embarrassing if I still cared about such things.

Her name is Vandy, which no doubt accounts for my tolerance of her uncomplicated chatter. The first time I heard it, a look must have crossed my face, because she volunteered the information that it was an old family name, from an out-of-the-way village in the old country, and that her ancestors had come to America almost a hundred years ago.

I actually remember these particular ancestors. They both came from good families, who periodically produced exceptional individuals, as were the two in question. The young man was a fine storyteller, and the girl a beauty who had been promised to the simple-minded son of one of the village nobility. They would have been her great-great-great-grandparents, I believe. Theirs was a scandalous romance (to their immediate families, of course, everyone else found it rather tedious), and to the general population, the most memorable thing about them was their decision to flee the village, as opposed to accepting their predetermined role as a focal point for a protracted family feud that had every indication of supplying scandal, gossip, and eye-rolling entertainment to the community as a whole for an entire generation.

Leaving one's village was a rare occurrence in those days. Most people lived their entire lives never traveling more than twenty kilometers from where they had been born.

You hear a lot of moaning about the loss of the ubiquity of small-town life, and a condemnation of the lonely anonymity found in big cities. People long for the days when "everyone knew your name." This is because they have never experienced a day-to-day existence where not only did everyone know your name, but your marital relations, your medical history, the workings of your digestive system, your amorous proclivities, your finances, your vices, and every foolish mistake you had ever made since you were a toddler. Of course, you knew everyone else's as well, which meant that, for your own survival, you were engaged in a constant game of dominance, influence, and brinksmanship; not to crush any enemy in particular, but just to assure that *you* were not the one everyone else talked about.

Back when our little mountain village first heard about the Americas (which was in the early 1800s, as I recall), everyone who didn't dismiss it as a fad, or simply another tall tale, seemed to focus on how *large* it was. The stories that engaged them were the ones about vast rolling plains, endless forests, and the enormous homesteads that ordinary people could carve out for themselves just by doing what they were doing here already, without having to share a bedroom with Great-aunt Màrinǧà, whose garrulous presence dampened the ardor of even the freshest of newlyweds.

No, Vandy's ancestors made the right choices, as had their subsequent progeny, if the result before me was any indication.

I had expressed an interest in her family history and discovered that the gift for storytelling had been deftly passed down through the generations, and our evenings were frequently graced with the old family stories of an isolated village and the monsters of the night that watched over it.

It is most peculiar to see yourself reflected thus in a mirror darkly so far from home. Occasionally, I remember the actual events from which her stories sprouted, and names and faces that I have not thought of for centuries would suddenly live again in my memory, like a trunk discovered in a junk shop that unexpectedly contains memorabilia from a life and a family you had been separated from long ago.

I'm sure that maudlin nostalgia factors highly in regards to my fondness for the girl. Yes, that must be it. There can be no other reason I've endured listening to her endless recitations about her schooling, her dissatisfaction with her hair, her life, and her constant inability to find a young man who recognizes her sterling qualities, which are patently obvious. Even back in that isolated village, the women of her line were sought out for their hips alone, not to mention her family's head for business. It's criminally underutilized here, but there's no denying she has the knack for it. She keeps track of every sale in her head and her books balance perfectly every night. Her future husband's business, no matter what it will be, will make her bride price back within the first year, if I'm any judge. I do not understand what is wrong with the young men of this country.

I have tried discussing it with Bone Cat, but he is probably one of the few entities more clueless about the finer points of romance than I am. Any penchant I may have had at that particular art when I was a young man has no doubt atrophied over time. But sometimes, listening to her, I get the distinct impression that couples who are thinking about keeping company together only discuss future finances and business strategies in the most shallow and superficial of ways. At times, I could believe they don't discuss them at all! No doubt I'm just not up on the current slang for such things.

She is also one of those peculiar people who are fascinated by Zenonland itself. Its history and its legends. To her delight, I appear to be equally obsessive, as I can talk knowledgeably about incidents and minutiae from decades past. Tonight, of course, she asks me about the events at the Happiness Machine. I welcome this, as it allows me to reinforce the story I disseminated earlier. I look forward to presenting it to Mr. Shulman. Vandy listens closely, and a frown settles on her face.

"Is there a problem?"

"I didn't think there were still any active gas lines in the park." I stare at her blankly. She meditatively winds a lock of hair around her finger. "Weren't they all decommissioned in the eighties?"

They most certainly were. I realize that I have foolishly allowed myself to fall into an old habit. Natural gas had long served as a convenient excuse for any amount of death and destruction that I had not publicly wished to own up to. We even had some naturally occurring incidents in the first few days that the park opened. It was decades ago, of course, but I had reached for it unthinkingly. Mr. Mortimer would have been quite disappointed in me. "It must have been an old line they missed." It is an implausible and unsatisfying excuse, as it obviously doesn't explain why there was still enough gas present to produce the observed explosion. But I am aided by the fact that Vandy doesn't expect me to actually have all the answers. I shall have to work on this.

Eventually Vandy finishes up. The boxes are stowed, the register is tallied, and everything is wiped down until it sparkles. I then walk with her, because it is on my way, to the nearest door down to the employee tunnels, where she'll clock out before heading home.

I offer her my arm as we walk, an act that I still find extraordinarily strange, and one that even today has me looking about for an outraged chaperone. We started doing it about a year ago, when the fool girl twisted her ankle while getting down off a stepladder. Obviously I couldn't just let her hobble along, and she wouldn't let me carry her, and the feel of her warm little hand upon my arm stayed with me for hours. She seemed to expect it the next night, even though she had been competently taped up by the park physician, which was surprising, considering the jackanapes couldn't keep his pop eyes off of me, even though she was the one sitting right there in front of him. Probably because I had mentioned that he would be very, very, very sorry if he did a shoddy job. Afterwards, when her ankle was quite healed, there simply wasn't a polite way to tell her to not do it.

She seems to be walking slower today, like she has something on her mind. I'm sure I'll hear about it eventually; if she wishes to say something, no power on Earth will stop her.

We stroll down the boulevard, occasionally dodging golf carts full of maintenance crews. Despite the bustle, the park itself seems lonely. It was designed to have endless rivers of humanity pouring through it, and much like a riverbed during a drought, it is obvious that it is not doing what it should be doing.

Vandy clears her throat in an artificial fashion. Heavens, she's actually quite nervous about something. I give her a pleasant smile of encouragement. "So, Sheriff," she says, "I'm assuming you have the same work schedule as me?" A reasonable assumption, since I'm always here when she is. The company is very strict about employees adhering to a five days on, two days off schedule. God forbid you accrue any overtime. "Which means you're off tomorrow, so I was wondering if maybe you'd like to go out for a drink. Or something." This last is delivered in a breathless voice that rapidly ascends into a squeak.

I ...

I stop and look at her. Her hand is tight on my arm and her eyes obviously want to look away, but they don't. They look into mine and what I see there is a fierce determination. There is fear, but it is an exotic flavor that I discover I have no wish to taste. "I ... I cannot."

She slumps. "You have other plans? That's cool ..."

"That is not it. You do not understand. We are too different."

"Look, if it's the age thing, I *know* you're an older guy. I'll be honest, I find that kind of hot—"

I actually gawp at her, caught up in a mélange of emotions that almost causes me to trip over a curb. "You have no idea how old I am." Something in my voice obviously gives her pause.

"... So tell me."

A wave of sadness crashes over me, because I am about to tell Vandy the truth. I like her too much to lie to her and this meant that I would probably never see her again, or else I would have to kill her. I really hated it when that happened. I hadn't told anyone the whole truth (who wasn't part of the upper echelons of the company) for almost thirty years. It hardly ever ends well.

"You will not credit it." She looks at me expectantly. I sigh. "I'm not sure how old I am, but I was born sometime during the reign of Basil the Second, the Bulgur Slayer, while he was the Emperor of the Byzantine Empire."

Vandy looks at me blankly. "I'm sorry, I was prelaw. We didn't spend a lot of time on political history."

I roll my eyes. "Basil died sometime in the year 1025."

She frowned. "So you're supposed to be, like, a thousand years old."

Bone Cat gave me a nudge. "She's taking it well."

She pulls her hand away from me with a flash of anger that freezes my heart. "Look, I know I said I like older guys, but you don't have to be a jerk about it."

I spin her about and grip her arms. She is alarmed now. I allow my voice to drop down into my hunting timbre. "I am not lying to you. I am over a thousand years old. No, I am not a 'jerk,' nor am I human, though I *was* once, a long time ago."

She looks at me and a trickle of uncertainty fills her mind. She has heard stories about me, of course, rumors passed down via the employee grapevine through the decades. I encouraged them once. Perhaps it is time to refresh them.

"Let me show you." She opens her mouth and I launch us upwards, unfurling myself into the night. Vandy gives a strangled *whoop* when we take off, but afterwards concentrates on maintaining her grip, as if I would let her go. Still, I appreciate it, as the screamers can be very distracting.

We soar upwards until the whole park lays shining below us. I pause at the height of my arc and slowly spin in place. Her eyes are wide and she radiates a combination of awe and terror that I find exhilarating to experience. I then allow us to fall freely. She squeals and clutches at me for several seconds before I snap my wings open and swoop downwards, spinning us around the tip of the volcano and then bringing us in toward the upper battlements of the castle.

Everyone assumes that the Castle is just an empty structure. This is not true. Aside from the guest suite that can be rented for an exorbitant fee, there are offices and a control room that monitors several of the nearby amusements. One of the otherwise inaccessible towers contains one of my resting places. Though thousands of people see the window and its snug little balcony every day, it does not appear in any of the park's plans, and it is there that I set her down as I coalesce back into my human shape.

Vandy watches everything. She doesn't cower, or even consider jumping. I am encouraged. I feel the familiar shape of Bone Cat precipitating out onto my shoulder, and I take a deep breath (more for the show of the thing), face her, and because I have lived in Southern California for over half a century, I cannot resist spreading my hands and softly crying, "Ta-dah!" It has the desired effect and her shoulders relax slightly, but she is still looking about the snug little room we are in, no doubt seeing if there is a possible escape route.

In this, she is not reassured. There is no door. All it contains is a chair, a bookcase stuffed with an eclectic mishmash of books, and ... the coffin. The coffin was not my idea. I would have preferred a bed, but this particular room had been designed and furnished by Mr. Mortimer, who had always considered himself a bit of a wit. I kept it for the ambiance, and to remember him by. I just make sure that no one ever lifts the lid to see the Posturepedic® mattress inside. Seeing no way out, she keeps her back to the balcony and shrugs. "So what are you?"

This ... was not quite the reaction I had expected. Don't get me wrong, I certainly didn't want her to start fainting or attacking me with assorted religious symbols, or even worse, prostrating herself before me, while begging to be allowed to become my dark servant or some such idiocy. Oh, I can tell that she is incredibly nervous, which was only to be expected. But I have to give her points for equanimity.

"He doesn't know, toots," Bone Cat interjects. "Heck, we know more about me than him."

She stares at Bone Cat and purses her lips. "One mysterious creature at a time," she declares.

Bone Cat nods. "Sharp thinking." To me, "I see why you like her, chief." He turns back and assumes what he thinks is a professorial stance. "So, I'm apparently some sort of manifestation of—"

"No," she interrupts. "I want to hear about *you*," she says to me.

Bone Cat looks mortally offended that anyone wouldn't find him the most fascinating thing in the room, and, with a snort, dives into the open coffin and slams shut the lid behind him. Vandy folds her arms and waits.

"Supernatural creatures come from many places, but they are not produced by the evolutionary forces that shape the natural world." I realize I'm trying to overcome my nervousness with pedantry. I take a deep breath and try again. "I used to be as human as you are, a very long time ago, but I do not even know if there is a name for what I have become. I am not a vampyre, although I do sleep during the day. I do not drink blood. I eat ... fear."

"Fear." Vandy considers this. "How?"

The coffin lid slams open. "He scares it right outta dem," Bone Cat shrieks. Vandy jumps. I slam the lid back down, pick the coffin up, spin it in place, and drop it back down on its lid. Muffled screams of rage can be faintly heard.

I carefully readjust my hat. "He is not incorrect," I admit. "When a person is afraid, it ... it sort of flows out of them, and into me. The more intense their fear, the more sustaining it is."

She looks at me strangely. "That's why you're always so creepy whenever you catch somebody stealing something." She thought about this. "Ew."

I clear my throat. "I was brought here when the park was being built and charged with its protection." I grin at her. "I keep the other monsters out." A bit of an oversimplification, that, but I figure that the mere fact of my existence was already a lot for the girl to absorb. "But part of ... the deal is that I cannot leave the park."

Vandy frowned. "But you don't look that horrible." She blushed. "I mean, you look human." She glanced up at me. "And who would know?"

I sigh. "It's not a question of choice. I *cannot* leave the park. It is a magical compunction; a mystical legal contract called a *geas*. I cannot even cross the street."

"Wait. When the park was being built? That's over fifty years ago!"

I nodded. "I told you it was a very long time ago."

"Wow." We stood together and stared out over the park. "I mean ... you say a thousand years, and that ... that's hard to wrap my head around. But fifty ... that makes you older than my dad." She thought about this. "Ew." She was using that word a lot. "So ... you're like an eternal security guard."

"Depressing, when you put it like that, but I cannot argue."

Tentatively, she reaches over and threads her arm through mine. "Well, it's kind of weird, but you seem pretty together, as far as monsters go. I mean, you've been here for over fifty years, so it's not like you go around killing people."

"I do, actually." I was expecting the surge of fear that boiled off of her and I resolutely shunted it aside. Consuming it would have been ... wrong. She whips her arm away and scrunches herself to the far side of the balcony. I'm pretty sure she wouldn't be foolish enough to try to jump, but I'm ready, just in case.

I continue to gaze out across the park. "Every now and then we do get a monster in the park. This is Zenonland. A cultural touchstone known around the world, and every now and then we get someone who sees the face the park shows to the world, the openness, the innocence, the childlike joy, and they want nothing more than to be the evil at its heart. The serpent in Eden.

"They come here expecting to find helpless children guarded by nothing but loving parents and simple humans." I turn and smile at her. "But they're not. They're guarded by me, and no one expects me."

"But ... you *kill* them?"

I look away. "I didn't at first. Mr. Bartholomew ... Mr. Zenon was very much against the idea. I was to just *scare* them. Scare them very much, and then turn them over to the police." I paused. It was easily fifty years ago, but the memory was still painful. Some memories last far, far longer than the people that forged them. "We didn't really understand back then. What sort of person would want to kill children in a place of innocence ... *needed* to ..."

Vandy astonished me by putting her hand on my arm. I took a deep breath. "I found one of them about to kill a child and I swooped in and filled him with such terror that I thought his heart would stop. But ..." Even after all this time, I still cannot explain it. "But there was more inside of him. Reserves that I did not reach. A ... a core of arrogance and self-belief that could never be breached." I lean wearily against the railing. "After surviving me, he was convinced that *nothing* could stop him. Oh, we turned him over to the police. He was out on bail within six hours and before the day was out he had grabbed a child as they were about to enter the park and he ... killed him." Vandy already looked ill, so I spared her the details.

"He got caught, of course. It was in all the papers, and the next night Mr. Bartholomew Zenon himself stood right where you are standing this very moment, and he turned to me and he said, 'If you ever catch another bastard like that, you crush it like a black widow.' And so, I do."

I neglected to add that the next words from him were, *"And for God's sake make sure the body is never found. At least not inside the park."* Mr. Bartholomew always had his practical side.

Not the most heartwarming story, I'll admit. I tried to think of something positive, to lighten the mood a bit. "I don't kill children," I volunteered. Vandy gasped. Drat. I really am not very good at this. "I can't, actually. It's part of the same geas." I thought for a minute. "Luckily, I've never felt the need." There. A positive thought! I smiled at her.

"I'd like to go now," she said levelly.

Oh dear, well, I'd known this was going to happen. "I have to carry you down," I told her. "There's no other way."

To her credit, she didn't argue, or whine, or even check, she simply held her arms out. I sweep her up and we flow down to the street. It was like carrying a wooden statue. I gently deposit her upon the ground near the closest door to the underground. She blinks in surprise as Bone Cat rematerializes upon my shoulder. She glances up at the tower.

"Naw, it's me," he says reassuringly. "I only exist when this palooka's feet are touching the ground. See, apparently I'm a manifestation of—"

Vandy turns to go while Bone Cat is still talking, which was for the best, really, since if she waited for him to *stop* talking, we'd be here until the sun rose.

No, this is good, really. If she's smart, she won't return. She'll go back to college (a lawyer—I'd never have guessed), find a nice, human paramour who will respect her brain and make use of those hips and eventually take her and their children to *King Dinosaur's Reptile Circus and Salamander Aquacade*, which I'm told is located down the street, and she will become one of the hundreds of people I have known throughout the centuries who had laughed and loved, cried and sang before falling before whatever instrument fate utilized to assert their mortality— remaining alive only within the corridors of my memory, because I knew I would never see her again.

CHAPTER TWO

This chain of thought takes me down my own well of memories. As you might assume, I have quite a lot of them, although I will admit that there are entire centuries that blur together because of their overwhelming sameness.

Even stand out events like wars, plagues, and natural disasters start to evoke not terror, but déjà vu. You see enough supposedly Apocalypse-heralding comets, and you become a jaded connoisseur.

But things began to change in the beginning of the nineteenth century. Alchemy was being superseded by this newfangled Science, and its products were appearing even in our remote little village.

However, we didn't have a lot of use for most of it, and when combined with an ingrained belief that "what was good enough for old grandfather was good enough for us," the people of my village continued to be amazed by the occasional traveler who lit their fire with something other than flint and steel.

Oh, new ideas and devices infiltrated our little world, but we were easily a hundred years behind the curve.

In the twentieth century, the modern world began to seek us out. Whether we wanted it to or not.

The first taste of this came in what most people today call World War One. The Germans began stomping through the country and, with typical thoroughness, even invaded our village.

Now dealing with invaders was one of the few activities that allowed the people of my village and myself to openly work together. I am the first to admit that the relationship between myself and the people of my village had been a rather odd one. In the beginning I had tried to fit in, staunchly declaring that I was still one of them, but that particular fiction broke down after the first century.

For a while, I was tolerated because I still had family to vouch for me, and by the time that was no longer the case, there was no denying that I had helped them innumerable times, and, honestly, there was the unstated fact that none of them could have defeated me. After a few generations, I was simply a cornerstone of their existence. I had been a part of the village forever, and had protected them from bandits, invaders, natural and supernatural disasters, and kept the Grumbly Witch away.

This last was rather easier than most, as the Grumbly Witch was simply a folkloric anthropomorphism of unspecified biblical-level disaster. As such, it was a name that was familiar all through what people these days call Eastern Europe.

You would think that over time, I would become accepted, and perhaps even honored for these efforts, and to be fair this did periodically occur, especially after I had interceded in a particularly showy way. But then a new generation would grow up and, as new generations do, sweep away the old and look at established institutions with fresh eyes. Invariably, I would be tied to those old institutions, and the fact that my very presence was disquieting certainly didn't help. I would once again find myself marginalized. They never actively turned against me, but I was regarded as a sort of universally shared creepy uncle, to be avoided until I was again needed.

It was during these periods when I questioned why I even stayed. Theoretically, I could travel anywhere I liked. While I had once been tied to the village by the bonds of actual family, a rather nasty bout of plague had eradicated the final, admittedly rather diffused, remnants of my bloodline, sometime in the late fourteen hundreds.

In the year 1575, I went so far as to actually leave. I had been taken by an urge to see the ocean, which I had heard about from a Romany peddler who had spun outlandish stories about it around a campfire, as well as a hundred other wonders to be found in the world, unaware of an additional listener ensconced in the treetops above.

It did not go well. Invariably, wherever I went, an extraordinary number of priests always seemed to appear, as if from nowhere, determined to send me "back" to some unspecified pit, or at the very least, drive me out of wherever I was comfortably sitting.

On the other extreme, I encountered a depressing number of bullies, thugs, corrupt officials, and otherwise ordinary people who, once they saw that I was both alone and "not from around these here parts," would attempt to make my life miserable in any number of ways, ranging from the petty to the murderous.

By my reckoning, I had travelled less than a hundred miles and killed twice that many people before I finally gave it up as a bad job and returned home. Little Āniakă Vellistĭnkeffrősş saw me arrive, made the sign against the evil eye, and then asked me what the young girls in the next village over were wearing.

It was then that I realized that while my relationship with my village was not ideal, that while they were uneasy in my presence, they never actually *questioned* my right to be there, and indeed, if pressed, took a perverse pride in the fact that I was watching over them.

This epiphany actually did quite a lot to improve my mental outlook about my place in the world. The villagers wanted a monster, something that united them, something that could be, according to the clergy, rendered harmless by prayer and a devotion to traditional values, helping to affirm their faith in an otherwise indifferent deity. Something that would, in times of obvious trouble, come to their aid. This was a role that I could play. Paradoxically, once I stopped trying to pretend that I was simply another human, albeit with peculiar dentition, when I embraced my role as "guardian monster," I found that I was more accepted. People knew what I was and knew how to deal with me. And thus, the last several centuries of my relationship with my village had been rather pleasant.

When the Germans came, everyone pitched in, and we became a center of anti-German partisan activity. It was the first time that the modern era really intruded upon my world. The Germans had weapons that seemingly never had to be reloaded, and it was the first time anyone in my village saw airplanes.

It was my penchant for bringing these down that made us stand out, I think. We obviously had no artillery, but easily half of the planes sent at night simply never returned. Eventually, someone in Berlin did some cost analysis, and the German army learned to go around us, and we sat out the last two years of the war as spectators.

After the war, we had a few German visitors, mostly family searching for soldiers who had been reported missing in our area, as well as a few obvious military types trying to figure out how we'd kept their army at bay. They seemed to genuinely appreciate the small, respectable graveyard that held their bodies.

And then, seemingly in the blink of an eye, it was early 1940, and there was another war with the Germans.

But it quickly became apparent that these were a different breed of German than those we had seen in the last war. Much more grim and efficient, and a lot less tolerant of interference by the locals, and that was saying something.

They had obviously studied the notes those military types had taken years ago, so when the area again became a hotbed of rather unnerving and effective partisan activity, they were easily able to deduce the center of that activity. But whereas we had assumed that they would go *around* us, as they had learned to do twenty years before, this time they decided to *eliminate* us. One of the differences between a war fought for economic reasons and one fought for ideological ones, I suppose.

The initial artillery barrage had started just as I was forced to retire to my hidden cavern by the dawn. Now, I am not entirely unaware of my surroundings, even at the height of the day, and thus in my dreaming, I felt the earth shake. The barrage continued right up until the first of the Panzers crested the roads up to the town and opened fire. Behind them came almost a thousand foot soldiers, all determined to take no prisoners.

Mr. Mortimer later told me that my people accounted for themselves very well, and that the German losses were very high. I don't know. He might have just been trying to make me feel better. But no matter how well they fought, the Germans had tanks and we did not. The outcome was inevitable. Within six hours, everyone in the town had been hunted down, and every building had been blasted into rubble. The army then left a token force and marched off with the sure knowledge of a job well done, and a message sent. The remaining troops then cleared a space in the town square, set up some perimeter guards, settled in, and began to search to discover the secret behind our little village's ability to strike at them so effectively.

At the first blush of dusk, they found it. Or rather, I found them.

I'm not proud of what I did to those men. Pride should accompany a sense of accomplishment. What I did was purely for revenge, a motive that I had always publicly discouraged, as, in a small town, I had seen that it can so easily lead to a never-ending cycle of tit for tat that poisons generations. Well, there would certainly be no chance of that here.

I ignored the sentries and started with the men who were off duty, most of whom were engaged in that time-honored soldier's hobby—casual looting.

The first one was a grizzled Sergeant, who had no doubt served in the army during the Great War. He was rummaging through the remains of the merchant Zîpôtskhin's once palatial abode and showed his experience by confining his efforts to small items, such as cash and jewelry. I let him scream for an unnervingly long time, and when his compatriots arrived, they found his mouth filled with coins and his eyes replaced with a pair of emeralds that the Lady Zîpôtskhin had been quite proud of.

The next was a rather officious-looking young fellow dressed in a black uniform examining the town records. This was the first time that I encountered a member of the *Schutzstaffel*, the elite organization within the German army that was responsible for a large percentage of the German atrocities. Today most people just know them as the SS. I knew nothing about them at this point, and so I must confess that I killed him much too quickly. An error I would never repeat, especially after I took the time to examine the man's essence. But the red of his viscera looked very striking against that black and silver uniform, and I was quite pleased with the effect it had on those who discovered him.

The rest of the night proceeded along a similar vein, punctuated with a few highlights, such as when I got a sentry to gun down one of his fellows, or when I prevented a sensitive young man from killing himself. No easy way out for him. I regard life as something rather precious, and the way he was begging for it by the end did my heart good.

Oh, and I fed well. By the end of the evening, I was so bloated with their fears that when I finally confronted their leader, as he made his last desperate stand huddled in the remains of the little church, I was able to project the combined fears of his own men, who had relied on and believed in him, into his heart even as I stripped his life away. I honestly believe that I may have scarred his soul so badly that it will never reincarnate, which is all to the good, in my opinion.

But, when it was finished, I saw that all I had really done was sully the ground of my beloved village with yet another score of mangled corpses. Then I realized that there was no one left to care. Everyone I knew was still gone. This was something I had gotten used to, over the centuries, but this time, another generation carrying their blood and memory would not be rising to take their place.

The Grumbly Witch had arrived in my little village at last, and I had been unable to stop her.

I found myself sitting on the edge of the fountain in the town square, staring at the dismembered head of Demeter, the statue that had, for over five hundred years, been standing demurely at the center of said fountain. I was remembering the day it been installed, a gift by the merchant Křêmetķin, who had had the thing hauled here all the way from Rome itself. There had been a festival to celebrate its unveiling, and the local girls had secretly sewn up outfits influenced by Demeter's rather skimpy toga and had appeared in them to perform a final dance number. The effect, when worn by actual people, was nothing short of scandalous. But Křêmetķin loved it, and even Father Ɵrkëśpatstín, that old reprobate, had only pretended to be outraged, and every one of those girls was married to a well-connected young man before first snow. Demeter, or variations thereof, became a popular name in those parts for three generations.

But there would be no more generations, and the fountain was in ruins. The water was spreading out over the slate and ceramic tiles of the town square, puddling around the bodies and flowing into the craters that marred the ground.

So I was sitting on that fountain, fastidiously cleaning my claws with a German bayonet, and idly wondering if I would actually bother to seek shelter before the sun rose.

Now you may be wondering how this tale of old-world death and destruction leads to my living several thousand miles away in an amusement park. That connection was made now, on this, the worst day of my life, when I met a man who did not exist: Mortimer Zenon.

In our isolated village, we had never heard of the American Bartholomew Zenon, the beloved showman and animation pioneer who, through a rare combination of utopian ideals, artistic vision, and a cutthroat business acumen that took no prisoners, would build a company unlike any ever before seen on Earth.

The aforementioned Mr. Mortimer was the third Zenon brother. Many people have been surprised to learn that there was a *second* Zenon brother, Mr. Raphael Zenon. I shall go into more detail about him later.

All of that said, the aforementioned *third* brother, Mr. Mortimer, achieved his anonymity honestly, by working very hard at removing any trace of himself from the general records. This was a lot easier to do back in the early 1930s, when everything officially written about your average person was inscribed upon less than a ream of paper, which was scattered piecemeal throughout the world in assorted dusty file cabinets.

To this day, I cannot understand why Mr. Mortimer dared to approach me, especially after everything he had seen. But approach he did. I looked up, and there he was, a nondescript-looking fellow with mouse-brown hair, wearing an outfit that in those tumultuous days would be noted and immediately forgotten anywhere between here and Tirana. His hands were where I could see them, and he had divested himself of any weapons, which, when I saw him putting them back from where he had carefully stashed them, must have taken him no small amount of time.

When he spoke, it was obvious that whoever had tutored him in our language had been one of those republicans that had backed the failed coup against our glorious Queen about thirty years ago. They were all from the more industrialized lowlands and tended to pronounce *V* as *B*, and then wondered why everyone else laughed at them. I'd heard that the survivors had emigrated to America *en masse*.

"Salutations, my good fellow," he said. "Please don't kill me; I am not with these people." I could read that he was terrified, to be sure, but more important, I found no trace of guilt (astonishing, considering what I learned of him later), and so I merely stared at him, and listened to him talk. "I am from America," he said, pointing somewhere towards the West.

I considered this. "I didn't know the Americans were involved in the fighting." I thought some more. "And, if you *are* an American, shouldn't you to be wearing a bigger hat?" I held my hands about a yard apart. "A Cow Boy hat. I've seen pictures."

He paused, and then shrugged. "I had to leave it at home, along with my horse. I don't want the Germans to know that anyone from America is here."

Mr. Mortimer was—well, I guess you'd have to call him a spy, of sorts. He was never fond of that particular label but was always loath to choose another. Today people are accustomed to thinking that there are secret levels of clandestine operations that never make their way into a government's official budgets, but in the first third of the twentieth century, this was a new idea, and as his brother was a pioneer in the field of entertainment, so Mr. Mortimer was a pioneer in covert operations.

"May I sit?" he asked. Silently I indicated a spot on the fountain wall, and, unhesitatingly, he settled in beside me. Together we regarded the carnage in the square. Eventually, he began to speak. "While my country is not yet in this war, my superiors are convinced that we soon will be. I have been sent to see what it is that we will be fighting against." He poked a German with his foot. "And I must say that we are all rather distressed at just how good the German army is."

He glanced at me. "So when the German High Command

labels this area as a particularly worrying one because of its surprisingly long history of successful resistance to outside invasion, I was bery interested." He sighed and leaned on his knees. "I was already on my way here when I learned that the Germans were about to attack." He looked directly at me. "I tried to get here in time to warn you, but they have clamped down on civilian travel, and ..." He made a weak gesture. "I am so sorry."

I could tell he was sincere. Actually I could always tell whenever he was being honest, which was a great source of vexation to him. But whenever he got mad, I pointed out that it was due to this ability that he was still alive. That always annoyed him as well.

He then stood up and faced me. "When our people first crawled out of the Great Mountain, the First King, Tak, stayed behind ..."

I stared up at him in astonishment as I realized that he was beginning the traditional bereavement ceremony that our village used at the death of a family member. It was then that I cried, something I had not done for centuries, as I realized that this town, which had contained every earthly remnant of my family, as well as all of the other families that I had adopted as mine, that I had looked over and protected, tended and nurtured, had been exterminated, root and branch, and that there was no longer anyone on Earth that I could count on not to recoil from me and what I was. I cried for them, and for myself. Who, I wondered, would keep me in touch with the remains of my all-too-fragile humanity?

Suddenly I felt arms around me, clasping me tightly. It was Mr. Mortimer, who had finished the oration, and had actually sat beside me and enfolded me in the traditionally accepted "Hug of Death" while I wept, like a stoic uncle holding a child who has seen his family taken from him. Even as I cried, I marveled. We were not really a very demonstrative people, to the point where flagrant public hand-holding between spouses had been the subject of thunderous sermons from the pulpit. No one had willingly touched me for centuries, and with a shock that redoubled my sobs, I realized how much I had missed it. The touch of other people, in tenderness, in sport, in anger—simply as an acknowledgement that you are another person—is such an essential part of being human that you do not think of it. When it is absent, you do not realize what it is that you are missing, even as its lack is felt. And then, suddenly, to have this basic need unexpectedly filled so selflessly, regardless of the risk involved (and Mr. Mortimer must have known how insanely dangerous a thing this was to do), was overwhelming.

I do not know how long we sat there, but when at last I looked up, the fingers of the dawn were beginning to touch the top of the mountains. I felt remarkably better.

I took a deep breath. "I will not kill you."

Mr. Mortimer visibly relaxed. "I am bery glad to hear it." He took a deep breath. "Would you like a job?" And thus began my time working with Mr. Mortimer as an unofficial "consultant" for the Americans.

I found my time with Mr. Mortimer to be eye-opening, to say the least. As I'd said, I'd never traveled much. After my last attempt, I had settled into my life in the village, and had taken comfort from its habits, rhythms, and rituals that I had learned to know, day after day, year after year, century after century.

The first time we arrived in an actual city, Mr. Mortimer was positively embarrassed. He said I gawped like a country bumpkin, and he had to steer me around with a firm grip under my arm like the exasperated parent of an oversized, addlepated child. I can believe it. I was completely overwhelmed. Oh, not by the things around me, even up in our isolated little town we had seen several auto-mobile machines grinding and stinking and looking very fine as they passed through, and while the height of the buildings was quite alarming, I always had the memory of my beloved mountains to measure them against.

No, what gobsmacked me were the people. Vast, never-ending, rolling *crowds* of people that filled the streets and the markets—even after midnight! And they were all strangers! A thousand different skin colors! Outlandish ways of dress! A roaring wall of undecipherable languages—and the emotions! An unchecked seething ocean of emotions, containing everything the human mind is capable of experiencing, flowing out at full strength. I have found that when two people do not share a common language, they allow their emotions greater expression, as these can often convey essential messages that mere words cannot. I was buffeted from every direction, and it was a stew well larded with assorted fears. Not just the usual pedestrian fears one finds in any large gathering but fears that were exotic to me—fears of crowds, of strangers, of being discovered, of *not* being found; fears about the future, the past, of strange languages or music or false idols or unclean food; about what they had done, or failed to do, about what would happen to them, or what they would be forced to do.

Imagine you've eaten nothing but your own home cooking for a hundred years, and then you are force-fed a scrumptious buffet of exotic, foreign delicacies. You quickly become aware that you should taper off a bit, or better yet, sit back with a charcoal biscuit and a cool cloth over one's eyes, but viscerally—oh my goodness! Tastes you've never experienced! Subtle nuances on old fears that you had thought well explored that reveal delightful new complexities making you appreciate them afresh! Toothsome, sweet, and delivered to you guilt free!

By the time we lurched into our hotel, I thought I was going to die. As soon as we entered our room, I collapsed onto the bed just long enough to regurgitate a pool of half-digested dreads. It was with a rather ill grace, I thought, that Mr. Mortimer managed to haul me up and stuff me into a lovely cedar-scented wardrobe from which I did not emerge for three days. An inauspicious beginning, to be sure.

After that, Mr. Mortimer and I spent a great deal of time just talking, interspersed with frequent nocturnal excursions. He wanted to know what I could and could not do, and what could and could not harm me. Not knowing what I am was certainly a bit of a problem, but it was a fascinating experience, and I learned many things about myself, such as when I discovered that I could hide inside a person's shadow, something I had been completely unaware of. It would prove very handy in the years to come.

Our first practical exercise took place in a small, out-of-the-way town in Silesia. It had been a part of the German Empire since the 1700s, but after a rather extended period of political back and forth, it had wound up a part of Poland in the 1920s. Naturally, Germany now wanted it back. Why, you may ask, would anyone care? Well, if you *did* bother to ask, you would hear an awful lot about ethnic tradition, and historical precedent, and natural geographic boundaries. Hardly *anyone* would deign to mention the plethora of gold, silver, copper, and coal mines located beneath all of that national pride.

When we first appeared, on a rather stormy night, we were just another pair of refugees from a rather unfortunate town upriver who, like many others, were displaced by the war. We found local work as night laborers, but despite Mr. Mortimer's quite excellent grasp of the language, and papers that convinced the authorities, the locals held us a distance. Possibly because they were aware that we were not from where we said we were, or possibly because they found me too disturbing. What can I say? I was still learning how to hide that I wasn't human. Overall, I think I did a rather good job. Unfortunately, I must concede that I made a particularly strange and unnerving human, and thus our problem. This was unacceptable, as we had arranged to meet with some locals, but everyone steered clear of us. We argued about the best way to circumvent this problem but were not able to come to a satisfying consensus.

Eventually, Mr. Mortimer decided to spend a boisterous

evening in the local drinking establishment attempting to cultivate some *bon homme*.

I decided to be a bit more proactive. I waited until midnight,
used my abilities to surreptitiously collect the four most hated
German officers, arranged their corpses together in rather
embarrassing positions, snuffed out the gas lamps—my first use
of this particular trick—and then joined Mr. Mortimer. The
small, timed explosive device he had taught me how to use
worked perfectly, drawing the attention of the town's firefighters
without disturbing my tableaux. After the initial uproar, the
German authorities said remarkably little about the whole thing,
and all of a sudden, everyone wanted to be our friend, if only
because our alibis were so ironclad. Things proceeded remarkably smoothly after that.

I could tell that Mr. Mortimer was of two minds about the
whole thing. On the one hand, he chided me for potentially
announcing our presence. On the other hand, he had to admit
that it had been very neatly done, and quite admired how the
Germans themselves had worked hard to cover it all up.

In time, these embarrassing "accidental" deaths became our
calling card, as it were, serving to announce to those in the know
that Mr. Mortimer and I were in town. It was better than
handing out free cigars. Concocting ever more elaborate and
amusing scenarios filled many an otherwise tedious hour.

And so, for the next six years or so, we fought Nazis. This
was no sop to me; everybody was fighting Nazis. Well, anybody
worth talking to.

I was never able to determine just how big Mr. Mortimer's
organization actually was, what it was called, or where exactly it
fit into the American espionage hierarchy. For all I know, it died
when he did (which would be so very much like him), but there
was no arguing that it was well connected within said hierarchy.
We were supplied with information and equipment, safe houses
and informants, and, up until the end, we worked harmoniously
with the intelligence agencies of over a dozen countries.

Mr. Mortimer did his best to keep my true nature a secret, which was quite a challenge, considering that everyone we hobnobbed with was the sort of person who couldn't resist unraveling a secret. In all our time together, only one ever managed to figure it out, and she had a bit of an unfair advantage.

We met her in 1942. Mr. Mortimer and I had been sent to Leningrad to babysit an American Senator who was part of a committee assigned to oversee the way that our Soviet allies spent the money we sent them. At least that was the cover story. The last few such overseers had returned with positively glowing accounts of the frugality and thrift of the Soviet agencies they were dealing with, which, frankly, flew in the face of experience, expectation, and, in one particular case, photographic evidence.

An open-and-shut case of corruption, one would think, but there was no evidence that these men had been compromised, and the last one had been selected because he was a rabid anti-Communist. It was very odd, and so they called us. Between Mr. Mortimer and myself, we were able to keep the Senator under observation for twenty-four hours a day, but even then, we almost missed it.

The Senator was a diligent fellow, and for easily twelve hours a day he worked in an official capacity. He left the usual rounds of committee meetings and hearings to his subordinates, and spent his days pouring over ledgers and account books. He remarked that once his hosts understood that he couldn't read Russian, they seemed to assume that he couldn't do math, either. The rest of the time he spent touring museums, dining well, and listening to music, firmly eschewing any offers of companionship.

He quickly found evidence of money being siphoned. What appeared to annoy him was not that money was being stolen, which didn't surprise anybody, but at how clumsily it was being done. His discoveries resulted in fresh questions, which he relayed through said subordinates. These were answered by unconcerned apparatchiks with rather blatant lies. This was when Mr. Mortimer and I sat up. Usually, in a situation like this, the next step would either be an attempt to bribe, blackmail, or assassinate.

What it actually was, was a barber. We had been in the Soviet Union for two weeks, and the Senator told the hotel that he wanted a haircut. Fifteen minutes later, Mr. Mortimer opened the door, and a professional-looking young woman, leather case in hand, tightly cut smock emblazoned with the hotel's logo stretched across her figure, smiled and curtsied on our doorstep. Thirty seconds later the Senator was sitting in an armchair, a sheet tucked under his chin, while she was asking him, in charmingly broken English, if he had ever met Errol Flynn.

It was her voice that precipitated things. While my appreciation of the fairer sex has been an abstract one for longer than I care to remember, appreciate them I do. Curious to see who possessed such a melodious voice, I silently stepped out of the back room where I normally stayed when we had casual guests.

Thus I, and I alone, had a perfect view of her discreetly pocketing a lock of the Senator's hair. I grunted in surprise, and she whirled about, scissors raised. As we later found out, she was used to being able to spot hidden people but had missed me for the rather obvious reason. At the sight of me, she hissed in surprise, and the hand holding the scissors made a complicated motion. Reflexively, I batted aside the minor curse she sent at me. It bounced back with a squeak and shattered a mirror.

"She's a witch," I informed the rest of the room. In one smooth motion Mr. Mortimer jerked the Senator from his chair, bundled him into the bedroom, and slammed the door behind him. He then blocked the exit.

"She was collecting a lock of the Senator's hair," I informed him. "With that there are over a dozen ways she could charm or influence him into writing whatever her masters wished."

Mr. Mortimer nodded in satisfaction. As far as he was

concerned, the mystery we had been engaged to solve was closed. As for the woman herself ... "Dangerous?"

In the beginning, Mr. Mortimer's knowledge of the supernatural had some shocking gaps, but this was, at least, an understandable one.

There are many different types of witch. Most of them are simply people who are able to nudge the unseen world in a direction they find more to their liking with greater or lesser degrees of efficacy. They run the gamut of good to evil much like any other segment of the population.

But a few are much more than that. The old alchemists referred to them as *"Magnam Pythonissam"* or "Grand Witches" when they dared to refer to them at all.

"This one most certainly is."

At this, the woman, who had been watching us closely, laughed and deliberately dropped her scissors. "That is quite true," she said, in markedly better English. "But I know when I am no longer the most dangerous thing in the room." Mr. Mortimer and I glanced at each other. The truth of that statement would remain an open question for over a decade to come.

This was our introduction to Madam Polina Urakhov. She was a Soviet agent, who claimed descent from a long line of witches, and, possibly, bears. She seemed to expect some sort of retribution from us, but after Mr. Mortimer made sure that she had divested herself of the Senator's hair, he merely remarked that she was wasting her talents on us when she could be confounding fascists, and politely showed her the door.

The Senator then went home and produced a very damning report that resulted in exactly one official, who happened to have Trotskyite sympathies, being very publicly executed, and then, the United States was assured, there was no more corruption to be found in the Soviet Union.

Whether it was because we had so easily rumbled her, or because she took Mr. Mortimer's words to heart, it was less than a month later that we were standing back-to-back-to-back with

Madam Urakhov in a sewer in Prague—an otherwise quite lovely city by the way—observing the fruits of our first collaboration, which in this particular case was a cell of Nazi sympathizers finally realizing that they had been the unwitting pawns of a particularly loathsome spider cult. As a result of this, everybody was busy fighting everybody else, and doing a bang-up job of it. Now normally I quite enjoy a situation where, usually through Mr. Mortimer's machinations, one batch of enemies was busy slaughtering another batch of enemies, but in this instance, both camps were still trying to kill us.

It did allow us to assess Madam Urakhov's fighting abilities, which were quite respectable. Interestingly, she mostly used a 1920 Colt .45. Witches are not really known for being hands-on fighters. They tend more to the laying on of curses, enchanting weapons for others—that sort of thing. But Madam Urakhov showed herself to be an excellent shot. Perhaps the runes inscribed on her pistol had something to do with it.

She watched me crush the throat of—if his ridiculous spider hat was any indication—one of the High Priests and took note of how I plucked his poisoned ring from where it was imbedded in the back of my hand and flicked it into the eye of a fellow enthusiastically waving some sort of kuris as he ran towards us, screaming. As his screams briefly took on a new urgency, she pursed her lips. "What exactly *are* you, my little enigma?"

I shrugged. "I don't know." This was as true then as it is now. Wherever you go in Europe, it is not unusual for isolated hamlets to concoct a local night creature or two, but over most of the continent these tend to fall into rather broad categories: vampires, lycanthropes, ghosts, ghouls, and the other relatively familiar things that go bump in the night. But Õllaĵeękǎ, the mysterious girl who turned me all those years ago, claimed to have traveled extensively across the world in her time, and never mentioned where it was that she herself had been created.

Often I have wished that she was still here, if only because she could have answered many questions, but I killed her immediately after she created me. I regretted it instantly, of course, but she had warned me that it would happen, and that she had no regrets.

Madam Urakhov found the whole thing quite intriguing. She said that there were vague stories about creatures like myself but up until now, she had believed that stories were all they were. In the remaining years we worked with her, she never did find out anything, and if she did after we went our separate ways, she found nothing about how to kill me, as I'm sure she would have used it if she could.

Grand Witches, of both the male and female variety, do not, as a rule, make for boon companions. They tend to regard other people more as things to be utilized, a trait that gets worse the older they grow. But there *are* exceptions. It's rare, but it happens, and it appeared to be happening now. There was something about Mr. Mortimer that fascinated Madam Urakhov, and the feeling was clearly mutual. We met her every couple of months, which apparently suited Mr. Mortimer and her just fine. Sometimes it was official, but almost as often we would be killing time between assignments somewhere, and, lo and behold, we would turn a corner and see her sitting at a café table, or she would enter a train compartment to find us idly playing pinochle. The only one who was ever really surprised by this was me. It would have made sense to have us permanently assigned together, and occasionally I still wonder if things would have turned out better if the two of them had managed to establish a more stable relationship. I like to think so. But it was not to be.

When we did work together, things tended to get weird, and not quietly weird. Big, ostentatious, call for air support weird. The after operations rulings always declared that we were justified in our actions, and we were commended through gritted teeth and surreptitiously awarded medals accompanied by certificates labeled "TOP SECRET. BURN AFTER READING." But as the war progressed, both of our higher-ups tried very hard to discourage these sorts of showy operations. It didn't look good, and they were terrified that they might become known to the public. Even before the war started, it was widely known that the Nazi inner circle dabbled with diabolical forces, which made our ... well, *my*, very existence suspect in some Allied circles. Even the German soldier on the ground, not to mention the Americans, British, and Soviets that pushed them back, had no tolerance for anything that smacked of the supernatural. And so an effort was made to keep Madam Urakhov and ourselves separate, which I think was a mistake.

None of us were happy with the situation, but, for the first time, it forced me to see how this prejudice against the supernatural affected the creatures of the night. Very quickly, I realized that I was one of the lucky ones, because I had official government sponsors and protectors, and, more importantly, I was already on the move, as it were. Monsters associate with humans, and so it should not be surprising that they often *act* like humans in many ways, especially those who were in stable arrangements with their communities and had been for generations. You could *tell* them that an army was approaching and that they should relocate, or at least be a bit more circumspect, but, also like humans, they would rarely listen. They would refuse to leave their homes, and thus were exterminated because they were "unnatural."

Sometimes this was seen as a positive thing, certainly. Many a region was freed from a vampyre clan that had claimed a monthly victim, for instance. But this was before anybody really understood the concepts and mechanisms of a functioning ecosystem. Today we understand that where there are checks, there are also balances, but back then anyone would have scoffed at the notion, especially when it came to monsters. Occasionally I was able to convince beneficial entities to leave ahead of the advancing army, but, even then, the question remained: Where could they go? They were refugees that no one would willingly accept.

I remember one incident in particular, a charming little town just inside the border of Moldavia, where Mr. Mortimer and I intercepted some secret plans and killed the head of the Nazi robotics project for the first time. What makes it stand out in my mind was that it was the home of an ancient Naiad, whose very presence purified the lake enough that the town was able to use it as a healthy water source, even after dumping assorted sewage, industrial runoff, and farming by-products into it for over a hundred years. For performing this service, all she required was the voluntary sacrifice of a young man every five years or so, which, in my opinion, was very good value for services rendered.

Naturally, when the German army learned of it, this could not be allowed to stand. Mr. Mortimer and I begged her to let us get her to safety, but she was betrayed by her own townspeople and killed by the Germans before we could convince her to leave. The locals actually celebrated being freed from her "yoke of tyranny." Less than three years later, most of them were dead, killed by a combination of dysentery, cholera, and heavy metal poisoning.

This incident, sadly just one among many, remains in my mind because the Naiad was close to my own age, and it is not often I that I find someone who can still appreciate a good Prester John joke. I did not know her for long, but I still miss her.

She was only one of any number of beneficial creatures of the night (some of them only beneficial in hindsight, I'll grant you) who were removed from the stage, and the nights became quieter and, for some of us, lonelier.

This does not mean that they became less dangerous—at least for us. Mr. Mortimer and I continued our work even after the German surrender, dealing with Nazi holdouts, collaborators, and black marketers. If this seems like rather small beer for the likes of us, well, you are not wrong. The war with the Germans might have ended, but everyone "in the know" was aware that all too soon the Soviet Union would be declared the new enemy, and when they were, our work would continue as it had before.

I was wrong about that. Oh, Russia was indeed a recognized problem, but actual war was never declared. The Atomic Bomb saw to that.

The other big change was that the armies of the four biggest industrialized nations had ground through Europe, and the Europe they left behind was different. It was at this time that I first heard myself described as a creature of an age now past, and it was not a good thing to be. There was now a de facto "zero tolerance" policy when it came to creatures of the night. My true nature was revealed to the intelligence fraternity at this time. How it was revealed, we did not know. Madam Urakhov swore it was not her, and, for what it was worth, I believed her. It wasn't her style. But however it happened, it quickly became apparent that even people whom I had helped and regarded as allies now felt uncomfortable in my presence, and one or two of them actually tried to kill me.

This type of shift in appreciation had happened to me before, so the one who it bothered the most was Mr. Mortimer, who despite dealing with Nazis, still had a fundamental belief in the goodness of human nature. Thus, when people we had trusted began to turn on me, and by extension, us, he grew positively morose at times. The Soviets, if anything, were even worse. We actually worried for Madame Urakhov's safety. Well, to be honest, Mr. Mortimer did. Sometime during the war, he had developed feelings for her, which, as far as I could tell, were sincerely reciprocated.

This made our inevitable falling out all the more unpleasant.

It was in the spring of 1947. We met in Prague, a city we were all quite fond of. The Soviets had claimed Czechoslovakia, and everyone was waiting to see what would happen. We met at our favorite restaurant, a small establishment deep in the Artist's Quarter. Mr. Mortimer praised their wines, Madam Urakhov was particularly fond of the chicken paprika, and I enjoyed the view.

It was a foggy night, so I couldn't concentrate on said view, which possibly changed everything.

Both Mr. Mortimer and Madam Urakhov were ill at ease, though they both tried to hide it. We started with small talk, but even a rather hilarious anecdote from myself about flushing out die-hard Nazis who had refused to surrender by strolling through the area shouting, *"Zahlmeister,"* which is German for paymaster, utterly failed to defuse the tension.

Finally, the owner brought us a complimentary round of prewar Tokay. I sniffed it for the appearance of the thing, and a subtle, unwelcome note caught my attention. Unhurriedly, I reached over and covered Mr. Mortimer's glass just as it was about to touch his lips. "Drugged," I said quietly. Madam Urakhov had not even pretended to drink, and when she saw that the jig was up, sighed and poured her glass onto the floor.

"By this time tomorrow," she said with a shrug, "I will be expected to kill you. I was given this one chance to capture you, and perhaps, with time, convince you to defect."

Mr. Mortimer leaned over the table and gently took her hands in his. "This particular door swings both ways, Polina. You could come back to America with me." He looked at her directly. "I would keep your secrets. You would just be another spy. Debriefed? Of course, but afterwards, we could do whatever we wished. Go wherever we wanted." She was silent, and Mr. Mortimer gently added, "You don't truly believe that Communism will accept you for what you are?"

"Don't be foolish enough to believe that Capitalism will be more accepting," she snapped. "They will not permit your tame little monster to roam freely, and when it has been removed, you will also come under suspicion. Guilt by association, darling." She sighed, and gracefully stood up.

"At the moment, Russia is cursed." She patted her chest. "Trust me, I know the signs. If I am to help free it, I cannot do it by running away." Her voice dropped to an almost imperceptible whisper. "Which is what you should do, right now." We looked around, and when our heads swung back, where Madam Urakhov had been standing there was now nothing but a rather ornamental coat rack.

Perplexing, but when the four men with guns burst through the doors and windows less than three seconds later, Mr. Mortimer and I were ready for them.

Over the next five years, she was a thorn in our side, although I like to believe that we gave as good as we got. Mr. Mortimer never stopped trying to get her to come over, even after she made several attempts to actually kill us. He was always convinced that she was under orders, and that Stalin had her heart hidden in a duck egg or some such, which he was using to control her. I would have tried harder to convince him that this wasn't really how these things worked with witches, but I doubt he would have listened; the foolish man still sent her blue roses every year on her birthday.

We never attacked her, but I will admit that whenever she came after us, Mr. Mortimer did his best to kill her. Personally, I thought that showed a lot of respect. But all witches are hard to kill, and Madam Urakhov was a very powerful witch indeed. However, "hard" is not "impossible."

The end came in a chemical factory somewhere in Belarus, where some very shortsighted person had rediscovered the papers of Albertus Magnus, the alchemist, and was planning on ending the cold war by crashing the economies of both the Eastern and Western blocks by producing entirely too much gold. Naturally, he sent a manifesto to the United Nations, so he shouldn't have been surprised that he had agents from, by my count, eighteen different countries trying to kill him, capture him, or simply steal his notes.

It was rather depressing, actually; many of these people were ones that we had worked with. That were still, ostensibly, our allies; and yet here I was, punching through the chest of a very nice fellow from the Netherlands, who had once shown us the proper way to cook tulip bulbs in the middle of a famine. He was not the only one whose heart was no longer in it, let me tell you.

By the end of it, the would-be alchemist was dead, and only Madam Urakhov and ourselves faced each other with the files everyone had died for sitting on a small table on a catwalk overlooking the laboratory, which was in flames all around us, chemical vats roiling and venting great gouts of poisonous steam. I eyed a number of pressure gauges that were reporting that there was a race on to see which boiler would explode first.

"Polina," Mr. Mortimer shouted. "This is perfect! You can 'die' here, and no one would ever know differently!" He held out his hand. "Come with us. With me. Please."

"And allow Capitalists to possess the secret? Never!"

"Is that it? Is that what you're worried about?" Without another word, he swung his pistol up and shot out one of the table legs, sending the files over the edge and into a vat of boiling mercury, where it burst into flames.

But Madam Urakhov only reacted to his initial movement. She saw his gun come up, ducked, and shot Mr. Mortimer where he stood. I snarled, and flowed forward, faster than she expected. I raked her side with my claws, but she spun and drove a small dagger into my arm, and I felt pain like none I had experienced in the last millennium. My arms locked into place and I fell onto my side. She laughed in triumph and pulled a second dagger out from her sleeve and strode towards me, confident that she had won, which is why it was so very satisfying to lash out with a well-placed kick, scything her legs out from under her, and sending her over the edge, screaming, into the same vat of mercury. I ripped the dagger out of my arm with my teeth, flowed to the ground, fell actually, and managed to slam the lid down on her and secure it tight. A boiler at the far end of the room exploded. Getting to Mr. Mortimer and pulling him free before the entire complex went up was a very near thing.

It was only after I got us far enough away that the remaining explosions were more entertainment than threat that I was able to determine that while Mr. Mortimer was severely wounded, he would survive.

Over the course of our association, we had saved each other numerous times, of course, and by this point, we no longer bothered to keep track of who owed whom. But Mr. Mortimer took this particular instance to heart for some reason, and I believe that it was at this point that he began to seriously plan for my future in the new world.

CHAPTER THREE

As I mentioned earlier, I had initially been sheltered from the anti-supernatural feelings that were growing in postwar Europe. We were aware that this feeling was growing stronger, even in the Americas, but I did not consider myself at risk. Proof that even I, with all my experience, was still susceptible to tunnel vision.

This changed early in 1953. Mr. Mortimer had a meeting with a fellow from Washington, and when he returned, he was angrier than I had ever seen him. There was a new president in America, and apparently this administration was determined to sever ties with anything "ungodly." I had been mentioned specifically.

Mr. Mortimer was frank. "They do not want you around," he said, "But I have done such a good job of talking you up that they will not let you go. They will not feel comfortable until your file is closed."

And so he killed me.

It was very well done, in an out-of-the-way castle in Bavaria where (the reports later explained), the Nazis had secretly stored some extremely combustible and satisfyingly pyrotechnic chemicals. It took three of the new administration's agents assisting Mr. Mortimer to do it, but only one of them lived to witness my operatic demise (and keeping him alive was a challenge, let me tell you). And so the deed was done, and Mr. Mortimer, understandably shaken by the whole thing, returned to the United States for the first time in almost two decades.

I took a more circuitous route by sea, where I was listed on the manifest as a particularly large cask of Madeira, which was being aged the old-fashioned way. It was a delightful trip, as I had never done any ocean travel. The ports the ship visited were always interesting, and it fed my recently discovered delight in the exotic. I even managed to dispatch a couple of Nazis who had attempted to hide from their pasts in more tropical climes. I thought of it as a little something extra to help repay the cost to the Americans of my extended cruise.

What with one thing or another, it wasn't until early in 1954 that my ship docked at the Port of Los Angeles. Less than ten hours later, I first saw what would later be known as Zenonland. It was still under construction, of course, but even then, the size and scope of the place was evident. Still, I was a bit underwhelmed. "A night watchman." I looked at Mr. Mortimer askance. "How glamorous my retirement shall be."

"When it's finished, it'll be larger than the village you were happy to spend several centuries in."

Well, there was no denying that. I examined the paper life that Mr. Mortimer had presented to me when we had met earlier in the evening. I had every confidence that it would all pass muster, but ... "Your brother is okay with me being here?"

"Bart is so pleased that I actually asked him for a favor, that he's perfectly willing to help you out."

"Even after you told him ... everything?"

At this Mr. Mortimer looked uncomfortable. "Well ... there *is* one condition ..."

"I won't have to wear one of those platypus hats, will I?"

"He wants a geas placed on you."

I stepped back. "A geas? On me?"

Mr. Mortimer looked uneasy. I had never seen him so

discomfited. He ran a hand through his hair. "My brother knows just enough about supernatural creatures to think that he knows everything. He ... he wants something that would prevent you from attacking children."

I was outraged. "What does he think I am? How *dare* he?"

Mr. Mortimer waved his hands trying to placate me. "No! It's just that ... Like I said—he's *heard* things." I opened my mouth. "Not about *you*, of course! But on the other hand, nobody knows what you are! That's the problem!" I frowned. Encouraged, he continued. "These days everyone refuses to believe in the existence of the supernatural. If you think of monsters, you think of those ridiculous things they call vampires and werewolves in the movies—And there is a codified mythology about them. Can't go out in the light! Afraid of crucifixes!

"Whereas you ... what *are* you? Even you don't know. Now Bart trusts me—but there are limits. This place he's building— It's a place where people are supposed to be happy. Be safe. He thinks people will *need* a place like this. So he demands assurances that you are safe to be around."

"But this is pointless. I would not attack a child."

"Then you should have no problem with me putting on a show to reassure him?"

Well, he had me there. I didn't like it, of course. We'd seen geas's at work during the war, and they could be nasty things. But I trusted Mr. Mortimer. I did.

So, I acquiesced, with poor grace, I'll admit, and several weeks before the park officially opened, we traveled by train to the city of New Orleans, in the state of Louisiana. An odd little city. I'll be the first to admit that my experiences with American cities is quite limited, but as I stepped down off of *The City of New Orleans* into the newly opened Union Passenger Terminal, for the first time since I'd arrived in this country, I felt like I had been transported back to Europe. Well ... Sort of. A strange, idealized reflection of a Europe that never was, I should say.

There was magic here. Oh, not the subtle, workaday magics

that are present in even the most mundane of human habitations. As we debarked, I saw a tall, skeletal figure wearing an improbably large top hat lounging upon the roof of the building across the way from the train station entrance. When he saw me looking at him, he sat up quickly, tipped his hat, and strode off across the rooftops, his legs stretching out to carry him away. Subtle it was not.

We climbed aboard a sleek electric streetcar that rumbled along through the night. "So," Mr. Mortimer asked idly, "any interesting ghosts hanging about?"

I sighed. When I squint in a certain way, I can occasionally see ghosts. Thankfully, I have to make a bit of an effort, as ghosts can be incredibly needy if they know you can perceive them, and you really shouldn't bother as they tend to be gloomy, dour, and, frankly, a bunch of whiners. "Sometimes I wish I'd never mentioned that."

"But my dear fellow," Mr. Mortimer chided me. "When we arrive in a new town, they're the one group that can't be bothered to lie to us."

Arguing with Mr. Mortimer was an exercise in futility, so I squinted, and gasped in surprise. The ghosts of New Orleans were all around us. Hundreds, thousands of them. But unlike any spirits I had ever seen, they whirled and danced and strutted up and down the streets, playing instruments and obviously having a roaring good time. I blinked and they vanished. I squinted again, and they reappeared, engaged in a street party that stretched for miles, and which, in all the time I was there, showed no sign of flagging. I dutifully reported this to Mr. Mortimer, who vainly craned his head about. "Are you sure?"

I squinted again and saw our streetcar roll through a gigantic skeletal alligator, easily thirty feet long, which was carrying a troop of the dead gyrating to some unheard music. As we passed amongst them, Mr. Mortimer's fingers began unconsciously tapping out a tune, which, I realized, perfectly matched the movements of the dancers. I saw that the other riders were all smiling and swaying slightly in time as well, and I realized that the positive energy—what we here in California now call good vibes—generated by this ongoing, post-life bacchanal is so overwhelming that a minuscule amount of it was actually managing to leak through the barriers separating life and death. The result is that it gives everyone in the city a bit of an extra bounce to their step, and a bit more apparent *joie de vivre*, which is rather amusing, all things considered.

"I think you're just making it up," Mr. Mortimer said petulantly.

"Look at the people on the sidewalks," I said.

Mr. Mortimer checked his wristwatch in that manner he had that allowed him to surreptitiously see everything around him. "More people standing about than I would expect for this time of night," he remarked. "Are they really all watching us?"

"They are, but I assure you that the only ones watching are not actually people." And this was certainly the case. While they might be unnoticed by the humans strolling among them, there was an unnaturally large percentage of nonhumans taking the night air, and all of them were keenly watching our trolley as it rolled by.

Mr. Mortimer looked interested. "Do tell. What's that one?" he asked, pointing to a tall fellow.

"Some sort of lycanthrope. You can tell by the ears."

Mr. Mortimer shook his head. "So you keep saying, but I just can't see it." He pointed to a rather shapely young woman in an abbreviated coat. "Her? Is she ...?"

I rolled my eyes. I don't how he always managed to find them. "Yes, she's a succubus. Well spotted."

Mr. Mortimer tapped his fingers upon his knee. "Now what is so interesting about us?"

In the trolley seat next to us, an elderly man had drifted off to sleep. At Mr. Mortimer's question, he raised his head and grinned, and I saw that something unnatural smiled out at us from behind his eyes. His mouth opened and a voice redolent with humor rolled forth. "Well, suh, der ain't many dat would go face-to-face wit de Queen of N'awlins, suh, much less pay fo' de priv'lege, an' to some, dat's worth seein'."

He looked me up and down. "Plus, a ting like you, suh, in de nawmul way o' tings, you'd ha been challenged or recruited, let us say, be'faw you had gone ten steps. But de Queen's word, she be out, and you is to be ... unmolested." He gave us a dazzling smile. "Welcome to N'awlins, gennulmuns." With that, he slumped back into his seat. A moment later, a gentle snore broke the silence.

The rest of our trip passed uneventfully.

When we arrived at our lodgings, we were met by a tall, elegant, shell of a man. In a voice as dry as dust, he told us that he was here to escort us to le L'Enfant.

I am always amazed at the number of ordinary people that have heard of the original Selene L'Enfant de Lune. She was such a product of this country, an astonishing mix of deepest secrecy and effective marketing. Everyone "knows" that she was the "Moon Queen of New Orleans," but most people don't really understand what that means.

If you can perceive magical influence, you will know that the entire city is enmeshed in a protective web that grows stronger and more complex the closer you get to the French Quarter. It is a subtle protection. A hurricane or atomic warhead could still destroy the physical city, but the essence—the heart, the soul, the knowledge that *somewhere* there *is* a New Orleans—will remain, and those ghosts, their numbers greatly swollen, no doubt, will joyously dance throughout eternity.

Personally, I don't really approve. There is a cosmic cycle to human lives. You are born, live, learn, die, and then return, hope-fully, to do it better the next time around. But this ... this pocket afterlife filled with endless celebration feels to me like—if you'll pardon the expression—a dead end. How long before the endlessly dancing celebrants begin to wonder if they are in Heaven or in Hell?

The energies become practically palpable when you stand on the L'Enfant's doorstep. I'm told that there is an emporium where one can purchase Selene L'Enfant de Lune souvenirs, harmless hedge magics, and questionable house blessings, but this was a solidly bourgeois residence on a respectably quiet street, with no hint of the powers that resided within.

The original Selene L'Enfant de Lune had died over seventy years ago. The name and the office had passed down the matrilineal line, and in this year of 1954, the current L'Enfant was the fourth to carry the name and the burdens of the office. I paused at the entryway and marveled at the intricacy of the magical weaves incorporated into the very house itself. There were indications that it had been first constructed over a hundred years ago, and yet it still stood firm, running without the original mage present to refresh and renew it. Old magic tends to decay piecemeal. As it collapses, you can get dangerous or intriguing echoes of what it was supposed to do. But there was no sign of that here. I could have been convinced that these spells had been renewed within the last month. This spoke well of the current L'Enfant whom we were coming to see.

Certainly power tends to run through families, but genetics is a tricky thing, and it's rare that a familial line maintains that unknown *something* that allows one to manipulate the world for more than a century or so. My estimate of the power of the original L'Enfant went up another notch. I could only imagine what the place had been like back when Selene was still alive.

The door opened and we were escorted inside. Our guide gestured us towards an inner door and then the animating force drained from him, and he slumped back against the wall. The far door opened and a graceful young woman, less than thirty, stepped inside.

Magical power is something that I can see—or perhaps I should say perceive, if I'm going to be technical about it, though of course there is a trick to it—and this woman *seethed* with it. If she was but a shadow of the original L'Enfant, then Selene herself must have been terrifying to stand before. Physically, she was surprisingly short, maybe five feet tall, certainly no more. Her skin was a rich golden brown, indicative of the type of genetic mélange that one finds at a crossroads of the world.

Despite the heat, she was wrapped in a heavily embroidered shawl, the threads of which flashed and writhed disquietingly whenever she moved. She was covered with assorted bits of jewelry. Gold and gems nestled amidst plain twists of copper and strips of intricately folded paper chains. It may have looked like a demimondaine's junk drawer, but it was a conduit for forces that I could see skittering across her body.

The room was sheathed in dark velvet, and lit with several dozen candles. There was a small round table, inlaid with assorted designs of wood and bone. A silver bowl sat in the center. She silently indicated that we should sit, and we all observed each other in silence for almost a minute.

When she spoke, it was with a delightful French Creole accent that I found most charming, and we spent a pleasant half hour or so engaged in polite conversation, which in retrospect, we realized, consisted of us regaling her with our biographies and philosophies, while she revealed ... nothing at all. It was very well done, and afterwards, Mr. Mortimer acted positively starstruck. However, I myself had a growing feeling that something was off.

I had initially been thrown by the panoply of charms and amulets she wore, but while Mr. Mortimer talked, I allowed myself to concentrate on the person beneath the aura. While there was no denying that the woman before us had a great deal of magical ability, it was becoming evident to me that all of it was *learned*, as opposed to being *innate*. This puzzled me. The weave I had sensed over New Orleans, even the one that enveloped the house—not only could this person not have constructed it, but I found it hard to believe that she could have maintained it so perfectly. There was a mystery here.

Suddenly a bell faintly chimed, although I saw none in the room, and L'Enfant stated that she would like to talk to each of us separately, starting with Mr. Mortimer. I was shown to a comfortably appointed room, where the hollow man said that refreshments would be provided. I demurred, naturally, and was soon examining what, in retrospect, remains the most interesting collection of books I have ever encountered, when I suddenly realized that I was no longer alone.

I turned, and there in the doorway was a young girl child, no more than ten, if I was any judge. She was dressed in a simple shift, and her hair was contained within a bright orange kerchief. A black rag doll was clutched under one arm. It was obvious from her facial features that she was related to L'Enfant, and she examined me with the same dark and unnerving gaze.

I bowed slightly and gave her a closemouthed smile. *"Bonsoir, Mademoiselle."*

Never breaking eye contact, she gave an elegant curtsy and replied, "Good evening to you, *Monsieur Monstre.*"

A perspicacious child. I settled down onto the sofa and examined her. Interesting. The L'Enfant had an obvious aura of magic. This child did not. Unnaturally so. As a rule, people have at least a flicker of the arcane to one degree or another in their makeup. I have heard it debated that it is this ineffable *something* that elevates humanity above the animal. But this child, the probable daughter of the current L'Enfant herself, presumably conceived, born, and raised here in the heart of New Orleans, had nothing.

"My name is Celeste," she volunteered. "What is yours?" I told her, and she surprised me yet again, by repeating it back perfectly. "That is a very old name," she said.

"It was brand-new when I got it." This actually produced a smile. "Shouldn't you be in bed?"

"Le zombie brought me here." I was not familiar with that particular term at the time, but I assumed she was referring to the hollow man. She tilted her head to the side. "I think you're supposed to eat me."

Three seconds later, I was in the hallway, about to tear the hollow man in half, when I felt a small hand on my arm. It was Celeste. I was astonished. She was calm and, indeed, had a small smile upon her face. After my explosive exit and furious attack of the hollow man, I would have expected her to be scared, or, at the very least, surprised. She was neither. "Please put *le zombie* down," she said seriously. "If you rip him up, his spirit will be confused, and it will take a long time to get him back to where he belongs." She paused. "And I'd have to sweep him up off the carpet."

"What is going on here?" I demanded. "What do you think I am?"

"I still do not *know* what you are, *Monsieur Monstre*, but I'm beginning to get a better idea."

I wheeled upon her and snarled, exposing my beautiful teeth. "I do not like games at my expense."

At once I was thrown back, as if I had been struck by a physical force. Eldritch power filled the room. I realized that this child, far from having no power at all, possessed so much that she had been able to hide it from me. I had never heard of anyone who could do such a thing. But I am not without resources. I gathered myself and flowed *between* the lines of magic she wove and stopped inches from her face. *That* startled her, and she took an uncertain step back, but I still felt no fear. I looked into her wide eyes and the old soul I saw within was something quite special. Enough so that I pulled myself up short.

Usually a soul "lives in the moment," as it were. The part of you that identifies itself as Johan Smyth, wheelwright, for example, will have no problem the next time around identifying itself as Kim Lee Sun, locomotive engineer. But the soul before me was under no such illusion. It knew who it was, and who it had been. I stepped back, and again made a bow, slightly lower this time. "Madam Selene L'Enfant, if I may guess. This is an unexpected honor."

The child gave a very adult sniff of displeasure. "Call me

Celeste, *s'il vous plaît*." She glanced back at the doorway and lowered her voice. "*Ma merè* doesn't deal as well as she should with unexpected phenomenon when it affects *la famille*. She's been like that ever since she was *ma petite bébé*." She smiled wistfully, and then focused her attention back at me. "But you. You have abilities I was uninformed of." I had no idea of who her informants would have been, but the icy tone of her voice seemed to cause the very shadows in the room to shrink back slightly into the corners.

"As do you," I said. We returned to the room and I again settled onto the sofa and regarded her with interest. "Do you remember all of your incarnations?"

"Only the last two," she admitted. "I believe I am older than that, but I did not become aware of *le grand cycle* until I was the first L'Enfant. I suspect that it is a combination of this family's bloodline, combined with something unusual about my own psychic composition." She sighed. "I do not detect anything similar about the intervening generations, so I must assume that it is something about *moi même*."

"Fascinating," I mused. "Do you have any Tibetan in your family tree?"

"Tibetan?" The girl shook her head. "I've never heard of that. Is it a family name?"

I waved a hand. "A kingdom in the mountains somewhere near China, or so I've been told. I only ask because in my travels I have heard similar stories of serial reincarnation pertaining to some of their holy men."

Celeste considered this, and then climbed onto the sofa beside me. Companionably, she patted my arm. "You have the potential to be an endless source of wonder and surprise." She looked up at me. "We should be *les amis*," she said seriously.

"I would like that."

Her mouth tightened. "As would I, but we shall see," and I thought I detected a touch of inexplicable sadness. "So you are willing to put yourself under this geas your friend is proposing?"

I shrugged. "I am not thrilled about it," I admitted. "But as I do not condone attacking children in the first place, I do not see as it being a hindrance. And, if it puts Mr. Mortimer's brother at ease, then so much the better." I looked at her and steepled my fingers. "Do you think I should not?"

She let out a huge sigh and fell back into the sofa, looking at me with an unreadable expression. "You are a strange one, you know. The idea of being under a constraint causes you to bristle, yet, as I understand it, you willingly confined yourself to a small village for centuries."

I acknowledged the dichotomy. "It was where I belonged."

"I see. Yes, that *is* important. Well, ever since your Mr. Zenon specified what he wanted, I have been consulting auguries and asking a great deal of advice from the higher powers."

"I don't think it merits *that* much effort."

"Nor did I, when I started, but rest assured that every indicator shows me that, as you so well put it, this Zenonland will be where you belong."

"Well, I certainly appreciate the effort."

She leaned in and looked me directly in the eye. "Hold that thought."

And thus, less than a week later, the elder L'Enfant, Mr. Mortimer, and I stood at the geographical center of the soon-to-be park, and as the moon rose, words were said, documents were signed and burned, and Mr. Mortimer (as a blood representative of the family) and I did the little dance (which neither of us was one hundred percent sure was really necessary, but Celeste had included it in her instructions). We shuffled about like a pair of inept vaudevillians, and to my shock, when the last heel had been turned, I felt a *smack* on the back of my head that, although it caused me no pain, drove me to my knees.

Mr. Mortimer stared down at me owlishly, and then gave a deep sigh as he offered me a hand up. "It is done," he said to no one in particular.

I noticed that L'Enfant, even though I had seen her do nothing, looked exhausted. "Are you all right, Madam?"

She looked up at me and smiled weakly. "*Merci.* I will need a chance to rest."

I never got to know the woman well. Celeste told me that the interstitial L'Enfants, who by any other metric would be considered powerful practitioners of the Art in their own right, suffered from being all too aware that they were mere placeholders, and they retired as soon as their reincarnated daughter reached the age of majority. People who work with Magic do not like being around another magic user who is better or more powerful than themselves, if only because when the situation is reversed, they tend to exploit the weaker person unmercifully. One would hope that such a dynamic would not apply within a mother/daughter relationship, but magic users do tend to be very unpleasant people. As I collected up the paraphernalia, she took Mr. Mortimer's arm, and we headed towards the exit.

I could tell that Mr. Mortimer's emotions were in turmoil, which was very unusual. He took a deep breath. "I want you to know that I really think this was for the best."

I waved a hand. "I understand. Hopefully your brother will feel more secure."

He stopped and looked at me with genuine distress upon his face. "No, I am first and foremost concerned with *your* safety, my friend."

We came to the sidewalk outside. "I don't know why you always think I need protecting—" Which was when I first ran into the barrier.

Mr. Mortimer and L'Enfant continued on past, and then turned back to face me. "Well," he said, "you're still too trusting, for one thing."

I couldn't see it, the night air still blew in my face, but I couldn't go forward. I stepped to the side—again I couldn't go forward. I felt a touch of panic. "What have you done?"

L'Enfant spoke up. "In addition to preventing you from

attacking children, I have placed a restriction upon your movements, *Monsieur*. You cannot leave Zenon property." She glanced towards Mr. Mortimer. "As I was engaged to do."

I was trapped. Trapped in a place that I knew nothing about. "How dare you?" I snarled. "You said nothing of this! Why would you do this to me?"

L'Enfant disengaged herself from Mr. Mortimer's arm. "This is now a conversation between two old friends, *oui*? Our business is done."

"You cannot leave me like this," I screamed. "I did not agree to this!" But without a backwards glance, she moved off towards a waiting car, which, after she entered it, drove away into the night.

Mr. Mortimer saw her go, sighed, and when he turned back to me, looked years older. "Why have I done this? Because, my dear friend, everything goes in cycles. You taught me that. Politics, fashions, and most importantly—tolerance. You've seen what I have, these last few years. For whatever reason, western civilization is increasingly determined to turn its back on the things of the night and embrace the mathematical surety of pure science.

"Unfortunately, by your very existence, you call that surety into question, at a time when they do not *want* questions. Rather than try to deal with you, understand the things that you represent, they will try to scrub you from existence."

"Let them try," I screamed. "I have lived for a thousand years! What can they do that hasn't been tried hundreds of times?"

"I don't know," he said firmly. "Because after they try everything old, they'll try something new. Something from *this* century —something you and the rest of the world hasn't even *imagined* yet! Things are changing! Things are different! Do you think— honestly now—do you believe that something like you could show up in an established community and remain undetected for another thousand years? There are libraries now. Telephones.

Science. No! Anywhere you go, you'd be exposed and exterminated in less than a month!"

"And yet you've trapped me here in America. In the heart of this science-land!"

"No. He has trapped you in a place that science will overlook. A place where you will be safe," a delicate voice from behind me said. I whirled and there was Celeste. When I saw her, I roared and reached for her—but just before I touched, I doubled over in sickness and agony, and my face slammed into the concrete. I was close enough that I alone heard her quiet sigh of relief, but the face she turned to Mr. Mortimer was calm and self-possessed. "Your geas has now been demonstrated to be fully operational, *Monsieur*. Make sure that your check clears."

"You are no child," I swore, as I climbed unsteadily to my feet.

Celeste raised her chin and let the force of her personality flow free. "I am in every way that is important, *Monsieur Monstre*." She then astonished me by placing her tiny hand upon my arm. "You feel betrayed. Tricked. Trapped. That is *naturellement*, if only because it is true. But your Mr. Zenon, and I, we did this to you *because* he is your friend, as I wish to be." Celeste turned to Mr. Mortimer. "Let me speak to him, *monsieur*."

Mr. Mortimer looked off into the distance. He was clearly troubled. At the time I had thought it simple guilt. If only ... But he said nothing, and so the girl walked back into the park. Deliberately, I turned my back on Mr. Mortimer and followed her. I regret that now.

We walked silently, side by side, until we arrived at the mechanized tower that stood before what would be known as Futureopolis. I had noticed it before, a gigantic amalgamation of gears and pistons that, when activated, moved in a hypnotic dance that did nothing. There she turned to face me. "Look at this ridiculous thing." She shook her head. "It evokes Science like a voodoo doll evokes a living man. But a voodoo doll is *not* a living man, hey? Just like nothing here will really be what a scientist would call Science.

"No, like everything here, it is a celebration of magic. Fairy tales! Ghosts! Spaceships! All equally make believe. Oh, I am not saying that Science is not real. It is a legitimate way of knowing the world. Looking at it. Learning from it. But the all-powerful Science that the people of this age desperately want to believe in —the Science that will give them their houses on the moon and their mechanical zombies—that is as much dreamstuff as my old twopenny love potion."

She sighed. "But I sold a lot of that particular dream, because it was something that people wanted to believe in, and today they still want to see Magic, but—and this is the important part —they want to call it Science.

"I cannot deny that the old magic has a lot to answer for. There used to be a reason you wanted cold iron over your door. Why the smart huntsman kept a round of silver bullets in his belt pouch. People remember the bad old things, and they embrace Science because it tells them that these things do not exist, and the people, they do not *want* them to exist."

I considered this. "But they *do* exist."

Celeste nodded. "*Oui.* An inconvenient truth, and a part of humanity, a deep part, knows this, knows that there are things that do not answer to science, and thus, at that deep level, it needs to believe that there is still good magic to help protect them against the bad." Celeste waved her hands to encompass the park. "And that is the wondrous thing that this *Monsieur* Zenon is doing, though I cannot think that he is doing it deliberately. Oh, he has his vision of what this place can and should be, of course, and it's a charmingly utopian one, but even he does not know what it is that he has created." She looked at me and shrugged. "I could almost believe that he is some higher power's catspaw, unwittingly doing what needs to be done."

I was in no mood for philosophy. "So what *is* he doing?"

She placed her fingertips together and spoke slowly. "He is

creating nothing less than a place where the concept of good magic can continue to openly exist. Where it can lodge inside a child's brain and heart and take root and be passed on as a viable idea. Dismissed as mere entertainment, of course, but kept alive within the memory of mankind will be the knowledge that there is *something* that can keep the Bad Things away."

I stared at her. "You still haven't explained why I've been trapped here."

"Because this will be a place of magic, hidden in plain sight from a larger world where real magic will not be tolerated. You and your magic will simply be another accepted wonder. You will be safe here, and ..." She looked off into the distance.

"... And?"

"And"—she looked at me with a serious expression—"you will be *needed* here." She shook her head. "I did not trap you here lightly. I know what it is to be bound by a web of obligations so strong that you can move in but one direction, as I myself will be again. But every augury I consulted told me that what I was doing was The Right Thing To Do. So I did it."

"So you say, but I do not wish to be trapped here forever!"

At this Celeste actually smiled. "It will not *be* forever, *mon ami*. Your Mr. Zenon stated that you comprehend the nature of cycles better than most. Think! A denial of the true nature of the world this extreme cannot hold for long. The names of the monsters may change, but they do still exist, and in time it may well be humanity's cherished Science that proves their existence.

"As for your immediate future within this park, well, for that all you need is a little patience. Whatever purpose it will serve regarding humanity's relationship with the Secret World, it is still a business. Twenty years ... possibly thirty, and it'll be old and forgotten. Shut down, sold, and the geas dispersed. You'll be free to go wherever you want. But in the interim, you will have had a chance to safely learn about this new world and have a better idea of how to protect yourself when your Mr. Mortimer is no longer there to guide you."

At this point Celeste pulled a thick envelope from an inner pocket and poked me strongly in the stomach with it until I took it. "And do not deceive yourself, *mon ami;* your Mr. Mortimer *is* still working to protect you." I opened the envelope. The top sheet held a map of the park. Several locations were numbered. According to the next sheet, these were sanctuaries that Mr. Mortimer had prepared for me, to allow me to avoid the sun. There was more, much more, but I couldn't bring myself to look at it.

I suddenly felt the weight of my accumulated years upon me. With a sigh, I sat upon a low wall. "I know he has protected me. He has from the moment I met him, even when I thought I was protecting him." I stared upwards at the stars. In those days, there were less than fifty of them that managed to shine through the smoggy California night sky. "And then he goes and does something like this. What is he thinking?"

Celeste had the look of a teacher working with a particularly slow student. "He is thinking that he will not always be there to protect you. Furthermore, he must now devote his remaining energies to protecting himself."

"What?"

Celeste sat beside me. "Your friend and you made any number of enemies, but you were both protected by agencies larger and more dangerous than you." She spread her hands. "But he is now retired, and everyone who knew of you thinks you are dead. Surely some will want revenge."

"Oh, yes, but Mr. Mortimer is very good at protecting himself."

"To be sure. But the most effective way to protect himself was to stay close to you. However, he has chosen to protect you instead of himself. I hope you appreciate that."

I stared at her, and then erupted upwards and headed back towards the sidewalk where I had left Mr. Mortimer. But even as I swooped in, I saw that he was no longer there. I saw a small object lying upon the unfinished sidewalk. I darted towards it but crashed into the unseen barrier ten feet short. A few minutes later, Celeste ran up. She saw the object, picked it up, and brought it to me. It was, as I had thought, Mr. Mortimer's fedora. But of Mr. Mortimer himself, there was no sign.

We searched, of course. I scoured the building site, though I knew it futile. Celeste did what divinations she could on unfamiliar ground, but if her spells were to be believed, he had never been there at all. This indicated deliberate magical interference, which for L'Enfant made it personal.

Over the years, as I settled in and gained influence within the local supernatural community, I constantly made inquiries, and many creatures who felt that they owed me made great efforts on my behalf to try and locate him. Magic aside, conventional means were certainly employed. Both of Mr. Mortimer's brothers did their part; Mr. Raphael insisted on employing detective agencies to try to locate him, and Mr. Bartholomew informed some of his contacts in government that one of their spies had gone missing under suspicious circumstances.

However, years passed, and no trace of my dear friend, Mortimer Zenon, was ever found.

CHAPTER FOUR

As in so many other things, Mr. Mortimer had been quite correct in his assessment of the postwar world's determination to eradicate the denizens of the night. You could follow it in the news. Oh, no one actually *said* anything flat out, of course. But I grew to recognize the language used to describe the hunting of my ilk. The European and American newspapers of the fifties and early sixties in particular unwittingly supplied a grim report of a war that the vast majority of humanity never even knew it was fighting.

I kept a file cabinet full of such newspaper articles for a while, but it grew too depressing. I actually remember the article that broke the camel's back, as it were; it was an empty-headed piece in some Sunday newspaper's travel section. It extolled the virtues of the caves of Slovenia, or whatever they're calling the country now. But while it went on at great length about the well-established caves, it did go out of its way to mention the Drakjan Cavern, which had been only recently opened to the public after being studiously avoided for centuries.

The reason it had been avoided was because it was the home of a particularly inhospitable rock giant, who wanted nothing more than to be left alone to sleep away the summers, sculpt the winter mountaintops, and race avalanches. Mr. Mortimer and I had found him by accident in 1945 when we were in the area, along with a Polish mining engineer, one Dr. Antczak, searching for an obstreperous gang of kobolds who were interfering with the Allies' railroads for some reason. (It turned out that they couldn't resist all of that refined metal lying about unprotected. After the war we convinced them to relocate to the Moscow sewer system, where they cheerfully went about their business, inadvertently creating a great deal of havoc.)

He was almost too slow to notice us—giants operate on a much grander time scale than we do—but when he did, he made a very credible effort to smash us flat. We let him be, but I always remembered his amazing crystal caverns.

Dr. Antczak had remembered them as well, as the article went on to mention him by name as the man who had proved that the legends around the cavern were baseless and that it was safe for the public. Dr. Antczak had been a dab hand at explosives back when we knew him, and I could not help but note that the photo of him also showed a peculiar crystal formation mounted upon his desk that I, at least, recognized as a rock giant's eye.

That was but one of hundreds of examples. There was never a declaration of victory, per se, but every time I read about how some heretofore shunned village, picturesque wood, or hidden cave system was actually quite charming, and certainly didn't deserve the terrible reputation that older locals had hung upon it, I knew that another supernatural entity was dead or fled.

It became *my* problem because Mr. Bartholomew was a great believer in advertising. There was a time when one could not go five minutes without hearing about Zenonland being the "Kingdom of Magic and Mystery" and other such claptrap on the radio or in newspaper advertisements. Paltry stuff to be sure, but as Mr. Mortimer and Celeste had predicted, there was a definite anti-magic bias that was gaining strength throughout the world, and here was Zenonland, publicly proclaiming itself a land where magic was welcome. Of course the ad agencies, Mr. Bartholomew, and even I, to be honest, had no idea how this would appear to a desperate population of threatened creatures who had been displaced from their homes. They tended to be scared, innocent (in their own way), and vulnerable to the grandiose claims that modern advertising promoted.

Thus, over the years, I found any number of them at the front gates, stunned at the realization that this was not an autonomous kingdom at all, but simply an amusement park. Oh, I'm sure it *sounds* hilarious, but watching a Litch-King cry, while the remnants of his skeletal army shuffle back and forth, trying not to notice, is just embarrassing for everybody.

Naturally, dealing with them fell to me.

The first ones to appear did so almost as soon as the park opened. Within the very first week. They were a colorful group of creatures that I discovered after following the sounds of drumming and drunken revelry. They were camping out on what I shall always think of as Monte Cristo Island, an acre of land topped with a small castle, rocks, and eucalyptus trees, which, until the eighties, supported the famous Zenon koalas. It sits in the middle of the whimsically named Not-So-Great-But-We-Like-It-Anyway Lake.

I had never seen anything like them before. They were an odd collection of spirits. Some could easily have passed as bizarrely dressed humans, but there were also a few garrulous animals, and an assortment of startlingly anthropomorphic household objects.

When I approached, a slim girl wearing a kimono and an oddly blank-looking face mask stepped forward and challenged me. I saw no weapons and held up my hands in a nonconfrontational manner—and found myself sailing through the air and into the lake.

The next time she tried to grab me, she discovered that I was now immaterial, except for that part that gripped the front of her outfit. This suddenly turned so cold that I felt patches of skin rip free when I hastily pulled back. This threw me off-balance, and again I wound up in the lake. The others found this very amusing.

So much for being nice. I blended into the shadows and flowed through the darkness to her feet, reached up, and grasped her ankle. She shrieked, and a great spike of pure fear burst forth. I caught hold of it and held her frozen in place while I manifested before her. "Hello," I said. I turned towards the others, who now stared at me without moving. "This is the only chance I will give you to have a conversation instead of a fight." When they still didn't move, I tweaked the girl's fear, and she moaned. This broke the spell, and as one, the rest of them knelt before me.

As a group, they referred to themselves as *Yōukai*, which, I came to understand, is what supernatural creatures are collectively known as in Japan. Apparently, where Zenonland now stood, there had been a thriving community of Japanese immigrants. Many of them third- or fourth-generation Americans. During the last war, these people had been hauled off to internment camps simply because they had Japanese ancestry. This was the first time I had heard of this, and as a person who had seen his share of internment camps in Europe, my faith in the American government took a palpable hit that day.

While they were interred, their lands had been stolen through very legal means, and had existed in a sort of regulatory limbo, without inhabitants, until the Zenon Corporation acquired them. I honestly believe Mr. Bartholomew, at least, had no idea about the land's history. That wasn't the sort of thing he worried about. But now that there was something concrete here, now that people had returned, the spirits had begun to return as well, looking for their families, and I was informed that if they could not find them, things around here would get very nasty indeed.

I probably could have eradicated them. None of them were as strong as myself—but I was moved by their plight. It took several months, and a private investigator paid for by a reluctant-at-first Zenonland front office, but eventually I was able to locate all of the *Yōukai's* lost families. The biggest problem was getting them back to them, but the iron teapots and other objects could be mailed, and we sent the rest by taxicabs. How pleased the families were with the return of their old spirits I cannot say, but Mr. Bartholomew and I were certainly relieved. On the whole, the *Yōukai* had been as patient as creatures like that can be, but even casual historical research will reveal that the first few months of Zenonland's operation had been plagued with an inordinate number of humorous (in retrospect) accidents and malfunctions.

However, no sooner had *they* departed, than an ogre, clutching a slab of granite with the words "AMERICAN PASSPOIRT" laboriously carved upon it, showed up, generating a fresh set of problems—and so it went.

Thankfully, most of these creatures were willing to listen to reason, once I demonstrated that I could subdue them (they were still monsters, after all). As a rule, they were the ones that were used to being able to control themselves, which is how they had managed to live among humans for as long as they did.

In many cases I found them to be simply at the end of their rope. Discovered, hunted, sometimes the last of their family, driven from their traditional homes, only to discover that people were filling up the spots that they would have naturally claimed. The first few reasonable creatures that appeared I was able to help to a degree, thanks to the lessons I had learned about establishing covert identities from Mr. Mortimer. But there were problems. It was all very well explaining how to keep a low profile in the community, but this was useless if you did not already have a place within that community.

Now, I'll concede that establishing oneself in a new place was a lot easier back then. A person could arrive from "out of town" and unless they aroused the interest of law enforcement, their past remained a closed book. People living today will not believe how casually people lived and did business back in the day. With nothing more than cash in hand, you could open a bank account, secure an apartment, travel via airplane, buy and sell on the open market, and your history would remain your own. Things have gotten infinitely more complicated now, what with a person's records being accessible instantly via the internet.

But even in those more relaxed times, if you wished to permanently engage with society, by attending school, or trying to secure any form of employment more rewarding than simple day labor, there were documents that you simply had to have that were difficult, if not impossible, for a monster to acquire on their own. This was the sort of rigmarole that occupied more and more of my time, and because of my own lack of mobility, I feared that things would fall apart. Then I had a stroke of luck, though I failed to recognize it as such initially.

When I checked in at the Zenon offices one evening in 1955, I found a young woman waiting for me. She was about thirty, with black hair, gold-rimmed spectacles, and a rather unfortunate squint. She was dressed in a plain outfit that did her no favors. I found us an unused office and we sat, looking at each other. Bone Cat was desperate to escape my coat and see what she looked like. I had had a surprisingly strenuous evening, helping to chase down a pack of hogs that had accidentally been released from their pen in the Frontier Zoo, so keeping my face entirely human was a bit of a strain.

I offered her something to drink, and she demurred, setting a large, overstuffed leather briefcase upon the table and releasing the straps as she talked. "Thank you for meeting with me, Mr. —" She paused.

I could tell that she was one of those people that hate doing something wrong, so I pronounced my name for her. She carefully wrote down a pronunciation guide and thus is one of the few people who has never mispronounced my name.

"I am Miss Ottilie Dawkson. I am a caseworker for the AAAApex Employment Agency."

Upon hearing this, I felt the first stirrings of unease. By this time, I had helped almost a dozen monsters and assorted entities obtain passable paperwork, and had confidently sent them out determined to, among other things, get a job in the human world. Back then, the quickest way to find a business was to look it up in a thing called the phone book, which was an actual book, which contained a listing of every business and household in the area that possessed a registered telephone. Unfortunately, the first creature I had helped in this way had torn out the page that contained most of the listings for employment agencies. The preceding page had only one remaining listing in that category: AAAApex.

Thus, AAAApex received a string of rather odd people, all with *barely* satisfactory paperwork, who had almost identical resumes and recommendations from the same place and the same person—me. All of these odd people had been assigned to the same caseworker, Miss Dawkson, who was considered by her employer to be a bit odd as well.

She leaned forward and regarded me closely. "When I brought this statistical anomaly to the attention of my superiors, I was told, 'See who else this guy has got.'"

This pleased me. Say what you will about monsters, but the ones I pass along are determined to fit in. They work hard and receive high marks from their employers. Just the other day, I had received a photograph of my PASSPOIRT-clutching ogre being honored with a plaque as Employee of the Month.

I tapped my fingers together. "Well, I *do* have a young lady looking for night shift work in a hospital or blood bank ..."

But this was not at all what Miss Dawkson wanted to hear. She frowned and aimed her squint in my direction. "There is something going *on* here. Something involving you, and the Zenonland Corporation as well. Possibly, it is a perfectly benign operation that is using an amusement park for children to hide what it is doing. Possibly." She sat back. "I shall give you this one chance to explain everything before I take my suspicions to the press."

What can I say? This was close enough to the speech that I tended to give to potential combatants that I hesitated to call her on it. Furthermore, I was impressed at her ability to discern that something was going on, and I had to admit that if I could "turn" her, as we used to say in my espionage days, she would be very useful. Reading her, I sensed a total determination to see this through.

I took a deep breath. "Very well, Miss Dawkson. I trust that once you hear me out, this will go no further."

She looked surprised but stayed quiet as I explained. About halfway through the recounting of my efforts to resettle the *Yōukai*, I ground to a halt, as I could not help but note that Miss Dawkson was beginning to get very angry. "Is there a problem?"

"Is this something Humpfrey set up?" I later learned that Mr. Humpfrey was one of her coworkers at AAAApex. "Are you making fun of me?"

"Why would I do that?"

"Here I thought I'd actually discovered something *interesting* ..." she muttered.

"You have," I protested.

"You have been wasting my time with stories about ... about *monsters!*"

"But it's all real."

She furiously snapped the latches shut on her briefcase. "I don't know what you're *really* doing here, but I'm going to send these files, along with inquiries, to every federal agency in my Rolodex, and *then* we'll see—"

I dropped my glamour entirely and roared at her. "SIT. *DOWN.*"

She slammed back into her seat, her eyes probably as wide as they would ever get, her hands clasped over her mouth. I stared at her and clicked my claws upon the table. "Now what am I to do with *you*," I muttered.

"Don't kill her!" Bone Cat wormed his way out of my coat and crawled up onto the table. Miss Dawkson's eyes actually ratcheted infinitesimally wider.

"I'm not going to kill her," I snarled. "But she has put us in a very difficult position."

"You're the one who spilled the beans."

"She *sounded* like she knew what she was talking about!"

Suddenly a high-pitched squeal interrupted our argument. It was Miss Dawkson, who was positively vibrating with what, to my astonishment, I realized was excitement and delight. She pointed at me. "I was *right!*" She pointed to Bone Cat. "I was *right!*" She leapt up onto the table and did an impromptu victory dance. *"I'm not crazy,"* she cackled. Bone Cat and I glanced at each other. That remained to be seen.

Miss Dawkson, I later learned, was what people today call a conspiracy theorist; one of those people who are always convinced that there are "things" going on that the general public are not privy to. Secrets and hidden plots infinitely more interesting than the humdrum affairs that filled her own, rather pedestrian, life, and because she had expressed these theories once too often at work, she was subjected to constant pranks at her expense. Apparently, the existence of Bone Cat and myself, and the heretofore hidden world that we represented, validated everything that she had ever imagined. Except for the part about space aliens.

After a bit more dancing, we were able to talk her down, in every sense of the phrase, and the rest of the evening was spend explaining our predicament. Before long, Miss Dawkson was excitedly making suggestions as to how we could improve things, and before the sun rose she declared herself a member of our secret society. Whereas we did not, in fact, *have* a secret society at that moment, we did by the end of the week when she strode in and presented me with a set of incorporation papers for—

I looked up at her. *"The Council of Shadows?"* The pain in my voice must have been evident. Miss Dawkson snatched the papers from my hand.

"It's a perfectly good name for the sort of thing we want to do."

Grudgingly, I had to admit that it did possess the sort of clubhouse-for-ten-year-olds vibe that would appeal to the sort of babe-in-the-woods monster that would most need our assistance. I sighed and picked up a pen. "Very well," I said as I signed. "But I want it made clear that I was not there when you came up with that name."

As it turned out, of course, it was the perfect name. Vague enough that it draws little outside attention, and, for those in the know, it makes them feel like they belong to something mysterious and special, and that alone helps keep some of them on the straight and narrow, so who am I to judge? But seriously, *the Council of Shadows?* Don't even get me *started* about the logo on our stationary.

Whatever my opinions regarding her mental stability or taste, Miss Dawkson proved herself a treasure, though a rather exhausting one. Because of her, I found myself at the center of a loose, but growing, support network that was able to give newly arrived creatures advice, aid, and shelter while they learned how to find their own place in this modern world.

Miss Dawkson continued to work for AAAApex for a few years, but eventually was able to quit in order to run our organization full time. At this point, through her efforts, we had managed to infiltrate a number of other employment agencies, and had ownership stakes in a bank, a travel agency, and a realtor, and had come to an understanding with several sympathetic medical professionals.

Miss Dawkson positively blossomed as an individual and was very happy right up until her death in 1994, and she surprised absolutely no one by immediately manifesting as a ghost who continues to diligently work for the Council until this day. Thanks to Miss Dawkson, once I intercepted a monster at the park, the day-to-day practical difficulties of assimilating them quickly passed from my hands, which was fine by me.

I'm still a part of the organization, of course, and everyone we've helped tries to show up for our annual conclave at the park. (And no, it's not All Hallow's Eve. That would be trite.) It's now a combination potluck and professional development sort of a thing, where we can catch up on gossip, see who is available as far as the supernatural dating scene goes, and, frankly, just take comfort in the simple fact that we are still here. We don't get as many newcomers as we used to, but we haven't lost a member in over a decade, which is a genuine cause for celebration.

All very jolly, but some monsters, of course, are *not* reasonable. These are, as a rule, the truly dangerous creatures. The ones that are several steps beyond feral. These I fight. Usually reluctantly, because even early on I was aware that the supernatural creatures of the world were facing extinction, and that even some of the more monstrous things that I faced surely deserved a place in the world. Several of them, once they were subdued, I had arranged to be transported to the world's wild places, places that humans will never go. A select few lie sleeping in sealed chambers beneath the park. Too extraordinary to kill, but too bestial to let roam free. I don't know what I'll do if they ever excavate the place.

And some, of course, I have no choice but to put down.

The worst one that I remember arrived in the early spring of 1966. Sometime after 3:00 AM, Bone Cat and I suddenly heard a shriek from the area of the ice rink. "Death is here," Bone Cat announced, "and he's moving fast!"

When we got there, it was in time to see a huge creature, covered in matted fur, finish dismembering Mr. Husain, the second security guard, who, like us, had come in response to the death scream of Mr. Leroy, the first. It looked vaguely human, but when it turned its face towards me, there was no intelligence within, only an insane, animal cunning. It also had absolutely no fear. Even when I ripped one of its arms off, it merely snarled, snatched it from me, and attempted to bash my brains out with it. I had to fight him using nothing but speed and strength, tooth and claw.

Over the centuries, I have occasionally wondered if I could die by simply being beaten to death—trust me, with enough free time on your hands, one considers all sorts of things—but by the end of the evening, I could definitively put that particular fear to rest. At the time, I had to wonder if this was a plus or a minus, as the creature had broken numerous bones, ripped at least two square feet of my epidermis off, and had battered, smashed, and flung me onto half of the hard, sharp, and unyielding surfaces in the park. It couldn't kill me, but I was in a great deal of pain. Another security guard, Mr. Kevin, died while attempting to help me. I *told* him to stay back—to call somebody else. At this point I cared nothing for the dictates of park policy regarding secrecy about actual supernatural events, and would have welcomed the Los Angeles Times Press Corp if they'd come in swinging their typewriters. But Mr. Kevin ignored my words, and charged in, only to be crushed in one terrible hand. I will charitably assume that he had fears for my safety, and there is no denying that his sacrifice distracted the beast long enough that I could actually formulate a successful strategy.

I defeated it by essentially dismantling it, removing its limbs one by one until, with no little satisfaction, I finally tore its head clean off of its neck. This was not as risk free as you would assume. Even without the rest of its limbs, the damned thing flexed like an eel, and its jaws bit hard enough to crack concrete. The head continued to glare, its terrible mouth trying to bite me, for easily a half an hour after I had separated it from its torso.

The monster may not have killed me, but I was so ripped up that it was a terrible effort to move. I could easily have lain there until the sun rose. Instead, driven by Bone Cat's constant harangues, I tottered to my feet, collected up the bloody bits of the creature, and hid them from sight. I just had time, before I had to retire, to call the park manager, tell him about the dead men, and warn him that they would not want to open that day. As it turned out, the damage was so extensive that the park had to be closed for three days. The excuse given to the public was to repair "minor earthquake damage."

When I finally reappeared on the second evening, Mr. Bartholomew was present, personally overseeing the repairs. I landed a few feet away from him—there were certain people I went out of my way not to startle. When he saw me, I could tell that he was scared. More so than he'd ever been in my presence before. This was understandable, of course. He was afraid that the death and damage had been caused by his mysteriously vanished brother's pet monster suddenly running amok, as he was well aware that there had been no actual earthquake.

But he put on a brave face as I approached. Either he had enough trust in me that he was willing to listen, or else he had an unrealistic faith in his own abilities. Powerful people often do.

"What the hell happened?" he asked.

"A monster broke in. It killed three security guards. Kevin—"

"I know who died," he snapped, "I had to call their families, and I had to give them some horseshit story about an earthquake."

"I feel very bad about that."

"Oh, really?"

"Yes," I said, looking him in the eye. "Because their families will never know how brave they were, how they unthinkingly came to my, and to each other's, aid. They deserve better epitaphs than 'crushed by debris.' They were killed by a monster."

"I know that," Mr. Bartholomew said. "My only question is *which* monster?"

I couldn't even be offended. I'd expected it, actually, but still, I took no small amount of satisfaction in revealing the hidden remains of the beast to him. The California climate is not conducive to the storing of the dead, so it was rather a good thing that the park *had* been closed until now. We could smell the creature from over fifty feet away. I have smelled any number of dead things, human, animal, and otherwise, over the centuries, but this outdid them all. Mr. Bartholomew had his handkerchief out and over his face before I had the door open, and even then his eyes were watering. He stared at the creature and any objection he may have had about my actions shriveled at the stench.

"What the hell is it?" he said from behind his hand.

I gripped the head by the hair and held it up to examine it closely. "I have no idea," I confessed. Behind me, I heard Mr. Bartholomew being sick. Can't say I blamed him.

"There's magic here," Bone Cat announced.

I glanced back at the head in my hand. "No, really?"

"No, no, I don't mean the usual 'Hey, hey, I'm a spooky bugbear' or whatever. This chump used to be a human being."

I had to look closely to see it, but it was, in fact, there. Transformation Magic always leaves an imprint. But it tends to fade after the actual metamorphosis. It's only so apparent on lycanthropes and such because once they get into the habit, they tend to change back and forth several times a month, renewing the magic periodically. This creature had changed only the once, and, from what I could see, it had been quite a while ago. "A curse," I said. "That should help in figuring out what it is."

But it actually took several years before the answer to that question came. It was a Wendigo, which is, indeed, a human who has been transformed into a monster by a long-standing area effect curse triggered by said human indulging in cannibalism. But while its identification solved one mystery, it opened the door to several more, because Wendigos ... Wendigi? (The fact that I am unfamiliar with the plural form rather illustrates my point), are extremely rare, and are usually only found in northern Canada. I don't believe that our neighbors to the north have more of a problem with rampant cannibalism than other places (though I've never been there, I'll admit), but rest assured that people eating people has been going on for as long as there have been hungry people, and yet the Wendigo is unique to that region. What one was doing in southern California remains a mystery.

As for Mr. Bartholomew, after we got him cleaned up and back on his feet, he confounded me by vigorously shaking my hand. "I have to apologize," he said. "Mort told me ... he told me all sorts of things about what you and him did during the war, but ..." He shook his head in wonder. "I always figured he was mostly pullin' my leg, you know?"

I knew. Brothers are brothers, and certain things never change.

"But this ..." He looked at me and his lower lip nibbled at his mustache. "Was it *all* true? Nazi monsters and witch spies and robot ghosts, and you guys shooting the original Stalin, and *everything?*"

Where to begin? I smiled. "I don't actually remember any robot ghosts ..." And that was the first of many conversations about Mr. Mortimer that the two of us had before Mr. Bartholomew passed away. I could count on him being there to greet me when I rose at least once a week. He was thirsty to hear about the things his brother had done and took great pleasure in my constant assurances that I wasn't embellishing things much at all.

Part of me cynically wondered when there would be a movie based on Mr. Mortimer's exploits, and what species of hilarious cartoon animal I would be transformed into. But when I mentioned this, Mr. Bartholomew shook his head. "This is family history. Mort worked his whole life to keep it all secret." He sighed. "Besides, people would think I'd gone crazy, telling a story like that."

The other change was that as far as the supernatural went, Mr. Bartholomew began to understand that I was not some one-of-a-kind freak—that many things like myself really existed, and could show up on his doorstep. I knew he was taking it seriously because he gave me a raise in salary.

While creatures had shown up before the Wendigo did, it was if its death had sent out some sort of signal, as immediately afterwards, the displaced creatures of the night began to show up with much greater frequency. At the peak, we had monsters—both reasonable or not—showing up four nights out of every seven. It was exhausting.

And it was during this period that the monsters that I *did* allow to stay arrived. There aren't very many of them, of course, only three, four if you count the gremlins as a unit, which is really the only way *to* do it, as even they seem to have no idea how many of them are squirming about in the dark down there. And then, about midway through the seventies, the stream of monsters arriving began to slow to a trickle, and in 1981, there was a period of over six months where none showed up at all. These days, we rarely see a new creature from one year to the next.

But I find myself drawn back to the present as I realize that this reminiscing about the past has lasted long enough that the maintenance crews have finally finished with their regular cleanup of the area I need.

The Night Crew is much in evidence tonight, a work force of almost ten thousand men and women bustling about the park's streets. Now this is actually fairly standard, but tonight everyone is cranked up and feeling keen between the Scylla of new management (who might already have observers in the park) and the Charybdis of the Happiness Machine's failure, which was apparently not as well maintained as it should have been.

The ruined ride is the main focus of everyone's attention. However, that is no reason to be complacent when Bone Cat and I dispose of tonight's *corpus delicious*. I have, over the years, cultivated a number of ways of disposing of the dead without having to worry about them being found later. I poke at one of the avoidance *gris-gris* that Celeste and I had carefully hung about, and there is a slight shudder that spreads out. And for the next hour or so, people will avoid this particular section of the park without even realizing they are doing it.

Even at the height of the day, the back end of Monte Cristo Island is one of the quieter places. I know that there are people, never children, who appreciate a place where there simply is nothing to see. I myself have opinions on this, but concede that there should be idyllic spots where a wisp of tranquility can be imagined. At night it is positively isolated. There are no lights, and the few crew who venture to the shores of the lake never approach the North side. It took a bit of effort on my part, but over the years I have worked with successive Heads of Park Security to ensure that this is one of the few places where there is no electronic surveillance. Once we arrive on the pebble beach, I drop my burden to the ground and carefully brush my coat. I realize I am merely delaying things and, with a deep sigh, whistle the three-tone call.

For a moment, nothing happens; then there is a burbling out upon the surface of the lake, and then, with a grace that never ceases to surprise me, a tall, gelatinous pseudopod lifts free of the water and waves coyly. It is only thanks to my long experience that I know not to stare at it, but instead at the water on the other side of me, which is why I see the remainder of Orsynn silently breaking the surface.

He is like a wall of ambulatory gelatin, and within him I can spot assorted objects slowly moving about. Several of these converge towards me, break the surface of the skin, and assemble themselves into a workable face which lights up in an unmistakable grin.

"It's my friends! How are you? I was thinking about you today! I was! And now here you are! Isn't that great?"

This is delivered in a voice that positively quivers with obsequious goodwill. Like he is amazed and flattered unto death that I would even consider talking to him, and he has been like this for over forty *years*. It is infuriating.

"Heya, big guy!" Bone Cat gets along with Orsynn wonderfully. So much so that at times I suspect he does it just to vex me.

"And what's this? What's *this*?" One of his tentacles, or whatever they are, has discovered the wrapped body. Orsynn looks at us and his expression is one of pleased exasperation. "I keep telling you, my dear chums, that you don't have to bring me something to eat *every* time you come see me! We're already boon companions! You don't have to buy my friendship with tasty snacks. That's what the power of friendship is all about!"

Less than ten seconds later, the dead bomber is fully engulfed by Orsynn, and while he could still be seen, it was obvious that there were chemical reactions already at work. Orsynn's features were a picture of bliss. He moaned in delight. "Oh, my friends," he crooned, "you cannot imagine how good this tastes!" He rippled slightly. "I believe that this rascal was a vegetarian. It really does make a difference, you know. And the cooking method—You shouldn't have gone to all that trouble!"

Bone Cat piped up. "That charring? It's called Cajun Style." I went to give the wretched creature a smack, which he easily avoided.

"I assure you we did no such thing."

I don't really know anything about Orsynn. Oh, I don't mean his hopes and dreams, philosophical ponderings and firmly held beliefs; no, he makes sure that we are fully informed about every thought that blunders its way into the softly throbbing nodule that I am pretty sure serves as his brain. No, I meant what *was* he? I'd never seen or heard of *anything* like him before. How old was he? Where did he come from? Were there more like him? Was he going to get any bigger? (I had no way of telling just how much of him remained below the surface. However, after all these years, there was still more water in the lake than there was Orsynn, so I think that was one worry I could dismiss.)

I include him amongst the monsters I have allowed to stay, but that's rather a disingenuous statement, as I really don't know when he arrived. We first encountered him in 1968, and he had been much smaller. Bone Cat had been shocked the first time he bubbled to the surface, and I rely on him to know when anything odd is in the park. Even more disquieting, he claims to have trouble "seeing" Orsynn. Thus, he can't tell me if he's magical, or something completely natural. Even Orsynn doesn't know anything about himself. His concrete memories stretch back about five years and then sort of dissipate. As far as he knew, he'd been in this lake for his entire life.

Frankly, I was not even sure that I could kill him if I had to. Luckily, he accepts my dictates regarding his behavior, at least so far, but he does have one worrying concern: He wants to try eating children. I don't know why; maybe because it is the one thing that I have forbidden him from doing. I would have added "don't show yourself to other people" but despite his outgoing personality, the idea of being seen by the general populace seems to terrify him. He has overcome this the few times I have personally introduced him to others, but him revealing himself to the world is not something I worry about.

It's a shame I find him so annoying, really. While he is simpleminded, he is always cheerful, and should be a refreshing tonic after dealing with other members of the supernatural community, who are, more often than not, of a more gothic temperament, but his unrelenting determination to eat children so annoys me for some reason that at times I can barely keep a civil tongue in my head. I don't even know that he *needed* to eat, per se, sometimes almost a year would go by without me feeding him some reprobate, and I never heard him complain about being hungry. Perhaps he gets the bulk of his nourishment by filter-feeding the detritus in the lake, in which case, he is certainly doing a poor job of it.

"Excuse me, my friend?" Orsynn had scrunched himself up. Apparently he thought that this made him look more winsome or something.

And now we come to the conversation about children. I took a deep breath. "Yes?"

"I have been thinking. You're the one who kills these people, yes?"

I blinked. This was a new conversational tack. "Yes. They die while I'm eating the part of them that I require."

"Have you ever tried eating a dead one?"

"Ew! That's disgusting!" Belatedly I realized whom I was talking to. "I mean, it wouldn't work. That which I consume is only there when they are alive."

"Ah, so you feeding is what kills them?"

This was a level of intellectual thought that I was unaccustomed to *vis à vis* Orsynn. I found it most disquieting. "No, I *can* feed on their fear without killing them. Why?"

"Oh, I was just wondering what it would feel like to eat a person while it was still alive."

Marvelous. The last thing I wanted was to give him a taste for living flesh. I occasionally push my luck transporting the dead ones as it is. However, it *was* possible, and while I drew a hard line at children alive or dead, I certainly had no moral objection to making a pedophiles' final moments a bit more terrifying ...

But this level of conversation from Orsynn was disquieting all by itself. "Are you ... feeling all right?"

He actually considered this, which was strange in of itself. "Yes," he said. "But I ... I have been *thinking*." He drew himself up proudly. "All by myself."

I stare at him, and then swivel about and stare at the remains of the Happiness Machine sitting on the other side of the lake. "Just in the last few hours, I'll wager."

"It makes my head feel all fizzy."

I don't even know if this is something I should be worried about or not. "Well, try not to overdo it, especially if you're not used to it. As to the live food thing ... I will see what I can do," I said grudgingly.

Several tentacles whip around me and squeeze hard enough

that I feel my head bulge slightly. "You are the best friend Orsynn could ever have!"

I don't need to breath, as such, and a good thing, as it was an agonizing several minutes, during which I had to endure the Friendship Song, which is a song that Orsynn composed about us being "the bestest friends in the whole world because I brought him dead people to eat and didn't throw rocks at him." I only know that it was supposed to be a song because he stretched the words out the same way every time. He couldn't carry a tune in a bucket.

Eventually, he released me, and Bone Cat joined him for the big finish, "We will be friends foreeevvvver!"

I suddenly realize that there was a very real possibility that this might be correct. The Vandys and the Mortimers that came into my life, the all too rare bright bits of color and joy that illuminated my existence down through the centuries, would continue to be snuffed out before their time, or else simply recede into the distance of memory, while Orsynn showed every sign of being as eternal as I was.

"No," I snarled. "We will *not* be 'friends forever,' you super-abundant clot of mucus!" I picked up a large rock and threw it into the lake. "You are naught but an overly familiar garbage disposal! I wish I had never met you, or Mr. Mortimer, or Vandy, or *any* of you!" I looked for another rock and saw that there weren't any. With a crunch, Orsynn helpfully placed the one that I had just thrown back at my feet.

I brought my fists down, shattering it into fragments. I realized that I was screaming, my fists clenched and aching, my teeth long and my wings unfurled. I was screaming at Orsynn and Bone Cat and Mr. Mortimer and the park and even the stars, who had slipped away from me, one by one over the years. I screamed until I ran out of air and then realized that I had dropped to my knees and clawed deep furrows into the rocky shore. My throat felt raw and it took a bit of effort to get my teeth to retract.

When I looked up, I blinked. Orsynn and Bone Cat had vanished. Slowly I stood up and realized just how far from human I had allowed myself to shift. My neck straightened with a soft crack, and now I saw a single terrified eye poking up from the surface of the lake. I opened my mouth to speak, and with a *glurp* the eye vanished from sight. I stood there a moment, feeling a bit sick and rather ashamed of myself.

It seems the loss of Vandy had affected me more than I had thought. I slowly shrugged myself back into a semblance of human shape, feeling quite awkward as I did so. I had started out, all those years ago, with a fairly defined human shape. I believe it was because that was the only shape my body *remembered*, as it were. But over the years, I have had to come to grips with the fact that my memory of it is not what it once was. Oh, it is still easy to mimic the shape of the people around me, but when I am preoccupied, or in moments of stress, the real me appears, and I do not like it. Bone Cat's disappearance was not without precedence, but it did not make me feel better. Occasionally, according to him, my thoughts and feelings are so … inhuman that he cannot stand to be near me. I now know how he feels.

I think of trying to call them back, but there are times when time and time alone will ease the embarrassment of the moment, so I launch myself into the night and hope that a brief flight will clear my head. As I slide through the sky, I find I cannot properly relax. That emotional explosion is very unlike me …

I come to a halt and hang in the air. Orsynn was not himself as well. Now, in his case, he was merely being thoughtful and less of a jelly-brained clown than usual, but after several decades, any change is significant.

I swoop in over the remains of the Happiness Machine and contemplate it for several minutes. It's a fact that supernatural creatures are more sensitive to outside influences. But this is worrying. If it being offline for less than eight hours has affected

Orsynn and myself to this extent, what is happening to the other permanent inhabitants of the park?

I think it high time I found out.

Which one to visit first? I am closer to the Lost Temple, and thus my choice is made for me.

The Lost Temple is at the heart of Kukuanaland, the jungle explorer section of the park. From the beginning, its popularity made it a keystone ride. Despite its ostensible African setting, the interior also unashamedly displays architectural elements and art from India, China, Mesoamerica, Cambodia, and, so we are told, Atlantis, all revolving around a central image, a great winged serpent. I alight near the door. Bone Cat does not appear. I do not know if it's because of my earlier outburst, or because he and this particular tenant do not get along.

I find my way to the great central hall and approach the altar at one end. Out of politeness, I extend a claw, and stab the palm of my hand, and a drop of whatever it is that serves me as blood falls into the central bowl. For a moment there is nothing, then a faint mist pours forth from the bowl, and a skeletal snake rises from the center.

"*Hola*, Young One," it whispers. "Bow Before Your God."

Obligingly, I go to one knee. "Hail to thee, mighty Xochemilchic." Normally, I don't coddle the monsters that I allow to live here so outrageously, but Xochemilchic is a special case.

After Mr. Mortimer disappeared, Celeste and I tried many different things in an attempt to locate him, but none of them had produced results. By the third night, Celeste's efforts were starting to range further afield than they ought. I awoke to find her and her mother hammering a copper pipe into the soil. They then spent almost two hours constructing an elaborate mandala around it, using colored chalk, sand, shells, and twelve small jars that, upon examination, I saw contained a variety of insects, lizards, snails, and small fish. "What exactly are you doing?" I asked.

"I am evoking the Spirit of the Land." She carefully traced out a handprint in red chalk. "It should be able to tell us *something*."

I glanced around at the industrial moonscape that would be Zenonland. I knew a little about how these things worked. "As far as the Spirit of the Land goes, I fear you may be a bit premature."

Celeste snorted. "There is something here. I can *feel* it." She paused. "Although I will admit that I am a bit uncertain. I cannot tell if it is very old, or very new."

"That," her mother said, "is because this is not your land. None of your power comes from here, my daughter. None. You are a stranger to this place and should walk the path of the supplicant, not the interrogator."

"Merci, mère," I heard Celeste mutter under her breath, "but I *have* done this before."

The elder L'Enfant possessed either superior hearing, or a shrewd understanding of her daughter. "But you have *not* done it here. Have you even bothered to introduce yourself to the spirits here? You have not."

Celeste was, by almost any metric, an old sorceress, wise in the ways of the unseen world and humanity, and should certainly have known better. However, doing something to spite ones know-it-all mother is an all too familiar epitaph. Thus, at midnight, she paced about the great circle, touching each of the jars in turn, and as the last one was touched, there was a rumble and a pop, and the creature we would know as Bone Cat appeared. Needless to say, this proved a great disappointment for any number of reasons, and Celeste had to admit—in front of her mother no less—that she had erred, and I gave it no more thought.

Until exactly one year later, when Bone Cat gasped and fell over. Before I could reach him, he rose into the air, and then was pulled away through the air like a kite on a string. I followed after him, and when we reached the spot where Celeste had performed her failed ritual, which was now the courtyard in front of *Missy Mammoth's Magic Tar Pit* ride, I saw a gigantic skeletal snake rising from a crack in the earth. It snatched Bone Cat from the air and shook him vigorously. "Return It To Meee," the creature hissed.

I tried to intervene and was swatted aside like an annoyance. Bone Cat was whining in a most pitiable manner, and so I did the only thing I could think to do—I rose into the air. Bone Cat faded away, and the serpent furiously swung about trying to find him. When it couldn't, it astonished me by collapsing to the ground and starting to cry as it began to dwindle in size.

I approached carefully, and, eventually, it raised itself upright and began to talk. Its name was—well, its full name was almost fifteen minutes long, but it would gratefully answer to Xochemilchic, and it was a god. A genuine old-school deity that had been worshipped under one name or another for over fifteen thousand years by a long line of pre-Columbian civilizations. He gave me a list of the peoples that had worshipped him, but I had to confess that their names meant nothing to me.

I suspect, from things he's said since, that he was there to greet the people who still—metaphorically speaking—had their feet wet from crossing the Bering Strait, and once, when I had brought him a cask of tequila, he hinted that they were merely the first *humans* who had worshipped him, but about this fascinating subject I could get nothing more out of him, as when it came to drinking, he is a bit of a lightweight. He is used to being offered something called *pulque*, which is to tequila what a firecracker is to nitroglycerine, and after that one experience, which resulted in him ultimately attacking (and losing to) the *Skittering Teapots* ride before passing out, he refused to touch it again.

For the last few centuries, since the Spanish conquests, he had survived by spreading himself out through the land, harvesting spare scraps of belief. In another century, at most, he would have faded into oblivion. But when Celeste had performed her ceremony, she had stolen a part of Xochemilchic's hard-won essence, which had crystallized into Bone Cat, and the shock had galvanized Xochemilchic into coalescing here to try to get it back. Having formed here, it was trapped. It no longer had the energy it needed to leave.

It was Bone Cat who came up with the idea of installing it in the Lost Temple. Originally, the idea was just to give Xochemilchic a place that was familiar, so that it could die in peace. But then, something odd happened. At the climax of the ride, you see the explorer, "Digger" DuQuesne, returning the stolen idol to the altar, thwarting his evil rival, who throughout the course of the ride states that "It belongs in a museum!" Well, when the animatronic Digger finally replaces the idol, there is a flash of lightning and a roll of thunder, and in that flash, visitors began seeing an enormous, winged serpent.

No one could figure out how they did it, and, soon enough, thousands began flocking to the ride to see the mystery for themselves. The park went along with it, and designers began adding representations of the mysterious winged serpent to the walls, and Xochemilchic began to grow stronger. Once again, people are beginning to Believe in him.

It will be a long and slow road, but I have a great fondness for him. He is the first and only "god" I have encountered, which no doubt explains my fascination. I have heard it said that gods should be avoided, but even almost powerless I have found him to be a font of wisdom, and I enjoy talking to him, though I dare not do so often, as it tires him out quickly.

"Why Are You Here?" Xochemilchic whispers. Actually, the Happiness Machine might be difficult to explain. Xochemilchic still tends to rail against the out-of-control futuristic technology embodied in the wheel.

"You have heard the song that makes people happy."

The snake raises itself up and swivels about. "The Song Is Gone." There is the beginning of interest in his voice. "I Had Noticed That Something Was Different But Had Not Realized What It Was. Why Has It Stopped?"

"The instrument that made it was broken. Does this affect you?"

Xochemilchic regarded me. "Only In That When People Are Happy, They Have No Need Of Gods. Will It Be Repaired?"

I nodded. "It will."

"It Uses Wheels, Doesn't It?"

"A few."

He sighs. "I Cannot Say That I Am Surprised. Must You?"

I nod. "I really think I must."

Xochemilchic sighs again as he fades away. "We Are All But Tools In The Hands Of Greater Powers." Not the most comforting of thoughts.

I exit the temple and find Bone Cat waiting for me. We say nothing about my outburst, and he leaps up onto my shoulder as if nothing had happened. We head towards the *Mountain of Madness* ride. I stop before the secret door, and reflexively look about, to make sure no one is about, then grasp the door handle. If that sounds odd, it's because the doors are only "secret" in that they appear to be a perfectly normal set of steel doors, with large hinges bolted to the wall. And, if you open the doors outward, you will merely find a small chamber that holds large spools of the electrical cables that maintain the ride.

However, if you knock thrice, ignore the large friendly sign that tells you to PULL, and instead *push*, there will be a bit of resistance (as if the doors suddenly weighed several hundred pounds), but with a groan, open they will. You will then find yourself at the head of a small flight of stairs that leads into an immense space. One that appears to be larger than the footprint of the mountain itself. I am assured that this is simply a very well-executed *trompe l'oeil*. Within this space is a vast heap of books, and, stretched out upon it, a dragon.

I had heard of dragons, of course, and had talked to other creatures that had once seen and dealt with them, but everyone agreed that they had mostly given up on our world several centuries ago and travelled on to greener pastures.

Be that as it may, I had been flying high over the park one evening, early in 1970, when she had appeared—as if from nowhere—blotting out the moon above me. She moved gracefully for a creature her size, easily fifty feet from nose to tip, and she regarded me as her wings beat deceptively slowly.

One thing everyone had been very sure to mention was that dragons appreciated politeness. I swirled in place as I doffed my hat. "Welcome to Zenonland," I said. I then introduced myself and waited.

She nodded and gave her wings a very impressive sounding roll and snap. "I am Cormangwöld," she said in a booming contralto voice. "A Dragon of the Forty-Third Percentile and the Last Warden of the Singing Trees." She waved a taloned hand at my expression. "Don't worry about it, the Singing Trees were cut down over two thousand years ago, and I never bothered to replant them because, frankly, I found them rather shrill." She stayed with me and executed a neat turn at the park's border when I did. "Ah," she said, sadness evident in her voice, "I see the weave of the geas upon you. It was crafted to restrict you to a given locale. I see now that it is to this tiny area, which is the 'Zenonland' I had foolishly allowed myself to think might be something grander."

Dragons are like that. At least this one is. Able to glance at a scene, see the magical underpinnings, and instantly understand the greater significance. Cormangwöld explained that like many a lesser creature, she had come here hoping to find sanctuary.

She and her mate had lived high in the Sierra Nevada Mountains for many years until prospectors had begun to loot their treasures. They might have been able to shrug that off—despite what you might have heard, while dragons do accumulate wealth, they make no real effort in that regard, nor hold any real attachment to it when it is there; it just sort of *happens*—like a shell accreting around an oyster. But the final straw came when their mountain valley home was scheduled to become a ski resort. The war they waged upon the developers had lasted for over a decade, but, finally, her mate had been caught in an avalanche triggered by dynamite.

According to her, Cormangwöld lost the will to fight, and so found her way here. Now, I probably could have found her another place to go, but frankly I was a bit starstruck, if I must be honest. And so, impulsively, I offered to let her stay, with the warning that at the moment I really wasn't sure *where* I'd be able to put her. As it turned out, the offer itself was enough. Dragon Magic is powerful but works best when it does not work in opposition. At least that was gist of the incredibly long and dry explanation Cormangwöld insisted on giving me. What this meant was that by offering the dragon access, I had allowed her to be able to work her magic within the park, and so construct her own safe haven.

The books just sort of accumulated over the years. I was never sure how. They range in subject, from cheap romance novels to textbooks on physics. Some of them are hundreds of years old, and I once found one with indicia that indicated that it had been printed three years in the future. It was *probably* just a misprint, but it *was* a collection of essays by Jorge Luis Borges, so one never knows. Disquieting to be sure, but it meant that I could always find something interesting to read.

As I entered today, I found Cormangwöld awake, a science fiction paperback in one hand and an immense pile of steaming barbecue beef ribs on a golden platter beside her. I also have no idea how she gets those delivered, even though she graciously provides several tons of them, both spicy and mild, every year for our annual get together.

When she sees me, she fussily lays a glowing feather in her book to mark her place. "Sheriff." Cormangwöld knows my name and can pronounce it perfectly well, but using my title seems to amuse her for some reason. She nods towards Bone Cat. "Annoying animal."

"Cute," he huffs. "*Cute* animal."

I tip my hat. "I came to see how you were feeling."

She regards us while lazily picking up a beef rib and crunching it down in tiny, bone-cracking snaps. When she is done, she fastidiously blows a small jet of flame onto her hand, burning away any errant grease. She then nods slowly. "This is about the music ceasing."

I don't even feel surprised, but simply nod back. She selects another rib, then puts it back down. "I *have* noticed a change in my emotional state," she said dryly. "I have been thinking more and more about Slarrmahgo."

Slarrmahgo had been her mate. She never mentioned him much. "Would you like to talk about it?"

She considered this, and then nodded. "Yes, I think I should." She settled herself deeper into a nest of books. "We had seen the announcements for Zenonland for some time," she began. "When we started having problems with those real estate people, Slarrmahgo thought that we should come here. He declared that once humans set their eye on a place, it is almost impossible to deter them.

"But I had lived a more academic life. Had less actual contact with humans. I was convinced that after a decade or so of trying, and failing, they would lose interest. But I was wrong about their tenacity, which meant that Slarrmahgo—a Great Dragon of the Seventh Radius—died at their miserable little primate hands. He was right one final time."

She selected another rib, but instead of eating it, spat a thin jet of flame that actually caused it to begin burning, bone and all. She regarded it critically as she continued to speak. "I burned the engineers who set the trap that killed Slarrmahgo. Then I followed the lines of causality back to their office and burned that as well. Then I followed the lines back towards the company that had hired them to develop the property in the first place." She swung her head towards me. "That was the Zenon Corporation."

I vaguely remembered an early attempt by the company to diversify into more traditional holiday resort businesses. But there had been endless, unspecified delays with the flagship project, and then some sort of huge mess that involved insurance companies ... "That part of the corporation was disbanded—and the people fire—ah, removed."

She continued as if I hadn't spoken. "But the closer I got to this place, the more I felt my fury slipping away. I didn't know that I could feel anything other than fury." The bone crumbled in her hand, and the final ashes fell as light powder. "I still felt sadness, of course. But the mindless rage was gone." She flicked her talons and the final bits of ash disbursed. She cocked her head as she looked at me. "Well ... not gone. Not entirely. But banked, like coals that you do not want to actively feed but may wish to save for another cold day.

"One of the biggest problems that dragons have with humans? We experience time very differently. Humans are so quick. They think fast. They move quickly. They solve puzzles in a flash. By their reckoning, dragons do everything very, very slowly. Humans seem to breed almost continuously."

She smiled. "At the time, I was rather ashamed at how quickly I was able to reconcile myself to Slarrmahgo's death. How soon I was ready to declare humanity's responsibility paid off. I mean, seriously, there was hardly any real death or destruction at all." She shrugged. "I ascribed it to age, and to a certain moral deficiency in my own character ..."

Her head suddenly snapped towards me, and her glare was unlike any I had ever faced. I dared not move. "But that wasn't the case at all. It was the music machine. The music it played. It soothed and relaxed, allowed me to forgive and forget. To move beyond the vengeance that I was rightfully due." She broke eye contact as she shook her head in admiration. "I've never seen or heard of anything like it. Magnificent." She sighed. "But it's broken now. There is no more music."

She shrugged her shoulders, and her wings opened with a boom. "Of course, I've been subjected to it for decades. Therefore, I calculate that it will take me a few days to completely throw off its stupefying effects, but I can feel my rage growing anew, and soon ... soon I will be perfectly willing to leave my den, whatever the consequences, and burn this park down to the bedrock, along with as many humans as I can." She selected another rib and tossed it into her mouth, then regarded me as she slowly chewed it to meaty fragments.

I stared at her, and then slowly closed my mouth, which had been hanging open. "Why ..." I realized that there was something here that did not make sense. "Why are you telling me this?" I considered further. "Why are you *waiting?*"

Bone Cat had been frozen in place beside me. At this question he furiously smacked my leg. "Shut *up*," he hissed.

Cormangwöld, however, nodded in at him in satisfaction. "No, no, my little *stultus loci*, that is a *very* good question." She turned back to me. "It is because when I *do* destroy this place, I imagine the humans will try to destroy me."

"I think they'll try very hard."

She smiled ruefully. "Yes, I agree. And they might even succeed. I fear I might be willing to accept that, once the full fury of my rage has been allowed to blossom and consume me. But—" She surprised me by gingerly climbing to her feet. Lying within the nest of books, we now saw three ruby red eggs, their shells seemingly made of cut crystal, each close to three feet across. After allowing Bone Cat and me a good look, she settled herself back down. "While I am still sane, I do not want that to happen at all."

I stared up at her. "I'm sure they'll have the ride repaired as soon as possible."

Cormangwöld savagely scooped up a huge fistful of bones and dropped them into her mouth. She then regarded us as we stared at her, mesmerized. She slowly chewed the impossibly large mouthful, mindless of the shattered fragments of meat and bone that dropped to the floor. She noisily swallowed. "That would be a very good idea," she said.

Ten minutes later we were inside the Happiness Machine,

staring at Punch-Press as he lounged upon the bed of an inactive stamping press. "What do you *mean* you're not already fixing it?"

It was quiet. Oh, there was no music, of course, which was still unusual enough that it begged to be noticed, but there was nothing. No machinery, no hammering, no gremlins running and yelling and doing things. It was positively unnatural. Even more alarming, I couldn't help but notice that a great many of them were slumped upon the floor, large tankards to hand.

"Inspectors," Punch-Press belched. "We're gonna have every goddamn human who knows how to *spell* inspector poking around here trying to figure out what happened." He raised a hand. "Until they're done, the only thing we can do is seal the rest of the complex off. Unless they bring in a fucking ground penetrating radar rig, which they might."

"Why would they do that?"

"To find some cockamamie exploding gas pipes!"

"Ah. You heard about that."

"Gas? Seriously? You moron, everything here is electrical, and three-fourths of *that* we get from solar! *Nothing* in the park runs on gas anymore! They'd have to retrofit *everything*, and nobody even *wants* to, because a couple of decades ago, *somebody* convinced everybody that we were susceptible to *earthquakes*!"

"Ah. Sooo ... what *will* they think caused the explosion?"

"If we could figure *that* out, we'd be that much closer to start puttin' it all back together."

I snarled, and then caught myself when I saw Punch-Press's startled face. "Sorry, but it is vitally important that we get the Happiness Machine back up and running as soon as possible."

Punch-Press looked at me and slowly pulled at his nose. "You're feelin' edgy. Impatient." I hesitated, and then nodded.

"My boys are feelin' that way, too. We'd thought it was because the number seven beer vat got blown up, but that ain't it at all, is it?"

"No. I think it's because the machine is shut down. I don't know why it's happening so *quickly* ..."

"*That* I can tell you." I looked at him in surprise. He waved a hand. "Hey, before I retired out here, I worked in advertising. Whenever you artificially manipulate people's emotions, it usually starts out just fine. Your brain is still grinding out negative stuff, but it's suppressed. But your body is used to a certain level of negative, so when it ain't gettin' it, your negative gland starts workin' *harder*." He smacked a wall. "It's why even with this thing working for fifty-some-odd years, there's still war and stuff. You people *work* at it. But if you *stop* suppressing things, then all the extra negative stuff your brain has been naturally grinding out suddenly got nothing resisting them, and they sorta backwash all through the system. It'll balance out after a while, but you'll be kind of a jerk for a few weeks." He glanced at Bone Cat. "More of a jerk."

Bone Cat picked up a wrench. "When your doctor asks why you have a *second* asshole? Remember to tell him 'I *asked* for this.'"

I take the wrench away. "It's not me I'm worried about. It's the dragon." I take a deep breath. "She's starting to get *angry*. Angry at Zenonland and everyone in it. I'm talking Burn Everything Down Until The Army *Kills* Her angry."

Punch-Press stared at me. Gremlins knew about dragons. "We'll do what we can out of sight," he said fervently. "But I ain't letting my boys get seen by inspectors." This was sensible. When inspectors discover a colony of gremlins, it's a toss-up as to whether they call in the EPA or the exterminators first. In either case, there would be no hope of getting things repaired on time.

"Do your best," I said. "I will see what pressure the front office can bring."

Punch-Press looked like he wanted to say something but settled for a simple: "Good luck with that, Old Tool."

"What is the status of the Prognostication Engine?"

Punch-Press shook his head. "Weird. We've had it disassembled and slapped back together three times today, and it's *still* acting weird." This worried me.

CHAPTER FIVE

As I headed towards Mr. Shulman's office, I mentally tried to arrange tonight's news into a gentle progression of increasing awfulness. It bothered me that by any metric this meant I'd be putting the fact I killed someone into the "good news" slot. Oh, well, some nights are like that.

I'm not really sure *why* I had to tell him I'd killed someone, as there really wasn't anything the company could *do* about it, but back at the very beginning, Mr. Bartholomew had been adamant that he wanted to know whenever I had done so. Mr. Bartholomew was long gone, of course, but the dictate was still there, and the assigned recipient of said bad news had, over the decades, devolved down to the current head of Park Security-Night Division, which was Mr. Ira Shulman.

I didn't relish this particular task, as it always seemed to depress him. He had worked his way up to his current exalted position about ten years ago, and aside from the initial period, which had frankly, been no rockier than any new start, we had developed a rather pleasant working relationship that continued to the present day. Unlike many other people, he seemed rather unsurprised that something like myself existed, and considered me simply another trial placed upon this Earth. Perhaps this was because during his climb up the Zenon corporate ladder, he had carefully amassed detailed files on everyone of interest within the company, and thus had seen much about humanity that, according to him, had disappointed him. These dossiers had proven useful often enough that they now occupied two locked, steel file cabinets that he had acquired when the FBI sold off some surplus office equipment.

These had actually helped us "bond," as it were. When these cabinets had originally been used by the government, they had been equipped with amusing little booby traps. These had, of course, been deactivated before the cabinets were sold to the public. But thanks to my time with Mr. Mortimer, I had been able to show Mr. Shulman how to reinstall and reactivate them, which pleased him no end. At the time, I had thought this simply one of those little secret joys. Like having a hidden compartment in one's desk, or a trick walking stick that hides a tube of brandy. In retrospect, I must admit that his understanding of human nature still manages to surpass my own on occasion, as there have been at least three incidents where he or I have entered his office to find an overly ambitious underling unconscious after attempting to peek inside those cabinets. What most impressed me was that instead of firing them, he promotes them, and as a result his influence within the company is far-reaching. This is the sort of insight that makes him worth knowing, and I find myself trying to shield him from some of the minor annoyances I encounter, which seems to suit Mr. Shulman just fine. Tonight, however, was in a league of its own, and he would have to be informed about everything, whether he liked it or not.

My first surprise came when I slipped into his outer office and there was a new secretary behind the desk. A no-nonsense young lady with long blonde hair and a penchant for turquoise jewelry. I hoped that Mr. Leonard, the person I'd normally expect to find here, was all right. I'd not heard that there were any new flu bugs delivered to us by our guests, but whenever a new one appeared, Mr. Leonard was one of the first to catch it. I decided not to startle his replacement. There are some things that temps should not have to deal with, and so I passed unseen into the inner sanctum.

Again I was surprised. The office had been stripped bare of Mr. Shulman's personal touches, and a new person was seated behind the desk, intently scrutinizing the monitors. This put a new spin on Mr. Leonard's absence, and meant that my evening would be even more depressing. I had truly enjoyed working with Mr. Shulman and felt the first stab of resentment against the new management. Oh, they often shuffled things around, determined to shake things up and establish their dominance within the organization, but there was usually a grace period, where they learned who was superfluous deadwood, and who knew where the bodies were buried, a bit of corporate speak that had a bit more relevance in our company than in most. Mr. Shulman fell within the latter category, and I dared hoped that his disappearance bespoke a promotion. Personally, I would not be surprised if Ira was our mysterious new CEO.

But I was again sad. I was used to people leaving, of course, but in these modern times, I had gotten used to the luxury of being able to say goodbye. Well, the least I could do in his memory was not take my annoyance out upon his replacement. I studied him, as he remained unaware of my presence. He was a young man, tanned, clean-shaven, with a nicely tailored black suit. He was obviously new to the job. After an initial period, the Head of Park Security-Night Division tends to realize that one almost never has to deal with either the public or management, and, within six months, he would no doubt adopt the semiofficial "Bermuda shorts and aloha shirt" uniform worn by his predecessors, as seen in the row of photographs that adorned the secretary's office. At the moment, his desk was covered with file folders and security logs. In the corner, a rather elaborate-looking coffeemaker burbled quietly to itself, and a large china mug was already making rings upon the otherwise spotless desk blotter. It was the quintessential portrait of a man trying to get up to speed in a new position, and I was resolved not to terrorize him; indeed, I was happy to provide him with a bit of a break. I tucked Bone Cat inside my coat. A person can only take in so much strangeness on the first day.

From behind his chair, I quietly cleared my throat. He froze, and then slowly turned to face me. This was encouraging. I find that people tend to fall into two categories when they meet me; those who freeze, and those who scream and run around. While the latter can be entertaining, it's tedious having to wait for them to calm down so you're not interrupting. So far? No screaming.

I smiled at him. "Hello! I certainly hope you're not a burglar!" I widened my smile. It's a little joke that always seems to get things off on the right foot.

This time was no exception. "No!" The young man shrank back into his chair. "I work here! I'm the new Security Chief!" Frantically he grabbed at his nametag and held it up before his face like a protective talisman, which, in a very real way, it was.

It was so close that my eyes had to cross slightly in order to read it. *Mr. Sebastian Donovan. Chief of Park Security-Night Division.* I looked back at his face and nodded. "Welcome aboard, young man."

I glided around to the front of his desk.

Mr. Donovan made a rather game try at pronouncing my name. I corrected him. "At your service," I added.

"I didn't ... Janis ... my secretary didn't tell me ..."

"She didn't see me. No one else knows that I am here," I reassured him. This did not appear to reassure him at all. "I am impressed that you know who and what *I* am."

Mr. Donovan stared at me. "Are you joking?" I must have looked perplexed. He took a deep breath and straightened himself up in his chair. He was still staring, but the naked fear was fast receding. "Thirty-six hours ago, I was in the Chicago office. In the space of thirty minutes, I was summoned to my boss's office, informed that I was being promoted and reassigned, given a rundown of my new duties, and then told that I was expected to be behind this desk by seven o'clock this evening. Then I was shown the door. Fully five minutes of that meeting was devoted to explaining you."

I waved a hand apologetically. "No written records allowed," I said with a sigh.

Mr. Donovan paused, and then nodded. "I was assured that you are more than capable of 'filling me in' on … what it is that you do."

I noisily sucked a tooth as I considered this. "This all seems rather rushed. The whole surprise promotion and transfer, I mean. This isn't some new management trend or something, is it?"

Mr. Donovan snorted. "No. And you're right. A move like this? They're supposed to give us a couple of weeks' notice, at the very least. I've got a goddamned condo I have to deal with!"

"What happened to Mr. Shulman? Your predecessor?"

Mr. Donovan shrugged. "I heard that Ira got the same treatment. Both him and his secretary got transferred to Tokyo." He shook his head. "I wish I'd had a chance to talk to him about …" He tried to not look at me. "… Stuff."

I was glad that the new management had let Mr. Shulman take Mr. Leonard along; they'd been having a clandestine romance for the last five years, after all. Oh, everybody knew about it, of course, but, officially, the company frowns on employees dating other employees.

"I *do* know that he wasn't the only one." He held up a printout. "According to this, *all* the senior park staff got rotated out at once, which is just stupid." He tossed it down and went to select another, but instead just waved his hand in disgust. "According to my guys back east, things have been stupid all over ever since Mr. Zoiden took over."

Ah, the name of the new CEO. Nice to know. I could see that this particular corporate takeover was going to be more vexatious than most. When it came to Zenon power politics, I had gotten used to going to Mr. Shulman for my gossip, who, as I mentioned, immersed himself in their intricacies like a palace courtier. He *had* mentioned that there was something "tricksy" going on at the upper levels of the company, but there had been no indication that a grand game of musical chairs was in the offing. Even I, who would be hard-pressed to make a going concern of a lemonade stand, recognized that removing all of the park's senior staff in a single day was insanity. "Well," I said with a sigh, "I suppose we shall just have to soldier on together and be prepared for the inevitable catastrophe."

A normal person might not have noticed it, but a thousand years of observing people let me see quite plainly that Mr. Donovan was suddenly very nervous. His heart gave an imperceptible skip. A faint dewing of sweat appeared upon his brow. And was that fear? Indeed it was. I had said *something* that caused him to worry. About me. "Well, thank you for dropping by," he said, clearly hoping I'd take the hint. "I plan on talking to *everybody* here, not just yourself, but first I wanted to familiarize myself ..." He trailed off and indicated the folders.

I nodded affably and headed towards the door. "Of course. I'm just supposed to report whenever I kill someone, and I'd assumed you'd want to know about it, but I see that the details can wait—"

Mr. Donovan's chair crashed into the wall behind him, so quickly did he leap to his feet. "They were *serious?*" He stood there staring at me. "You actually *kill* people?"

This was a reaction I had seen before. Like any organization, a newcomer was occasionally subjected to some form of hazing, and certainly our company had a rich set of traditions along those lines. There is an amusing little object, easily fifty years old by now, cobbled together out of a coat hanger, a plumber's helper, and a hand-powered drill that is still solemnly presented to new park employees as "The Platypus's Ear Tightener."

Occasionally, a few of the people who were informed of my

true nature smugly believed that I was simply another story. This rarely lasted long, but in the beginning, I will confess that I had done my part to string them along, just to see how long I could. That sort of thing ended back in '67, with the fellow who, after a bit too much to drink at his birthday party, attempted to forcibly remove my "false teeth." It was the most amusing party I've ever attended.

I glided over to him. "Yes. I really do." Purely for the show of it, I lengthened the claw on my little finger and delicately picked away at an incisor. "Not often, and I only kill those who prey upon children."

Mr. Donovan took an uneven breath, and suddenly I was behind him. Before he realized it, I had encircled his arms with my hands and effortlessly held him as he tried to break free. His head tried to crane about in order to see me, but it was simple enough to stay outside his field of vision while leaning close to his ear. "On the other hand, that still leaves me a great deal of latitude when it comes to dealing with people who are not forthright with me." I gave his arms a squeeze. "This would be a shame in your case, as I think we would have worked very well together." I sighed dramatically. "But if that is not to be, at least neither one of us will have to get used to an untenable situation."

Mr. Donovan had again gone still, but he was pouring forth a tasty torrent of fear that was growing stronger by the second. Now you might think that this would be a counterproductive way to begin a relationship with a new coworker, especially one that, ostensibly, I reported to. But sad experience has shown me that this really is for the best. In this amazing country and in these modern times, people are taught that, in the abstract, we are all equal. Reassuring, yes, but in the same breath it is pointed out that a blindly rigid society of pure equals is patently dysfunctional. Thus, society must, reluctantly, establish artificial differences such as boss/employee, or General/Lieutenant, and so on, in order to facilitate the smooth functioning of said society. This is presented as a universally recognized fiction, and thus all are reassured that the people in charge are there because of luck, and anybody could get lucky if they keep their head down and follow the rules. It's very well done, really.

Anyway, it means that a nice, simple demonstration of my capabilities, emphasizing that I am *not* "one of them," allows people to quickly come to grips with the fact that I am, as it were, not part of their system. They are not my equal, let alone my superior. This is not to say that I haven't gotten along with the other people who have sat behind this desk. Many of them were intelligent enough that once this little dance of dominance was trod, we communicated very well. Some of them, in fact, confirmed that knowing me enriched their lives in unexpected ways. Mr. Shulman, for instance, remarked that my very existence made him reconnect with his childhood faith, which made his mother very happy.

Mr. Donovan would no doubt fall into line. He was already ahead of the game in my eyes, what with the not screaming and such. "I don't understand," he said faintly. "What do you want?"

"I believe that there is something that you are not telling me," I said. "And call it a failure on my part, but I am a person who does not like surprises."

Mr. Donovan closed his eyes and took a deep breath. I did that clicky thing I do with my teeth. "You're going to be fired," he gasped.

I blinked in surprise and released him. "I'm *what?*"

He cowered slightly. "It's not my idea! But I ... I was told that I wouldn't have to ... to put up with you for long, because you're going to be fired." He shrugged. "Corporate considers you an unfortunate legacy from the previous management's reign." He coughed. "Or something."

I nodded amiably. "Ah."

He flinched. "Please don't kill me," he whined.

I rolled my eyes. "I am not going to kill you." I paused. "Unless ..." I draped a friendly arm over his shoulder. "You do not take pleasure from the killing or molesting of children, do you?"

"No! I like grown-up women! Women with great big—" At this point Mr. Donovan realized that he *might* be sharing a bit too much and looked at me with wide eyes. I gave him an avuncular smile and patted him on the shoulder before releasing him.

"That's quite all right then! If you have a steady partner, even if you're not married, per se, don't forget to register them with Human Resources. Here in California, there are some very useful benefits available to them."

Mr. Donovan blinked. "Aren't you ... you don't care that you're being fired?"

I waved a hand dismissively. "My dear sir, I've been fired from this fine company more times than you've had hot dinners. It will pass." I was being flip, but inwardly I was sighing. Being fired was inconvenient. Oh, it always worked out rather quickly, but it usually meant that I lost the use of my beloved office for a week or two. Well, at least I had a heads-up this time. While I would certainly have no objection to returning to the private sector, unless those in charge could abrogate my geas, this newest dictate was as irrelevant as all the others.

"Thank you for your frankness, Mr. Donovan. I look forward to working with you. Now let us talk about something important. The explosion that took place tonight—"

Mr. Donovan glanced at his desk. "The gas explosion in the *Itty-Bitty Planet* ride. I heard about that. There was a girl who was thought to be inside, but ..." He paused, and I could see the connections being made. Oh, how *nice* it was to work with competent people. "*You* were the one who delivered her to her parents. *And* gave them Lifetime passes?"

I nodded. "That was no gas explosion. It was a bomb. The bomber is the man I killed. He had taken the little girl hostage." I held up a hand. "She will not remember this. You are the only human who knows. The inspectors will not find any evidence of a bomb."

"They won't find any evidence of a gas explosion, either."

I cleared my throat. "A mistake on my part. I'm rather hoping we can put that behind us and get the inspectors gone as soon as possible."

Mr. Donovan rubbed his neck. "They'll demand to know what blew up ..." He went still.

"What are you afraid they'll find? More bodies?" I waved a hand dismissively and chuckled. "Don't worry about *that*, my good fellow, no one *ever* finds the bodies."

Mr. Donovan did not look reassured. "The bomber. Who was he?"

I shrugged. "I have no idea." I held up a preemptory hand. "I do not know if he was working alone. I have no idea what he wanted. All I can tell you is that no one was hurt, and that his body will never be found."

"I need more than that."

I leaned forward. "What *you* need is to figure out how a guest was able to get an explosive device into the park through gate security." Mr. Donovan blinked. I recognized the look of a man who, while he might be well versed in the theoretical, had never had to actually use the machinery of his office. I snagged a chair and brought it behind his desk, and then gently brought enough pressure on his shoulder to get him to sit. "Here, I can help you get started."

We then spent a very instructive hour or so, accessing the camera feeds that cover the park, and bringing them up on his computer. "Naturally, you can also do this from the central security station when you brief your staff," I told him. "But first let us find how our man got in."

I long ago memorized the codes assigned to the camera grid, and so am able to soon call up the archived feeds that are located near the Happiness Machine. Spooling through the archives was the most time-consuming part of the exercise, but suddenly I see our man. He was approaching from the *Muskrat Minuet* ride, and what was important was that he was talking to someone. A tall man wearing wraparound sunglasses and a Zenonland manager's uniform. I freeze the image. "That was your bomber," I informed Mr. Donovan. "You'll want to backtrack and see how he got in, but I'm guessing that *this* man"—I tapped the image of his companion with the sunglasses— "was how he did it."

"He's an employee." Mr. Donovan's voice conveyed both disbelief and anger. "A manager." A quick check of his emotional state showed that he was properly fired up.

"Not for long, I suspect." I stood up. "I assume you'll want to deal with this yourself?"

Mr. Donovan nodded. I was not surprised. Catching something like this on his first night would look mighty good to his new bosses. He hesitated. "If I need your assistance ... May I call?"

Oh, he and I were going to get along very well indeed. "Of course, sir. I do report to you, after all. My office is down the hall, and here is my cell number. Though I wouldn't rely on that getting through." Marvelous things, cellular phones. I don't carry mine much, as it tends to fall to the ground when I become immaterial. As I prepared to depart, Bone Cat popped his head out from my pocket, and with a toothy grin said, "Welcome to the Zenonland family, chump!"

Mr. Donovan stared. I stuffed Bone Cat back into my pocket. "We have *lots* of other things we should talk about when you've settled in," I said gently, and with that I opened his office door. I was prepared to introduce myself to the new secretary, but she had apparently stepped out. I glanced at her nameplate for future reference before I headed back to my office.

"He took me well," Bone Cat opined from inside my pocket.

"I think you timed your appearance perfectly." This rare compliment so pleased him that the rest of my evening passed with a semblance of peace.

I head for my office. The majority of the visitors to the park never really think about the mechanics of how it works at all. This is either because the system is functioning so smoothly that they never have to consider it, or because they are blessed with a simplicity of thought that allows them to believe that the park runs on fairy magic. This is absurd, as I have never met a fairy capable of a hard day's work in my life.

For many guests, the idea that thousands of their fellow humans work very hard behind the scenes to keep the park functioning is simply beyond their comprehension. For them, the magic is all too real. Thankfully for civilization as we know it, they are a minority.

On the other hand, there are a healthy number of our guests who *are* aware that there needs to be an industrial infrastructure, and have heard that there is, like an iceberg, a vast complex hidden beneath the visible park. These people no doubt imagine something analogous to a Bond villain lair, with recessed lighting and mysterious functionaries in quasi-military outfits gliding through the spotless corridors in bubble-topped golf carts. To be honest, that was probably what the original designers had in mind, but sixty years, entropy, and the mildew-friendly California climate have drained a bit of the romance from the place. Oh, don't get me wrong, it's certainly not as squalid as it got in the early eighties, but today there's more of an acknowledgement that you're backstage at an amusement park as opposed to the heart of an enterprise determined to reshape the world through technological innovation. Mr. Bartholomew had big dreams.

However, he always had problems relating to his employees. It took me over five years to get my own office. For the longest time Mr. Bartholomew apparently assumed that whenever I wasn't menacing the unworthy, I would be content to hang from a rafter in the castle by my ankles or some such foolishness.

Now I am the first to admit that it is not much, as offices go. It is about ten feet square, and of course there are no windows, but I have a desk, a phone, and since the late eighties, a computer. Most importantly, I have a door with an only *slightly* misspelled version of my name on it that I can shut. This gives me a palpable weight and visible existence within the Zenon organization.

The décor in my office has changed over the years. Originally, I covered the walls with travel posters and photographs of exotic locales. Cities I had been to, like Prague, or New Orleans, or of places I wished to see, such as Rio de Janeiro during Carnival, or Las Vegas. But after ten years, they merely drove home the fact that I was not going to be visiting them anytime soon.

In the seventies, I was determined to prove the stereotypes correct. I painted my walls black and filled the room with assorted bones, skulls, and arcane trash one could purchase from the advertisements found in the backs of a certain type of magazine. It was all nonsense, of course; the only genuinely interesting thing was the executive mushroom farm, and no one I knew dared eat them.

These days, I have discovered that a monster working out of a perfectly normal-looking space is far more disquieting. The walls are a tasteful bone white. A little bit of faux diabolism seems to be expected, and these days you can buy enough fantasy and supernatural kitsch online that a respectable necromancer would fire his decorator. Thus, I allow myself to display the stuffed head of the Wendigo upon my wall. Everyone assumes that it's something I pilfered from the props workshop. There's a jolly travel poster of Transylvania (it keeps people guessing), and a charming little Bavarian clock that, frankly, I keep because I enjoy the sound of the ticking. The furniture is standard corporate issue. I even have a fern.

I have a hook upon the wall from which hangs an overly large, black, cowboy hat. In all our years together, Mr. Mortimer never let me forget my disappointment that he was not wearing one at our first meeting, and I discovered this one waiting for me in the castle chamber he had prepared for me, tucked neatly into a large, round Stetson box, with a note claiming that I obviously needed one, now that I was an American.

The one thing that people never even notice was the surprisingly fat pedestal table that holds my fern. If you did examine it closely, you *might* find the secret door, and if you managed to open *that*, you'd find a small freezer compartment that contains the frozen head of Bartholomew Zenon.

There are many people who have heard the persistent rumor that Mr. Bartholomew had himself frozen after he died and is now ensconced somewhere under the park, waiting for his beloved future to develop the technology to resurrect him. Well, that was certainly Mr. Bartholomew's intention, but, unfortunately for him, the cryonics company he signed on with turned out to be an edifice of smoke and mirrors, and thus his fatally degraded remains were eventually interred in the family mausoleum at Woodlawn Cemetery, the same as many a lesser mortal.

This did not sit well with Mr. Bartholomew, which is why he returned from wherever afterlife he had been cooling his celestial heels in and began haunting the place. Explaining to him that there was as much chance of resurrecting a pig from a festering ham sandwich as there was of reconstructing his body —let alone his actual functioning brain—from his moldering corpse, was pointless (the dead are remarkably immune to logic). To make a long story short, he would not be laid to rest until someone dug up his head and put it in a freezer. Naturally, once it was there, it gave everyone who knew that it was there a severe case of the heebie-jeebies, so they moved it out of the employee break room refrigerator, and it eventually wound up in my office. I owe Mr. Bartholomew a great deal, and it feels nice to be able to pay some of it back by allowing him his eternal rest.

I settle in behind my desk and take a moment to rest my head in my hands. I must not allow the absence of the Happiness Machine's effect to so exaggerate the distress caused by Vandy's departure. Annoying he may be, but Orsynn certainly did not deserve that over-the-top display of rage. In many ways he is like a child himself. A child I had—however unintentionally —frightened.

If he didn't annoy me so, Orsynn had the potential to be my favorite amongst the refugees here in the park. All of the monsters here are quite efficient when it comes to disposing of extraneous human bodies, but the Gremlins insist on them being chopped up, Xochemilchic is only happy if you drain all the blood out and offer it to him separately, and Cormangwöld won't *touch* them unless they are wearing a hennin, one of those ridiculous, tall, pointed princess hats. I do not know if it is just an affectation, but I put up with it because she does such a good job of managing my mutual funds.

Orsynn, on the other hand, happily gobbles them down, clothes, electronics, prosthetics, and hats, whole and entire. If I examine my feelings, I must admit that the whole child-eating thing aside, Orsynn gets up my nose simply because I find him too overly familiar, and always have. I like to choose my friends, but Orsynn entered my life convinced from the get-go that we were "friends to the end."

I'm told I have elitist tendencies and accept this as one of my few character flaws.

I am not often subject to feelings of guilt, but I feel it now. I shall simply have to go apologize in a few days. Perhaps I'll make the effort to keep the next miscreant alive. If that doesn't work, at least he'll forget all about it in five years or so. This last thought so thoroughly depresses me that I slump even further, and it is easily ten minutes before I can raise my forehead from my desk blotter.

I do so only because I feel the hesitant patting on my arm that is as close as Bone Cat ever gets to trying to offer solicitude. It is not much, but I appreciate the effort. I sit up and scratch his ridiculous earbones. Wallowing in misery will accomplish nothing, and I still have things to do before the sun rises. I deal with my email, catch up on my reading (I might lose access to my computer for a day or so while they tried to fire me), and downloaded my project files onto a thumb drive.

Ah ... my project. I briefly considered just letting the people who would no doubt sweep through and clean out my office delete it, along with everything else, but, no, I still thought the idea had merit.

Allow me to explain—it's something I've been thinking about for quite some time. Basically, I contend that a significant percentage of the park is *underutilized*. Because of what I am, I can tell that there are places in the park where our guests feel neither excitement, or fear, or ... anything, really. It wasn't an issue sixty years ago when the park opened, but more and more I've sensed a growing impatience with these dead areas. Like I said, I didn't really notice it when the park opened, but the wiring inside people's brains is always changing. The interesting difference these days is that the changes are now recorded.

All you have to do to see it is to compare the editing in modern television and movies—all jump cuts and three-second pans—to the slow, leisurely takes of vintage films. Both are valid expressions of the film medium, but younger viewers increasingly find these older films almost unwatchable. Kids these days don't watch enough opera, that's the problem. The salient point is our park was designed and built by people who were a product of that more genteel mindset. They expected things to take a more leisurely pace, and this expectation is baked into the very architecture.

Oh, the newer exhibits seem to be dimly aware that people have less patience, and the lines for the rides have become much more of an interactive experience. But there are hundreds of areas *within* the rides, or even just scattered about the grounds, where there are nothing but blank walls. I believe that if we want the park to engage future generations, then we have to increase the *density* of the experience.

Let me give you an example: the pirate ride. I find this one especially inexcusable since they refurbished the whole thing after the success of the movie franchise. Oh, the set pieces are all very well done, but there are all these dark, empty stretches that the boats glide past, where I can't help but think they could have put in *something*. I'm not saying wire the place up for another animatronic tableaux, but a diorama, a skeleton with glowing eyes, a wanted poster that winks at you—*something* to catch the eye and engage the mind.

Now you would think that this would be a fairly simple idea to explain, test, and execute. If only to shut me up. But I have been banging my head against this particular brick wall for almost fifteen years with nothing to show for it.

Bone Cat thinks I'm missing the point of what Zenonland *is*. He says that what I have never understood is that for many people, the Zenonland Amusement Park is, first and foremost, a park, and that a park should have areas that relax a person. He says that the problem with today's world is that there is so much going on, so much instantly accessible entertainment, that people do not have a chance to get *bored*. If they don't get bored, they never try to create.

I myself am skeptical about this. I have seen what children throughout the ages have done when they get bored, and it tends to involve recklessness, mischief, and hooliganism, often against perfectly innocent creatures who have no reason to expect their favorite bench to be weakened, or who wake up to discover that while they slept, their resting place has been filled to the roof with dandelions. No, I fail to see the benefit of this sort of behavior, and so, on this, as on many other subjects, we have agreed to disagree.

But as for management, at this point I am beginning to believe their refusal to even consider a test of my ideas to be some form of childish revenge for my invariably terrorizing the man in charge the first time I meet him. This was a revelation that I was loath to accept for quite some time, as it displayed a level of obstinacy and spite that I had not seen since I had left the old country, but purely for the sake of open-minded scientific experimentation, I had resolved to try to be positively pleasant when I met the next new owner. Well, it looked like *that* was foredoomed to failure, what with the looming attempt at firing me and all.

As it always does when a new boss appears, the faint hope that the new owner might actually have a way to break my geas, and thus allow me to actually leave, blossoms. That would certainly put a different spin on things and would definitely make for a better retirement gift than the traditional Preston Platypus watch (Though I still want one of those. They are pretty nifty). I snuff this particular line of thought out hard. I have tried for decades to find a way to short-circuit this particular spell, but every line of research has led me to the conclusion that my only hope lies in the actual dissolution of the company, and short of some sort of sci-fi, civilization-ending apocalypse, I just don't see that happening.

It's depressing. I mean, I do not *want* to be one of those strange people who live in Idaho hoping for some unspecified catastrophe to turn things so topsy-turvy that they would, by default, be considered qualified to rebuild some semblance of society. I *like* civilization. I am well aware that it has problems, but I can assure you that they are, as a rule, a better class of problems than the ones most people had to deal with several hundred years ago.

So, no. While indeed somebody someday might be able to break this particular enchantment, to allow myself to hope leads to nothing but bleak disappointment, and I've certainly had my fill of negativity today, what with Vandy and Mr. Shulman leaving, my shouting at Orsynn, the possible threat of Cormangwöld, and the ample evidence that the incoming administration will be bringing in its own bag of problems.

Suddenly, the thought of being cooped up in this miserable little office, which is merely the smallest of the confining matryoshka dolls I inhabit, was too much to bear. I may be trapped here forever, but I will not stop trying to break free. I erupt upwards and outwards, through the ceiling vent, out of the decorative grill hidden in one of the faux cacti in the *Land of the*

Lone Prairie and up into the night sky. Upwards, ever upwards, I flew. Desperate to crack the invisible barrier and free myself from this place.

It has been over a decade since I tried this. Surely if any part the spell holding me were to weaken, it would be up here, far from the artificial and arbitrary lines constructed by mankind. Upwards, ever upwards. I once carried an altimeter up with me and saw that I was able to ascend over three miles straight up before I was dragged back to earth.

I feel a tightening on my flesh, and frost forms. I grin in exhilaration. I can feel the cold now. Refreshing. My coat goes stiff, and the wind whistles through it as I continue to rise. How I miss the freezing winds of the mountains. I miss snow. I miss everything. I am sick unto death of my entire world being confined to seventy-five hectares of artificial reality. Higher. Higher. I *will* break free of this one way or the other. Even if I have to sail off into space itself, I long to be free of this place where no one even wants me.

It is a strain now, to continue to rise. I have no idea how I fly. I've never been scientifically minded, which the gremlins tell me is for the best, really, but as I shudder at my apogee, I find my lack of knowledge frustrating in the extreme. As a rule, I never bother with exploring my limitations, because I tend to settle into a lifestyle where I never have to know what they are. I suppose it's analogous to a human knowing exactly how many push-ups they can do. But in this case, I don't even know what it is that I should be doing more *of*.

Suddenly I realize that I am straining as hard as I am able, and yet am not actually moving. I feel fatigue beginning to seep through me. This is a rare feeling, and one I welcome, as it quells the desperate fury that drove me upwards. I feel myself beginning to calm down, and since it is why I am here, I glide towards the west—

And again smack into the invisible barrier. Seriously? I throw my head back and again scream into the night—though a faint and thin scream it is, at this altitude. I am then suffused with a great wash of sadness, which causes me to draw into myself. I shake my head, bemused at my foolishness. Not at my inability to break free, but at this evidence that I still had that most terrible of dangerous emotions: hope. I had thought I had managed to crush that completely. Obviously not. Obviously not.

I spin slowly, preparing to return, and received an unexpected reward for my efforts. The stars. Far above the smokes and lights of civilization, they are still here, as they were in my youth a thousand years ago, as they will be when I am dust. Here they are, before me in all their magnificence, and I lose myself for a timeless space and bask in their eternal glory.

Suddenly an unexpected lance of pain impacts upon my consciousness. I detach myself from my gazing. It takes a bit of effort to turn, as the frost that rimed my muscles has now solidified into actual ice; parts of me have started to freeze solid. Serves me right for not paying attention. But that is not the source of the pain. It is the sun. I feel a moment of panic, and then realize that it was merely a fluctuation in the horizon's atmosphere that allowed a premature shaft of light to wash over me. Actual sunrise is still a way off, but it is definitely time to return.

I spin and dive, aiming for the deceptively small patch of land surrounded by the not quite sleeping city. I roar downwards, exulting in the sensation of speed and motion. I have never gone this high before, and for an instant I wonder ... what would happen if I did not slow down, if I allowed myself to strike the earth like a meteorite, smack dab in the center of the park. Would I die? Would this be enough to keep me from slowly coalescing back to consciousness? Probably not.

So I spread myself out and begin to control my fall, turning it into a magnificent swooping glide that takes me around and around my home, my prison, my world, in a series of slow, looping spirals that allows me to see every inch of the place that I know every inch of.

When I touch down, a great weariness fills me, both of the physical and mental variety, and I seek out one of the more reclusive of my resting places. Mr. Mortimer was a man who insisted on redundancy, and we always had more than one safe house in any given location. Thus, while there are the "official" locations that Mr. Mortimer had prepared for me, bless his heart, there are also secret ones that I have constructed myself. Hidden even from the Zenonland records so that, when I must, I can brood and not have to worry about the outside world. I have been in these moods before, but moods are all they are. I slide into my chosen resting place, and seal it behind me. After a second, I feel a hesitant pat-patting upon my hand. "You okay?" I say nothing, but make a space for Bone Cat in the crook of my arm, and he flows up against me and begins to purr. Tomorrow cannot help but be a better day.

I sleep.

CHAPTER SIX

I awake the next evening with Bone Cat still tucked within my arm, and take a moment to examine him as he sleeps. Our relationship was not always so cozy.

If you have even a passing acquaintance with Animism, you are no doubt familiar with the idea that all things have spirits. Well, I've lived with one in my pocket, as it were, for the last sixty-some-odd years, so I'm here to tell you that whatever you think you know, you probably have it wrong.

I had long been familiar with the basic concept, of course, even back before I knew there was a name for it. Any person who has ever had dealings with an obstinate drawer or appreciated a sheltering tree cannot help but subconsciously assign it a personality, no matter how dormant. After long observation, I believe that this is a universal trait amongst humanity. Certain cultures take it to a greater degree than others. The Japanese, to cite just one example, believe that if you discard a long-used tool or other manufactured object in an inappropriate manner, then it could turn evil. Some special places are also said to have a spirit to them. This is rare, especially these days, if only because Americans don't tend to think in these terms.

However, on that long-ago night back in 1955, Celeste awoke

very strong magics indeed and did so regarding a very specific part of the land.

Places like Zenonland, a place where people congregate and routinely pump out strong emotions, *can* generate their own spirits. But these are usually crafted by the people who use the space for a long time, sometimes over generations, such as a secluded glen with excellent lighting that is used for magical ceremonies. A place like that can acquire a natural spirit that exemplifies the feelings of the congregants, and there is a sort of feedback loop that, over the years, can result in very impressive manifestations indeed.

There are not a lot of places like that in modern America. Things come and go so quickly here that in the space of a week, even the holiest of places could be razed for a fried chicken restaurant.

But the L'Enfant reversed the process, as it were. When she bound me to this spot, she had to give the spot she was binding me to a shape, a purpose. Now, everyone *knew* that Zenonland was going to be this magnificent place, and so that was the expectation that she gave to the land. The result was that she created an ... idea that might have taken generations in both time and people to generate naturally, and because there was this idea and an expectation waiting to be filled—the land filled it. Usually, places that have spirits acquire them through use, as it were. But L'Enfant gave shape and self-awareness to the place that would become Zenonland before it even *was* Zenonland.

As a result, when our very first guests came through the gates on opening day—no, even as the workers and construction crews were putting the finishing touches on the park—they knew, *everyone* knew, that this was a special, a magical place, one that warmed people's hearts and satisfied a spiritual need that most of them didn't even know they were lacking. The park was a success from day one.

And when a magical place is established, and used for generations, an "animus spirit," one that incorporates all of that emotion, can form. In my time I have encountered innumerable nature spirits occupying glens and pools and caves. Shy, gentle creatures that formed spontaneously over time.

Again, Celeste took that process and turned it on its head. She artificially created a niche where an animus spirit for the land would have naturally formed over time, and the land responded as if the emotions of the people were already there and manifested. When she attempted to pull forth a *genius loci* in order to ask about the fate of Mr. Mortimer, she actually *created* one on the spot from the dissipated wisps of Xochemilchic.

Unsurprisingly (in retrospect), the Spirit of Zenonland manifested itself as one of Mr. Bartholomew's cartoon animals. I don't know how it chose the shape it did, but it appeared as Bone Cat, the very first character that Mr. Bartholomew animated back in the early 1930s.

These days everyone knows Preston Platypus. He was Mr. Bartholomew's breakthrough character, and there is no denying that it was his famous animated short, *Ain't We Got Guns,* that began Zenon Studio's climb to success.

But before that, he started with Bone Cat, a scrappy, mischievous, reanimated cat skeleton that bedeviled antagonists and delighted audiences through six shorts that are themselves a treatise on the early days of animation. Each one is significantly better and more sophisticated than the one that came before, as Mr. Bartholomew and his ragtag crew of filmmakers learned, and in many cases invented, the art of animation as they went.

But when Mr. Bartholomew was trying to lock down his now famous distribution deal with the owner of the Apogee Theatre chain that got Zenon cartoons in front of audiences from New York to Los Angeles, the owner, Mr. Jupiter Applegee, made but a single demand: He wanted to see something new.

And so Bone Cat was retired, and Preston Platypus bounced into the hearts of America and the world. But Mr. Bartholomew always held a particularly warm spot for Bone Cat, so it made perfect sense that he became the form that the spirit of the park assumed.

Because he is tied to me, he only appears when I am in contact with the land. Whenever I fly, he fades away. To where? Even he does not know, and thus he berates me whenever I contemplate flying instead of walking. Interestingly, he remains even if I am only *technically* on the ground. Standing atop a building, or even sitting in a chair, and he is still there.

Which meant that I had acquired a new friend, and a garrulous prankster of a friend at that. It took some getting used to. Before my association with Mr. Mortimer, I had been a bit of a loner. Then for fifteen years I had been part of a team. Oh, there was no denying that Mr. Mortimer had his puckish side, but on the whole he was a sober and steady fellow.

Bone Cat is his antithesis. It took some getting used to, and no mistake. To be honest, in the beginning, there were entire evenings I spent flying about over the park because the idea of the little fool capering gormlessly around me made me want to break things. Our first decade or so together was a strained one. This only began to change when I thought that he was dying.

I first noticed it on the night that Mr. Bartholomew himself passed away, in 1967. His death was no surprise—the man had lung cancer, after all. But there was a great deal of worry amongst the employees, and, from what I gathered, the general population as well. The Zenon Corporation was so closely associated with the man who'd created it, that the idea of it continuing on after he died was seen as unlikely, at best.

When I awoke that evening, Bone Cat did not move from his usual resting place, which was, at that time, curled atop my sarcophagus. I fluttered the lid, in order to get him to move. When he did not, I slowly opened it all the way, which resulted in him sliding to the ground and exploding into a pile of loose bones.

I was terrified, and spent several minutes scrabbling across the floor, scooping all the bones into my hat, which was the only thing I could find. My fears eased slightly when I noticed that the bones were slowly rearranging themselves into his normal shape, but he still refused to rouse.

Mr. Bartholomew died at 2:12 AM. At two thirty, Bone Cat startled me again, by abruptly sitting up on my desk, where I had deposited him. For almost a minute, he did nothing, merely sitting and staring into space, until I poked him with an extended claw. He batted it away. "Barty-boy's dead," he informed me matter-of-factly.

I nodded. "Is that why you were ... comatose?"

He nodded. "Yeah. Me and a few of the others thought we should be there. You know, to see him off."

"Others? What others?"

"The other characters. You know, Preston, and Wenceslaus Weasel, and Count Honkula, and Missy Mammoth, and—"

"The other characters that Mr. Bartholomew created? They're *alive*?" I waved my hands. "Or whatever it is you are? Am I going to have to deal with a whole *pack* of you?"

He grinned. "You should be so lucky. Nah, most of them went with him. Me? I'm still tied to the land."

"So ... You're saying that a creator's characters ... when they die, they meet them ..." I thought of some of the embarrassing deaths that Zenon villains had succumbed to over the years. The evil unicorn Dyspepsya, who met her doom strapped onto her own automatic pencil sharpener at the end of Zenon's acclaimed retelling of *The Lady of Shalott* stood out in my mind. I had thought it moronic, at the time. But to be held *accountable* for it ...

"Oh, not everyone you're thinking of showed up," Bone Cat assured me. "A lotta Zenon movies, he just signed the checks, y'know? But the early stuff? The characters he created himself, the ones he put something of himself into? We were there."

As I have said elsewhere, I do not know what happens after people die. That said, the few hints that occasionally come my way continue to surprise me.

Bone Cat claimed that he was now fine, but I paid a bit more attention, and I noted that for the next few years, he seemed to go into a bit of a slow decline, which mirrored that of the park, and indeed the company itself.

As far as Zenonland goes, I personally believe that if the park had been an autonomous place, unconnected with the corporation, it could have survived perfectly well, possibly even better than it did, serviced by a volunteer "priesthood" that would have maintained it and preserved it for future guests. It has that kind of a hold on people. But, of course, that was not what happened at all. And so, as I promised, Mr. Raphael Zenon now enters our story.

If you look in a dictionary for the term "middle manager," it should be illustrated with a tiny little picture of Mr. Raphael, trying not to be noticed. However fate did not allow him the genteel obscurity he craved. By the dictates of Mr. Bartholomew's will, he was made the new CEO of the Zenon Corporation.

Mr. Raphael does not really receive enough credit in the Zenonland histories. There were many people who figured that he would be quickly swept aside, but whatever his personal inclination, when faced with adversity, he displayed the legendary Zenon family tenacity. While he lacked Mr. Bartholomew's idealism, he remained loyal to his brother's vision.

There is no denying that the company declined under his rule, but there were extraordinary circumstances that would have tested the mettle of anyone stepping into the position, and all things considered, the amazing thing is that the company survived at all.

Mr. Raphael's is not a name familiar to the general public, which is how he would have wanted it, but his tenure is still studied at the better schools of business, albeit for all the wrong reasons.

It was undeniably true that under his watch, the Zenon Corporation reached its nadir. The malaise spread to Zenonland, which began to suffer as the company's stock price fell. Maintenance was deferred. Corners were cut. The shine began to rub off. The magic began to dim. This naturally impacted how our guests felt about the place, which, in turn, was reflected in Bone Cat's behavior. He became listless and out of sorts. Towards the end, there were entire weeks when he could hardly be bothered to rouse himself.

Now it would be very easy to blame all of this on Mr. Raphael's mismanagement, and many histories of the company do. But what few people know was that he was restricted in every important way by his departed brother's dictates from beyond the grave. Oh, there was no denying that Mr. Bartholomew had been the man with the vision of what the park could and should be. Call it genius or deluded, idealistic or fascistic, precognizant or overly nostalgic, but Mr. Bartholomew had thoroughly articulated that plan, demanded that everyone adhere to it, and had fully expected them to do so even after he was gone. And adhere they did, for a while.

But as I have mentioned, because of the whole cryonics cockup, Mr. Bartholomew had taken to haunting the corporate offices. While he was primarily obsessed with the location of his body, this occupied only part of his time. The remainder he spent trying to run his company.

Unfortunately, those dead who barely comprehend that they are no longer alive, certainly do not have the mental flexibility to understand how things that happen in the outside world can make their core dictates irrelevant, impractical, or even illegal.

The upshot of this was that Mr. Bartholomew was often in a bad mood. It was very disturbing, because when you were talking about something innocuous, he would be quite businesslike, and several of his former associates had trouble remembering that he was actually dead. However, if you innocently suggested a change in the way things were being done that crossed any of the thousand and one invisible lines that existed in his head, he would roar and shriek and fling about every detached item in the room, smashing furniture and windows and, in several cases, almost injuring people.

Everyone at this level of the company was heavily invested in Zenon stock, and so they had great incentive to see that news of this haunting did not get out to the public. It was barely whispered about within the company, and, in fact, *I* did not find out about it until one evening when I opened my office door and was astonished to see Mr. Raphael himself, huddled upon my guest chair.

We had met, of course. Mr. Bartholomew himself had brought him to the park to meet me, shortly after the incident with the Wendigo. We did not hit it off.

Mr. Raphael was one of those persons who embraced the scientific worldview that was currently on the ascendance. It was neat and tidy and did not require the presence of invisible creatures that one was expected to petition for protection or favors. It was a universe as dull as he was, and that was exactly how he liked it. Naturally I, and the reality that I represented, flew in the face of everything that he wanted to believe, and rather than having to change his worldview, he found it much easier to pretend that I did not exist. Thus my surprise at finding him here.

It took almost an hour, a cup of coffee heavily laced with some of the brandy that the current Head of Park Security kept hidden in his desk, and a great deal of uncomfortable small talk before the reason for his visit was dragged out into the open. It was then that I learned of Mr. Bartholomew's disruptive, post-vital shenanigans. Suddenly the reason for the retention of the many policies that encumbered the park, as well as the corporation itself, was explained—

"No, wait a minute," I said. "Your brother died almost a decade ago ..." I stared at Mr. Raphael aghast. "You've been putting up with this for *ten years?*" It was then that Mr. Raphael truly broke down. He had adored his brother, and had, with some justification, seen him as the source of everything positive that had happened in his life. However, things had gotten to the point where indulging his brother's spirit was no longer realistically possible. The changes that Mr. Bartholomew's shade was railing about were no longer simple things like tweaks to artistic style, or whether women employees should be allowed to wear trousers. He was now protesting changes that were needed to keep the Zenon Corporation in compliance with the law. Sociologically, it had been a tumultuous decade, and the company's rules and regulations regarding things like the hiring of women for executive positions, the hiring of minorities, handicapped access, the permitting of unionization, adherence to safety standards, waste disposal procedures, and a hundred more, were grievously out of date.

None of this non-corporeal drama was known to anyone except for the inner corporate circle. To the outside world, it simply looked like another case of a company that had been ruled by a single man foundering without his strong hand on the tiller. A rather ironic interpretation, actually. But the result was the same—the company continued its downward spiral, and, by the late seventies, I had great hopes for its dissolution.

But Mr. Raphael realized that the choice he faced came down to continuing to obey his beloved brother and watching the thing that Mr. Bartholomew had created be destroyed, or destroying his brother, and letting the company that carried his name, live on. The answer had been obvious, but it had taken him another year to build the resolve needed to come to me.

"Why me?" I asked.

He looked at me as a man trapped in a bog, about to be sucked under, would stare at an overhanging tree branch that might—or might not—sway to where he could grab it in time to pull himself free. "He's a ghost," he said slowly, like he was explaining something to a child. "I don't know how to deal with ghosts. None of us do." He sighed. "But *you* do, don't you?"

And indeed I did. Naturally, I couldn't do any of the actual leg work, as it was all off-site. But through agents, people were paid to look the other way, and Mr. Bartholomew's head was covertly removed from its grave. A suitable container was fashioned, and with great ceremony, before the gaze of Mr. Bartholomew's shade, placed into a small freezer. Thereafter it was conveyed, within a refrigerated truck, to Zenonland in the dark of the night. As the truck pulled away, the shade left the Zenon offices, and although everyone who saw it swore that it appeared to be walking normally, it effortlessly kept up with the truck through the city and up to the gates of the park.

Bone Cat and I were waiting at the entrance when they all arrived. The truck pulled up to the curb, and a second later Mr. Bartholomew stepped out from behind it. I could tell that he was a ghost, of course, but it was still a shock, seeing him after all these years. He saw us, as they were unloading the truck, and strolled on over. "I'm told you're responsible for finally straightening this out," he said, as he gave Bone Cat a pat.

"Your brother did all the work," I said. "I just told him what needed to be done."

His eyes never left the freezer that was now being wheeled towards the gates, but he nodded. "Yeah, that's Raff in a nutshell." He sighed. "I probably leaned on him harder than I should've."

"You think?"

"Tell him I'm sorry, and thanks for everything." I was about to tell him to convey this himself, but as soon as the freezer cleared the turnstiles, Mr. Bartholomew gave a great sigh that never ended, and he dissipated from the inside out, vanishing into thin air. And that was that.

Now, I myself thought that things between Mr. Raphael and myself would revert to normal. But to my surprise, the very next evening, he was again waiting in my office. He already looked better. He was sitting up straight, and he had the look of a man who has finally gotten a decent night's sleep. "He's gone," he said simply.

His gratitude for my assistance in freeing him from the

shadow of his brother, who had always been a commanding personality, made the next decade or so much easier on me. This was also when I received my second raise in pay.

I also saw improvements being made in the park, which were reflected in Bone Cat's rapid improvement. It was during this period that the Night Crew began to grow into the army of people, thousands strong, that it is today. All very good, and no doubt some would regard the resolution of my relationship with Mr. Raphael to be so saccharine that it was worthy of being made into a Zenon picture in its own right.

But there was one very important consequence of all this; the park did not close after twenty years. It did not close after thirty. It was no longer a mere company; it was well on its way to becoming an institution.

Eventually Mr. Raphael bowed out, and, for the first time, the Chairman of the Zenon Corporation was not a Zenon family member. History says many things about Mr. Michael's tenure as CEO, but as one looks about today and sees a globe-straddling megacorporation that has absorbed half of the world's entertainment properties while single-handedly bribing enough of the United States government that they cheerfully gutted their own trademark laws for our benefit ... well! You have to admit that he did all right by our shareholders.

Which is a problem for me, as I am still trapped. Now don't get me wrong, I certainly earn my keep, and it's not like I object to my job, but I want my freedom. My only hope is Celeste. Oh yes, we have stayed in touch. She is in her seventies now and has been the official L'Enfant for over fifty-five years.

Her mother's reign was a short one. In the early 1960s, another sorceress, a Lady LeChow, attempted to become the new Moon Queen of New Orleans. An important part of this plan involved the eradication of the old Queen, which she did in a rather messy fashion.

This was supposed to let people know that the new Queen was serious and would suffer no sass. She was very surprised when she discovered that Celeste was the actual power in New Orleans. Now there may have been a bit of generational friction, but Celeste had been very fond of her mother. I am told that in a certain New Orleans voodoo-themed tourist trap, there is a room where the casual tourists are not allowed to go. One of the things you'd find there is a cunning little doll trapped inside a cage of nails. This contains the Lady LeChow's spirit. When it is not moaning in pain, or begging to be released, it will relate her whole, sad story for a dollar.

Celeste is once again (as far as she's concerned) the undisputed Moon Queen of New Orleans. She comes to visit, every decade or so, and I quite enjoy it when she does, the whole geas unpleasantness aside. She once addressed the Council of Shadow's annual fiesta, and her speech was even more popular and inspirational than the one delivered by that charming Elvira woman, and I'd thought that a bar impossible to clear. She has brought her own daughter, and later her granddaughter along as well, both of them rich with the family power. I am convinced that the carnival of the dead will be strutting through the streets of New Orleans for generations to come.

Anyway, several decades ago, when it had become patently obvious that the Zenon Corporation might very well outlive western civilization itself, I had once again begged her to undo the geas. Unfortunately, when my geas was originally crafted, part of what made it so strong was the understanding that no L'Enfant will ever undo that which a previous L'Enfant has wrought.

Higher magic is all about tricking reality into behaving against its better interests. As a result, when done correctly, it reads like a contract between insane lawyers. And, like an innocent man caught up in the coils of the law, I have pleaded, threatened, and railed against her about this, all to no effect. The upshot is that while *she* cannot abrogate the geas, there is the possibility that some *other* sorcerer could actually undo the damned thing, but apparently no one *powerful* enough is willing to do so, at least not within the United States.

If you are unlucky enough to spend any time amongst the magical community, you will realize that these people have *issues*. Everyone who has the slightest ability to sidestep the observable nuances of cause and effect is a large ball of thin-skinned insecurities. Thus, if you dared to unweave another sorcerer's geas, it would be seen as a challenge of some sort, and you'd wake up to find all of your handkerchiefs trying to strangle you or something.

Thaumaturgy is a filthy business, and the schadenfreude I experience whenever I hear about some magus being dragged down through the floor or going up in a ball of green flame is well earned, I think.

Celeste has sworn that she would not go after anyone "foolish enough to dare to challenge the might of the L'Enfant," but just the wording of that ostensibly benign declaration should tell you all you need to know. Be that as it may, I cannot deny that she did her best to get me out on a technicality.

This attempt was made in 1988. Mr. Raphael was in the hospital with pneumonia, and it was an open secret that he was not expected to last for much longer. Celeste had informed me that she was arriving, and I met her at the main gate. She explained that she might be able to retroactively *tweak* the geas so that it would only bind me while a family member of Mr. Mortimer's generation still lived. The downside was that there was a thirty percent chance that when Mr. Raphael died, I would as well.

To make a long story slightly less long, I accepted.

Again there were words in the light of the moon. Oaths and declarations, potions and another dance step that left me stretched out upon the ground, panting. Celeste looked at my reflection in a smoked mirror and declared the enchantment in place. She even waited around until Mr. Raphael slid peacefully into his final slumber. I had an unpleasant moment there, when he actually died. I felt a great tugging from nowhere. But after a minute, I realized that I was not going to die, and with a joyful shout, I leapt up into the sky and sailed smack into the ever-present barrier.

Celeste was quite embarrassed. To the point where she did not even bill me.

In fact, the most immediate and long-term effect was a souring of the relationship between Bone Cat and myself.

He glowered at me after Celeste left. "Did you even *think* what would happen to me iffin you died?"

I looked at him in surprise. "Not really," I admitted. "I have had several close calls, like when I fought the Wendigo, and you never mentioned it."

"That was different. You was doin' your job. I respected that. But this ... 'Oh, fuckin' boo hoo, I'm so sick of being stuck here that I'm okay with gettin' snuffed for nothin'.'" He sneered. "You wanna be pathetic, you do it on your own time."

I felt stunned. It was true. I had never even considered what my death would do to Bone Cat. He only manifested when I touched the ground. And now that I thought about it ... "What *would* happen to you if I actually managed to sever my geas and leave the park?"

He leapt up and smacked me across the face. "Thirty-three years and change before you even *thought* about that? You *asshole!*" Obviously he had thought about it a lot, and for the next few years, our partnership was an uncomfortable one.

It was ten years before Celeste got back in contact with me. To my surprise, it turned out that she had been working on my problem for a large part of it. L'Enfant de Lune does not like failure.

We met up at *Bayou Wonderland*'s homage to New Orleans' Café du Monde, which is famous for chicory-infused coffee and a particularly beloved variant on humanity's eternal love affair with fried and sugared dough, called a beignet.

Apparently, when it first opened, the beignets here were

rather awful, if young Celeste's reaction was anything to go by. However, she paced out a little cantrip around the building, and with my help, inscribed some symbols on the roof in red chalk, and now any employee who produces less than perfect pastries or coffee has an increasingly horrible series of dreams explaining how they're going to metamorphose into an alligator unless they flee or their work improves. This has proved so effective that the whole alligator thing only happened once, to a troubled young lady who had a very well-hidden herpetological fetish. She was actually rather pleased when she transformed into a majestic albino alligator who is now treated like royalty at the local zoo.

It was kept out of the papers, of course, but a transformation like that leaves a residue, as it were, which can linger for over a century in the right climate. What it did here was give those dreams *credence*. As a result, pastry chefs have traveled here from the original Café du Monde to see how it is that the Zenonland bakers are now producing better beignets than they are.

So there we were, sitting together. The café was crowded, as always, but magically, as it were, a small empty table was waiting for us in a corner. Celeste sat and listened to Bone Cat, who enjoys having a new listener for his ramblings, while I fetched us a large plate of pastries and a couple of coffees. Naturally, I myself do not have to eat or drink, but there is the public appearance of things to consider, and Celeste does not want to look like the kind of woman who would plan on eating a dozen beignets all by herself (Although that is in fact what she does, all the while making a great show of reluctance about doing it. It is a performance that never fails to entertain.).

As for myself, I surreptitiously sprinkle a little powdered sugar down my front and simply allow people make the obvious assumption. Incidentally, I have found this to be a very useful psychological trick whenever I want whomever I am talking with to be more at ease in my presence. Tastefully small dabs of mustard and salad dressing work equally well, but ketchup has rather the opposite effect.

So Bone Cat and I sat back and watched as Celeste plowed through a half a dozen pastries (without a speck of powdered sugar getting anywhere near her black outfit) before she paused and looked me in the eye. "I have been working on your geas, *mon ami*. Ever since Raphael Zenon, *paix à son âme,* died."

I shrugged. "Magic is, by its very nature, tricky."

"No." She surprised me with her vehemence. "No, it *should* have worked. We did everything correctly. You agreed to the price. It was *accepted*. I *saw* that in the mirror."

"So what happened?"

Celeste hunched down and selected another beignet, which she delicately nibbled on. "There are several possibilities. There is no mistake about Bartholomew and Raphael Zenon, but we must now acknowledge the possibility that *Mortimer* Zenon is not actually dead."

I felt shock at this declaration. I was convinced that Mr. Mortimer had suffered some terrible fate the night I had been bound to the park. If only because I could not believe that if he were alive, he would have stayed away. I had let it be known, through Celeste, and the rest of my contacts, that I had forgiven him. But in all the intervening years, I had heard nothing. I looked over at Bone Cat, who was engaged in attempting to steal one of the L'Enfant's beignets. He shrugged. "Sorry I can't help you answer that one, chief. Barty-boy was the only member of the family *I* ever cared about."

This was certainly true. The two had had a most interesting relationship. Mr. Bartholomew had been thunderstruck the first time he'd met Bone Cat, and apparently—I had stepped out to allow them a modicum of privacy—had spent an inordinate amount of time apologizing for "throwing him over for Preston." Artists worry about the strangest things.

"I find it hard to believe that he might still be alive," I said carefully.

"As do I," Celeste said regretfully, selecting another beignet.

"It would make things ever so much easier, but all of my researches have told me that he never left the city."

"Then he *could* still be alive, albeit a prisoner. He'd be in his late eighties, but—"

Celeste waved a hand. "I have dreamwalked. Through this city, through the state, through the upper world." She sighed, and suddenly looked as tired as if she had continuously lived every one of her lives in one long stretch. "It was difficult. But even if he was drugged, I would have found his sense of self. No, even if his body was alive, Mortimer Zenon is no more."

I had thought that I had come to terms with the idea that Mr. Mortimer was truly gone, but the sick feeling in my chest let me know that I had still held out hope. I slumped in my chair, and Bone Cat gently patted my arm. "Very well ... so?"

Celeste sat back, glanced at the beignets, and with an uncharacteristic grimace, pushed them away. Bone Cat took this as permission to begin wolfing them down, to the fascination of several young children at the next table.

"It is possible that one of his parents had additional children, of which mayhap even the three sons were unaware." She shrugged. "A premarital indiscretion secretly given up for adoption. The hidden fruit of an extramarital affair. Magic delights in exploiting these sorts of surprise loopholes."

I sat back and considered this. I had never met the elder Zenons. But everything I had read implied that they were simple, hardworking people you would have unironically described as "the salt of the earth."

They had been immensely proud of what Mr. Bartholomew had built, although I'm told that they were worried that it was all some sort of gigantic confidence trick, as the idea that his fame and fortune actually resulted from simply drawing an endless succession of cartoon animals seemed improbable to them, at best. I would have said that neither of them seemed the type to produce mysterious, heretofore unknown offspring, but there are certain things that continually surprise me as far as people are concerned, and a depressing number of them have to do with sex. I sighed. "So we are back to waiting for someone to die. How cheerful."

Celeste shrugged. "But it is a step in the right direction. Everyone *does* die."

I considered this. Both of the elder Zenons had died in the 1940s, both in their eighties. I could not realistically see any contemporary kin of Mr. Bartholomew being younger than seventy-five already. "Well," I grumbled, "they're certainly taking their time about it, but the next ten years or so should be sufficient, yes?"

"Oh, yes," Celeste assured me, "There is a very good chance you'll greet the new century free and clear."

And yet, once again, she was proven wrong. It has been over twenty years since that night, and as my recent flight confirmed, the geas that binds me to this place is as strong as ever. Whomever it is that the geas binds me to either has access to superlative medical treatment or else, and this is the thought that troubles my dreams, is being prevented from dying. There are any number of curses that could do that, though you don't usually see that kind of old-school malice much these days. Those types of curses tend to extract a terrible price on those foolish enough to cast them. However, if I am honest, I must admit that during the time of our association, Mr. Mortimer and I earned that level of enmity several times over.

I only wished that I had been there to help him as he had helped me.

CHAPTER SEVEN

I extrude myself from my sanctuary and pause. I can feel it. Something is different, but what?

It looks like it's going to be another pleasant California night. The crowds ebb and flow in their usual patterns, but there is something odd. An out of place note in the overall symphony of the park. Bone Cat gives a yawn that looks like it would split his head in half and darts out into the twilight.

It is still a bit too bright outside for me to fly up and survey the park *en toto*, so I step out and extend my perceptions. The visitors are normal. A few wisps of vague dread about the cost of this vacation or fretting about the report they really should have finished that is still on their desk, and there is a ubiquitous, but low-level fretting about gas explosions, which makes sense, I suppose—thin fare to be sure, but until I know what is wrong, I prefer not to get too full.

Suddenly something that has been right in front of me snaps into focus. All of the park employees are wearing new badges. The first concrete sign of our new masters. It has a lovely holographic image of the Castle that sparkles as it tilts, but it seems like an odd expenditure, the old badges were still quite service-able ... The mystery clears a bit when I see another employee attempt to use one of the service doors, only to find it locked. They roll their eyes and dip slightly in order to bring their badge within range of a newly mounted reader. The door gives a gentle buzz, and they step inside. Ah, I have read about these. In addition to allowing only employees entrance to backstage areas, they can also tell security which employee is opening which door.

Initially I think this to be Mr. Donovan's doing, in response to yesterday's infiltration. But even a minute's thought is enough to dismiss this idea. The paperwork alone for a job this extensive would have to be undertaken days—if not weeks—in advance, especially if you want it done within the space of a single day, which it appears that they have.

I debate whether to get my old badge replaced immediately, or to wait until I head down to my office after the park closes. On the one hand, I do not want to give the impression that I am worried about the state of my "job" (I fully expect to find my office—gasp!—locked), but on the other hand, I do not function in a vacuum. The security people that I work with are touchy enough about my status that they appreciate the fact that I bother to hew to the form of things, and actually wear my badge, pay my Union dues, and fill in my time card. This is one of those occasions when I want to remind people that I am a "team player," plus I expect that no matter how tight a lid has been kept on things, the news of even a minor explosion on a Zenonland ride will be all over the news. The park will be swarming with outsiders, newspeople, and those damned inspectors, who do not know who I am ... So—let us force the issue. To the office it is.

That is, until Bone Cat rockets back around the corner, grabs my coat, and drags me forward so that I can see that there is scaffolding around the castle tower. This is a shocking lapse to begin with. Repairs and maintenance are, of course, going on all the time, but to exhibit the mundane artifacts of this; to admit to the public that this place of magic and moonshine is subject to entropy and California State Building Codes is practically unheard of. I assume that someone is taking the gas leak threat all too seriously—until I notice that the focus of the scaffolding seems to be my chambers.

I step into the shadows and skirl my way up to the window. What I find is so surprising that I almost coalesce enough to once again be subject to the forces of gravity. My room has been, well, foamed. It's the sort of insulation stuff that they squirt between walls, which swells and hardens, filling every nook and crevice. I extend my senses and can tell that the room's furnishings are still there, just entombed in foam. The casket has been opened, and thus, even if I could somehow phase through several meters of solidified foam (which I cannot, of course, no ephemeral ghost or phantasm am I), it would provide me with no useable sanctuary.

I do not for an instant believe this to be some misguided attempt at repair or renovation. This is an attack upon myself. With this realization, I dart out into the night and head for my next closest registered resting spot. My suspicions are instantly confirmed. This place has also been destroyed.

An hour later, I finish my survey of the park. After the first three destroyed resting places, I began to travel more surreptitiously to try to avoid leading anyone to places they might not already know about, but that particular horse has already left that particular barn far behind. All twenty of the resting places registered with management have been destroyed. Of the additional twenty-three I had thought secret, only seven remain untouched. No, someone wants me dead, not fired. This is no longer amusing. While I am perfectly willing to play through the whole being fired farce, I have no patience with anyone who tries to kill me. It is definitely time to have another talk with my new friend, Mr. Donovan, and examine the park camera recordings.

I am outside the nearest employee door when I pause. Additional reasons for the new badge/lock system belatedly present themselves. It is obviously only a minor inconvenience, but it is an unexpected one, and it forces me to seriously consider what other modern tricks and traps may be waiting. In my time here I have allowed myself to feel invulnerable. I have been encouraged in this because when I act this way, it makes a good first impression, and this is such a theatrical culture that many of the people I deal with wouldn't recognize a subtle threat if it set their shoes on fire. However I myself am not deluded. Close calls with the sun and fire have convinced me that either would work quite well, and, as the Wendigo proved, whatever I am, if you pummel me long enough and hard enough, I will take serious damage. My geas demonstrates to any potential foe that I am susceptible to curses and magic, and I must assume they will use them if they can. There is a time to be brash, and there is a time to be subtle, and this is one of the latter. Hopefully, this will catch my foes by surprise, as no one is really used to me being subtle.

I start by taking a more circumspect route into the offices, infiltrating myself into the ductwork and flowing along, silently. The offices I peer into seem to be functioning normally.

Then I come to my own. I pause in surprise. All of my belongings are still in place. Even more alarming, a small boy—no more than ten years old—is seated at my desk, idly surfing the web on my computer! While eating caramels! I don't know what foolishness this portends, but I cannot and will not sit by and let this imp get my keyboard all sticky.

I prepare to flow down into my office. However, when I shift my position, I get another unpleasant surprise. Set up behind my door appears to be a large bank of powerful lights. From where I am, it is easy to see that things have been set up so that they would be triggered as soon as the door swung open. I sharpen my gaze and see that these are full-spectrum lights, the type used on movie shoots, possibly even more potent than genuine sunlight. That many, at that close a range, could very well destroy me. This oblivious child, sticky fingers and all, is obviously bait. Admittedly bait that whoever put him here must be all too aware that I cannot physically harm, but surely there must be some sort of consideration as far as psychological damage goes; on the other hand, this wretched child is now picking his nose and *wiping his finger on the arms of my chair*. This child *needs* to be terrorized, and I suspect that whoever set him here is hoping that I will. What kind of person am I *dealing* with?

I take a deep breath and continue onwards. To take my mind off the probable state of my office furniture, I contemplate my surroundings. I really should write a dissertation about air ducts. I mean, they're such a standard staple for covert travel in fiction that you'd think people would demand a greater level of veracity. The flaw in this plan is that they're not all that interesting. They're a lot smaller and dirtier than the ones you see in the movies, for one thing, but if we're being honest, that description applies equally to everybody and everything in the entertainment business.

This line of thought keeps me amused until I reach Mr. Donovan's office and cautiously peer in. I see no sign of traps or alarms. Mr. Donovan is slumped at his desk, elbows planted and head resting upon his cupped hands. A pose I often found Mr. Shulman in. It must be something they teach them at security school.

I flow into the room and coalesce behind his chair. Bone Cat materializes on his desk. We lean in and, in unison, whisper, "Good evening." But there is no humorous response. No response at all. I realize that something is seriously wrong. Even before I touch him I can tell that Mr. Donovan is quite dead. Unfortunate to be sure, but it's not the first corpse I have found lying about the grounds that I had nothing to do with. But there is something odd about this one. I tip his head back and Bone Cat squeals in surprise, actually falling off the desk. I can see why. Mr. Donovan appears to have died of fear. It's an expression I have some familiarity with, but seeing it cold gives even me quite a start.

"Whose turn is it," Bone Cat asks. I'm actually considering this until I realize that this body is really not my responsibility. I need to report this and let the corporate machinery grind along as it should. Bone Cat believes that we should take him anyway and give him to the gremlins. There is merit to this thought, as it is possible that they might still be holding the whole gas explosion thing against me, though I cannot see how they possibly could. On the other hand, I really don't know what they do with the bodies I provide them with already, so I'll acknowledge that I am not expert in Gremlin psychology.

We are arguing this very point when we step out of the office, and into the late Mr. Donovan's anteroom, eliciting a shriek of surprise from his secretary, whom, I belatedly realize, I never actually introduced myself to. My stepping *out* of Mr. Donovan's office without her knowing that I was *inside* must be quite disconcerting.

"Who the hell are you?" she then demands. Some people are like that. Get them flustered and they try to hide their embarrassment with a coarse bravado. These people are usually hard to deal with.

With a little effort, I can produce vocal harmonics that ensure absolute attention. I do so now. "Be quiet. Call the police and medical services, although I believe them to be superfluous. Mr. Donovan is dead." She claps her hands to her mouth and her eyes go wide. I assume that she came to California to get into the movies, and physically, she has potential, but watching her now, I must conclude that she learned how to emote from an intense study of Cartoon Network. "Yes, yes," I say, "you're very surprised. Now—"

But at that moment, the anteroom door slams open and a uniformed guard—one I was unfamiliar with—steps in, pistol drawn and aimed straight at me. "Freeze!"

I blinked at him in annoyance. "Thank you, young man, but —" And then he shoots me. I'm so astonished that the bullet throws me back against the wall. This is no nine millimeter "for show" pistol. This guard is packing heavy ordinance. A .45 caliber at the very least. I relax my cohesion in time that the next two shots pass through harmlessly and simply carve chunks out of the wall behind me. The fear boiling off the secretary serves as a tonic, focusing my mind as I flow towards the guard. This worthy stands his ground and continues to fire. I am counting his shots now, and I know that he is down to his last two. Evidently he knows it, too, as he straightens up, and with a sob, turns, and guns down the secretary.

I freeze in consternation. "What the hell did you do that for, you lunatic?"

"I saved her soul from you, you demon," he shouts, and then he swings the gun up under his own chin and pulls the trigger.

Even as his fool head explodes, I'm kneeling next to the secretary, to see what I could do for her, though I am afraid it would be little enough. A .45 at close range can kill a human through hydrostatic shock alone, and I see that she is dead.

"Demon" he called me. I'm beginning to think he may have meant that *literally*. Bone Cat is already on the phone in the secretary's desk, trying to call for the police.

I give the guard a cursory examination. I see that his exposed skin has an unseemly number of tattoos. This is not as unheard of as it used to be, as sometime in the last ten years or so the Zenon Corporation had rescinded its established hiring ban on people with visible tattoos, but even now they have to be innocuous. What I can see on the guard is anything but, as it appears to be a mix of crucifixes, bible verses, and handguns.

Bone Cat slams the phone down. "The line is dead," he reports. "The jerk must've shot it up."

But I don't see any damage ...

I think about the cellular phone in my desk—it's no doubt been used as a depository for chewing gum—and sigh in annoyance. I'm about to search the gunman for his, when a clatter out in the hall alerts us that more people are coming. Marvelous. I briefly consider facing them, but I remember that light setup in my office. If they're out to get me, specifically, then they might be better prepared than the fool at my feet.

With a grunt (that initial bullet impact still smarted a bit), I flow up and into the air vent. Just in time, as it happens, as when the door is kicked in, a flare of light fills the room. Even from where I am, the reflected glare is enough to make me congeal slightly, which is most uncomfortable inside that conduit, let me tell you. But I stick it out and am rewarded by a squad of uniformed security officers (none of whom I knew) pouring into the room, guns drawn, all equipped with head-mounted sun lamps.

Every now and then I realize that I have been immersed far too long in a corporate culture that takes its cues and social mores from the movies it produces. This was once again the case as I realize that I'm waiting for the men in the room to explain why they're after me, and, possibly, where they'll be meeting "the Boss." Don't judge me; I'd had a trying morning.

Needless to say, they do no such thing. These men are a step up in professionalism from their late, trigger-happy colleague, though there seems to be an unseemly amount of muttered prayer. This solidifies a growing suspicion; if you want to whole-heartedly hunt a "demon," then go out of your way to employ people who are already convinced that demons actually exist. While I admire the deviousness thus displayed, I also find it vexing, as it means that my chances of rationally talking to these people are minuscule at best. There can be no negotiating when you believe you are fighting a Holy War. God wouldn't like it.

If I'm honest, I can see how a credulous person, given a superficial outline of my activities and abilities, could be convinced that I was some sort of force for evil. It's been people's baseline assumption about me for almost a millennium, after all. But I really cannot fathom *why* the new owner has gone to all this effort to convince people that I'm *so* evil that the sin of *suicide* is apparently the lesser threat to their soul. Oh, any number of incoming executives have initially recoiled from me and my work here, but all too soon, they see the necessity.

Mr. Michael was one of the hardest to convince. He was the

first CEO who came from outside of the family, though he had worked his way up from within the organization. Now, Mr. Raphael was an excellent manager, but whenever possible, the policies of his brother trumped competing suggestions from well-meaning underlings, and Mr. Michael always had suggestions. So it was unsurprising that Mr. Michael had over a decade of buried resentment to work through, which manifested in a determination to do things his way.

He was incredulous when he first heard about me, and was convinced that I was not, in fact, a timeless monster that patrolled the park and killed those who would prey upon children, but some sort of scam artist. It was that notion that seemed to anger him more than the reality, and when the time came, he was quite eager to meet me.

The official transfer of power was to take place the next day. Mr. Raphael brought Mr. Michael to the park that last night so that we might meet. I had been told that the new boss was a bit of a skeptic, and so I tried for a flashy entrance. When I saw them waiting near the newly erected statue of Mr. Bartholomew, I swooped down out of the darkness and made a show of coalescing before them. It was all rather spoiled when I tripped upon the curb and sprawled at their feet. Mr. Michael stared down at me with contempt. "This is your monster?"

Mr. Raphael was obviously embarrassed, but helped me up, nonetheless. Mr. Michael peered upwards, no doubt searching for the wires he assumed I had lowered myself down upon. "I thought I'd tell you in person," he said, still looking upwards. "You're fired. You can leave now."

This was the first time someone tried to fire me. To be honest, it was a bit of a shock. "I don't think you can do that," I said. I looked to Mr. Raphael. "Can he do that?"

That worthy checked his watch. "The public ceremony takes place later today, but all the papers were signed a week ago. So, technically, as of midnight, which was five minutes ago, he is, in fact, your boss."

"But ... but it can't be as easy as that, can it?"

Mr. Michael leaned in, looking me in the face for the first time. "It sure can, pal. I don't know what kind of con game you ran on these guys, but it's done." He reached into his coat and pulled out a crisp tan envelope. "Here you go. All legal and above board. Your final check and your paperwork. You're done. Let's go." Without another word, he turned and we headed towards the gate.

Walking beside me, Mr. Raphael coughed quietly and pulled out an envelope of his own. "I'm not really sure that this will work," he admitted, "but if it *does* ..."

Inside I found another check and an admittedly vague, but glowing, letter of recommendation, signed by Mr. Raphael himself. Before I could say anything, he waved a hand. "It's the least I can do."

We passed the gates, and just before we reached the sidewalk, I ran into the barrier. No easy way out for me. "This is as far as I can go," I said with a shrug.

"The hell you say," Mr. Michal growled. He grabbed my arm and attempted to jerk me forward, almost flying off of his feet when I didn't move. "I've heard of stuff like this," he said with a sneer. "Bracing yourself against the ground." I had no idea what he was talking about. But apparently Mr. Michael had come prepared for any unpleasantness. He waved his hand, and doors opened on a sleek limousine parked at the curb. Four large men in dark suits hurried towards us. A few muttered instructions from Mr. Michael, and they all grabbed me. Curiosity stayed my hand, and I allowed them to try to push, pull, and eventually, lift and carry me across the invisible line. All to no avail. The largest of the men finally threw up his hands. "I dunno *how* he's doin' it, sir, but he's doin' it. We can't move him."

Mr. Michael's eyes narrowed. He glanced over at Mr. Raphael, as if he thought the older man was playing a joke on him. Then he squared his jaw and nodded. "Fine. Let's see how he does it when he's unconscious. Tony—" He pointed to the leader of the men. "Get this trespassing bum outta my park."

Mr. Raphael looked alarmed. "Michael, don't!"

The men surrounded me and their grip was harder. Enough. I flowed out from between their fingers, and with two punches, a shove, and a kick, sent them flying back towards their car. I then swooped down on Mr. Michael, grabbed him by the collar of his very expensive suit, and hauled him high into the air. The two of us hovered above Electric Avenue. On the ground below, the five men stared upwards, their mouths open in amazement.

I'll give him this, Mr. Michael didn't scream. At least, not until I turned to face him and he saw my true visage. Then he screamed quite a bit. I don't know what he expected me to do, but what he got was an argument for why, since I could not leave the park, I should continue to be employed there. I thought it was rather reasonable and well thought out, considering I had to deliver the whole thing off-the-cuff as it were. Naturally there might have been a few places where I needed both hands for proper emphasis, but I always caught him quickly.

In a remarkably short time, he agreed that the terms of my continued employment were more than fair, although I will confess that I used my current advantageous position (approximately 150 feet up) to wrangle a modest raise in pay. No doubt there are those who would call this sort of behavior towards one's boss impertinent, and not really conducive toward long-term employee/management relations, and I cannot, in good conscience, argue. But evil? Worth trying to *kill* me evil? Ridiculous.

Oh, I suppose someone could be under the misapprehension that they are settling my karmic hash *vis-à-vis* the whole killing people thing, but to be honest, over the years, incoming CEOs are less fazed by the fact that I kill pedophiles than by the fact that I dare to contradict them. I do not know what they are teaching in management schools these days, but apparently humility and anger management are not in the curriculum.

But I have not even *met* the new owner, so I really have no idea as to why he should have taken so much trouble to cast me as a villain. These were my thoughts as I flowed through the conduit. I really had no particular destination in mind, but I thought a general reconnaissance was in order. I head towards the main security monitoring station. It was usually occupied by one or two bored guards, along with a multitude of screens displaying ever-changing views of the park and the underground complex.

Today it is packed with security people, both uniformed and not. The one in charge is explaining that I am dangerous and am to be destroyed on sight. On the main screen is an endless loop of myself coalescing behind Mr. Donovan and lifting his head to reveal his shocking visage. To me it's obvious that I had done nothing, but to a more excitable person, I have to concede that you could interpret it as a monstrous attack upon a sleeping man. No wonder everyone is so upset. It doesn't help that I have yet to see a familiar face amongst the security forces. There is no one with any experience in dealing with me to reassure them that, while I was creepy, yes, and certainly an inexplicable thing that was a power unto myself within the park itself, I cause no actual *harm* ...

It is times like these when a person realizes that they have been inexcusably lax when it comes to the whole social media thing. I had rather gone out of my way to cultivate a mysterious persona within the company as a benignly dangerous entity bound by no laws but my own. Possibly it was time for a bit of a public relations makeover. Unfortunately, that would have to be postponed for the moment.

Below, the security officers present file out, and a fresh batch shuffle in. The room only holds ten people at a time. The man in charge allows the newcomers to get an eyeful of the damning loop on the screens before he calls for their attention. "All right, men." I belatedly realize that sexual diversity in this particular workplace seems to have gone by the wayside. "This is the demon you heard about when you were hired."

There are shocked exclamations and muttered prayers as the scene loops a few more times. "Yes, it's real; no, they were not kidding. It's been infesting the park for less than a week." He faces the new officers and taps his podium for emphasis. "Your test results show that you know how to keep a secret. Here's your chance to prove it. You don't talk about this to anyone outside the job. You don't talk to non-security personnel. You don't talk to the press. You don't talk to family. You don't talk to your priest.

"You wanna be able to face the Lord on Judgment Day and say that you had a hand in taking this abomination down? Then a buttoned lip is the price of admission. You can't do that? You walk now." None of the assembled men stir. It is obvious that they want to be in on this. The presenter nods in satisfaction. "Your most powerful weapon is the Light of the Lord." He hoists up what appears to be an overly large flashlight. Seeing it, I pull back quickly, and thus when the expected flare of light fills the room, I'm safely beyond its effects. He clicks it off and I drift back. "That's God's sunlight, and the creature will do everything it can to avoid it. You will each be issued one of these, as well as a head-mounted unit." He puts the light down. "And now," he says with a smile, "let's talk about ammo."

An appreciative murmur goes through the group. The presenter holds up a cardboard box. "The Zenon Corporation has got your backs. These are the most nonregulation bullets you're ever going to see. Ceramic-tipped dumdums that deliver a payload of holy water, silver, and cold iron." The crowd applauds.

Bone Cat looks at me with raised eyebrows. I shrug back. I don't know if those would kill me, but I know they would hurt. More and more, avoidance sounds like the strategy of choice. I look out at the excited men milling about, examining their newly acquired equipment. They are totally unlike the security officers I am used to dealing with. Their eyes are practically glowing with religious zeal at the idea of being able to take down an actual creature of darkness. I think about these yahoos striding about the park like vigilantes, each determined to be the one to take me down, and I feel ill. The next few days will be dangerous.

A new thought intrudes. These men are dangerous to *everyone*, not just myself. I will be astonished if they don't shoot one of our guests, or one of the other employees, within twenty-four hours. Whoever is behind this is an idiot. My eye falls on Bone Cat and I'm forced to reconsider. I know what an idiot looks like, but a genuine idiot would not be able to take over the Zenon Corporation. Everything I'm seeing tonight is indicative of a subtle and convoluted mind. One that has been planning and committing significant resources to this for quite some time. Aside from the material costs for lights and ammunition, they obviously had the power needed within the company to transfer, hire, and fire personnel at will. They also appear to know a great deal about me, while I do not even know why they are after me. How I wish I still had access to Mr. Shulman and his files.

Suddenly, I realize that I very well might. Company policy states that when personnel are transferred, personal office material was be crated and shipped to them within a week, but the lads down in the shipping department tended to act as if that one-week interval was mandatory. Therefore there is a very good chance that those information-stuffed file cabinets are still here, waiting to be sent out along with the rest of Mr. Shulman's things. If they *are* still here, they will be on the south loading dock. They will be locked, and booby-trapped to be sure, which will mean that it will take longer to go through them, but it is a concrete plan of action.

One convoluted journey via conduit later, and I am looking down at a large shipping pallet, stacked with recognizable bric-a-brac from Mr. Shulman's office, and nestled at its heart are the two familiar orange file cabinets. There are also a half-a-dozen guards standing about, festooned with lights, looking like they are guarding a high-security facility in a bad science fiction movie. As if I would exit or enter through the loading dock. I mean, seriously, what are they thinking? I don't even own an auto-mobile. But absurd or not, here they are.

Those damned lights change the equation enough that the best thing would be to draw them off. I think I can do that.

Thus, for the next several hours, until the park closes, I make a point of flitting about the northern sector. This is a bit of a risk, as two of the resting places they have not yet discovered are here, but I want to be seen as far from this particular loading dock as possible.

As I take pains to be seen skulking about, I cannot help but notice that even though I'm now believed to be a crazed demonic force of some kind, the park remains open. It displays a shocking disregard for the safety of our guests if they truly believe me to be as evil as all that.

I pause. It *is* shocking. Criminally shocking. *Unbelievably* shocking. The fallout from a monster rampaging through the park would be *catastrophic*. But upper management has *not* closed the park. Another moment's thought and the answer is obvious. Whatever problem the mysterious Mr. Zoiden has with me, he has already shown that he knows all too much about me. I must conclude that he knows that I am not a monster, per se. He *knows* that the guests are perfectly safe, but he has manipulated perception to make it *appear* that I am dangerous. For the first time in a very long time, I am getting *angry*.

I continue to make my presence known. I assist two lost children, and excessively terrify one pickpocket (I do not know when I will next get a chance to eat properly), who I turn over to a lone security officer in full sight of a gaggle of kindergarteners. As it is, I almost overestimated the fellow's self-control. For a moment, I fear that he will actually draw his weapon in public. Bone Cat distracts him at a critical moment, and I remove myself quickly. I resolve to keep my distance from these cretins for the rest of the evening.

However, my antics do have their desired effect, and by the time the parade is winding down, the northern sector is crawling with security personnel desperately trying to look like everything is normal. I cap off the evening by allowing myself to be seen as I dart into the stand of wood that girds the lake. To call it a forest is an insult to those vast, dark refuges that covered Europe for most of history, but it will be different enough terrain from the rest of the park that my pursuers will proceed cautiously, at least for a little while, which should be all I need.

I drift surreptitiously towards the nearest vent, and soon enough, I am once again observing the loading dock. Despite my best efforts, there is still a remaining guard. I grin. One is all too easy. Suddenly I feel the prickle of boney claws on my arm. I glance at Bone Cat, and he silently draws a finger across his throat. Death is near. I hear Mr. Mortimer inside my head, an unexpected echo from almost seventy-five years ago. *Does it look too easy?* he whispers. *If they are still bothering with guards at all, there will be more than one.*

I pause and examine the room more thoroughly. I extend my senses. Oh yes, there *is* someone else here. But ... I cannot tell where they are hiding. I ooze around the edges of the room, examining the hidden nooks and crannies. Nothing. Whoever they are, they are very good. Still, there *is* only one hidden person. I'm pretty sure about that. And one-on-one, even without Bone Cat, I have a great deal of self-confidence.

I slide around until I am nestled within the lone guard's shadow, then quickly flow upwards, engulfing the lower half of his face, along with his arms. He almost gets a shot off, but I insert myself behind the trigger and he pulls in vain. I feed quite well in the short time it takes him to pass out, and I lower him silently back into his chair. It is done so quickly and smoothly that I am confident that anyone making a random check on the monitors will notice nothing amiss. There is always the possibility that I was seen as I took him down, but I hear no alarms. I have Bone Cat scoot outside the door to keep watch.

There is no reaction from the rest of the room. This does not make me feel better. I can still sense the aura that intelligent beings surround themselves with, but I'm not getting any emotions. Anticipation. Boredom. Anything that might give me an indication of where this fellow is would be useful, but there is nothing. I wait for a minute, but I cannot assume that things will be quiet for long. I abandon subtlety, and head straight for the file cabinets. It is but the work of a moment to sweep aside (carefully, of course) the detritus blocking the drawer I want. The lock proves a slight challenge, but nostalgia and a healthy sense of mischief have kept me in practice over the years, and it quickly snaps open. I slide open the drawer—

And a punch tosses me halfway across the room. I had allowed myself to solidify more than I had thought. While my head is clearing, I see a massive form unfolding itself out from the file drawer, and then standing upright. This explains much. The second guard was not human, and—

Oh, for pity's sake. It's the McGoon. I feel a flash of annoyance. Whenever a member of the established supernatural community enters the park, they are supposed to let me know, out of courtesy, if nothing else. Obviously this was a trap, and the McGoon is here on behalf of the new owner.

In any organization there are those members who actually enjoy punishing back-sliders and recidivists. Amongst the local supernatural set, the poster child for that particular mindset was the McGoon. I never bothered to learn much about him. He claims that he was known as the Ketch back on that Emerald Isle he's so excessively fond of going on about (Although if memory serves me, a ketch is actually a type of boat. I try not to judge. America is all about reinventing oneself). He actively enjoys hunting people, and the one thing I do remember hearing is that if he gets ahold of you, he does not let go. He is also excessively large, unbelievably supple, and capable of patience.

Oh. And he can also extend his arms in a seemingly impossible fashion, as he demonstrates by reaching for me without moving. I dissipate almost completely, and his oversized, clawed hands close on little more than mist. I then feel a terrible ripping pain as he retracts his hands, and a handful of my essence goes with him. Ah. He really *doesn't* let go once he has a piece of you. This is a magical attack I have never encountered before, and it's a good one. I lose precious seconds coping with the unexpected pain.

Again his great hands stretch out, but this time I avoid them. The McGoon chuckles. "You can't run, me lad," he rasps in that bubbling liquid voice of his. "I hunt. It's what I do." He elaborately passes one of his hands under his enormous, pointed nose and sniffs deeply. "And I have the scent of you now. No matter where you run, no matter what burrow you rattle yourself into, I can find you and dig you out. Even under the light of the glorious sun." He rubs his hands together. "So why don't you just come here and let's end this early and with a modicum of dignity, hey?" He then cracks his knuckles with a sound reminiscent of shattering walnuts.

Like many humans, the McGoon loves the sound of his own voice. With any luck, he'll say something useful. He starts to circle the room, sniffing deeply as he goes. The sound of his sniffing may as well have been designed to brew terror in those trying to hide from him. I nod in admiration. I never could pull off a good sniff like that. Don't have the sinuses for it. But I can appreciate artistry when I see it in others. Oh, but now he's talking again. "I don't really care why you went bad, old son. It happens. You look around and see the humans and you remember the good old days ..."

The Good Old Days is a topic that, ordinarily, would keep the McGoon blathering for hours. Best to move things along. I alight upon a ceiling girder. "I did not 'go bad.' You're being used."

His hands move like quicksilver. Flowing towards me like impossible raindrops running up a windowpane, faster than the mind can comfortably comprehend. But I'm not there when they arrive. He gives a sharp-toothed grin. "Could be." He shrugs, producing another set of rumbling pops. "But the client, you see, he knew the words. He paid the price. And he overpaid it enough that I'm willing to let any irregularities slide, if you know what I mean."

"Client? What client? I thought you worked as a bouncer when you weren't tracking down oath breakers for the Council of Shadows?"

The McGoon laughed. "Bouncin' is fun, and no mistake, but the pay ain't enough to keep me in style. Workin' for the Council used to do nicely, but there ain't too many oath breakers these days." He shook his head. "No new members a'tall for a few years now, and the old-timers are either settled in, or else they cracked and I dealt with them a while ago."

Suddenly he spun, and with perfect aim, his arm shot out and grabbed hold of me. It was neatly done. I allowed myself to be towed back. "So you're hiring yourself out as an assassin?"

The McGoon spat. "That's what the client called it, but that's a fancy word, and I don't cotton to it. I prefer hit man. It's ever so much more accurate, don't you know?" And then he hit me. I suppose he thought it was clever. It wasn't, but the punch still hurt.

He had me within normal arm length now. I had to hurry. "Who hired you?"

As I thought, the McGoon couldn't pass up an opportunity to talk. "He called himself Zoiden. Hans Zoiden." He looked at me shrewdly. "And I can see you're not surprised."

I wasn't, and now I know that Hans Zoiden is a man who was willing to deal with other supernatural creatures, but not me. "Did he say why?"

At this the McGoon frowned. "He did, but it didn't make no sense. He said you had to face an assassin."

I waited, but that seemed to be all he was going to say. "... I don't understand."

The McGoon smiled. "Well, I'm right pleased to hear you say that, old son."

"You are?"

"Here I thought he was just bein' a clever bugger. But if a smart feller like you, me lad, don't get it, then myself, I don't feel so bad. My thanks."

"I have to face an assassin."

The McGoon nodded. "That's it." He grinned again. "It don't mean nothing to me, so as far as I'm concerned, you get to die for nothing."

That sounded final, and I couldn't count on us being alone for much longer. Time to wrap this up. As I feel his hands begin to tighten, I extend my neck and open my mouth, revealing my beautiful teeth. That startles him. You see, whenever I deal with the extended supernatural community, I endeavor to look as human as possible. If for no other reason than to try and set a good example. However, as a result, many of them have never seen the monster behind the façade.

I sink my teeth into that great sniffing nose of his, and he gives a scream like a horse set on fire. And there it is, a beautiful spike of pure fear that I latch onto and begin consuming. Almost instantly, the fear is replaced by rage, but it's much, much too late. If I'm making direct contact, and latch onto a being's fear, I can keep it flowing from that terrified part of my victim's brain. Pull it forth. Grow it. Strengthen it. Amplify it so that it begins to overwhelm the other emotions.

But the McGoon will not go easily into that long good night. His hands tighten, and I think he's trying to crush me. Futile, as I can become as tough as old boots. But no, he has me in both hands, and he is not letting go; in fact, I can *feel* his fingers digging into me, and then with a tremendous shock of pain, I feel him start to *pull*. He's making an effort to literally rip me apart, and the pain is almost overwhelming. I pour as much of myself as I can into the slowly widening gap between the

McGoon's hands, but it's agonizingly difficult to get past those terrible fingers.

I bite down harder, and it is the McGoon who cracks first. His right hand lets go and he desperately tries to rip me free from his nose, but my beautiful teeth have burrowed deep. The fear is running from him like a torrent now. Usually the McGoon is too stupid to feel fear. It requires a healthy dollop of imagination. But he feels it now, and he does not like it. He begins smashing himself against the walls, trying to scrape me off, rolling on the ground, and finally just clawing at me with ever-weakening hands. This is surprisingly effective, and I'm damned lucky he didn't begin with this tactic. As it is, he's peeling shreds of me off every time he swipes at me. But it is too little, too late. The fear is everything now. It fills his entire head and heart, and so unused to the feeling is he that the final shuddering spasm happens much quicker than I had anticipated. Not that I'm complaining, mind you. The McGoon contorts one final time, and then collapses to the floor and begins to crumble.

As I've mentioned, some monsters are born from human imagination working upon perfectly normal things that they didn't understand. They will insist upon anthropomorphizing these things, trying, at a subconscious level, to animate them, sometimes for generations. Occasionally, these things oblige by coming to life. But almost every monster of this type still has that original mundane thing at its heart; a wounded animal, a slightly mad recluse, a skeletal-looking dead tree ... Something like that, ensnared in local lore and rebuilt into something malevolent and cunning by unfettered imagination and wild magic.

The McGoon was reverting to that ur-state now. Once the life was stripped from him, the magic holding him together begins to dissipate as well. His flesh dissolves into stinking mud and his bones are revealed to be thorny sticks that would have caught and pulled the unwary, and with a final squelch, the terrible McGoon melts back into nothing more than the remnants of a peat bog, with a few stained brambles. His *anime vitae* remains buried until the bitter end, then makes a desperate dash for freedom. I snare it easily and study it with great interest.

Old in years and experience, this is still a young soul, in that this was its first time through. I usually try to make some allowances for first timers, especially when they get ensnared in one of these unfortunate animism situations. They never end well. But this entity had centuries to try to develop a little sympathy for the creatures around it. I find nothing like empathy within the thing flickering in my grasp.

However there *is* terror, and a new understanding that it is not omnipotent. A very important lesson for the young. I reinforce it with a final breath, infusing a touch of dread into its being that should make it a bit more cautious the next time around. I let it go, and it dissipates off to wherever things like that go. And seriously, I have no idea what happens after one dies. I mean, I *know* that there is some sort of recycling mechanism at work, it's obvious, really, especially when you meet the same souls once or twice, but the specifics are a mystery to me, and, quite frankly, I'm okay with that.

I straighten up and realize that my body is a symphony of assorted aches. I haven't had a workout like that in over a decade, maybe more. But enough self-pity. Time is short. I go to fly over to Mr. Shulman's precious file cabinets and collapse to the ground. I am more seriously wounded than I had thought, and no mistake. Bone Cat gets behind me and pushes as I crawl over to the opened file drawer and begin riffling through the files. Time may be short, and I may be seriously injured, but at least that fight wasn't a complete waste of time, as I actually acquired useful information. Zoiden ... Zoiden ... There are a surprising number of files under *Z*, but here is Mr. Zoiden's!

It is not very thick. Suddenly the sounds I've been anticipating, the thunder of approaching boots and the clatter of people laden with weapons, arise from the main corridor. I envelop the folder within my coat and swoop up towards the nearest vent opening. Ow. The swine sprained my lifting muscles and carrying a material object makes things even more painful. The late McGoon did a thorough job on me, and no mistake.

I'm so busy fretting about my lifting that I almost don't understand what I'm seeing. There appears to be something moving jerkily within the air vent ... I roll to the left just as a cluster of lights blaze on within the conduit. With a snap, I drop and then jink to the right and head for the great rolling garage door. There are plenty of openings sufficient to let me escape, but most of them are small enough that if I am hit by those lights while I am halfway through—

I am not, but it is a near thing, as yet another crew is putting the finishing touches on a light assembly right outside the garage. The fellow in charge screams and throws the switch as I rush past, and half the lights—all of the ones facing the door— come on. The rest of the guards fire their guns at me ... smashing a fair number of the lights. Oh, it's Amateur Night at Zenonland Park, and no mistake.

I hang in the sky to consider my options, and immediately begin to fall. I am too wounded. I must find a sanctuary where I can rest. I land with an undignified thump upon the roof of the *World Is Made of Cheese* ride and consider my choices. I could wait for this to blow over ... while things have never gotten this bad before, there have been times I have considered abandoning my responsibilities. I have one bolt-hole no one would ever find, a natural cistern located deep within the earth, long dry, connected to the surface by a series of fault cracks and what I believe to be prehistoric gopher burrows. It's where I plan to go if they ever play the "Waltz of the Cave Bears" song.

Sorry, I should explain myself. If you've ever been a guest here, you've no doubt noticed that your stay is accompanied by an endless parade of musical scores from movies, cartoons, and stage shows playing over the park's sound systems. Very jolly. What most non-employees *don't* know, is that there are songs that are only played in certain situations. If there is ever a crazed gunman in the park (during daylight hours, of course), then the loudspeakers will alert those who need to know by playing the disturbingly jaunty "The Love-sick Jackalope" song.

There are other tunes for other situations, but if you are ever unfortunate enough to hear the "Waltz of the Cave Bears," then let the nice staffers herd you and yours underground, because the Missiles are on their way. Mr. Bartholomew really did try to think of *everything*. So that's always an option. But I could be stuck down there for a very long time.

I could just start killing all the guards determined to kill me. This has possibilities but would have to take place only after the park closes. These religion-besotted fools have already killed one innocent. I honestly believe they would consider themselves heroes if they had to gun down a dozen park visitors just to wing me. It wouldn't be sustainable, of course, the park would be shut down within the hour, and the Zenon Corporation itself might have to file for Chapter Eleven ... This chain of thought actually forces me to sit down. My freedom. It could be as simple as that.

But ... what price am I willing to let others pay in order to secure that freedom? Angrily, I dismiss the scenarios half-forming in my head. I *protect* the visitors of this park. That is who I am. But *that* said, I really see no problem with me taking out my frustrations on religious zealots determined to kill me, as long as I wait until after the park closes. It might take longer, but I'm pretty sure that if they haul *enough* bodies out of here, word will get out to the media (I can make sure of that), and there will be repercussions. This is certainly the more dangerous route, as the mysterious Herr Zoiden has demonstrated a distressing competence for utilizing both supernatural and advanced technological weapons against me. There is also the grim fact that my opponent's forces can lose multiple times, while I cannot afford to lose even once. I will have to step up my own game.

I require advice and information. Luckily, I have access to

clever fellows who possess both, and who owe me several rather large favors. The gremlins.

I stand up and promptly fall over, scattering files about me. I really am in a bad way. I need to rest and recuperate. I watch Bone Cat gather the files up. At least I'll have some bedside reading. As the moon dips towards the horizon, I stagger towards my chosen resting place. As I lie myself down, I page through my hard-won dossier.

Hans Zoiden. Born in Düsseldorf, studied at several different universities. Interesting ... earned an MBA and specialized in entertainment management. Joined the Zenon Corporation at our Paris branch. Managed the park there and did well enough that he was promoted. Promoted several times. Sometimes twice within the same year. Youngest ever member of the Board of Directors, and, according to this, a serious contender for the CEO position ... and I suddenly realize that what I am holding in my hands is a fake. A very good fake, and one that would easily stand up to casual scrutiny, but again Mr. Mortimer's tutelage comes to my aid. Someone has constructed a beautiful Horatio Algeresque fiction of a life filled with hard work and a love of children and entertainment so exemplary that his taking over the Zenon Corporation seems like the logical culmination of their life story.

But I can see the cracks. The inner inconsistencies. It is very well done, but I do not believe a word of it.

I feel a sudden chill as I wonder whether Mr. Shulman's sudden transfer actually happened, or whether he made the mistake of voicing suspicions where he shouldn't have. If he is, in fact, in Tokyo, I will send him a message to watch his back. If he hasn't noticed something wrong, he soon will, and I am convinced that Herr Zoiden will kill him for simply asking the wrong questions. I toss the file aside. While I have learned nothing factual, I have learned yet another important thing about Herr Zoiden tonight. I can trust nothing about him.

As I begin to doze, I ponder this business about facing an

assassin. Despite what I told the McGoon, there is something about it that is bothering me. A bit of lore is stuck in my brain— just out of reach—like an obstinate seed stuck in one's teeth. It will surface in its own time. All I am sure of now is that it is important. But I cannot let it distract me. I have to be on my guard now. Tomorrow I will revisit The Happiness Machine.

CHAPTER EIGHT

The Happiness Machine was originally commissioned by a bottler of soft drinks for the 1964 world's fair in New York City. It appeared to be a jolly little boat ride that promoted the idea of world peace and human inclusiveness through puppetry and song. In actuality, it was a diabolical machine designed to broadcast a newly discovered form of ætheric wave that, in laboratory tests, gave everyone within a five-mile radius an uncontrollable urge to consume vast quantities of soft drinks.

To the disappointment of the sponsors, however, once it was activated in the field, it did no such thing. It simply made everybody in the world slightly *happier*. Not everyone believed it at first, and they ran numerous experiments, but by the time the fair closed, there was no questioning the results. When the machine was running, everybody in the world felt happier.

The soft drink company considered it a tremendous failure, and was planning on scrapping it, when the United States government quietly stepped in and bought it from them. You might think this an unusual purchase. But you must remember that the world had just teetered on the brink of thermonuclear war (the Cuban Missile Crisis), and seriously clever people became rather determined to keep anything like that from happening again. Towards that end they were pursuing any number of different strategies. Some admittedly more outré and experimental than others.

The next problem was where to put it. This was solved when someone remembered Mr. Bartholomew. He had worked with the government during the last war, making propaganda cartoons, and was well regarded. He agreed to have it installed in Zenonland and received a very nice tax break for doing so. Mr. Bartholomew knew how to drive a bargain, and the fact that he was helping to prevent nuclear war was a bonus. Thus, it can now be mathematically proven that Zenonland is, in fact, "the Jolliest Place on Earth."

In case you haven't already guessed, I am, of course, referring to what most people know as the *Itty-Bitty Planet* ride. The one that was blown up. I have to admit that before I discerned that there was actually a coordinated effort to kill me, I had wondered if our suicide bomber had belonged to some sort of doomsday cult that was doing its bit to bring on Armageddon. I abandoned this notion fairly early on, because if someone was sufficiently in the know to be aware of the *Itty-Bitty Planet* ride's true nature, then it would follow that they would also be aware that Mr. Bartholomew was a great believer in redundancy, which is why there are copies of the Happiness Machine in every Zenonland park on the planet, all reinforcing each other. None of these other machines have been attacked to date, and so I must conclude that it's all about me. That's good, I guess.

Anyway, a machine like that takes a great deal of maintenance. When the park was in its decline in the late seventies, the clandestine maintenance crews from the US military stopped coming. I couldn't believe it, at first. One would think that keeping this machine running would be something the American government would do even if the park itself was shuttered. The only plausible explanation we could come up with was that after that unfortunate business in French Indochina, the United

States military was in such disgrace that it lost control of its secret budget.

According to Mr. Mortimer, every military has its secret budget, financing hidden bases or questionable weaponry research. After the second world war ended, but before conflicting ideologies tore our happy little group apart, Comrade Polina, Mr. Mortimer, and I spent a very productive couple of months going down a list of secret Nazi military projects that had been found in a hidden safe belonging to former *Reichsmarschall* Hermann Göring, who, no matter what else one may say about him, did seem to have a genuine talent for recruiting unpleasant creatures, both human and not. He was also a stickler for paperwork, which we appreciated quite a bit.

But some Senator somewhere no doubt got his hands on some of America's secret expenditures and realized he could demonstrably save the taxpayers some money by axing a vaguely defined maintenance program. It is a sad fact that politicians hate to pay for maintenance on *anything*. The idea of throwing perfectly good money at something that is still working seems idiotic. If it falls apart in the future, it will be somebody *else's* problem. Once you understand this, most of the decisions made by government make a lot more sense.

So the maintenance teams were reassigned, a few thousand dollars were spent on something bright and shiny within said Senator's home state, and the Happiness Machine started to go out of alignment.

If it had been almost any other tale of bureaucratic ineptitude, it might not have been so bad. As I mentioned, there was already another Zenonland down in Florida, with its own Happiness Machine grinding away. But we *are* talking about a device that was designed to alter people's mental processes. Just because it stopped working *correctly* didn't mean that it stopped being *effective*.

Luckily, in retrospect, when things started to go wrong, they did so quickly. In the autumn of 1980, something went off the rails in the heart of the machine, and for almost three days everyone who came within a hundred miles of it began to have terrible dreams. I had no idea the Happiness Machine was causing it at the time. To make things even more difficult, Bone Cat began to go mad, and most of my time was spent preventing him from attacking people, which gets tiresome, let me tell you.

I truly believe that things would have gotten very bad indeed if the local gremlins had not arrived. Up until this point, these particular gremlins had been a small, rather down-on-its-luck group of elders living at the local airport. They showed up at the park in great distress, claiming that they had heard the Happiness Machine screaming and were determined to get it to stop. In retrospect it was obvious that I wasn't thinking all too clearly myself, as I was equally determined to keep them out of the park. I'm not sure *why*, but at the time, I knew it was *very important* I did so.

But they persisted, managed to get past me, and repaired the Happiness Machine. I came to my senses, the nightmares ended, Bone Cat stopped trying to eat people, and we once again narrowly averted nuclear war.

(I only found out about that last one a few years later. Apparently one of the Joint Chiefs of Staff located in California had *such* bad dreams that he become convinced that the exploding of several hundred nuclear bombs would, and I quote, "scare off the moon." He had taken over a local launch facility and been industriously circumventing the fail-safes when he snapped back to sanity. This sort of thing happens more often than you'd think, and I, for one, am just as glad I don't know about it.)

And that was how the now world-famous (amongst certain, select circles) Zenon Clan of gremlins became established here at the park. We have a rather robust population these days. The feat that cemented their place here was when they constructed their own brewing engine. A proper gremlin brewing engine is hard to hide, and many gremlin communities in the New World are forced to make do with inferior ale because they don't have a place to hide one, or because of EPA inspectors. Our gremlins didn't even try.

Do you remember the great steampunk tower that vibrates so majestically at the entrance to Futureopolis? The one that Celeste used as an example of voodoo science? Well, several decades ago, the gremlins appropriated it. They redesigned it and rebuilt it from top to bottom from the inside out and these days it delights our guests by roaring and spinning and venting great gouts of colored steam into the California sky. It delights the gremlins by producing prodigious quantities of a very foul artisanal beer that is in demand around the world. (I suspect it is because they put old beignets into the mash.) Between the vintage rides and the beer, the Zenon Clan enjoys keeping the place running, and we've become a prime gremlin retirement destination. Over the years we have been of much use to each other. I have been able to secure them raw materials through my contacts within the Zenon Corporation, and they have supplied me with gadgets and valuable assistance over the years. I would not say we are friends, as such, gremlins don't see people that way, but we work well together, which is a trait that they value very highly.

CHAPTER NINE

I find myself standing within an ancient Mesoamerican temple. Huge stone blocks are cracked and warped by the roots of trees and vines that poke through. I look upward and see the night sky, but a sky that no one on earth has seen for hundreds of years. The stars shine forth in their unobscured glory, and I allow myself to enjoy the sight, until I realize that the constellations I see are unfamiliar to me. Then I try to remember exactly how I got here. I try to concentrate and realize that I cannot close my eyes—or rather, I *can* close my eyes, but it does not appear to change the view. Around me torches begin to burst into flame, and I realize that I am trapped within the dream of a god.

At the far end of the temple stands an ancient altar. No crumbled remnant this. It is straight and clean, and the inlaid precious metals and gems have been lovingly polished. Upon it is a familiar bowl carved from obsidian. As I walk towards it, I see blood begin to well up within the bowl, ooze over the lip, and drip onto the altar. Where it strikes, there is a hiss and great gouts of steam. More and more blood flows from the bowl, and the steam explodes outwards and upwards, filling the air above the altar. As it reaches the ruined ceiling, there is a low rumble, and I see a flicker of what can only be lightning causing the cloud of steam to briefly glow from within. The thunder grows in intensity. I can actually see forks of lightning now. They stab outwards from the cloud, growing in size and strength until, finally, there is a great bolt that crackles downwards, blowing the obsidian bowl apart to the accompaniment of a boom of thunder that rattles the ancient walls.

When my vision clears, I see a huge white serpent equipped with a magnificent pair of turquoise wings and glowing blue eyes staring down upon me. I clap enthusiastically. The serpent smiles in delight, and a blue tongue flicks forth. "Pretty Impressive, Eh, *Amigo?*"

"It truly was," I say honestly. "Thank you, O Xochemilchic, for allowing me to witness your glory."

"Glad You Liked It. It's Exhausting."

As I continue to walk towards him, everything begins to shift. The room begins to dwindle in size, the stars of the southern hemisphere fade away, as does the acoustical echo that one only truly gets inside a genuine stone building, that simply cannot be duplicated, even by the master craftsmen and masons employed by the Zenon Corporation, and within ten feet, I am recognizably within nothing more than the main throne room of the *Lost Temple* ride. I look up and pause. Xochemilchic is unchanged. I sigh. "I'm still inside some sort of dream or something, aren't I?"

The serpent blew out a great gust of wind when it sighed and lowered his head down towards mine. "Don't Make Me Lose All Of It," he whispered, in a voice that was noticeably more reedy than before. "Let Me Keep This."

I bow. "As the Great Serpent wishes." I look around. "So why have you entered my dreams?"

"There Are Whispers Amongst The Celestials. Whispers About This Zenonland."

I am unsure about what Xochemilchic means by Celestials, though from what I gather, they are a more ... rarefied species of supernatural creature. One that has less interaction with the mundane world, though they were still connected. "What do they say?"

His head slowly swayed from side to side. "I Do Not Fully Know. I ..." He dips his head, and I somehow realize that he is embarrassed. "I Am Not As Feared As I Once Was. Lines Of Communication Are Closed To Me. I Am No Longer Deemed Worthy ..." He pauses, and then snaps upright. "But I Know More Than They Think I Do. The Destruction Of Your Happy Wheel Machine. It Was *Planned*. It Is But The First Step In A Larger Undertaking." He looked at me. "One That Requires You."

"Me? How?"

His body ripples in what I recognize as his equivalent of a shrug. "I ... Cannot Say."

"What should I do?"

"Help Me Show Them That I Am Not To Be Ignored. Scorned. Belittled. *Here*."

And suddenly, in my hand, I hold an obsidian disc, a little over two inches long. A winged serpent adorned one side, while the other ... I realize that there *is* no second side. Every time I turn the coin over, no matter what direction I turn it, I behold Xochemilchic, right side up.

"When You Meet The One That Would Harm You, See To It That This Is On Their Person—And I Will Be There."

"But how—"

And then I woke up.

CHAPTER TEN

I swim upwards toward consciousness. This alone tells me that it will be a difficult day. As a rule, I tend to either rouse from a light trance, which has allowed me to unconsciously monitor the world around me, even as I maintained my somnambulistic state, or else I switch from total blackness into full wakefulness, like the switching on of a lightbulb.

Today it is neither. I feel stiff and sore in ways that I am quite unaccustomed to. The late McGoon pulled things I was unaware could even *be* pulled, and he pulled them quite vigorously. I am also famished. I had thought that I had fed deeply of the McGoon as I killed him, but either it was not enough, or the energy required to undo the damage he had caused me was prodigious. I feel something in my hand, and even before I see it, I know that it is Xochemilchic's obsidian coin. I slip it into a pocket. Normally I have to concentrate when I go immaterial to keep things from falling free, but, somehow, I know that this will not be a problem with this token.

I glance towards the small liquid crystal clock near my resting place, and do what to an outside observer would be a most comical double take (Hollywood culture affects us all when we least expect it, alas). The *time* is correct, but the *date* is wrong. Not actually wrong, of course, just unexpected. I have slept through an entire day. The McGoon's damage must have been worse than I had thought. No wonder I'm starving!

This is not good. When I am very hungry I tend to get a bit reckless, which is the last thing I can afford at the moment. If nothing else, my opponents will have had an extra day in which to prepare. I must be careful. At least they have not discovered this resting place. I hope they haven't discovered any of the others.

I drift to an observation port and spend several minutes looking about. This is one of the newer bowers that I have created. On the corner separating the *Land of the Lone Prairie* from the *Lost Shipyard*, there is a wondrous steam-powered music machine: *the Silverodeon*. Easily fifteen feet long and built onto a venerable old-time circus wagon. It contains over twenty-five instruments, including slide whistles and birdcalls, and displays of cunning little automata that perform an intricately choreographed dance number incorporating forty-eight state flags (Alaska and Hawaii were made states after the machine was constructed, so their flags have since been tacked up above the stage, because even people from Alaska and Hawaii have money). It has been a beloved feature of the park ever since we opened, and you can buy CDs of its musical repertoire in various shops.

However, despite the fanciful pedigree inscribed upon the plaque mounted before it that details its creation as a drunken collaboration between John Philips Sousa and Nikola Tesla in a misguided attempt to create the first transistor radio, it was actually something cobbled together from junk and scraps by Zenon Studio employees in their off time in the early 1930s. They had the technical ability. They invented and hand built many of their experimental cameras and projectors. They also drank a lot, and left no coherent notes. They are all long dead, so the first time the machine stuttered to a stop sometime in 1981, the technician who pried open the maintenance hatch found a hodgepodge of jumbled parts that looked as if Rube Goldberg had had a fight to the death with Heath Robinson and both had declared victory. He almost had a stroke. Even the Gremlins threw up their hands in defeat.

The machine spent the next twenty years out of order as often as it was up and running. Then, in the year 2000, a very clever sound engineer ripped out the mechanically powered musical horns and bellows and self-beating drums and replaced them with a computer chip the size of a quarter and an array of very good speakers with a bass cannon the size of a refrigerator. This left close to sixty square feet of empty space that no one was using, and as long as I make sure to slip in a set of earplugs, I find it very comfortable, with the added benefit that when I awaken, I feel like I've had a sustained, full-body massage.

According to my cursory inspection, the park appears the same as always; it's a normal crowd for a weekday, but—But there are noticeably more cameras in position. Ordinarily, the Zenonland staff have gotten very good at hiding cameras—inside gargoyles, or false coconuts, or whatever, but these are simply mounted on walls and roofs. Somebody wanted cameras up quickly and cared not a whit for stealth. This is a desperate act, as, even as I watch, I can see that guests are noticing them, and they do not like them. I'm sure the plan is to take them down after I'm gone, but I would be surprised if they are. The sort of mind that insists on surveillance is usually the sort that will never relinquish it once achieved.

But that is their problem. Mine is that I must assume that I will be seen leaving the *Silverodeon*, and thus its usefulness as a hiding place will be over. Unfortunate, but I do not think I have a choice. I make myself as insubstantial as I can and flow out hugging the ground, heading for the nearest pool of shadow.

Despite my best efforts, I see the nearest camera break from its programmed sweep and focus on me. Busted. If I am to get to the Happiness Machine unobserved, I fear I will have to do something I have been saving as a last resort for some time, and I'm afraid this situation qualifies.

Actually, I must admit that I have any number of improbable objects squirreled away throughout the park, ostensibly for unspecified emergencies and last resorts. Occasionally, they are actually useful, but the truth is that I couldn't bear to see some of this stuff destroyed.

Ten minutes later, a squad of heavily armed security officers cluster around the entrance to a maintenance shed that had been locked for over ten years before I entered it five minutes ago. Two hundred feet away, a similarly underused structure opens, revealing the eternally smiling visage of Badaxe Smoke-Eater, the Firefighting Barbarian®. I wave at a party of children, who stare at me blankly, and then ignore me. Perfect.

Badaxe's only movie, a criminally underappreciated animated musical comedy from the early nineties, titled *This Horde's On Fire*, had not been the commercial success the studio had expected it to be, so Badaxe (voiced by Brian Blessed) had proved to be a bit of a dud, as mascots go, and had been retired after a single season. I had appropriated the suit when it had been scheduled to be recycled. It should now allow me to move without notice.

In this, however, I am quite wrong. To my astonishment, I discover that sometime in the last ten years or so, *This Horde's On Fire* has been reevaluated by a new generation, and Badaxe himself has now become some sort of hipster icon. I literally cannot go three feet without being inundated with twenty-some-things who swarm around me like ants, asking for autographs, taking selfies, and breaking out into impromptu performances of "Flammable or Inflammable—Don't Make No Difference to Me," which was Badaxe's big song-and-dance number, and is now seemingly capable of drawing enthusiastic fans from all over the park. Naturally, employees in costume are encouraged to "go along with" these spontaneous expressions of *joi de vie*, and as a result, instead of quickly slipping away, it takes me an hour and a half to go 600 feet. It is the most nerve-wracking and ostentatious "sneaking" I have ever done.

On the other hand, it turns out to be the perfect disguise. Teams of security officers ignore me as they pass by, unless they insist on getting selfies with me.

As an added benefit, I am well fed. There is a certain type of parent who insists on posing their child with mascots, even when said child believes that their loving parents are, for some inexplicable reason, cheerfully surrendering them to a terrifying monster. There are hundreds of thousands of treasured family photos adrift in the world showing small children, their mouths unnaturally square, as they are forever caught in mid-scream from within the clutches of an iconic cartoon hero they had never dreamed actually existed.

I try not to feed off of the fears of children, as a rule. It feels morally questionable, in an indefinable way, but, more importantly, their fears are uncomplicated and primal. I could say that I have grown to appreciate the subtle and nuanced fears of older, more sophisticated people, but the unsavory truth is that their simple fears are raw and exhilarating, and it would be very easy to develop a craving for them until I was unsatisfied with anything else. There are reasons why the more disreputable class of monsters seek out children.

In any case, I am finally able to slip away through the cast member door in the back of the currently shuttered Happiness Machine. Once there, I am tempted to stuff the wretched costume into a furnace, but it is a poor workman who blames his tools. Thus, I take a deep breath and hang it to dry with all the vents properly open. I then slide through the access hatches into the technical side of one of the Park's most famous attractions.

I will be honest. I rather prefer this side of the ride. It's an insanely complicated bit of machinery, without a transistor in sight. The *Itty-Bitty Planet* ride is one of the more iconic rides in the park, and if Zenonland gearhead aficionados want to see the workings of any ride, it's either this or the *Haunted Monorail*. The

Gremlins were aware of this, and thus, over time, they created a sort of an art project.

When you examine the workings of the *Itty-Bitty Planet* ride, you'll find a mechanical time capsule that perfectly encapsulates the industrial design ethos of the early 1960s. It sends engineers and machinists into a positive swoon while they mutter about "The Evolving Functionality Esthetic of Mechanical Forces and its Evolution Due to Improved Alloys," or "The Lingering Influences of the Northern England Victorian Industrial Revolution, It's Slavish Devotion to Brunel, and the Inherent Shortcomings Thereof," and other such mind-numbing codswallop. Personally, I don't really "get it." Capital *A* Art has never really done much for me. I prefer representational art, myself. Plebeian tastes, I know, but I like what I like.

Most importantly, it keeps these very clever people from really noticing all of the modifications that the gremlins have made to the actual functioning equipment, which is now a level or two underground.

The space within the ride is quiet. Unnaturally quiet. To the despair of the accountants, the Happiness Machine ran twenty-four hours a day, seven days a week, even when the park was closed. It even has its own dedicated emergency backup generators. It's all silent now. Which makes no sense at all. I would expect people to be all over it. Where are the inspectors? Or if not them, then construction workers—*anybody*? I see no one.

I tap a small, easy-to-overlook button, and in a few minutes a gremlin appears. I know her. This is Wurmgear, one of the senior crew bosses. She is not smiling, which is very unusual, as gremlins take a great deal of pleasure in whatever it is that they are doing. In fact, her whole demeanor is different. If I had to guess, I'd say she was worried, which for a gremlin is almost unheard of, unless they are actually on fire. I glare down at her. "I thought I made it clear that the Happiness Machine was to be repaired as soon as possible. Where is everyone?"

She shrugged. "It ain't *gonna* be repaired. The new high

muckety-muck says it's to be torn down and replaced with a combat simulation ride or something." It should come as no surprise that the gremlins have listening devices installed in the corporate offices. No one likes a surprise inspection.

I had already concluded that Herr Zoiden was not a boss who worked well with others—but this is insane. We're not talking about replacing *Solomon Snail's Slo-Motion Speedway,* this is the *Itty-Bitty Planet* ride. It's one of the most popular rides in the park. Oh, yes, and lest we forget, one of the actual lynchpins to world peace. This cannot be because of some difficulties with recalcitrant inspectors. Whether it requires extensive repairs or outright bribery, this was the sort of problem that egregious corporate wealth was accumulated to solve.

I gnaw on my lower lip. "There has got to be someone I can talk to."

"I doubt it," Wurmgear says as she hops up onto a shelf before me. "You are poison, Old Tool." She continues, "The new guy in charge wants you dead and gone as of yesterday and has let everybody know it."

"I am aware of this."

"What did you do to get this guy so cranked up?"

"I have no idea. I've never even met him."

"Really? 'Cause he sent his goons chapter and verse on how to take you out."

This Herr Zoiden seems to know entirely too much about me. Up until now, few people even knew I existed, which, frankly, is how I prefer it. I have assembled a sketchy catalog of the things that will hurt me, but even I don't know everything that could kill me, and here he has a *list*? "May I see this list?"

Soon enough I am perusing a printout and it is very informative. They have sunlight, of course, down to and including a list of specific light bulbs that will generate the correct wavelengths. I can be severely wounded by being beaten, check, though it says here that I can only be beaten to death with an iron cudgel. Interesting. Ah, I see here that those ridiculous bullets are only expected to slow me down long enough so that I can be properly beaten to death.

Then we start to get into folkloric knowledge. Apparently I can be lured anywhere by the aroma of sour cream made from goat's milk. I'm rather surprised I never ran across that one before; back in my old village, they seemed to put goats' milk into *everything*. I cannot carry anyone if they have been blessed by a priest within the last twenty-four hours. The sight of a pure black rabbit will cause me to faint ... where are they *getting* this rubbish? I tapped the list with a finger. "Some of this seems a bit farfetched."

"*You* are farfetched, Old Tool." Wurmgear shrugged. "This is pretty straightforward stuff, as far as magical constraints go."

Well, she had me there. In my time I've seen behemoths taken down by being pelted by duck eggs, and a frost nixie that lived in an active blast furnace. It's a funny old world and no mistake. "Have they approached your people? Or any of the other residents?"

"Nope. I don't think they know we're here."

Because of our long-standing relationship, I don't believe that the gremlins would sell me out if my adversary had attempted to broker a deal with them first. There is nothing altruistic about this; they are scared to death of what I would do to them, so I would confidently expect them to allow me to make a competing bid. My being able to preempt my otherwise uncannily well-prepared opponent is a stroke of luck I do not intend to squander. "Then I would like to enter into a contract with your people, if I may. I will require intelligence, surveillance, and sabotage."

Wurmgear shuffles her feet and looks away. "No," she whispers. "We ... I've been instructed to say no."

I am taken aback, and no mistake. Gremlins are invariably arrogant, cocksure bundles of insouciance, but I can now feel shame, embarrassment, and, yes, actual fear emanating from her. "Why?"

For a moment, she's determined to not tell me, but I have the shape of her fears now, and I reach out and *encourage* them. This is an awful thing to do to one's acquaintances, but I must know. Her eyes bug from their sockets, and I can see that she'd flee if she could, but her feet no longer respond to her wishes. Without moving, I loom above her. *"Why?"*

"Because you're not here," she squeaks. "In the Future. *You're not here!*" I stare at her. She moans and drops to her knees. "The Prognosticator is still messed up, so they reinvented it ... differently." I'd seen this before. Gremlins are all about results. They have no inherent attachment to a particular way of doing things.

"They finally got a coherent readout. They were expecting something a bit abnormal, but the model that came back was completely whacked, or so they thought. There's a lot of death. There's a big shake-up in management, and you ... you're not in the Park."

"Is the company still in existence?"

"Yes! That was the first thing they checked! They ran it over again and again and again. You are not here!"

"It must be a mistake."

Wurmgear shook her head. "You don't understand. You being here—It ... it's one of the base assumptions that the system makes that helps it calibrate the rest of the readings, like the sun coming up, or the funicular railway schedule, or the nightly parade. It had to work really hard to make a coherent picture without you occupying your customary space. Luckily ..." She clapped a hand over her mouth and stared up at me.

A feeling of calmness settles over me. "Tell me."

"You're an integral part of the park," she whispers. "It ... it can't function properly with you gone. Too much would be out of balance. They figure that's why the old Prognosticator went wonky to begin with. But luckily ... lucky for the Park, you understand ... something takes your place. It all settles back into greased grooves. Just ... without you."

"When?"

"Within seventy-two hours."

I feel most peculiar. The refusal of the gremlins to assist me makes perfect sense now. I will lose whatever contest I will face in the next few hours, and the gremlins do not wish to start out on the wrong foot with my successor. Arguments about causality and whether I would, in fact, lose if they *did* assist me are pointless. I'm not saying this outcome *couldn't* be changed, changing unpleasant outcomes was rather the whole idea when they built the Prognosticator, but it's ... difficult to do; rather like trying to redirect a river, I'm told, and there are often humorously ironic "unintended consequences" that take a great deal of time and effort to rectify.

No, the gremlins have seen a future where *they* survive. The question of *my* survival, while of interest, is not important enough for them to jeopardize their safety. For what it's worth, I suspect they might actually feel bad about it, but ... I bump into a wall, and with a jolt of embarrassment I realize that I am in a bit of a daze. Suddenly I become aware of a droning sound, coming from all around me.

I snap back to awareness, and I see the gremlins. Hundreds, possibly thousands of them, all around me, lining the walls and floor, standing amongst the now frozen figurines of the ride itself. They are the source of the sound. They are singing. Gremlin songs, like so much about them, are different. This is a warm, wordless sound that fills the world and suffuses me with a feeling of belonging and purpose. Slowly rising and falling in a solid, comforting sequence, it is the sound of vast, idealized machines functioning perfectly, and, I realize, they are singing it to me. They are honoring me, as they would honor a lost engineer, or a well-made part that functioned right up until it could function no more. It is their highest honor, and I find myself deeply moved. Perhaps they will feel bad about me for longer than I had thought. You might think this to be cold comfort, but considering that I had always thought I would be forgotten and unmourned by anyone or anything, it is actually quite comforting indeed.

According to the clock mounted near the door, the Park will have closed. I roll my shoulders and they crackle comfortingly. No more hiding. There will be "a lot of death"? Very well. I do not know if it will be the deaths of innocents or enemies, but I shall do my best to tip the balance as far as I can from the one to the other, while seeing to it that only a statistically insignificant amount of it will be my own.

I step out and look around. "Where to, boss?" Bone Cat is uncharacteristically low-key. Of course. My death will affect him. How? We cannot know, but change is coming.

I gently swing him off my shoulder. He stares at me with his softly glowing eyes. "I have discussed your situation with Celeste. If ... when I am gone, she will attempt to bring you back. We do not know if it will work, but I wanted you to know that I have tried."

He stared at me and then, twisting, bit my hand. "Great," he groused. "So I get to hang around here without you. Thanks a heap." I realize that's the best reaction I could've gotten and pat his head before I again set him on my shoulder and look about.

How peculiar. I see the park with fresh eyes. How many times had I wished that I might never see it again? Now I effortlessly catalog a cherished memory for every place I glance. Now, admittedly, many of these memories involve me terrorizing or feeding upon some hapless villain, but not all of them. Not by any stretch of the imagination, thank you.

There are innumerable memories of children reunited with parents, treasured objects found, and interesting philosophical and metaphysical discussions with people over the years. Some were one-time incidents with random guests—almost every extraordinary intellect in the world has made its way here at least once. But some of the most interesting discussions were with colleagues and fellow employees, the effects of which tended to develop over years, like slow-ripening fruit. Some were moments of bonding with fellow creatures of the dark, whether through reasoned intellectual give-and-take or through a judicious use of applied violence.

And then there was Vandy. Ah, *there* is a universe of regret and unfulfilled possibilities. Masochistically, I turn my feet towards her station. I suppose I should be figuring out how to deal with the assorted security personnel ...

I stop short and look about, cursing my carelessness. I don't see any security people at all. Oh, there are the usual employees shutting down their shops, but I have been out on the street for several minutes now, and I'll admit that I had expected to be quickly surrounded by some sort of assault force. But there is nothing. A few of the older employees see me—and wave as they pass. Usually they stop and chat, but they all look like they have somewhere to be. I detect no fear of me. Evidently my status as a dark, soulless thing of evil was only revealed to the new employees. Understandable enough, they are the ones with the guns, but I don't see any of them.

Obviously, my enemy is trying a different tactic. I glance towards the nearest camera. It is tracking me without subtlety. So they know where I am, and they are biding their time. I glance about. The park is empty of guests; perhaps they are waiting for the employees to leave as well. Good. Now that I think about it, I suppose that it is just as well that they did not know of my friendship with—

"*There* you are," Vandy says. I stare at her in astonishment, and then rub my eyes furiously. It does not *feel* like a glamour, but—I feel her hesitant touch upon my arm, and I know it is her. Again I stare at her. I open my mouth but I cannot speak. What is she *doing* here?

"You didn't come by as I was closing, so I started looking for you, but then I realized that you could be anywhere. So I figured I'd just wait somewhere that had a lot of traffic and here you are!" She then poked me in the chest. "You sure took your time, Mister."

"But ... but you weren't here," I stammer.

"Yeah, I had two days off. Remember? I asked you—" She sees my face and a light dawns. She rolls her eyes. "Wait. Was I supposed to be all 'Oh my god, it's a monster!' and faint or move to Bolivia or something? Please. I've been seeing monsters and vampires and ghosts and aliens and fairies and ... and whatever on TV and in the movies all my life. It's not this big new idea, okay?

"See, *I* always suspected that the government encouraged all those types of movies and TV shows because it was trying to get people used to the idea of weird creatures existing and being all cute and intelligent and stuff so that when the *real* space aliens landed and were all 'Hey, yo, we're here to like, invite you into the Space Federation and here's a cure for war and acne,' people wouldn't be all like 'Zomighod bug-eyed monsters! Kill them!'"

She looked pensive. "Of course, if they *are* all totally evil and come here to enslave us and steal all our water, then somebody would have *totally* fucked up and—"

I enveloped her in a hug, which had the added benefit of checking her nervous flow of words. She gasped, and then returned it fiercely. I allowed myself several glorious seconds, then reluctantly pulled back and held her at arm's length. "You ... you shouldn't be talking to me. It's very dangerous."

"Too late," Vandy shrugs. "I already think you're pretty cool." She looks me in the eye. "So I'm only asking because if I don't, you'll probably take another two hundred years to get around to it, but are you one of those monsters that can, you know, fool around?"

Bone Cat starts to laugh, but then discovers that he cannot, as I'm compressing him into a ball approximately two inches in diameter. "I am serious," I snarl. "Someone is trying to kill me, which means *you* could be in danger."

"Death is here," Bone Cat whispers.

Vandy gasps, and looks around, and then starts to kick him. I stop her, and the look upon my face causes her to freeze. I realize that I have not sensed anyone else near us for quite some time. I speak quietly. "Were there any special instructions about closing tonight?"

Even before I am done, her hand flies to her mouth. "Yes! But I forgot when you didn't show up! They're fumigating the park or something. We're all supposed to be out before midnight."

It is easily past midnight now, and I don't believe this ridiculous fumigation story for a moment. I must get her to the nearest exit as soon as possible. Vandy gives a squeak as I encircle her with my arms and lift—And we both grunt in surprise as I crash back to earth, my lifting muscles twin stripes of pain. My encounter with the McGoon had been more damaging than I had thought. "Sorry," I mutter as we straighten up. "But we have to get you out of here." I point towards the west. "The closest exit is that way." I glance towards Bone Cat for confirmation that the way is clear, but he focuses on a spot immediately behind me, obviously seeing something I cannot, and slowly shakes his head. "He's ... I don't think there *is* a good way to go, boss."

Vandy says nothing, an indication that she is taking this seriously. As we move, I extend my perceptions until I can hear the worms humming their endless roundelay symphonies beneath our feet, and yet it is Vandy who sees the child in the distance. He is thin, dark-skinned, and indifferently dressed, leaning nonchalantly against a closed Weasel-Fruit stand. When he sees that we are aware of his presence, he silently dashes off towards the *Cavalcade of Mismatched Socks* ride.

This is certainly not the first time I have discovered a child determined to live the dream of making Zenonland their new home, but the timing certainly could not be worse.

I briefly consider ignoring him, but Vandy is already after him. I clash my teeth in frustration and catch up to her. My hand upon her arm stops her dead. "*I* will deal with this rapscallion," I assure her. "*You* get out of the park and inform a Night Manager that there is a child loose within."

The logic of this preempts any objection she might have, and she nods once. Then, before I understand what she is doing, she leans in and gives me a peck upon my cheek. She has kissed me.

"See you tomorrow, Sheriff," she calls over her shoulder as she trots off.

She has kissed me. What kind of foolish, misguided impulse led her to do that? She has no idea what I am capable of and that I am going to be dead or worse within hours and whoever thinks that they can simply stroll into my kingdom, destroy my resting places, kill innocent people, and try to prevent me from dressing Vandy down for that impertinent kiss are going to be very sorry indeed. I am in such a state that I am almost upon the young man before his behavior finally rouses me from my inner maelstrom.

We are in the Great Green Square, which was built as a direct architectural rebuttal to the Soviet Union's Great Red Square (occasionally Mr. Bartholomew's more patriotic ideas looked better on paper). I see him clearly now. For some reason I had thought him older, but as I study him, I see he cannot be older than twelve. I have a shock of recognition. This is the urchin who was sitting in my office. He is standing directly in the center and is just staring at me. Waiting. Not like a child who has been caught doing something naughty, but like ... a hunter.

Ironically, I have the McGoon to thank for my continued existence. Instinctively, I leap upwards, but stall out less than six inches up. Thus the shot the boy snaps off with the rifle he had concealed behind his back passes over my head, instead of catching me square in the chest. I shift to near immateriality just in time. A second shot rips through my center and I *feel* it burning as it passes through. These must be the "enhanced" bullets that were being handed out to the security personnel. Even though they wouldn't kill me, I dare not become solid enough that one can lodge within me.

I roar at him and open my senses to catch a hint of fear—Nothing. There is nothing. This child is as devoid of emotion as a charred log. No, I lie. There is a flicker of annoyance. Like you'd find in a bricklayer who saw that his spirit level was slightly off true. His eyes narrow and the next shot goes through my head, and it stings like a hot coal shoved up one's nose. Fury fills me now, but all I can do is turn and flee. I cannot touch him. If I tried, the geas would kick in and I'd solidify enough that the next shot would assuredly do permanent damage.

As I flow towards the *Buster Buttons House O' Chees-Cones*, a girl steps out from behind the Cheddar-hound statue. She looks like she's ten, but she handles the Uzi in her arms like an Israeli commando, and easily two dozen rounds burn through me before I can dive into the shrubbery. I want to pause and assess the damage, but I know better than to do that. Even so, the true horror of what is happening is rolling over me. Children. Herr Zoiden, I presume, is using *children* to attack me. Again, what kind of person am I dealing with? I wonder if I will last long enough to find out?

This trap was well laid, but since I am not dead, I have to believe that it is not yet complete. For a brief second, I'm suddenly overwhelmed by the most tantalizing aroma I have ever smelled. Unhesitatingly, I whip my hand up and brutally squeeze my nose closed. Through watering eyes, I peer through the foliage and see a third girl, twelve at most, standing upon the giant *Shogi* board. During the daytime it's occupied by the endlessly moving anthropomorphic pieces. But at night, just before the parade, they march off to their giant lacquered box. In this empty space, she is using what looks like some kind of powered caulking gun to methodically spray white goop in a circle before an array of lights, to which she holds an activation switch. This goop must be the fabled goat-derived sour cream listed in the Gremlin's notes. I would have succumbed to that if I hadn't been aware of its existence. One final gift from them.

Foliage rustles behind me. Closer than I can credit. These

children know how to move and track through vegetation, even at night. Who *are* they? A shot tears through my arm and I scream. The strain of trying to stay insubstantial in my wounded state is beginning to tell on me. A *fourth* assailant. I see him now. He is atop the reproduction of the information kiosk from Grand Central Station, wearing what looks like some very sophisticated night vision goggles. I lurch to the side just before he shoots a second time, and a spurt of fire buries itself in the ground beside me. He is using some sort of tracer rounds. I cannot imagine what *those* would feel like, and I have no wish to find out.

I run *towards* him, which he does not expect. Time seems to slow, and an age passes as his rifle swings down towards me. He is firing off shot after shot even as the gun moves. I flow past him and my perception of time returns to normal. The flat cracks of the rifle are joined by the sounds of the other weapons opening up as their owners catch sight of me. On the other side of the copse, the night turns into day as the girl triggers the lights. In anyone else, I'd suspect it was done out of frustration, but with these preternatural children, I cannot guess. The shots cut off—apparently the unexpected light has temporarily blinded them. I crouch down and move while I can.

Unfortunately, I am limited in my choices as to where to go, and they are well aware of this. Even as muted and dead as their emotions are, I can sense satisfaction. Now they are fanning out, trying to herd me in a specific direction. I analyze their actions. If I could fly, I'd evade them with ease ... I consider this, and then scoop up Bone Cat and fling him skywards. Less than ten feet up, he strikes something, and hangs there, thrashing, stuck on some sort of adhesive. I can see it now, almost-invisible netting, faintly silhouetted against the lights. Instantly he is caught in a crossfire that literally takes him apart before my eyes. I shiver. This is why I despise prognostication. I become all too aware that every trivial decision I make is becoming larded with the possibly that it could be the one that seals my doom.

Bone Cat reforms on my shoulder. "Asshole," he mutters. "That always hurts, you know."

Reflexively, I reply with the old Gilbert Shelton joke: "Nonsense. I've killed *lots* of people. It doesn't hurt."

But avoiding the net is only a short-term victory. I am still being successfully herded towards the lake. I point towards the stairway that leads up towards the *Land O' Milk and Honey,* and with a grimace, Bone Cat dashes towards it.

I keep going towards the lake. This seems like a poorly chosen trap. It will be an effort, but I can still become insubstantial enough that I can stride across the surface of the water, or, if worst comes to worst, although I'll admit that I have not done so for close to a thousand years, I'm pretty sure I can remember how to swim. As I arrive upon the shore, I hear Bone Cat begin to mangle the yodeling song from the Oscar-winning cartoon *'Alp! I'm Afraid of Heights!* followed almost instantly by a brief flurry of shots from behind me.

They found him rather quickly. This guess is verified as he reconstitutes himself upon my shoulder and smacks the back of my head. "That stung *too,* you jerk."

I ignore him as I take this precious moment to examine the lake. The lights of the *Submarine Racetrack* across the way shine cheerfully in the distance. *Too easy,* I can hear Mr. Mortimer mutter. My pursuers have not made a mistake so far; I cannot count on them starting now. Guided by nothing but instinct, I gingerly touch the surface of the water before I trust my weight to it. The pain causes me to pull back, hissing like a broken radiator. My finger gives off a wisp of smoke. Someone has blessed the water of the *lake.* The entire lake! It must have taken them *hours.*

Creating genuine holy water is not accomplished with just a flurry of hand-waving while shouting *domine* a half a dozen times. It requires salt, for one thing, and not just any salt. It must be pure. Then you have to consecrate it and *then* recite the proper prayers as you mix them together. This all takes time. And before you lose *all* faith in the scientific underpinnings of the world, let me assure you that the inverse-square law, at least, most certainly still applies. Thus, you cannot wave your hand about, toss in a saltcellar, and sanctify the ocean. For a lake this size, I calculate they must've repeated the ritual at *least* fifty times and poured in no less than a hundredweight of salt.

Ridiculous, but I cannot argue with the end result. I look about. Barricades have been erected to either side—just far enough that I did not see them as I approached. This was indeed planned out. The children are approaching slowly now. The three with guns are surrounding the one girl who is lugging a set of lights and what looks like a battery pack on, of all things, a small red wagon. They are taking their time. I am afraid I am out of options. I only see one thing to do, but I won't enjoy it. I turn and stroll along the lakefront towards one of the barricades. The children speed up slightly, and their eyes track me without blinking.

I come up to the barricade and examine it with a studied calm that I am not really feeling, but, at this point, appearance is everything. The barricade extends several feet out into the lake and is sheer enough that even I would be hard-pressed to get purchase, even if I wasn't being shot at.

It's been long enough. I turn, and there they all are, exactly where I expected them to be. I think about Xochemilchic's coin in my pocket, but these children are not the architects of my troubles. I clear my throat, which causes them to freeze. "This is your last chance," I inform them in a whisper, while slowly raising my hand. They stare at my hand, but there is no discussion; they simply start firing, while the girl with the lights continues to connect her cables.

Very well. I take a deep breath and—Ooh, I hadn't considered this last bit. In order to make a noise, I will have to solidify enough that my breath can register. There is no good option, but even in my immaterial state, their damned bullets are hurting me. I solidify, drop to my knees, and whistle—I feel a series of painful shocks—and suddenly the night seems to coalesce into a hulking shape enveloped in a great black cowl, its face hidden. It peers at me unsympathetically, the pain sharply increases, a sword begins to form in its boney hand, and I realize I'm whistling out my last breath. I collapse to the ground—

And the impacts I've been feeling stop. The great figure looming over me hesitates, and then with a shrug, turns back, and as it does so I see that it is not some ridiculous personification of death, but merely the equally ridiculous form of Orsynn that is now looming up in the darkness, the children struggling from within his deceptively strong coils. Even now the children say nothing. They thrash and grunt trying to free themselves, firing desperately, but they do it silently.

Orsynn, of course, has no such inclinations. "Hello, my friend! What is this? Are you still angry at me? Or are we having a party?" He licks his lips. "Something tastes salty." Suddenly he blinks, and peers down at the child firing steadily into him. When he speaks again, there's a new tone in his voice. "Are those *guns?* Are they *shooting* at me?"

Even as I drag myself upright to a sitting position and futilely strain to extrude the bullets lodged within me, I have to wonder —how in the world does Orsynn know what *guns* are?

Bone Cat bounds to my side. "Those little assholes *shot* me again," he swore. "Can't they see how goddamned cute I am?" He looks at me with concern. Numerous bullets are lodged within me. I'm not really up for our usual level of badinage. "Fade out a bit, boss." He seems very sure of himself, and to be honest I'm rather losing interest in thinking for myself, so I go as immaterial as I can, and he thrusts a clawed hand inside me. This adds an exciting new level of pain to my existence that jolts me a bit closer to the here and now. I can *feel* him rummaging about inside me, and when he pulls his hand back out, easily a dozen unnaturally shining silver bullets are clutched in his paw.

I take a deep breath and feel marginally better. That was

close. I look back up at Orsynn. "Yes," I answer him. "They are shooting at all of us."

Orsynn gets a strange look upon his features. One I've never seen before. "That makes me ... that makes me *angry*." The children within his grasp gurgle as he visibly *squeezes* them. I hold up a hand. "Wait. I need to talk to them." I almost think he is not going to listen to me, but after an interminable moment, I can see the coils slacking slightly. I point towards the girl who was in charge of the lights, and Orsynn swings her down towards me. Her gaze is unnerving, and she is still silent. "Who are you?" She glances at the other children, who are all silently watching, and gives a slight nod.

That is the only warning I get before several of the lights snap on. She still has the wireless switch clutched in her hand. The pain is terrible. Luckily, most of the lights are pointing towards the barricade behind me, but the reflected glare alone causes parts of me to start smoking, and I howl in agony.

Again Orsynn saves me, as a rope of muscle snaps out and smashes the lights with a crackle and a shower of sparks. The pain recedes but is still overwhelming. I again collapse to the ground, my head spinning, a roaring and screaming in my ears ... which, I realize, is something I'm actually hearing.

I roll over in time to see the last child engulfed. He thrashes briefly within the gelatinous mass and actually fires his gun one last time. The barrel was obviously plugged, as the gun explodes. I can see the ball of light that tears him apart and causes his prison to quiver once before it vanishes under the water. Orsynn actually hisses in either pain or annoyance, I am not sure which.

Making a supreme effort, I manage to snag the boy's essence as it breaks free. I spit it back out, like you would spit out an ice cream cone artfully sculpted from frozen vomit. I have never experienced *anything* like this. Not even from a die-hard Nazi. It is a young soul, as these things are reckoned, but it is as if it had died long before its current body had. There is no question of punishment on my part. This entity has already been to Hell, and anything that happens to it from this point onward can only be a blessing.

Orsynn looks down at me, and I see concern upon his features. "Are you damaged, my friend?"

"I am," I confess.

"Don't die!" he moans. "Please, don't leave me. We were friends again!"

I am nonplused. I was unaware that Orsynn worried about such things. Now, I am not very good at giving comfort, as a rule. I tend to be too honest. In many ways, Orsynn has the mind of a child, and while I have often been placed in a position where I am called upon to sooth a distraught manikin, I always know that if I fail to project sufficient amount of bonhomie, I can always turn them so they cannot see the bodies and then blur their memories, thus avoiding a fair amount of trauma. I do not think that is something I can do with Orsynn, so I will just have to do my best, which, considering the circumstances, what with my prophesied death and all, will be a bit of a challenge.

"It's not that big a deal, Orsynn. Everyone dies," I begin cheerfully.

"NOT MEEE!" he screams, and, rearing up, thrashes so hard that the water around him is whipped into foam. "NEVER MEEE! *I AM NOT ALLOWED TO DIEEEE!*"

Ah. You know, if I had more time, I suspect that this would be the seed of a *fascinating* conversation. But as it is, I'd best steer him onto another topic. "About those children ..."

Instantly Orsynn's mood changes. "I am sorry, my friend. Did you want to kill them yourself?"

"No, no. You had said that you wanted to try killing some yourself, remember?"

Orsynn stares down at me with a delighted look upon the various aspects that made up his face. "Why so I did! And you *remembered!*"

"Indeed I did. Well, as it happens, I had these obstreperous children trying to kill me, so I figured we'd satisfy two of your requests at the same time." All I can see of the children now are indistinct blobs dissolving within Orsynn's main bulk. "How did you like them?"

If Orsynn found them particularly succulent, this could be a problem. Not *my* problem, of course, but I'd hate to leave a situation like this behind. Luckily, Orsynn gives forth a deep sigh. "I will tell you, my friend, I cannot say that I liked them very much at all. You would think that they would be tastier than someone more aged, but I have gnawed upon old tires at the bottom of this lake that I enjoyed more. They were bad meat. Please do not bring me any more children."

Bone Cat and I gently bump fists in relief before I even realize what I am doing. When I do, I find that I no longer care about the ridiculousness of it all. "I can assure you that I will not bring you any more children, my friend."

Orsynn gasps. "What was that? What did you say?"

What *did* I say? "I said—"

"You actually called me your friend! You have not done that for *such* a long time!"

I rack my brains. "Wait. When did I *ever*—?"

"But now you have! We are really and truly friends again!" He blew a melodious trill of bubbles. "This is the best day *ever*!" And before I could ask anything, he has vanished beneath the surface.

Bone Cat and I stare out over the lake. A frustrating and ridiculous enigma until the end. Well, *my* end, anyway. I glance over and see one of the now ubiquitous cameras focused upon me. There's never been a camera there before. It appears to be slightly damaged by stray bullets, but I trust that whoever was watching was thoroughly surprised by Orsynn showing up. I have no idea who or what will be taking my place in the cosmic scheme of things as the gremlins claim, but I cannot count on them being able to protect Orsynn. His biggest protection, after all, was the fact that no one knew he was there. If that's gone ...

I grumble as I slowly climb to my feet. The world just keeps finding more and more reasons why I'm just going to *have* to kill

Herr Zoiden. When at last I am upright, I give myself a shake and find I am feeling surprisingly better. I walk back to the broken remnants of the light array. Who were those terrible, damaged children? In their own way they were more monstrous than half of the monsters I've met.

"Delightfully horrible, weren't they?" The voice booms forth from one of the park's many hidden speakers. It catches me by surprise, and no mistake, but I fail to visibly react. An outside observer might put it down to a jaded world-weariness, but the truth is that I am still in a great deal of pain, and sudden movements would only make it worse. At least I'm not expected to answer. These cameras don't have audio capability.

"Child soldiers," the voice continued. "My people found them in some wretched little conflict in southern Africa. Been fighting since they were six years old. Their commander sold them to me for five hundred dollars apiece." The voice sighed. "Apparently I should have picked up another dozen when I had the chance."

This will be Herr Zoiden, I presume. Soldiers ... now why is *that* word clamoring for my attention?

"So. Big monster in the lake. You keep it around to eat problem kids? I am super impressed. I knew about your geas, of course, but I would never have thought you were that foresighted." I ignore him as best I can. I need to find a place to rest, and with the park as wired as it is, that will be difficult. "Wow, now I'm kind of wondering what *else* you have stashed around the place."

A worry that will keep him up at night, I hope. There is one bolt-hole I doubt they'll find, as it is a hidden subcellar directly beneath the security room. Getting to it might be challenging, but if I can convince them that I was determined to confront them in some sort of macho, suicidal, Hollywood-type exercise ...

"Oh, I love your idea, by the way. The whole elimination of boring places in the park? You are so right! There is so much *potential* there. So *many* places where people could be startled, or shocked, or flat out *terrified*. People love that shit! I have any number of ideas already."

I'd grit my teeth but it would hurt to do so. It all sounds so ... *unclean* when *he* talks about it. Of course I must acknowledge that the whole "irrationally trying to kill me" thing aside, just the sound of this fellow's voice is raising my hackles. "Personally, I think our *Haunted Monorail Station* is a bit of a joke, don't you? Aside from the bit with the skeletal ticket takers, it's about as scary as a stroll in the park."

"Because this *is* a park," I mutter to myself. "People come here *because* it's non-threatening. The world has a surfeit of genuine terrors already."

"Oh," Bone Cat says, his eyes rolling with a sound like marbles in a ceramic dish. "*Now* you get it."

"So be honest—let me know what you think— *I'm* thinking of changing it to an abattoir-themed sort of thing? We'll keep the music, of course—and here's the *best* part—the riders can pick an animal to be slaughtered, watch the process, and then have it served up in an attached restaurant! I mean, you *can't* get fresher than that! Am I right?"

Without breaking stride, I shift direction. Zoiden is still talking, but I am no longer listening. To Hell with him and all the rest of it. I will find my prehistoric gopher burrow. I will pull it in after me and sleep in the dark heart of the Earth for a few years. By the time I return, this idiot will have transformed Zenonland into a rubble-strewn lot sewn with salt, and the demise of the Zenon Corporation will be a horror story told in college business classes for the next century. Then America will see the back of my boots and I will discover how just badly the last sixty or so years have treated Prague, which was run by a very civilized vampire queen who liked to dress in outrageous—

"Sheriff?" That is Vandy's voice coming over the loudspeaker now. She is scared and obviously uncertain about what is going on, unlike myself.

"Um ... I found a Security guy at the entrance, and he brought me here, but nobody wants to hear about the kid, and they won't let me—AAH!"

That was the unmistakable sound of a blow, a fist upon flesh, and then silence. I find myself vibrating with rage. Suddenly Zoiden is back on the air. "Can you *believe* this girl? I mean seriously, she never shuts up. I mean, *I* wouldn't blame you if you just left her here, because she is annoying as fuck." I don't move. I just listen.

"But I'm guessing you care about her, because she sure seems to care about *you*. Hoo hoo, you dawg, you! So here's the deal. You're going to let me kill you, and I'll let her go."

No, he won't. For a thousand reasons, but the only one that counts is that he knows that it will annoy me. "You don't believe me. Well, and why *should* you? But really, what choice do you have? Oh, well, sure, you could just walk away and let me torture her to death and *then* I'll just kill you *tomorrow*—Or you could believe me when I say that I would sincerely appreciate you saving me all that time and effort, not to mention messing up a good suit—and I'll show it by letting the little chucklehead go. Why would I lie? Seriously, who would believe her?"

He *is* lying. Lying through his teeth. I *know* this. I try to step back and be dispassionate about this; what *is* Vandy, really? A nostalgic infatuation who will be dead in less than a century, and doubtless extremely tiresome decades before that, no matter how well the women of her family age. I've seen thousands of people die, what is one more—

A muffled whimper comes over the speaker. "Wow, she is being super brave, but I guess that last one just kind of slipped out. You should *see* what she's enduring while you're just standing there, fucking around—"

"Fine," I shout. "I'll do it." I raise my hands in the universal symbol of surrender and walk to the middle of the Great Green Square and slowly lower myself to the ground. I face the East. I always said that I wanted to see the thing that killed me. In a bit less than four hours, I shall. Bone Cat walks up and stares at me. Zoiden is still talking, but thankfully the speakers are now too far away for me to hear his gloating.

I take another breath. Perhaps it is all for the best. I have been alive for over a thousand years, and have seen so many things die—people, towns, nations, ideas—that I can begin to reconcile myself with the philosophical concept that it is, at last, my turn. I have regrets, of course. Personally, I think that having regrets is yet another thing that separates sentient creatures from base *animalia*. But overall, I think I can be proud of what I have done with my time upon this sphere and must admit that I'm curious to see what will happen the next time around. Perhaps I will be a ballerina. I could—

A phone is ringing. It is possibly one of the few remaining public phones in California. The Zenon Corporation keeps them around because these days, they trigger as strong a sense of wonder and nostalgia as the monorail that circles the park. They still work, of course, and with a sigh I climb to my feet and go to answer it. If I don't, it's quite possible that it will ring until the sun comes up. I lift the receiver—"WHAT THE FUCK ARE YOU *DOING?*"

It is Herr Zoiden's voice and he sounds rather put out. I cannot imagine why. "I'm doing what you want. I'm waiting for death," I explain patiently. I wave at the nearest camera and make a production of pointing towards the East. "I'm in an open, exposed place. When the sun comes up, I will be unable to escape." Especially if I sit here for the next four hours, as I'm sure my legs will go to sleep; ah, well, dying is not supposed to be comfortable.

"No," Zoiden says petulantly at the other end of the line. "No, that's not what I need at all."

"Well, I'm sorry," I point out, "but I can't make the sun go any faster."

"NO, I mean you get your ass in here and I will kill you myself."

The first thing I feel is annoyance. What is his problem? This will work. I have staked out any number of photosensitive creatures—some of them in this very square. That stain they've never been able to remove from the pavement? Vegerax the Undying, thank you very much. The Sun never fails to deliver satisfactory results. Young people today have no patience.

The second thing I feel is hope. Foolish, but undeniable, hope. Is this idiot determined to try to kill me in some sort of elaborate death machine of his own cunning design that will enable him to play a round of before-I-kill-you-let-me-tell-you-my-diabolical-plan?

Oh, Hollywood, if this is the case, I shall never complain about you again. I've encountered people like this before, determined to make you appreciate the full breadth and scope of their genius instead of just killing you. This is always a mistake, for as long as one is alive, one has a chance. "All right," I say carefully. "Tell me where to go."

After I hang up, Bone Cat is still glaring at me. "What?"

"Once again you were ready to sit on your ass and just die. I'm losing patience with you."

"I'm sorry. I'll do my best." I grip his shoulders. "Please help me to get Vandy out," I ask simply, "and I shall try to not get killed."

He resists for a moment, and then pats my wrist. "I was gonna do that anyway, you jerk. I just wanted you to think about it."

Several minutes later, we find ourselves before the *Haunted Monorail Station*. "Can you figure out where Vandy is being held?"

He concentrates. "She ain't here."

That makes sense, I suppose. "Can you find her?"

He concentrates so hard he actually begins to fade out—then snaps back into focus. "I can find her, but ..." He looks at me. "She's still in the park, but she ain't close."

This will be tricky. As far as we can ascertain, Bone Cat is only able to manifest because of me, when I am in contact with the land itself. While he normally is within arm's reach, he *can* operate independently. However, the farther he gets from me, the more difficult it is for him to exist. He can do it, but I have to be actively thinking about him. This means that I will not be able to devote my full attention to whatever is happening to me.

"Don't worry about it, boss," he says reassuringly. "Thinking has never been your strong suit to begin with." I take a deep breath and raise my hand. Instantly he smacks it in an enthusiastic high five and scurries off into the darkness. I straighten up and examine the building before me.

The *Haunted Monorail Station* is considered the back entrance to *Futureopolis*, as opposed to the front entrance overseen by the Gremlin's brewing tower, and if you alight there from the park-encircling monorail, you actually have to make an effort to avoid going through it. The first time you hear about it, you may be excused for being a bit confused. *Futureopolis* is supposed to be everything that the 1950s thought Science was all about. Buildings that looked like they were built inside a wind tunnel, moving sidewalks, a total abandonment of spiritualism and superstition. It's diametrically opposed to the park's *Whitechapel Wonderland* District, both philosophically and geographically, with its twisty cobblestone streets, it's Victorian-Gothic architecture, and its collection of faux-scary and supposedly unsavory rides, such as the aforementioned *Pirate Cruise to Nowhere*.

The whole thing was a terrible mix-up. To this day, no one is quite sure how the mistake occurred, but where the *Haunted Asylum* was supposed to be to be built, the gleaming *Palace of Enlightenment* was constructed, and, on the opposite side of the park, the promised *Future of Transportation* ride had morphed into the now famous Charles Addams-designed *Haunted Monorail Station*. Mr. Bartholomew was furious when the error was discovered, but by that time the cost of correcting it would have been prohibitive, especially as the construction costs of the park were already soaring. Plans were made to grin and bear it and do something about it in a couple of years. Naturally, these changes were never made, as even before the park officially opened they so delighted visitors that everyone assumed that the dichotomy had been deliberate. It was hailed as a triumph of design, and they are now two of the most popular rides in the park. That said, Mr. Bartholomew was annoyed about it until his dying day —and beyond. I walk into the entryway, and a large video screen blinks on. I stare at the figure revealed and experience a most peculiar turn.

It is Mr. Mortimer.

CHAPTER ELEVEN

After a brief moment of existential disorientation, I look again, drawing upon a thousand years of experience observing the vagrancies and the peculiarities of genetics. Of course. This can only be Mr. Mortimer's son. He must be in his fifties, but he looks younger. Some of that can no doubt be explained by exercise and diet, but surely not all of it. This fellow is positively *radiating* good health.

He is examining me as keenly as I, him. He shakes his head. "Well, you certainly don't live up to your rep, old man."

I roll my eyes. He certainly has none of his father's subtlety. He is baiting me. I think about Bone Cat and try to look ineffectual. "You are a surprise as well." But his patrimony explained a few things that his file had not; his supposedly preternatural knowledge of the company's inner workings was a bit more plausible now. But there was still the central mystery ... "Why the name Zoiden? If you have a claim to the Zenon family name ...?"

Herr Zoiden smiled ruefully. "Technically, I suppose, I would be labeled a bastard."

Ah. That explained some things. The Zenon Corporation had always been rather leery about admitting that any of the founding family even knew what sex was. Oh, there are subsequent generations of the Zenon family hanging about, ostentatiously displayed throughout the company's organizational chart. But in actuality they were all too willing to sit back, cash checks, and forgo the tedious business of administration, or indeed, anything that might be mistaken for actual work.

Now even if our young fellow here was a member of the family, and passed the inevitable DNA tests, there was no getting around the fact that he was a wild card, raised outside of the familial politics that, according to Mr. Shulman, keep the rest of the younger generations of Zenons in line. A person with his lineage, along with his demonstrated business savvy, suddenly showing up to claim a piece, however theoretical, of one of the largest companies on Earth, would not be a threat taken lightly. Legally, his would be a Sisyphean task at best. But from what I knew of Mr. Mortimer, his place would have been secured, legalistic legitimacy aside, unless ... "Your father didn't know of your existence," I hazarded.

Herr Zoiden nodded and glanced off to the side. He was not alone, wherever he was. "That is true. I'm told he would have *interfered*."

Oh, my. Now *that* was a charge I had heard leveled against Mr. Mortimer any number of times, usually as someone's plans and/or death fortress was crashing down around us. But one of Mr. Mortimer's gifts was that, initially, you never suspected him capable of anything more than finishing his beer, and by the time you realized that he had destroyed everything you'd been working towards for the last twenty years and stolen *your* beer as well, it was usually one of those supreme moments of clarity that come to a person as they are hurtling face first towards a cauldron of molten steel or some similar Armageddon.

Very few people had the experience required to develop that level of paranoia regarding Mr. Mortimer, and only one of them might have gotten close enough to produce the man appearing before me now. "Hello, Polina," I called out. "It is a fine-looking boy you have there."

Herr Zoiden's face went blank, and he again glanced to the side. But this time there was a bark of laughter, and Madam Polina Urakhov stepped into view. Grand Witches are known to live for a very long time, though they tend to suffer unfortunate physiological effects as they age. But in Polina's case, it appeared that time was treating her extraordinarily well. I would have sworn her to be no more than thirty. She was wearing a severe black pants suit, and the only outré touch I could see was one of those westernized ladies' turbans that had not been fashionable for close to forty years. This was also rather unusual, as your typical witches' fashion sense seems to degenerate as they do. Older witches invariably favor a hodgepodge of rotting Romany finery and junk-shop new age jewelry.

"I quite thought you were dead," I admitted. To be fair, most people you encase in a sealed vat full of boiling mercury have the good taste to take the hint. "So did Mr. Mortimer or, I assure you, he would have continued to send you those roses." Ah, now that hit a nerve of some sort. She grit her teeth and opened her mouth—

"Is *he* the one who sent those?" Zoiden interrupted. "I always suspected."

"Don't tell me she *kept* them?"

"Every single one. I thought it was charming—"

With a snarl, his mother twisted her fingers into a knot and Zoiden acted as if he'd been punched in the stomach. "Shut up, you fool!"

Ah. This was one of those *happy* families. I filed that away and addressed her in Russian. "I must assume that trying to kill me is *your* idea, Polina. I confess that I don't know why. Surely whoever is really running your country at the moment doesn't care about me, and, come to think of it, I would be very surprised if they actually knew of *your* existence at all. That means it must be personal, which seems rather petty on your part. I mean, yes, we were colleagues who tried to kill each other, to be sure, but—"

Zoiden broke in, also in Russian. "I'm afraid I really didn't believe you, Mother, but you were right. He articulates every single thought he has."

She nodded. "It was one of the reasons your father kept him around. He made him look positively Machiavellian."

Grand Witches are particularly good at getting under one's skin, both literally and figuratively. "Where is the girl? Tell me or I am leaving."

Another screen lights up and I see Vandy. She is naked, which almost causes me to start breaking things then and there. She is strapped down on some sort of table, and a fellow in a set of medical greens is standing beside her. There is a rack of rather medieval-looking instruments to hand. Her face shows signs of bruising, and I can see several angry-looking marks upon her arms and torso. They are in a rather well-lit room that I recognize. It is, in fact, in the Palace of Enlightenment. They have chosen well. It is all the way across the park, and even if I *could* fly, it would still take me several minutes to reach her. I think very hard about Bone Cat and try to focus on Vandy's face.

Evidently this is a two-way connection, as she sees me. I cannot feel her emotions, but she puts on a brave smile. "Hello, Sheriff."

"Hello, Vandy." I shift my attention back to Madam Urakhov. "Cover her."

The witch shrugs. "You'll have to earn that, *Dehazzaki!*"

"Gesundheit."

The witch rolled her eyes. "No, you imbecile, a *Dehazzaki* is what you are!"

Well. That *is* interesting. I roll the word over my tongue. I wonder how she'd discovered it. "Thank you," I say. "Now I know what to put on my business card." I take a deep breath. "But seriously, Polina, what is this about?"

"Where is Mortimer Zenon?"

This was the last question I expected. "I assure you that I have no idea. I'm afraid that he's dead."

"He is *supposed* to be," she spat. "But you couldn't even do that!"

"... You've lost me."

"That fool was supposed to die," she said. "He *must* die! That is the final step!"

"Wait. Are you telling me that Mr. Mortimer is *still alive?*" I desperately tried to understand. Mr. Mortimer had always been the one who was able to work out even the most convoluted plan. "Why would *I* kill him? *How* would I have killed him? Do you know where he is? I never saw him after ..." I had a sudden flash of insight. "*You* grabbed him the night I was bound to this place, didn't you?"

She looked away. "Yes. It was the perfect opportunity. I knew he would never come to me of his own volition."

"May I point out that *you* were the one who broke our last truce. In Vienna? 195—"

"Cut her!" With a nod, the fellow next to Vandy selected a scalpel.

"Stop," I shouted, but to no avail, as he methodically made an inch long slice in her arm. Vandy tried to endure it, but a small scream escaped.

"Damnation, if *you* captured him, then why would you expect *me* to kill him?"

She stared at me, her jaw sagging open in a most unbecoming manner. "I thought the two of you had thwarted me," she muttered. "Had set one of his devilishly subtle plans into motion. The years I've spent trying to divine it ..."

Suddenly she screamed and pounded the wall beside her in fury. "You didn't figure anything out at *all*! You just didn't *kill* him?"

I shrugged.

She snarled, "Cut her again!"

I dropped to my knees, which so surprised Polina that she held up her hand and the technician paused, scalpel raised. "What do you want of me!"

The witch gave a vinegary smile. "To begin with, I don't want to hear any more of your endless prattle. All I want to know is: Where is Mortimer Zenon?"

"I don't know! You just said *you* had him! I haven't seen him since the night I was imprisoned! I swear!" Polina considered this, and then turned back to the screen, obviously about to order more torture. "*Why* do you think I should have killed him?"

She paused, and then her mouth closed with a click. "Because he would have been a monster and killing monsters that attack this park is what you do."

I stared at her. "You turned him into a monster?"

"Yes." The memories she was mining were taking a dark turn, it was evident from the look on her face. "Yes, I took him that night. I was prepared to give him one last chance to be together. Ideologically there truly was no longer any reason to fight. The Communists were as bad as the Fascists, and, secretly, they all wanted to become Capitalists." She shook her head. "He told me that back in 1943, but I didn't listen to him ..." Her voice ran down, and she spent almost a minute adrift in some other time and place, until suddenly her eyes snapped back towards me, and they were filled with hate.

"But while your last little death trap failed to *kill* me, it started my ... *changes* prematurely."

Oh dear. I knew what *that* meant. She made a complicated gesture, and her glamour—a glamour that had been so artfully woven that I had not even been aware that it was there —dropped.

Contrary to popular fiction, glamours and charms manage to survive things like mirrors or photography quite well, let alone electronic transmission. This is a good thing, since, as I have mentioned, I've been inadvertently photographed or filmed thousands of times over the years. It's hard to explain, but really it just takes some practice, Oh, there were some rocky patches in the beginning, when actual *silvered* mirrors first made an appearance in our remote little village, which was not until sometime after the first World War, if you would believe it. But I was able to train myself to overcome its effects. That said, I can usually recognize the signs of a glamour—a sort of shimmer, reminiscent of the ripples in the air one sees above pavement on a hot day—but more in the ultraviolet spectrum. These are conveyed perfectly well via television, as well as photography; you just have to know what to look for.

But Polina had taken the art to a whole other level. Which in this case meant that when she dissolved it, the revelation was even more shocking. I confess that I made a sudden hiss of indrawn breath at the sight of her true visage. Time had not treated her well after all.

Oh, she was still alive, which certainly counted for something, but like I said, Grand Witches do not age well, and Polina was either a lot older than I had thought or had had a particularly rough time of it. She had the nose, of course, and the hump, and now resembled nothing so much as a malevolent scarecrow made of dried apples and beef jerky. But even beyond that, she looked half melted. I had seen some rather extreme cases, in my time, but Polina eclipsed them all. Psychologically, it must have been very traumatic, as Polina, like all Grand Witches, started out as quite the ethereal beauty.

I suspect this is why Grand Witches, of either sex, have a tendency to turn mean once they begin to change, though there is no denying that some of them start that way and only get worse. You may think I'm being rather shallow and focusing on superficial appearance, but Polina, and every other young witch I'd met, had taken great pride in their ability to seduce, and there was no getting around that she was now extraordinarily hideous.

"Very pretty, don't you think?" She twirled with an echo of the sensual grace I remembered, which just made it worse. She glared at me. "I was supposed to have another *century* before I was reduced to this," she hissed. Grand Witches are very closemouthed about how and where they acquire their power, but one does get the opinion that it is bargained for. "In order to save my life after our last encounter, I had to burn through *all* of my youth!"

This offered some tantalizing clues as to how she'd managed to survive most of our other, admittedly more casual, deathtraps. Personally I had thought the whole mercury thing to be a bit extreme, really, but evidently it had not been extreme enough. Looking at the resulting ruin, I could only assume that what awaited her after death must be even worse.

Now, before you feel any sympathy for her, I want to make it clear that this was all brought about because *she* had betrayed *us* in that restaurant back in Prague, but I knew that pointing this out would cause Vandy nothing but pain. Under Mr. Mortimer's tutelage, I had learned how to project sincere contrition.

"I'm very sorry, Polina. No one deserves this, and least of all you. If Mr. Mortimer was here—" Even before the words have left my mouth, I realize my mistake. When they get this old, a witches' sanity is delicately balanced, and it doesn't take much to send it skittering about.

"I *gave* him a chance," Polina rasped. "Your precious Mortimer *screamed* when he managed to dispel my glamour! I *told* him not to! I *did*! But he *never* listened to me!" She spun about again. "Cut her," she screamed. "Cut her *face*!"

"No!" I roared, but of course Polina's servant wasn't about to listen to me. Mechanically he again applied his scalpel, and deftly sliced her cheek. Vandy screamed this time and strained against her bonds.

"So I wrung a child from him," she crooned, "and then I turned him into a monster. One that will give *me* control of this place."

I desperately tried to understand what she was talking about —and suddenly the pieces came together. "You're using *Inheritance Magic*!"

Oh, this explained much. Inheritance Magic is a sort of backwards curse. Terribly complicated, but remarkably effective.

Let us say that you have a King. Furthermore, said King has many sons. Your fortunes are tied to the fifth son. As things stand, it's a toss-up as to whether he'll be forced to take Holy Orders or be sent off to sea. Curses have been commissioned for far less.

So, by magical means, you have the King turned into a ravaging beast or some such, terrible enough that there is no question that it must be destroyed.

If you are feeling particularly vindictive, you arrange to have this "monster" slain by the King's best friend, loyal vassal, eldest son, or any other troublesome person you want to get rid of, one who is unaware of who the "monster" really is. But it must be more than killed, the body must be completely destroyed, traditionally by fire.

At this point, your designated heir must take an *Oath of Vengeance.* (I did say this was ridiculously complicated, did I not?) Meanwhile, the person who has unwittingly killed the King must be shown to be totally beyond the pale, and this is done by them killing an Assassin, a Loyal Soldier, and a Holy Man sent by said Designated Heir.

Yes, it all made sense now. The McGoon was the Assassin, those warped children were the Loyal Soldiers, and the Happiness Machine bomber was, in his own way, a Holy Man. She had sent them in the wrong order, but that did not interfere with the dictates of the spell.

"How did you know that I wouldn't get killed and ruin your plans?"

Polina waved a hand. "This is the *best* plan, but it is not my *only* plan. And if you were weak enough to be killed by those idiots, well, it's not like it would have been a complete loss."

Charming.

Anyway, once your killer's perfidy has been established, you send your chosen heir out to avenge their murdered sire, usually with some sort of magic weapon, and as soon as they righteously slay their parent's killer, they come into the worldly wealth, power, and lands that are their due.

No doubt you are asking, "Surely there is an easier way?" Easier? Of course. But what makes this so potent a magic, is that as soon as the "King" is "avenged," the inheritance is transferred immediately, without any tedious legal wrangling or challenge by any other heirs.

Considering that in this case we are talking about the Zenon Corporation, who are known for the quality and quantity of their lawyers, who would be perfectly willing to bill by the decade, I can see why Polina thought dark magic was the sensible way to go, and, to be honest, I don't blame her. It is a brilliant plan. I'd seen it used a hundred times in the old country, back when access to shape-changing magic was more common, but apparently, here in America, something had gone seriously wrong.

"So, if I understand this, you gave birth to Mr. Mortimer's son, and then transformed Mr. Mortimer into a monster. And then you unleashed him in the park." Polina and Herr Zoiden nodded. It certainly sounded plausible, but *which* monster? I had fought so many ... "What did you turn him into?"

That checked her, and she looked away. "I ... I don't know."

This seemed beyond sloppy. "How could you not know what kind of monster you turned the father of your child into?"

Herr Zoiden cleared his throat. "I'll tell this part, Mother." He faced me. "I was pretty young, but I remember that Mother had finished the spells. We brought Father here and ..."

"Why don't *I* remember—?"

Zoiden waved a hand. "Oh, you couldn't have known. We brought him here during the daytime. He was under a stupefaction spell, so all *we* had to do was buy him a ticket and push him towards the gates."

True. This would have been before they had any sort of serious security checkpoints.

"We were to find him a quiet place, and then that night he would transform and run amok." Zoiden sighed, like a child who had missed a promised show. "*He* went through the gates just fine, but when Mother went to follow ..." He shrugged.

"I could not enter," Polina rasped. "It wasn't a barrier; it was just a ... a ... there was this terrible *music*. I could not even approach the gates without starting to shake. I collapsed and almost lost my glamour."

"I'd never seen her do anything like *that*," Zoiden said. "I was only six at the time. I had to get her out of there, and my father ... well, he got away."

"Music, you say?" I considered her. "When did it stop? I mean, you're here now, so—"

"It stopped when I had that fool 'Holy Man' blow it up."

I paused. "The Happi—I mean, the *Itty-Bitty Planet* ride? You were the ones responsible ..." I looked at Zoiden again and imagined him in a pair of sunglasses. "You were the one who let the bomber in."

If ever there was a creature that I would expect to be repulsed by amplified waves of artificially generated happiness, it would be an evil witch. Even one of the young ones. Oh, I've seen my share of witches cackling in unholy glee, but once they go bad, genuine happiness seems to be anathema to them.

"It took us years to figure out what the source was," Zoiden volunteered, "and I didn't know for *sure* until I was high enough within the company that I was able to access the secret files."

"I waited ... and waited ... and *waited*. I became convinced that you *had* killed Mortimer, but had *hidden* it, somehow." Polina muttered, "So I sent the three against you, but the Inheritance Spell didn't activate. I was convinced that you had anticipated me. Prevented me from entering and rescued Mortimer and then hidden him safely somewhere within the park." She shook her head in disgust. "But you didn't even know any of this was happening, did you? You *must* remember him! He was designed to do *terrible* damage after he changed."

And then it hit me. The Wendigo. I had always rather *wondered* how it had gotten all the way down to southern California. Circumstantial, perhaps, but another thing that set the Wendigo apart from the other monsters that I have had to kill, is that *I did not destroy all of the creature's corpse.* I still had its head stuffed and hanging in my office at this very moment. Suddenly I realize the full enormity of what this witch is saying. A vast sorrow overwhelms me, and I drop to my knees.

"I do know the monster you mean. That creature was Mr. Mortimer? You had me *kill* Mortimer?"

The witch looks confused. "Wait. You *did* kill him? But the spell hasn't activated. You're lying." She raises her hand—

I shake my head. "No. I killed him." I looked up at her. "And I know how to complete your spell." Zoiden and Polina looked at each other. "But before I do so, you will release the girl."

Polina sneered. "You would say *anything*. How can you prove—"

"I did not destroy the body completely. I saved his head. It is mounted upon a wall in my office."

Polina's mouth fell open. She turned to Zoiden, who started to smile. "There *is* a monster's head on his wall. I'd thought it was a fake ..." He looked at me. "You *kept* it?"

"I didn't know it was your father's." I considered the situation. "I'd say I'm sorry—and I am—but not for anything you'd understand."

Zoiden rubbed his hands together. "Good enough!" He turned to his mother. "I can kill him now, right?"

Polina glanced at me and, for a brief second, I felt sympathy for her. "No," she and I said in unison.

"I ..." I tapped my chest. "*I* have to destroy the head. That is why your mother's spell didn't activate. Only *then* can you try to kill me." I deliberately sat down on the floor. "And I won't do it until you release the girl."

Zoiden glowered. "We could—"

"Torture her? Yes, yes, you could, and a very unpleasant few minutes she'd have—until I got there and ripped your minion to bits." For the first time, the man next to Vandy looked nervous. "I suppose you *could* kill her ..." I tried to ignore the gasp coming from the screen behind me. "But then I'd have no reason to cooperate with you at *all*"—I let my voice dip into my hunting register—"and I'll rip *all* of you to bits."

The witch toyed with a hair growing from a wart on her chin. "Why would you even consider doing this without coercion?"

I stared at her. "Because," I said, speaking slowly, "I value the girl's life infinitely more than I care about who is the CEO of the Zenon Corporation."

Polina looked at me blankly. "The Zenon Corporation."

I nodded at her encouragingly. "That's right. Big company? Stuffed with money? The thing you're after?" I looked over at Herr Zoiden and raised my eyebrows.

He nodded vigorously. "It's what *I'm* after," he confirmed. This worried me. Even in my short acquaintance, I had come to the conclusion that Herr Zoiden was a rather shallow individual. Obviously Polina was the power behind his unnatural rise within the company. And whereas I believed that he'd be quite satisfied with vast wealth and the ability to hobnob with movie stars, the more I thought about it, the more that didn't seem like the kind of thing Polina would care about.

Now, if this was a normal mother/son relationship, I could be persuaded that she was working diligently towards providing him with enough money that even he couldn't blow through it in his lifetime, but *that* didn't seem right either. I was again missing something.

As it turned out, so were they. We were all so caught up in what was going on, that when Vandy brought the heavy metal tray down on the medical technician's head, it caused us all to jump. As she slammed the tray down several more times off camera, Bone Cat jumped onto the table and waved the scalpel he had obviously used to surreptitiously cut Vandy's bonds.

I swung back to Polina and Zoiden and smiled. "Well, well, well. This changes everything."

Polina sneered and dipped a hand into a pocket and pulled forth a tag. With an unpleasant start, I realized that it was Vandy's Employee badge. She smiled at me. "This changes *nothing*." She gave the badge a squeeze, and Vandy's gasp of pain could be heard coming from the screen. Polina looks at me expectantly.

I sigh. "Very well. I will do it, but the girl goes free, and you do not harm her, nor engage or allow others to harm her." It's not perfect, by any stretch; witches love loopholes, but it's the best I can do. She nods.

"Swear by salt and by air, by your obligation and by your freedom." Polina snarls at this and again Vandy moans. Her son looks astonished. I cross my arms. When it comes to promises, there is almost nothing a witch considers binding. But what they *do* consider binding, binds them very tightly indeed.

You don't see Grand Witches these days. I really don't know why. For a while I had thought it was simply a case of the stories about what ultimately happens to witches gaining enough of a circulation in these more media-literate times that young people have become informed enough to not take the Deal.

However, living in America for the last couple of decades has convinced me that if one could deliver demonstrable power today, that was to be paid for in unspecified misery years later, then every incoming high school class would have a full woggle of witches by the end of September. Cynical, but there you are.

No, there must be some other reason that Grand Witches are dying out, but I, for one, cannot say that I will miss them. Any good they do in their youth is almost always overshadowed by their later actions. Polina was the first I'd encountered in a very long time, and may quite possibly be the last, for all I know. A pity, really. Back in the day I'd rather hoped that her relationship with Mr. Mortimer would keep her sane.

She glares, and then slowly vows by the Four. Although we

are in different locations, we all feel the same errant breeze gently whirl around us briefly and then die down. When it is gone, Polina is silent for several moments, and then she shrugs, and snaps her fingers. On the screen, I see Vandy toss the now visibly bent tray off to the side with a clatter. Bone Cat has found her clothing, and she quickly starts to dress. I eye the tag in Polina's hand, but the witch ostentatiously tucks it into a pocket.

"Vandy," I say. She pauses for a second, and then continues to dress without looking at me. I notice a blush working its way up her chest towards her face. "This is very important. You have to get out of here. Out of the park."

Zoiden looks like he's about to say something, but a glare from his mother shuts him up. "Forget that any of this ever happened. Forget about me. You should be all right. I have paid for your safety."

Polina looks like she has bitten into a lemon, but she nods reluctantly. I wouldn't put it past her to try to get at Vandy sometime in the future, purely out of spite, but I really can only do so much. I expect Vandy to say something, but she merely gives me an undecipherable look, and then turns and steps offscreen. Bone Cat gives me a thumbs-up and follows her. If she goes to the South entrance, she should be out of the park within ten minutes.

Eleven minutes later, I meet Polina and her son outside one of the entrances to the underground offices. Herr Zoiden is carrying a large sword slung jauntily over one shoulder. I try not to look at it. "I trust the guards will no longer try to kill me."

Zoiden waves a hand. "Taken care of. Everyone's been sent home. The last thing I want is one of those idiots wandering in and messing things up. By tomorrow most of them will be collecting unemployment."

We head to my office, and I cannot help but notice that the place does seem to be deserted. Good. Outside my door, I pause. The room must no longer be trapped, because they need me alive. I fish Xochemilchic's coin out of my pocket. "What is that?" Zoiden demands.

I hold it up and let them see it. "It's a charm your father gave me. It lets the bearer know if a mechanism is safe." I wave it at the door. "For instance, I see you've removed those lights." I open the door with more confidence than I feel, and it swings open onto an empty office. The light trap has, in fact, been removed.

Polina pushes past the two of us and strides over to the wall with the Wendigo. She gets as close as she can, impatiently shoving the fern in front of it to one side. I catch it in midair and place it on my desk. She closes her eyes and goes rigid. I idly consider killing her and her son at this point, but she again has Vandy's tag clutched tightly in her hand.

Herr Zoiden steps up. "Let me see that thing." With a show of reluctance, I hand the coin over. He grunts in surprise when he flips it over. "Where did he get this?"

I shrug. "Somewhere in Mexico, I believe." I hold out my hand, and with a smirk, Zoiden tucks it into his own pocket. "Let's just call this the first installment on my inheritance."

I open my mouth in a show of protest when Polina suddenly snaps back to life and whirls towards us. Her eyes are alight with triumph. "It's him!" She rubs her hands together. "The Zenon blood! It's here! I can *feel* it!"

I study the Wendigo. I had prepared it myself. For me, taxidermy was just one of those odd skills one sort of picks up over a millennium while living in a small community. I had set the face so that it was snarling, to show off the teeth to best effect. I'd had to order the glass eyes from a firm I'd found listed in the back of a hunting magazine. I think they were supposed to be a lion's or something. As an amusing aftereffect, I got targeted junk mail that alarmed everyone in upper management for close to a decade. I look at it afresh and I cannot see anything of Mr. Mortimer in its features. Not a thing. That is a bit of a relief.

I reach up and gently lift him off of the hook that holds him to the wall, and cradle him in my arms, remembering the first time I met him, when he did the same for me. "Let's go."

A few minutes later, we are again on the Great Green Square. Along the way, we had stopped in a maintenance shed and found some motor oil. I poured it over the head and realized that I didn't have a match.

Herr Zoiden guffawed and turned to his mother. "Just set it alight," he told her.

Polina smacked him. "*He* has to do it," she hissed.

She had her son pull a twenty-dollar bill from his wallet and hand it to me. Polina snarls at it, and the bill bursts into flame. I touch it to the oil-soaked head. It catches immediately and burns fiercely.

I don't bother with any sort of religious supplication. In all our time together, I had never heard Mr. Mortimer express any predilection towards one faith or another, and I was rather sure that his spirit had moved on long ago. Anything I said would be to the empty air. I keep an eye on Herr Zoiden, expecting him to start smoking, or itching, or displaying some form of distress, but so far I see nothing. What is Xochemilchic waiting for?

With a final soft pop, the last of the head crumbled into glowing coals. I turn. "All right, let us—" I hear a clang—and a sword erupts out through my chest. I gasp in pain—and realize that it is not as bad as I expected.

I look down and see that it is made, not of cold iron, but of black glass. Obsidian. This is not the sword that Zoiden was carrying at all. It is inscribed with glowing red pictographs that I recognize from the Lost Temple and it hurts quite a bit. Even as I scream, I realize that I have been betrayed. Xochemilchic is hijacking the spell. The disk I gave to Zoiden must have transformed into the sword and—I turn to look, and, yes, Zoiden is obviously possessed, his body rigid and his eyes glowing blue.

I see that Polina is in mid-gloat, but she is beginning to realize that something is wrong. A fresh agony rips through me as I feel the sword being twisted inside me.

"Why Are You Not Dying?" I hear Xochemilchic's voice even though he is operating Zoiden's vocal cords. "There Is No Power. I Feel No Magic!"

I sag down to my knees. Whatever is happening is, from my perspective, taking an annoyingly long time. Polina screams in fury and makes a sweeping gesture while stamping her foot upon the ground so hard that the pavement cracks. With a shriek, I see an enormous white snake, wings flailing desperately, rip free of Zoiden's body and go sailing off into the night with an agonized wail.

I hear another scream from behind me, followed by a meaty smack. Zoiden collapses on top of me. I turn my head in time to see Vandy now leaping towards Polina, brick in hand, about to strike again—and Polina crushes the tag in her hand. Vandy gives a squeak and thuds to the earth. Polina ignores her and stares down at me.

"Why *aren't* you dead," she mutters. She reaches out and smacks the sword that is still lodged within me. It really hurts. "Obsidian." Surprise washes over her ruined face. "That foolish creature used an obsidian sword—not cold iron at all! But even so ... the sword struck true, wielded by the hands of the first-born son and heir; it still should have worked. Why ..."

Her eyes go wide. She lunges toward the ashes of the Wendigo and gives a deep snort. When she turns towards me, her eyes glow red with rage. "A trick," she shrieks. *"This is not Mortimer Zenon at all!"*

She gives the blade a kick. I almost pass out. "Where is he? I *felt* him ..." She looks at me blankly. "Your office. Whatever is left of him is still in your miserable office!"

She makes a claw-like motion with her hand and drags it upwards through the air. I see Zoiden jerked to his feet. "Wake up, you moron!" She slaps him three times before he tries to pull back.

"I'm *up*, Ma," he mumbles. She releases him and he drops to the ground. But he is awake now, and staggers to his feet under his own power. His mother grabs his arm. "Come! I must find the remains of your father before something *else* happens, and I need *you* to get me in." She looks at me with annoyance. Zoiden looks back at Vandy and myself. "They're not going anywhere, and he will not die," Polina says. "As for the girl ..." She holds the crumpled nametag down before my face. "She is not dead *yet*," she snarls, and they hurry off.

I try to push the sword back out, but the dratted thing appears to be lodged on something inside me. I grit my teeth and try to lower myself to the pavement to *push* it out—but as soon as the tip of the blade touches the ground, a jolt of what feels like electricity arcs through it. I scream, I think. Things blur a bit.

I feel Bone Cat patting my arm. When I open my eyes, I see him dancing from one foot to the other, frantic with worry. "Can I trouble you to pull this sword out?" I rasp.

"I'll try," he says. "But I don't think that's a good idea, boss."

He bounces back and I feel him grab the sword—and another burst of lightning burns through me.

"Yeah, that's what I thought," he mutters. "This is all tied together with the very nature of the land or something. I'm a *part* of it, y'know? I ... I can't affect the outcome."

"That's disappointing," I whisper. "How is Vandy?"

Bone Cat hesitates long enough that my heart sinks even further. "Not good. That dame did a real number on her."

"Damn it, why did you let her come back? She was *free*!"

Bone Cat wrings his paws in distress. "I *had* to," he whines.

"Got a phone call." Vandy's voice is weak, but cognizant. With a terrible effort, I manage to swing myself around. Bone Cat was being uncharacteristically delicate. Vandy looks like a doll that has been crushed by a freakishly strong eight-year-old. She's looking at me in such a way that I can tell that she's in shock, which is a small blessing. Then her words penetrate.

"You got a what?"

"Got a phone call," Vandy says again. Her voice is beginning to drift into a dreamy cadence. "Her name was Celeste. Said she was a friend of yours. She seemed nice."

I look at Bone Cat, who nods. "It was her, all right."

"She is a ... colleague."

"Thass cool. Figured she was a magic person 'cause she had my number. Didn't even give *you* my number, Sheriff. Wanted to give you my number. Wanted you to call me ..."

"Vandy!" It hurts to shout, but she is starting to drift. "What did Celeste say?"

She rolls her head so she is looking at me. "She said I wouldn't understand it. She said ..." Suddenly Vandy shudders and her eyes go blank. Her mouth opens and Celeste's voice rolls forth.

"The witch bargained away her youth in order to live. She will do anything to save herself. Zenonland is a unique Place of Power. If she gains control of it, ownership of it, she will have the right to bargain *with it. To legally surrender it. It and everyone inside it. For a place this powerful, for that many innocent souls, she could ask for eternal youth, riches, power—whatever she desires.*

"The balance of the worlds seen and unseen would be thrown into chaos. You must deny her this. By whatever means necessary.

"I am on my way."

Vandy's head slumped to the ground. Her eyes opened and I saw that she was herself again. "She said you had to know," she whispered.

Ah. This made things much clearer. No wonder Polina was so desperate to carry through with this scheme. No wonder Xochemilchic had betrayed me to try to horn in on it. I smiled sourly. Magic is a filthy business. Oh, Polina may have indeed had "other plans," but once she had committed to this spell, all other venues were closed to her until it was either completed or definitively thwarted.

I gave a series of painful wheezes. Bone Cat stares at me. "Are ... are you *laughing*? What the hell is so funny?"

"A couple of things. If Xochemilchic had used the *iron* sword,

I would have died, and the witch would have lost everything. But I am still alive."

Bone Cat looked at me. "Ha ha?"

"There's more. The witch is *still* wrong," I whispered. "She truly did sense the Zenon blood in my office. But it was not from Mr. Mortimer, it was from the head of *Bartholomew* Zenon, his brother. In the freezer? Right *below* the Wendigo?" Bone Cat stares at me and nods slowly. He still doesn't seem to find it as funny as I do.

I wonder what will happen when they force me to destroy poor Mr. Bartholomew's head? It's been quite a while, but it is not inconceivable that the actual specter of Mr. Bartholomew will return, once his remains are removed from their resting place. But I fancy that will be someone else's problem, as I fear that neither Vandy nor myself will survive. Polina will use the correct sword this time. Oh, they swore to not kill Vandy, but that leaves a lot of wiggle room, and I will not expect Polina to be terribly concerned about her comfort, except negatively.

I look at Vandy again and my heart breaks. The damage is too severe—and it was inflicted by magic. Magical damage is forever tainted by the malice behind it, and under normal circumstances, never heals properly—if at all. I crawl closer, until our faces almost touch. Vandy is breathing heavily, and there is a liquid quality to it that I try to ignore. I gently touch her face and her eyes open. When she recognizes me, they soften with a happiness that fills me with fury. "It's really bad, isn't it?" Her voice is soft.

"Yes. It is really bad."

"See," she says softly. "That's what I found so cool about you. You never lied to me. About anything. That makes you so special ..." A tear wells up and rolls down her face. "I don't want to die. I mean, I haven't even gone to Zenonland Tokyo."

"Me neither." I look at her and I feel my heart freeze. No. I should not allow myself ... "You don't have to die," I say hesitantly. "I can ... I can turn you."

She looks at me so blankly that I feel a rush of terror that she has already died. "Which way?" she finally asks. I roll my eyes.

"I can make you the same as me. But ... it will not be pleasant."

"Will it be worse than dying?"

"I couldn't say. I've never died." I paused. "Maybe."

"But I'm all fucked up."

"You will be healed." I looked at her wounds. "Almost instantly."

"Soon enough that I can punch that bitch in the face?"

"I'm rather counting on it."

She closes her eyes and a small shudder runs through her. I cannot tell if she is dying or laughing. "Let's do it."

"This will be ... unpleasant." I hesitate. "You will hate me for what I am about to do to you. You will hate me so much that you will kill me yourself." Her eyes widen, and I put a finger to her lips. "And that's all right," I say gently. "That's how it is with our kind. I killed the one who created me, and now it is my turn, and I want you to know that saving you—Saving you will make it all worth it."

I reach out and hold her head in my hands, and ... there's nothing. I'm looking for fear, something I can latch onto so as to begin, but there's nothing. She trusts me completely. That won't do at all. "Vandy, I ..." She looks at me and her eyes are full of acceptance and what I assume is her idea of love. "This is going to hurt."

She closes her eyes. "I figured."

"Everything you have ever known is going to be different."

She smiles adorably. "That happened when I met you."

We don't have time for this. I was trying to ease myself into it, but I am afraid there is no kind way to do this, which is why I never have. I grip her head hard, allowing my claws to prick her skin. This elicits a sharp intake of breath and her eyes fly open, and she sees my true face, the one without glamour, without any disguise, the one designed to help me feed—

And she screams and the fear erupts from her, and there is so very much of it. I pry my way in and amplify every fear I can find, ripping them from their hiding places in her conscious mind. With a sneer I smash open her subconscious, exposing the things she dreams about and noisily begin sucking them dry, while continuing to burrow downwards, snapping up the fears that try to flee before me. I encounter her ego, and it is strong, very strong, and when it begins to buckle, the fears I find here are dark and sweet, flavored with horror and a growing despair. Her body is thrashing now. She would be screaming, but she has run out of air and is too terrified to suck in more.

The growing fear of suffocation, one of the most ancient of fears, strong and primal, allows me to ride down, down, down into the realm of her id, where the animal fears are buried. I uproot them one by one, cracking them free and pulling them into myself, but only with a great effort. I am choked and bloated with her fears now. Normally I would have to skim the fear from dozens of people to collect this much, but a human is a machine made of meat that is driven by fears when you get down close to it, and I'm so close that she can feel my breath hot upon her neck.

When I kill a person via fear, it's more of a riding roughshod over their heart and mind. I extract the important things in such a way that it does a lot of damage on the way out. With Vandy, I scour every nook and cranny of her soul until I discover that last little kernel of self, the brave little bit that believes it's immortal, because we cannot allow ourselves to believe otherwise, and I enfold it and prepare to crush it out of existence, and that last little bit feels my claws around its throat and it finally *knows* that this is it: The final death from which there is no return. And, with a small whimper, it surrenders, and by doing so ... moves beyond the Fear of Death.

And then ... then I hold her. Everything that motivates and shapes and makes Vandy the person I know and would recognize no matter how many times she incarnates—I hold that within myself until I can hold it no longer—without consuming a drop —while her mind and body begin to dissolve from within, because with absolutely no fear, a being has no purpose. No structure. No reason to go on ...

And then ...

And then, with a great exhalation, I release it all back. Every iota that I have stolen goes roaring back where it belongs ... and finds that it no longer quite fits, and to *make* it fit, she *changes*. She desperately tries to reassemble herself, cramming everything that is Vandy back where it belongs, back where it needs to be, back holding her mind and self in place, and she begins to realize, even as the last wisps of her fears slide back into place, that it is not enough. That it will *never* be enough, and that her body now knows how to harvest more. Eagerly she attempts to drain it from me, but against me her will splashes like a wave against a granite mountain, and she pulls back into herself—

And collapses to the pavement, gasping, and I am no longer alone in the world. She spasms in place, and for a moment I think she will vomit, but she sees me, and a look of rage fills her face. With a snarl, she smashes her hand across my face, and a newly grown set of claws rip furrows into my flesh. I expected that.

"What did you *do* to me," she screams. In a single flowing movement, she is on her feet, and she draws her leg back to deliver a kick ... And she remembers that her arms and legs were shattered. She staggers slightly as she looks at them in wonder. She stares at her hands, and seemingly without effort, they again form into elegant, needle-tipped claws.

While she is staring at them, I blink, and realize that what can only be Death stands behind her. I can see it clearly now. It looks confused and rather annoyed as it reluctantly pulls a great black sword out from her body. Vandy gasps as it pulls free with a final snap and drops to her knees. With a growing fury, the huge dark figure slowly turns and looks down at me. It gives a great smile of anticipation and that terrible sword swings upwards ...

I focus back on Vandy as she remembers that I am here, and again the memory of what I did to her burns through her brain. She snarls, and I see her teeth lengthen most alarmingly.

This is the way it is with us. It is the only truth about our kind that we are born knowing. That the one who created us must be punished for doing something so horrific.

I only faintly remember the carnage after my mysterious girl found me bleeding and torn on that mountain road so long ago and transformed me. She had never liked being what she was, and I am convinced that she had just been waiting for the chance to pass it along. I have always wondered if she had somehow set those bears upon me, but I never examined the circumstances too closely, as, long afterwards, I wanted to remember her fondly.

And now it is my turn. I had known this would happen, but Polina and Zoiden will not be expecting her. More important, they have no hold over her now. The spell using her nametag may be potent, Polina is certainly one of the most powerful witches I have ever known, but it cannot stop her now. Vandy is no longer the person that tag represents. In any sense of the word. After she has drained them of their fears and left them as mere husks, she will be free. Free to wander the world as I no longer could.

Vandy screams one final time and comes at me.

I only wish—

And suddenly, Bone Cat is there. He plants himself before her and the roar he gives forth almost splits his head in half. The wind of its fury pushes her back, and suddenly, I see a glimmer of sanity in her eyes. Bone Cat now leaps forward, latches himself onto the lapels of her shirt, and gives her a huge, sloppy kiss. "Happy birthday, toots!"

She spends several entertaining minutes spinning about, trying to dislodge him, but it's almost impossible to do, as I can well attest. Even if you sweep your hand through him, scattering his bones, they simply tumble back into place. However, this does seem to serve as an excellent way to burn off her initial fog of rage and betrayal, and eventually she is standing there, panting, for a moment more annoyed at Bone Cat than she is at me.

"You okay?" Bone Cat peers closely at her face, and then nods in satisfaction. He then turns towards me. "I think she's as sane as she ever was, boss."

This rouses Vandy, and she looks at me. "I *hate* you," she hisses.

Bone Cat shrugs. "Maybe even saner."

"Thank you," I tell him.

He snorts. "Hey. I told you, I got no idea what would happen to me if you die."

I'm at a loss, frankly. I hadn't expected to be still alive this long after Vandy had come into her power. Death, if that is what I saw, has vanished. As I am not ripped into bits, I can concentrate on other things. Like this sword sticking through me. I jerk a thumb towards my back. "A little help here?"

Vandy strides over and glowers down at me. "Does that hurt?"

"Yes."

She gives the sword a kick. "Does that hurt *more*?"

"Oh, yes."

She leans in. "Why shouldn't I make it hurt *even more*?"

"Because then you will be assisting the people who made it necessary for me to do this to you. Remember them?" A legitimate question. One of the horrible things about the process that Vandy has just undergone, as I remember it, was that, subjectively, it seemed to go on for days, and when one undergoes an experience like this, a lot of things about your life that seemed *very important* suddenly seem rather trivial or, indeed, you dismiss them from your memory altogether.

However, Zoiden and his mother are apparently unpleasant enough that their memory can still inspire action, as Vandy now reaches around, plants her foot on my back, and yanks the sword out.

With a groan, I roll over onto my back, and we look at each other. She examines the sword, and obviously considers reburying it in my chest. I am honestly not sure what would have happened if Polina and Zoiden had not chosen that moment to reappear. Zoiden is carrying the canister that contains Mr. Bartholomew's head, and they are arguing fiercely, which explains why they don't see us until they are rather close.

Once they *do* see us, Polina wastes no time, but makes a show of holding up the nametag, and visibly crushes it. Vandy screams and drops to her knees, and I can hear her bones cracking. Polina laughs and comes close enough that when I pick up her magical iron sword and hurl it at her, it easily passes through her midriff, stopping her cold. Zoiden takes one look and dashes off, proving himself smarter than I had given him credit for.

Meanwhile, Vandy pulls herself together, rubs her hands along her arms and laughs in wonder. She then flows towards the witch, grabs her face in one hand, and secures her hands in the other. She looks back at me. "So how does this work?"

I find I can stand up and walk over beside her. "Ah. First you want to find out what they're afraid of." Vandy looks at Polina and sees her as I do.

Oh, there are many things swirling about her. I'm sure that in time, Vandy would be able to pick her apart without problem, but I remember the confusion of my first few times.

"Polina here is easy." Vandy has very sensibly covered her mouth, but the witch's eyes are on me now, silently pleading. "Polina is afraid of death. There. Did you see how that spiked there? This is a very common fear, and you might think it's the best one to start with, but it is *so* easy, that you really should go beyond it."

I lean in and address Polina directly. "You see, Grand Witches are not really afraid of death, per se. She has seen far too much of that, haven't you, my dear? No, Polina is afraid of what is waiting for her *after* death, and well she should be." And yes, the fears of what must await her take shape and they are very rich indeed. Vandy eagerly reaches out and snaps at them, and the witch struggles in her grip. It's quite adorable, but—

"If I may," I murmur. I step in and begin to enfold her fields within mine. Vandy rears back with a snarl and shakes me off. I can feel her attempting to harm me, but the combination of inexperience and extreme hunger neutralize her efforts. I back off. Of course she's still too traumatized to allow me to get too close. "Sorry about that."

"Don't. Touch. Me."

"It will not happen again."

Thus, I stand back and merely watch. It is very frustrating. I see what she is doing wrong, but on the other hand, I had no one to teach me and I did not starve, so I bite my lip and wait.

There is a bit of trial and error, but she gets it eventually, and bites down just so. Beneath her hand, Polina screams and her eyes roll upward into her head. My word, the girl is a natural. A bit too enthusiastic, in my opinion, but it *is* her first time, and the change will have left her ravenous. This particular fear is so deep and all-consuming that even from where I am, I am easily able to siphon off some of the ancillary fears and regrets that come boiling off the witch without interfering with Vandy's meal. I catch her eye, and I can see that she is aware of what I am doing ... and the pleasure to be found while feeding so suffuses her that she does not mind. I have never dined together with someone. I can see why it is such a popular bonding experience.

All too soon the witch goes limp. Her soul makes a frantic last-second effort to escape, startling Vandy, but I ensnare it and present it to her for examination. A witch's soul tends to be different from other souls, and Polina remains textbook to the last. Hers is an old soul. One of those that has gone around again and again and again enough times that it thought it could game the system, as it were. I point out features of interest, and Vandy is an excellent student. Polina's soul's efforts to escape become ever more frantic.

"So what do we do with them?" Vandy asks.

"Normally we just release them. We could even release Polina here and give her a sporting chance." From within my grasp, the soul begs for freedom. I close my metaphorical grip a little tighter.

"However, she hurt you." I shrug. "And myself, and in cases like this, I have found it best to make an example."

A rough voice from behind us chuckles, causing Vandy to almost fall over from where she is kneeling. "And I honor and appreciate you for this, *Tovarishch*."

We turn, and Vandy gasps at the sight of an ancient black bear, easily ten feet tall, even though he is still on all fours. He is wearing an eye patch. I had been expecting the old fellow, and politely bow, as does he.

"Vandy, this is the late Madame Polina Urakhov's familiar." We had met once and had a very convivial conversation during a particularly portentous eclipse in Krakow.

The bear sits with a grunt. "Is true. Was very rough job. Will not be sorry to see it end. My little Polina was a very busy girl." He scratches his belly with huge black claws as he frankly examines Vandy. "So you are new *Dehazzaki*? There has never been two of you in the world at the same time before. A new thing." He grins. "Sometimes a new thing is good. Sometimes it is bad. But at least this one will be interesting I think."

A light dawns. "*You* told Polina about me. About my weaknesses."

The bear actually looks embarrassed. "Is true. But she wanted the knowledge, and giving her knowledge was part of the job. Until recently she was not willing to pay the price to get it.

"Was not easy to find, but everything is written down *some-where*. Am not proud of this; you always treated her with respect, and she did not reciprocate. I, for one, will acknowledge her sins against you and, as her Familiar, declare the accounts now balanced."

"Thank you."

He shrugs. "She was very desperate to avoid Grandfather Death, and I wanted to help her. It was all I ever wanted to do, but ..." He gave a great sigh that caused him to slump. "But she never listened to my advice. Even when it went against our Master's interests."

Vandy tentatively raised a finger. "Your ... Master?"

The bear raised a paw. "Don't worry about me, little *Dehaz-zaki*, the Master, he expects us to plot and scheme against him. It makes our failure all the sweeter." He leaned in and lowered his voice. "He is a total dick."

He is silent for a long moment and then gestures to the soul in my hand and sighs. "But now we must be off. He will be waiting, and we have very far to go."

I extend my hand, and the bear delicately plucks Polina's essence from my grasp with the tips of his claws. "Hello, my little girl. You never listened to me, and now? Now it is too late." With that he opened his jaws, wide, wider, impossibly wide and stuffed the frantically straining soul within, before closing them with a wet snap. He then clambered slowly to his feet and bows to us one last time. "I doubt we will meet again," he says with a shrug, and then pads silently off into the night.

Bone Cat leaps off my shoulder and hollers after him. "Don't forget to chew!"

Vandy looks at me. "How many *other* monster women who want to kill you are out there?"

"At the moment, I believe you're the only one left." I clap my hands. "But enough dawdling! We still have Herr Zoiden to deal with."

Vandy gasps and looks around. "Oh, he took off while we were ... feeding."

I held up a finger. "True. But the *way* he took off will take him the long way around to the exit." I extend my hand. "An excellent chance to learn how to hunt." Vandy stares at my hand, and then steps back.

"I ... I can't." She shakes her head. "What you did to me. I don't want to touch you anymore." I drop my hand.

Oh, there is much I could say, but Vandy is an intelligent girl. It is not logic that is at work here. "I understand," I say gently. "And afterwards, you will be free to do as you wish, but for tonight, at least, please allow me to teach you what you need."

She stares down at the ground and balls her fists, but then a thought suddenly hits her, and the look she gives me allows me to hope. "Can I fly?"

"Fly?" I laugh. "Flying is the *least* of what we can do." And this time, when I extend my hand, she takes it. Reluctantly, but firmly. I glance towards Bone Cat. I *will* teach her to hunt properly, but our remaining time is short enough that I will not eschew a little help.

Bone Cat closes his eyes. "The *Sorcerer's Breakfast* ride." And we are off.

Herr Zoiden provides a better hunt than I had foreseen. He has learned how to dampen his emotions. His mother's training, no doubt. He makes excellent use of cover, knows how to double back, and can move in complete silence. In fact, he actually makes it past the gate.

But then he allows himself to succumb to an inclination to gloat, while I hang helpless just within the boundary. Thus, it is so very satisfactory when Vandy stoops and takes him like an eagle taking a hare. It is very well done, and she graciously drags him back inside, where we have another lovely, shared breakfast.

We then have a final exercise. As I float overhead, Vandy tracks down the late Madam Polina's scalpel-wielding assistant all by herself. It's a very good first solo assignment, as he appears to be slightly concussed, but there is no denying that she does an excellent job, and even manages to snag the fellow's spirit before it can fly free. The girl has the knack, and no mistake.

I then escort her to the offices. A quick search shows that

Herr Zoiden did, in fact, send all of the employees home. Ah, hubris. We slip into the late Mr. Donovan's office, and using the backdoor codes that I installed a decade ago (I really do try to keep up on these things), send out a mass email under the imprimatur of the Head of Park Security-Night Division (which if you go by the Last Man Standing rule, I technically am), informing the new security staff that they are all fired.

I then send a note to HR telling them that they will have to refill those positions rather quickly. I strongly recommend that they work with the AAAApex Employment Agency. I also send out an emergency notification that we need night watchmen pulled from the corporate offices and nearby hotels immediately, because, at the moment, the park is deserted.

Before these worthies show up, we stow the bodies, I explain to Vandy that the peculiar feeling she is getting when facing the East is indicative that the sun is soon to rise, and that we must hide.

She sits abruptly, and actually cries for a bit. I can understand, even after all this time. Losing the Sun is perhaps the most difficult thing creatures like us have to face in the beginning. It is deeply ingrained in humanity that the sunshine represents purity, light, and safety from the things of the night. It is very hard to accept that you will never see the sun again, nor walk in its light, and that you are now one of the things that it is protecting humanity from.

And then, still slightly overstuffed, we stroll together down Main Street, past the closed shops and arcades. "What happens now?"

"I have a few resting places that have not been found. I will show you one"—I raise a finger before she can speak—"and then I shall go to another, and we shall sleep."

"I meant tomorrow."

"I know. But we have done as much as we can tonight. A lot has happened. As for everything else, we shall have to deal with that as we go. Remember, if nothing else, you now have time."

She nods and we say nothing more. I think about offering her my arm, but quickly quash the impulse.

When we come to the resting place I have selected for her, she gives me a skeptical look, and I can understand her reluctance. It is the pedestal that supports the statue of Mr. Bartholomew and Preston Platypus. An art deco façade of polished jasper and brass that appears quite solid, but it is, like so much of the rest of the park, hollow within. I have to teach her how to dematerialize while still retaining enough cohesion that she can flow through the small grate I had placed there when the pedestal was laid, but as in everything, she grasps the idea quickly, and she vanishes within. Shortly, I hear her close the light-blocking hatch.

I then head to my own chosen spot. I could fly, the repeated meals have done wonders as regards to my injuries, but I am still a bit sore, and chose to walk. Plus, there is enough time that I can indulge my need to talk. Of course, it's only Bone Cat, but he's better than nothing.

"Wow. Worst first date ever, boss."

—Or so I'd foolishly assumed. "It was what I had to do. The only thing I cared about was keeping her alive."

"Did you?"

An annoyingly germane question. I'm not actually sure if I— we—count as a species of undead, or if we are merely differently alive. "We can still talk to her without having to use a Ouija board, so I will consider this a win."

We came to tonight's resting place. I don't care for this one as much, as it's located under one of the roller coasters, but today, I believe I will be able to sleep through anything.

As I settle in, I feel Bone Cat curl up in the crook of my arm. I am almost asleep, when he murmurs, "You know, I still don't get it. If he wasn't that Wendigo shitheel, then what *did* happen to Mortimer Zenon?"

My last cogent thought is: *That is a very good question.*

CHAPTER TWELVE

When we awake the next evening, Vandy complains of being a bit stiff. I assure her that this has nothing to do with sleeping underneath a statue but is due more to all of the physiological changes she went through yesterday. Mentally, she will also still be coming to terms with becoming an apex predator, and the restrictions that will apply to her.

It is obvious that Vandy still hates me for what I did to her. She tolerates my presence, because she is intelligent enough to realize that I still have things to teach her, but it is an ongoing struggle for her to stay civil. In a day or two, a week at the most, I expect she will strike out on her own. I hope I can teach her enough before that happens. I wish we could discuss it, but I doubt there will be enough time before she leaves.

Neither of us is particularly hungry, what with yesterday's feast, so I try to ameliorate the annoyance she is feeling by showing her some of the more outré aspects of Zenonland, things that even the most rabid devotees of the park never suspected. This certainly puts her in a better mood.

After the park closes, we head towards the offices. Vandy would prefer to fly, but she's new to it, and would fly from dusk to dawn if she could. I explain that continuing to mingle with people is important, especially people we would see every day, like the employees of the Night Shift. There is no denying that we are different from humanity, but as long as we can *act* normal, most people won't *allow* themselves to see just how different we are. Vandy has an advantage in that her true form is still identical to what it was when she was still one hundred percent human. It will be a century or two before she will have to rely upon glamours to walk safely amongst them as I do.

As far as park-related gossip goes, the employees today are spoilt for choice. There were a number of things that we were not able to clean up before we had to retire, and thus the Morning Crew found themselves presented with a few exciting challenges, such as unexplained bullet holes, swathes of steel netting, and discarded weapons. The local police were called in, but there really was nothing else to find.

The park managers had been frantic, as it appeared that the entire security force that had recently been hired through questionable methods, had just as summarily been fired sometime last night.

But the employees here *are* professionals and in its own way, this *is* show business, and so people fill in where they must, and the job gets done. Meanwhile, pleading phone calls to former staff and employment agencies were made and with only a half an hour's delay, the gates are opened, and the show goes on.

Many, many people want to talk to Herr Zoiden about the hirings and the firings and a number of other irregularities as well. But it appears that the new CEO is missing, and the remainder of the board are acting as if they had awakened from some sort of dream. They are falling over each other to declare that *other* members must have voted him in, as they certainly would not have, and apparently both the SEC as well as the FBI have taken an interest and paid them the first of no doubt many visits.

While I am sure that their recent actions in this regard were the direct result of the late Madam Urakhov's influence, the general consensus seems to be that upper management was overdue for a bit of legal scrutiny.

Herr Zoiden's replacement has not yet been selected, obviously, but the smart money says that it will be my old friend, Mr. Shulman, who had already been recalled to the states after Mr. Donovan's death. I actually have a rather large chunk of Zenon stock in my portfolio, thanks to Cormangwöld. I usually don't activate my proxies, but, in this case, I will cheerfully throw them behind Mr. Shulman. I know I can work with him, and it will be a pleasure to see him again.

Vandy does very well, overall. She has a few rough moments dealing with crowds, but I know when to remove her to more remote locations so that she can recover. The only time she breaks down is when we stroll past her old pin kiosk. When she failed to report for work, someone else was slotted into that particular position without fuss, and as far as this tiny portion of the world is concerned, it is as if she had never been. She sits atop the Mountain of Madness and has herself a good cry, and I am relieved and pleasantly surprised when she rejoins me of her own volition.

Afterwards we sit at an empty table, a plate of untouched beignets between us, and she makes a list of the things she will have to deal with. We discuss whether she should keep her apartment, and how she will renew her driver's license, and should she go back to school, and what will she tell her family, and she begins to truly comprehend the thousand and one things that are *different* now, and that will stay different forever.

I give her Miss Dawkson's contact information and explain how she can help. I feel a great sadness, because I desperately wish to help her more than I will be able to. While I certainly had no mentor when I made the transformation so many years ago, it is a fundamentally different world now. Monitored, interconnected, and wired to an extent that would have been inconceivable even a century ago.

Vandy may be a child of this age, but for creatures like us, the interconnected nature of the times changes *everything*. So much of what we do is best done under cover of the darkness, away from the eyes of an uncomprehending humanity. My time here was a great gift. As Mr. Mortimer had predicted, it gave me a chance to learn, while being safely cocooned from the everyday world. Ideally, Vandy should stay here as well, learning how to deal with the world from a place of safety, but I know that it is too soon for her to able to stand being so close to me. Soon enough, she will leave. Possibly tonight.

Thus I make an effort to make the last chore of the evening, the disposal of the bodies, as magical as possible. Besides, we have other business to settle as well. First, of course, we invade the Lost Temple. While we progress, I explain to Vandy what happened. We are occasionally interrupted by a bit of minor seismic activity, and a few ghostly illusions attempt to scare us off, but all too soon we are standing before the main altar.

I fully expect that I will have to invoke the old god, drag him out of hiding by his ethereal ear, as it were, but Xochemilchic surprises me. There is a burst of thunder, and he manifests before us. No illusion this, he is here, battered looking, and his feathers a bit threadbare. But he straightens up and regards us with a roll and snap of his faded blue wings.

When he speaks, there is defeat in his voice, but also a determination to go out with dignity. "I Am Xochemilchic. I Wished To Extend My Miserable Life, But I Have Failed. I Will Not Crawl, Nor Beg For Mercy. I Will Give Neither Excuses, Nor Spin Fanciful Might-Have-Beens. I Have Betrayed My Benefactor, And Thus Deserve No Mercy." And then he dips his great head down and waits.

I reach out and find ancient fears so cold that I pull back and am surprised that a part of me does not snap off and remain behind. I glance at Vandy, and she is staring at him in wonder.

She then looks at me, and nods, agreeing with the decision I had made before we came here. I take a breath, and we both go to one knee and bow our heads. I reach behind me and haul the body of the medical technician forward, tossing it before us. "I give thanks to the Great Serpent, whose actions have saved us, as well as so many others."

Xochemilchic's head snaps up in astonishment. I can feel him tentatively reach out and he feels the truth behind my words. "Are You People *Loco*? I Tried To *Kill* You."

I shrug. "Because you interfered when and how you did, I did not die and the land was not claimed by the witch. If you had not done this, then the world would be a different and more terrible place."

"But ... I Did Not Intend ..."

I smile. "We are all but tools in the hands of greater powers."

Xochemilchic regards me for a moment, and then swings his head toward Vandy. "He Thinks He Is A Lot More Clever Than He Really Is."

"And probably more merciful than he should be," she replied tartly.

Xochemilchic recoils as if she had smacked him on the snout. "I Can See That I'm Going To Have To Be *Careful* Around You," he mutters. "Let Us Start Again."

He straightens up and his voice fills the temple. "In Recognition Of You Saving My Servant ..." Servant? Wait. Does he mean *me*? That wretched reptile! "I Will Grant You ... A Boon."

A boon? Now I am doubly annoyed. I'd had to appear to truckle to him for over a decade before *I'd* earned a boon of his choosing—and that had simply been the ability to appreciate American jazz music.

Xochemilchic rises to his full height, and suddenly his eyes glow so brightly that Vandy is caught in the beams. "YOU WILL ALWAYS BE HAPPY WITH YOUR HAIR," he roars. When he finishes, there is a final crash of thunder, and when the smoke clears, Xochemilchic, and the body of the technician, have vanished.

I turn to find Vandy staring at herself in a polished stone. Her hair looks fabulous. "Sorry about that," I said. "I don't think he really understands what people want any more."

Vandy gingerly touches her hair and smiles. "That's what you think, eh?" She shakes her head, and her hair flows gracefully from side to side. "I'm not surprised."

We bring the remains of Polina to Cormangwöld. She often complains that people today tend to run to fat, which gives her indigestion. The witch's remains, on the other hand, are rather gaunt, and should be a rare treat indeed. Vandy is scandalized at my affixing a cheap, gift shop princess hat onto the old witch's corpse, but I was determined to keep the dragon in as good a mood as possible. When we enter, it was obvious that this would be an uphill battle.

Cormangwöld is still sitting upon her nest, but every few minutes, she levers herself to her feet and paces back and forth across the room, smoke billowing from her nose and mouth, before she realizes what she was doing and settles back down atop her eggs. The heap of books is still there, but large patches of them are shredded, and I cannot help but notice that the titles I see now consist mostly of militaristic space fantasy and police procedurals. Not a good sign.

When she becomes aware of us, her agitation seems to fade slightly, and she swings her long neck down to examine the two of us. Vandy is obviously awestruck, which seems to please her. "There are two of you now," she says. "How interesting." She then blows out a stream of flame. "The music has not yet returned."

"I hope to have that rectified very soon. In fact, it's my next stop." I hold up Polina. "But in the meantime, I hope this will tide you over. This is the witch responsible for all the trouble." I toss her at Cormangwöld's feet. "I'll let you examine her and figure out what she was planning."

The dragon stares at the late witch and I can sense her calling forth her ability to examine mystical connections. Her breath hisses as she begins to see the scope of the late Polina's plans.

"Someone," she says slowly, as she lifts Polina up, "*someone* has been a very *naughty* little princess indeed." Her tongue flickers around her jaws. "Oh, you *want* to be punished, you say?" Suddenly she freezes, and glances towards Vandy and myself. "If you'll excuse us?"

Without another word, I snag Vandy's arm and drag her out. We can hear the dragon purring, "Don't act so surprised, Your Highness, you weren't on any *mercy* mission *this* time ..." The doors close behind us with a gentle boom.

Vandy stares at the door, then looks at me, an appalled expression upon her face. I raise my hands. "Even the fantastic occasionally need fantasies."

She massages her brow. "So ... this memory erase thing. Can I do that to myself?"

The subsequent discussion almost has the feel of old times and lasts until we come to the Happiness Machine. I knock but receive no reply. I knock harder and harder, until I am pounding upon the door. Eventually we simply break it down. Gremlins are lying about everywhere amongst shattered glassware and broken machinery. Initially I fear for the worst, but after examining a few of them, I realize that they are simply drunk out of their minds.

Eventually we find Punch-Press, almost completely submerged in a large tankard filled with a purple slurry that smells like beer that had been brewed from cat litter. I fish him out and spend several minutes slapping him against a table like a particularly inert lump of bread dough, until he finally cracks open an eye and looks up at us. "Hello, Old Tool. The hell are *you* still doin' here? Come to celebrate?"

Bone Cat peers down at him. "Celebrate what?"

"The asshat in charge is dead. The Prognosticator sez that everything is going to be great!" He hiccupped. "Mostly."

"Then I suppose that I have brought the perfect treat to the party." I dump Zoiden on the floor. "May I present the aforementioned asshat, the ex-CEO of the Zenon Corporation."

Punch-Press examines the body and gives a huge belch of approval. "Nice." He yells to the other gremlins lying about, "Time to brew up another batch of Number Three Sweet!" A ragged chorus of cheers fills the room, but none of the little figures stir.

"So, what are you doing? When will the Happiness Machine be repaired?"

The Chief rolls his eyes. "There ain't no rush. We been working on the deep down stuff first. I figure we'll be back up in ..." He shrugs. "A week. No more than two. Depends if we can get the parts."

I think of Orsynn, expanding the scope of his taste for human flesh, of my own irritability, and of the dragon, sliding closer towards a murderous rage by the minute, and of the gremlins' own unnatural inertia.

I lean in and give Punch-Press a *look*. "If you don't have enough duplicate parts already squirreled away to rebuild this thing from scratch, then you're no better than a gaggle of tinker fairies." The entire room gasps in outrage. I poke him in the chest. "You have twenty-four hours." I close my teeth with a snap less than an inch from his nose. "Or *else*."

Every gremlin present screams in anguish. It sounds like a calliope being pushed down a set of stairs, and then every one of them leaps up and runs off yelling orders at one another. Even before we leave the room, the floor begins to vibrate, and we can hear the boom and roar of buried machines starting back up.

"Marvelous creatures," I explain to Vandy as we head towards the exit. "But they work best under a deadline. The more impossible the deadline, the better they do. You will see. Tomorrow, we will return and—"

"*You* won't." We turn and there is an ancient gremlin.

"This is Lynch-Pin," I explain. "The Matriarch here. She has chosen the onerous task of being this colony's spiritual leader, denying herself the usual gremlin retirement." When they get to a certain age and status, gremlins are sealed into a mechanism where they are allowed to do nothing else but perform simple, repetitive actions until they die. It's their idea of paradise on earth. I try not to judge.

Lynch-Pin ignores Vandy, and stares at me intensely. "You will not be here, Old Tool."

Her tone makes me shiver. A very unusual feeling. "Surely things have changed. The witch is dead, as is her son."

She shrugs. "True. But we ran the Prognosticator this morning. Within twenty-four hours, you will be gone. Settle your affairs, Old Tool."

Bone Cat steps up. "What'll happen to me?"

Lynch-Pin stares at him and gently shrugs. "Like we care."

We go outside while trying to ignore Lynch-Pin's shrieking and Bone Cat's roars. I ponder the immediate future and turn towards Vandy. "I think I'm going to be ... gone soon."

She looks wary. "I thought you couldn't leave the park."

"It is true that *le monstre* cannot leave Zenon property." We both jump in surprise, and there is Celeste. She does not like to travel much at her age, but she has done so, and has not even taken the time to properly rest before coming to the park. She is in a wheelchair, which is a new development.

It is being pushed by her oldest granddaughter, Lunette, whom, I see, is visibly pregnant. Bone Cat skips out of the Happiness Machine, gives a whoop of greeting, and leaps into Celeste's lap, where she strokes his earbones.

I bow. "Madame, may I present my ..." I consider my words carefully. "My apprentice, Vandy. Vandy, this is Madame Celeste L'Enfant de Lune. She is the Moon Queen of New Orleans, and this is her granddaughter, Madame Lunette L'Enfant."

Vandy stepped back. "I am not your apprentice." She points

to Celeste. "You're the one who phoned me. How did you get my number?"

Celeste waves this question away as the triviality it is. She regards me through slitted eyes. "So, my friend. Do you know what you have done by killing this particular Grumbly Witch?"

I blink. Celeste is not being facetious. "What do you mean? Madam Urakhov was not the real Grumbly Witch. ... Was she?"

Celeste shook her head. "There is always a Grumbly Witch loose in the world, though different people call it different things; a creature determined to precipitate an unnatural disaster for purely selfish ends. This time, it was simply your Madame Urakhov's role, and she came terribly close to fulfilling it, and so, for a brief time, the Grumbly Witch was very real indeed." Celeste sat back and gave a satisfied smile as she regarded me. "And you had no clue what you were a part of. Unbelievable."

"He can't even see Death," Bone Cat said sleepily.

Celeste froze and regarded the thing in her lap with a touch more respect. "Unlike you? Do tell." She looks back at me. "As far as her reality in the broader sense, well, let us just say that she is no longer *as* real as she was yesterday, and thus you have altered the future in a very positive way."

Lunette looked at her askance. "Uh, yeah, that's *one* way you could put it." She looks like she is going to say more, but Celeste raised a boney finger and she stops.

"Well done." Celeste continued, "And as a result, you are no longer required to be here. Your job is done."

I feel a chill in the California night air. "What job? And are you saying you *could* have released me?"

She laughs. "Do you remember, *mon ami*, your first night here? I told you that I could see that you would be *needed* here?" She took a deep breath. "It has taken longer than I'd thought, but for the first time, I no longer feel that this is the case. You have done everything that you were required to do."

I frown. "I don't see how that changes my situation."

She shrugs. "I was not lying when I said I could not

undo your geas, and I *was* sincerely working towards that end. It was a very perplexing mystery, and I considered it a challenge." She waved a hand. "If I *had* managed to free you, it would have been simple enough to beguile you into staying."

"Oh, *would* it now?" I bristle—and suddenly realize that I am looming threateningly over an empty trashcan. I spin about and see Celeste blithely examining the tips of her fingers. She looks up at me and the corners of her mouth twitch upwards.

"Yes, I think so. Now as for your geas, I still cannot *remove* it, but it is finally time that I allow you to acknowledge that things have *changed* since you were first imprisoned here."

"Changed? Like what?"

"A moment, if I may." Celeste reaches into her sleeve and pulls out a small fetish, that has a thick bandage wound about its head. She begins to unwind it.

"You have to understand," Lunette spoke up. She is clearly worried about something. "*Everything* we saw said that you *had* to be here in the park at the correct time, or else there would be a *catastrophe*."

"But you've said that I *couldn't* leave the park. What's changed?"

Celeste removed the last of the wrapping, and I feel a new clarity of thought beginning to blossom inside my head.

"Simply the size and shape of the prison itself." She turns to Vandy. "When he was captured here, sixty-some-odd years ago, this property was pretty much all there was to the Zenon empire, aside from an animation studio building. Today ...?"

Vandy considered for a moment. "Well, as far as property goes—there's Zenonland parks in Orlando, Osaka, Chartres, Istanbul, Xian, Wellington, and Brasilia, as well as the holiday resorts on Hawaii, Fiji, the Galapagos, Costa Rica, and McMurdo Sound. I'm not sure how many hotels, office buildings, and shopping complexes they currently own, but—" She paused and a surprised look crossed her face. "If your geas acts like a legal contract, I would've guessed he should be able to go to *any* of them."

I am stunned. Vandy sees the look upon my face. She taps her head. "Prelaw, remember?"

"But how? If I cannot leave ..."

Vandy looks at me in exasperation. "Did you ever *try* to leave aboard one of those Zenon buses that takes people to the airport? Or the hotels? I mean. The company *owns* those, right?"

They most certainly do. As well as airplanes, cruise ships, and fleets of auto-mobiles. I feel a rising tide of fury as I turn towards Celeste. She stares up at me, convinced that she is as secure as she was when she was ten. "Yes, I placed an enchantment upon your mind. Restricted your ability to see, and as a result, Zenonland was not sold and the people inside it are still their own masters. Judge me as you will."

I stare at her for a timeless moment, and then abruptly sit down. "I don't know where to go first."

Celeste gives a faint sigh of relief, and then ostentatiously clears her throat. Wearing a relieved smile, Lunette pulls a small slip of paper from inside her jacket. "Through mysterious methods, that are not to be revealed to lesser mortals, I have come into possession of the name of a so-called sorceress in China, who titles herself the Empress of Blue Jade.

"She has often boasted that she could break any geas brought before her." Both Celeste and Lunette sniff derisively in unison. "Wisely, she has not dared to come here to America in order to prove it, but if you went to her, I'm sure she would feel safe enough to try it."

She raises a finger. "She will charge you a stiff price. Not an *unfair* price," she admitted grudgingly, "but a stiff price nonetheless." She then hands over the paper and I see a name, address, phone number, and email address, written in Celeste's elegant handwriting.

"Please thank these mysterious methods on my behalf. I

know that a pitiful creature such as myself dare not approach them, lest I be driven mad."

"Damn straight," Lunette said approvingly.

I face Vandy. "I know you don't want to be near me, and I accept that. But you should listen to me. Stay here. Zenonland will still need a protector, especially when it gets out that I am gone. Plus, there are people here who can help you. Teach you. I know I can't force you ..."

Vandy raises a hand. Her eyes are shining with excitement. "Do you really think they'd let *me* become the new Sheriff of Zenonland?"

I mentally switch gears. "The job comes with its own office."

Later, while Lunette and Vandy are off talking, about hair from what little snippets I overhear, I sit with Celeste, who is leaning back in her chair, eyes closed, slowly stroking Bone Cat, the picture of comfort. I have finished recounting everything that happened over the last few days.

Celeste listened quietly for the most part, though she did ask many questions about some of the things Polina did and said, insisting that I repeat them word for word. After I am done, the silence grows. It was a companionable silence, but there are things that have to be cleared up.

"I don't understand why the Gremlin's Prognosticator didn't warn us that this was about to happen."

"Their machine did what it was supposed to do. There was death, there was change, you will be leaving the park. They do not care about the greater scope. Your Madam Urakhov was a remarkable creature," Celeste replied. "Even the *threat* of a Dire Contract of this magnitude, it should have caused any magic user in North America with a touch of clairvoyance to wake up screaming. But she had constructed a sort of false future memory. I don't want to think about where she harvested the power to do *that*. It would have soothed the human seers, but a machine wouldn't have been fooled."

At least I could reassure the Gremlins that their devices were still functioning. I examined Celeste, and a realization came over me. "You'll be leaving soon."

It says much about our relationship that Celeste knows what I'm talking about. She nods. "Oh, yes. This body has had to endure for far longer than I had thought it would." She looks over at Lunette, who is examining Vandy's palm. "Children are waiting longer before they have children themselves," she said approvingly. "But I already feel some of my memories beginning to drift into their new home." She grins in satisfaction. "My next incarnation will be very powerful indeed." She taps the top of Bone Cat's head. "Prenatal vitamins. That's the secret." She looks at me. "Now let us talk about your problems, my friend."

"I still have problems?"

She closes her eyes and feebly waves her hands about. "I see that you are having problems with ... romance."

Bone Cat murmurs sleepily from Celeste's lap. "I didn't say nothin'. It's pretty obvious."

"Indeed it is," Celeste confirms. While she is speaking, she absent-mindedly weaves a small geegaw from thread. "Do you love her?"

I consider this. "I think I do. I wouldn't have changed her if I did not."

I glance over. Vandy and Lunette are still, examining something on the ground before them.

"You truly expected her to kill you?"

"Oh, yes."

"But you changed her anyway."

"She would have died if I had not."

"Then I consider her behavior most ungrateful."

I shook my head. "I don't. You have no idea what it felt like, what I did to her. I have earned this."

"I can fix it."

"What?"

She reaches inside her sleeve and draws out a small vial, corked with red wax. Inside was a deep green liquid. "Love potions were the *first* thing I learned, *mon ami*. Now this will not make her your slave, who wants that? But she will—"

I slap the vial from her hand, and I stand before her quivering in rage. "Don't you *dare*! Her mind is her own!" I say this so intensely that I am not surprised to hear it echo.

Then I realize that it is not natural acoustics that are doing this. I spin and see a small weave—identical to the one that Celeste had woven—stretched out between Lunette's hands. Vandy is staring at me and her face is a study in contrasts.

I wheel back to Celeste. "You interfering old swamp witch. I believe it high time for you to begin your next incarnation—"

She looks up at me without fear. "If you must. But first, let us talk about the fate of Mortimer Zenon."

Damn the woman. This is one of the few things that could have checked my wrath. "You know what happened to him?"

"You told me so yourself. The witch sent him in here. He is somewhere in the park."

"But he *wasn't* the Wendigo—" I stop as I realize what I'm saying.

"No, he wasn't." Celeste leaned forward. "He *should* have been far worse. But you never fought anything worse than the Wendigo. So ... *you never fought him*. Therefore, he is still here."

I am ashamed that it takes me almost fifteen seconds before my jaw falls open in realization. "ORSYNN?"

I give the three-note whistle and am pleased to see the expressions on everyone's faces as Orsynn rises to the surface.

"My friend! Hello! Hello! How are you today! Why it seems like it was just *yesterday* I saw you last!"

"It *was* yesterday."

He blinks his great stupid eyes at me, and then a grin smears itself across his lower face. *"I can tell time,"* he squeals.

His eyes then glance downwards. "And what's this? What's

this?" *This* was Vandy, Celeste, and Lunette, who all give a small wave. "I'm *sure* I keep telling you that you don't have to bring me someone to eat *every* time you visit, my friend." Vandy and Lunette look startled and quickly step behind me. Celeste chuckles.

"Especially ..." Here Orsynn actually looked hesitant. "Especially since you have again called me your friend ..." The question hangs in the air, and I take a deep breath.

"Of course you're my friend, Mortimer."

He freezes. "Mortimer? Who is that?"

"That is you. You may not remember it, but your true name is Mortimer Zenon, and you are my oldest and best friend ever."

His eyes grow round with amazement. "It *is true*! I can *feel* that this is true!" Mortimer crows and thrashes about. "I *am*! You have always been here, and I have always been Mortimer, and I have always been your friend!" He looks at me glassy-eyed. "I think I might pass out now."

"Breathe in," I said with a sigh, "and don't pass out, because I have some people to introduce you to. They are not food. They are *new* friends."

I had not thought that Mortimer's eyes could get any rounder. I am proven wrong. "*New* friends? I will have *more* friends? *Is this even possible?*"

Bone Cat shook his fist. "Hey! I'm your friend, too, you jerk."

Mortimer considered this. "Yes, but you make fun of me, and you look creepy."

"Creepy? I'm *cute*, you asshole!"

Vandy stepped up. "Hello," she said.

Mortimer goggled at her. "A girl!" He looked at me. "She is a girl." He looks at her again. "You have very nice hair." I roll my eyes.

Mortimer sidled towards me. "I am surprised. You were never good with women, my friend." He sidles over towards Vandy. "He is very bad with women."

"I know."

"But he is the best person to have as a friend! I am Mortimer, and I would be happy to be *your* friend, too."

We all agreed that this would be a fine thing, and then we all had to endure being hugged and listening to Mortimer sing the friendship song, and, to my astonishment, Vandy, Celeste, Lunette, and Bone Cat joined in, and no doubt they would have continued on until morning if I had not grudgingly come in on the final chorus.

"And this," I say afterwards, "is *Madame* Celeste L'Enfant de Lune."

Mortimer pauses. When he speaks, I can almost hear the voice I remember from so long ago. "I know you," he says slowly. "You're a magic person." He squints at her. "You were shorter."

Celeste nods. "Indeed I was. So were you."

"Yes. Yes, I was. I ..." He looks off into the distance. "I had to go away." He shivers and then looks back at us. "You took care of my friend. Thank you, *Mademoiselle*."

Celeste snorts. "It is *Madame*, you ignorant Yankee."

Mortimer smiles. "I will always think of you as *Mademoiselle*." This charming moment stretches out—and is broken by Mortimer rearing back and groaning. "My head hurts sooooo much!" And he submerges in a splash and a flourish of bubbles.

Vandy stares out at the lake. "And *he's* the ravening monster the witch was trying to unleash?"

Celeste bites her lower lip. "That is the part that still eludes me. He should have been a thing of madness and fury."

I nod. "And indeed he would have been, I have no doubt, except that he had escaped the witch's direct influence, and exchanged it for *this*." I gesture, and they all see that we're next to the Happiness Machine.

"As near as I can figure, Polina must have brought him here right after the machine was first activated. It was why she couldn't enter the park. After wandering around for a bit on his own, apparently Mr. Mortimer fell into the lake.

"He lay there for who knows how long, gestating into what

he has become, marinating the whole time in the point-blank emanations of the Happiness Machine."

As we walked back to the entrance, I ask the obvious question. "Can you break Mr. Mortimer's curse?"

Celeste and Lunette look at each other and have a silent conversation consisting of twitches, shrugs, and grimaces until they both sigh deeply in unison. "It will not be easy," Lunette says.

"It will not be quick," Celeste adds. "Getting rid of that excess mass alone will take decades."

"But it can be done?"

Again they looked at each other. "We shall see."

As we stroll along the roads towards the entrance, I ask Vandy to take over the operation of Celeste's chair, and beckon Lunette to fall back with me. I have another curse I need to deal with.

It is a sudden ætheric sound wave booming out across the park that awakens me the next evening. After a pause, I can hear the level of shouts and laughter from the crowd tick up a notch.

The Happiness Machine is back up and running. I imagine Cormangwöld blowing out a final snort of flame, and then settling back down upon her nest, and I feel a wave of relief.

When Bone Cat and I step out onto the promenade, it is to discover teams of technicians removing cameras. Upon questioning them, I discover that Mr. Shulman has returned, and my faith in him had been justified, as this had been his first order.

Mr. Leonard was positively beaming as Vandy and I enter his office, and he insists on showing us a new engagement ring. It seems that Mr. Shulman felt that the new CEO of the Zenon Corporation should show that he could publicly commit to things.

Evidently he heard us laughing and congratulating Mr.

Leonard. He pops his head out of his office with a frown on his face, but when he sees who we are, he smiles, holds up a finger, and retreats. A moment later, several men and women, whom I recognized as members of the Zenon board, file out, trying very hard not to stare at me as they pass.

I introduce him to Vandy as we sit down but save any other information about her until I bring him up to speed on everything that has happened in the last few days. After the first minute, he starts taking copious notes, many of which I am sure will wind up in his file cabinets. When I was done, almost two hours have passed.

He sits back and puts his fingers together. "So. You're leaving?"

"I am. I hope to come back, but it will be without constraint."

He nods slowly. "You know," he said idly, "I wasn't in Tokyo for very long." He looks at me. "But there were ... things I was informed about regarding our operation there that made me wish you were there as well."

I say nothing. He examines his fingernails. "Over the years, I've also received reports—nothing official, of course—about ... incidents at some of the other parks." He looks me in the eye. "I don't suppose, once you're footloose and fancy-free, that you'd be interested in staying on the Zenon payroll?"

I sit back and consider this. Even if I manage to acquire my freedom, it's a big world out there, about which I know shockingly little. There could definitely be benefits to having one of the world's largest corporations watching my back. I agree.

Mr. Shulman recalls one of the men who had been displaced when we came in, and we then spent a rather tedious hour going over contracts. Vandy, who is graciously reading through documents on my behalf, (because, as she tartly informs me, a lawyer does not have to like her client) clears her throat several times, and makes corrections that, as far as I can tell, involve little more than the shifting about of commas, but they seem to vex the man quite a bit.

Mr. Shulman, on the other hand, finds it all very amusing, and he and Vandy hit it off immediately. After everything was signed and witnessed, he formally offered Vandy my old job, which she gleefully accepted.

He then spent yet another hour making phone calls, while I showed Vandy my—now her—office, and in a surprisingly short time, I found myself walking down Main Street with Mr. Shulman, possibly for the last time.

Upon my head is the black cowboy hat that Mr. Mortimer had purchased for me all those years ago, and I saw many people giving me admiring glances as we walked by. My old hat now hung on the hook in my office. Vandy could do with it as she wished.

"So," Mr. Shulman asked, "where will you go? I mean if this thing in China works out and you can go anywhere? Straight to Tokyo?"

"Prague," I said without hesitation. "I have dreamed of it frequently. It was ruled by a very nice vampyre queen who I have lost touch with. I would like to make sure she is all right." I sighed. "I'm sure it will be much changed, but that applies to everything, doesn't it?"

I'd had a long conversation with the L'Enfants, and Lunette had offered to take Vandy under her wing. Between her and Miss Dawkson, Vandy would have an easy time integrating into the local supernatural community. She would be in good hands, and with Lunette advocating on my behalf, eventually I might be able to return, and then we would see what we would see.

Mr. Shulman cleared his throat. "There'll be a coffin waiting for you at the airport. I got one with padded velvet on the inside. Solid oak. Built in cell phone and Wi-Fi."

I looked at him askance. He waved a hand. "Rich *schmucks* will buy anything. You'll like it. If you need anything, money, whatever, you just get in touch, okay? Our people should be there every step of the way to make sure things go smoothly. And, oh. Before you go ..." He then reached into a pocket and fished out a small box. "Here. You always said you wanted one."

I open the box and find an official Zenon Corporation retirement watch.

I startle him by enveloping him in a great hug. "Thank you, Ira. You are, and always have been, a good friend."

Mr. Shulman freezes within my embrace, then hesitantly gives me several small pats on the back. "*Shalom*, Sheriff."

I look about. "You must excuse me for a moment. I have a bit of business I must see to."

Mr. Shulman checked his own watch. "Don't take too long."

I walk for a few minutes until I was alone, and then clear my throat. "You're upset. I can tell."

Bone Cat pops into existence before me and folds his arms. "Gee, I wonder why?" He kicks a pebble that arcs up and bounces off of my nose. "Maybe it's because I'm gonna be *dead* in a few minutes."

"Is that what you're worried about? You're not going to die. You heard Celeste. You are a manifestation of the land. You'll live as long as the park does, and possibly much longer."

"Oh, sure, in some airy-fairy disembodied ghost mode where I don't even know I exist. You *know* I don't manifest unless your fat stupid feet are on the ground."

"Like now?"

"Yeah, like ..." It was then that Bone Cat notices that I am in fact hovering at least six inches above the pavement. His lower jaw drops to the ground and shatters. It instantly reforms back in place, but it is still quite gratifying. "What ... How?"

I pull aside my coat and reveal the amulet Lunette had waiting for me when I awoke, filled with earth from beneath the statue of Mr. Bartholomew. I don't think it's any more magical than soil from any other part of the park, but I thought it a nice touch.

"Normally, I don't think this would actually work, but Ms.

Lunette has assured me that she and her grandmother have called in quite a few favors from the spiritual plane to ensure its effectiveness." I rolled it between my fingers. "As I understand it, it won't even drop off when I turn completely insubstantial." Another miracle of the modern age. "So as long as I maintain contact with it, you will be able to be as annoying as ever."

Bone Cat stares at me. "Boss ... I ... I don't know what to say."

"I doubt *that* will last." Before I know it, he has leapt into my arms and for several minutes, we engage in a prolonged bout of back patting. This lasts until we come back to the entrance, and as Mr. Shulman had promised, there is a Zenonland bus quietly idling just inside. To my surprise, Vandy is standing beside Mr. Shulman. She makes a point of not looking at me.

Bone Cat bounces onto Vandy's shoulder and gives me an evil grin. "Don't worry, boss," he sings out, "I'll always let'cha know what color underwear she's got on."

In one smooth movement, Vandy scoops him off her shoulder and stomps him into fragments. Yes, I think she'll be just fine.

I bow in farewell, and turn to go, and Vandy astonishes me by putting a hand upon my arm. "Let me know when you get where you're going," she says, her eyes not meeting mine. "Just so I know you got there okay." She finally looks at me. "Okay?"

I smile back. "Okay. Good luck, Sheriff."

I step up to the door and it folds open. The driver peers down at me and checks a small clipboard. "Are you ...?" He stares at the name and then holds it up before me. "... him?"

"I am," I said.

"You got any baggage?"

I turn and look back at the place that has been my kingdom for the last sixty years. I know every inch of it and know that it is time to move on. I glance at Vandy, Mr. Shulman, and the newly reconstituted Bone Cat, who gives me a final thumbs-up. I am leaving the place in good hands.

Oh, I would be back, but when I came, it would be under my own terms, as my own person, beholden to none, and free to do as I chose. I take a deep breath. It has been quite a while since I could say that.

I turn back to the driver and smile, showing him my beautiful teeth as I step aboard. "None whatsoever."

ABOUT THE AUTHOR

Phil Foglio is known primarily as a cartoonist, and is the first to admit that drawing pictures is way easier than poring through the thesaurus looking for the correct word. He has been active in the science-fiction and gaming community since 1973 and has never had a real job. He lives in Seattle with his  wife, Kaja, their two children, and a variety of animals. As far as the cartooning thing goes, it has resulted in him winning a number of Hugos and getting to see a bit of the world. To check out *Girl Genius*, the comic that he and Kaja have been working on for 20-some-odd years now, please go to www. girlgeniusonline.com.

OTHER TITLES FROM THE PRINCE OF CATS LITERARY PRODUCTIONS

MacGyver:
Meltdown
Eric Kelley & Lee Zlotoff

Or Even Eagle Flew
Harry Turtledove

Seventh Age:
Dawn
Rick Heinz

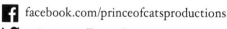 facebook.com/princeofcatsproductions
twitter.com/PrinceLiterary
 instagram.com/princeofcatsbooks

Printed in Great Britain
by Amazon

69791261R00168